His Lordship's Coachman

Maxime Jaz

To my heart horse, gone too soon. I love you forever.
To the horse who now has my heart.

Book Cover by Maxime Jaz, design consultant Bjorn Larssen.

First edition 2023

Preface

Having grown up loving horses and riding, having been influenced by books such as the 'Black Stallion' series by Walter Farley and 'Black Beauty' by Anna Sewell, my books often include horses, but maybe this one has real horse protagonists too, for the first time. As the human characters, they also have a role to play in their life, and in this forbidden romance love story, in a time when horses were an integral part of everyday life, often abused and neglected, worked to the bone, just like lower-class humans who often had the same fate. Horse and man, linked together by the strings of their heart, just as the protagonists are, despite of all their differences, the danger that represents such a love, and the challenges they have to face. Someone said, Darren loves horse more than people, and it could not be more true, save for Archibald, who is his entire world.

For my regular readers and fans, this book might seem less steamy than the others, but as ever, I don't build my books, I just follow the story my characters show me. This might be a slower burn, but that passion is there under the surface, inevitably, as the main characters have to hide their love, but rest assured, the steamy scenes are filled with passions.

Finally, a word on the language used. UK English spelling was used for this book as it is set in 19th century England, so please read it accordingly. Words in UK English have a different spelling, sometimes from US English (and other variations of English) and those are not spelling mistakes. Whereas the language at the time was more formal than in the book, it has been simplified to suit a wider audience, hence might not be historically accurate. A thorough research was made on the time period the story is set in, but I am not a historian, nor a scholar in 19th century England. I hope, however, that you will still enjoy this romance in a historical setting, which I would not label historical romance in good faith.

Love and horses. Horses and love. What could be better? I hope you enjoy this story of a love that is as strong as that generous animal's heart.

Content notes

This book contains graphic depictions of violence, abuse, death and grief, as well as explicit sex scenes.

For a more detailed list, please scan this QR code or follow this link.

https://maximejaz.weebly.com/his-lordships-coachman-content-notes.html

Contents

Chapter 1

"I'm sorry, Darren... her ladyship's health is paramount, so I have no choice. We are leaving England next month and moving to London this week for the final preparations."

Lord Shackleton watched his stable master's drawn, pale face, still pulled into a mask, that man of thirty-five who had served his family even as a young boy, grown into an adult with him aging towards sixty. Blue eyes of a peculiar shade under his black hair, he stood, waiting, and Lord Shackleton sighed, his hands behind his back to keep them from trembling.

"I have made sure you all are cared for, so you are moving with the horses to Lord Edward's estate. He was in need of a new stable master, but as his mansion is smaller than ours, you shall also serve as his coachman. Knowing your reputation, he was delighted, of course, when I told him you were available." He forced a mild smile on his face, watching Darren struggle with his tears. "Much smaller stables too, so you will not have that many men to order around, but he has two stable boys, which is a bit of a help. I also sold the carriage to him, the large one. He will be at the estate next week, moving his family from town for the winter to escape the fog and pollution of the city. The young Lord is frail of health, unfortunately, and needs to regain his strength. Do you remember him?"

Darren swallowed, trying to find his voice. "I am not sure, Milord, I might have seen him ten years ago, as a young boy..."

"Yes. A young boy of fifteen... well, he is twenty-five now... how time flies..." He quieted, holding back from hugging the man tight. "Take good care, Darren. I will never forget what you did for our family during all these years. I trust you will not disappoint your new master."

"Of course not, Milord. I will do my utmost to serve Lord Hampton and his family." His voice drowned in tears, so Darren shut up, still not letting any rogue tear spill.

A mild smile. "Very well. Farewell. I shall write to Lord Edward to get and give some news."

"Wishing you all the best, Milord." He bowed and left quickly, almost rushing down those long corridors, out in the crisp autumn air.

At last, he could breathe and let his tears spill, the stable buildings a blur as he pushed the door open, that comforting smell of fresh hay and straw laced with the horses' sweet scent ramming into him. Warmth, soft neighs as they recognised his steps, his scent. He hurried to one stall, a beautiful bay gelding's head poking out above the grates, sniffing his hand. The horse pushed his nose into his soaked chest and nudged softly.

Darren laughed through his tears, stroking the animal's head. "We're leaving, Dandy."

His chest tight, because despite everything, this was the only home he'd known, growing up here, taking over from his father who had died young, his mother following, her heart shattered from sorrow. He stroked the horse, his soft nose, and loose lips, gently nibbling for treats, then left to pack his scarce belongings. Alone in their family home, that small house wedged against the stables, two rooms only, but it had been everything. His eyes drifted to the double bed, and they welled up with tears. *Maybe it's for the better... not see that bed anymore...* see those horrific pictures flashing in his mind, the screams... sheets soaked in blood... He shook his head, pained, breathing against that tight cage around his ribcage. *Leaving... next week...*

He drove the carriage to Lord Edward's estate, that mansion a lot smaller than Lord Shackleton's, but still of an imposing size, and stopped it in front of the large stairs leading to the front doors. The steward hurried to greet him, eyeing the horses, Dandy, and a dappled grey pulling the carriage, and a black, and roan one tied to the back with a small pony.

The haughty man pulled a face. "The horses don't match... I am not sure his Lordship will tolerate this."

Darren shrugged, his heart in his throat. "They are reliable and sure-footed. His Lordship... Lord Shackleton valued these over colour..."

"Lord Hampton will decide their fate." His eyes roamed Darren. "Your reputation is flawless, so I have hopes that you will be of good use to his Lordship and his family. The stables and fields are that way. We only have two horses, the rest got sold." He gestured to a young boy standing on the side over, his shoulders hunched. "This is James, he is one of the stable boys. He'll go with you and show you around." The boy hurried past him before he could get a swat on the head, and stood next to Darren, his fearful eyes carefully checking him out. The steward could barely hide his contempt. "These boys are lucky that they still have a place here. They are extremely lazy. Make sure you are severe with them and harsh. That is the only way."

Darren just nodded, already mildly fed up, but he pushed that brewing anger down, his soft despair.

The steward rubbed his hands together. "Very well. Please go and settle. I shall see you around later." He turned and left, hurrying up the stairs, and the boy's grey eyes turned to Darren.

"Just follow me, sir... I'll show you..."

Darren smiled at him. "Come, jump up. No need to walk, we'll be faster this way."

The boy's eyes widened, but he didn't dare argue, and jumped next to Darren, the horses pulling with a light trot straight away to the clack of his tongue. Leaving that huge mansion behind, they made their way towards the back of the park, to the stables.

Darren pulled on the reins and halted the carriage in front of the large double doors of the stable building. That unmistakable smell of ammonia in the air, and he frowned slightly, watching as another boy emerged, this one with red hair. He stood next to the other one, waiting.

Darren sighed. "What's your name?"

"I'm Travis, sir."

"Smell this, boys?"

The boys looked at each other, wide eyed, and Travis turned to him. "Smell what?"

Darren walked into the stables, gesturing for them to follow. He stood in the main alley, breathing hard against the stench which made his eyes water. "This."

Travis shrugged. "It's urine, sir. Smells like this on any given day."

"Does it?"

James had understood, his voice soft. "It is not properly cleaned, right, sir?"

Darren looked at him. "Who taught you?"

Travis grinned. "The former stable master... he got kicked out though... drinking and all..."

Darren towered over him. "Well, no more of this. We clean again today, and you better get it right. And no drinking either. I catch any of you, you are out. Understood?"

The boys looked at each other, but then just nodded, scared a bit. James risked a smile. "I'll show you your quarters, sir. Follow me."

They went outside to a set of wooden stairs leading up to the stable's roof, and Darren followed him a bit wide eyed when he gave him a key.

"This is your door, sir."

Darren opened it and pushed the door in, the smell of stale wine and cigarettes pouring out, laced with dust and age-old grime. His face fell, looking at that single room under the roof, two small windows milky with dust. A bed on the right and a stove on the left with a table and two chairs, a trunk right next to the entrance, and a cupboard. Empty wine bottles lined the wooden floor, and a cup had been used as an ashtray, filled to the brim.

James shrugged, embarrassed. "The former master, well, he didn't clean, sir... so..."

Darren just breathed, trying not to lose it completely, his eyes roaming that room from the threshold, but there was no time to mourn, and no option to leave, so he sighed and looked at James. "No worries. The horses first, boy. Then this place..."

James grinned. "I'll help you, sir... just don't beat me up."

Darren smiled wryly and ruffled his hair.

They went to the stables after having settled the horses in a field, and worked hard, the afternoon dipping into dusk, but the stables smelled of fresh hay and straw, and James and Travis had shown him where the grain was, the well. There was also a small vegetable garden patch, completely neglected, and a chicken coop, so Darren had some hopes, even if his heart was in pieces, that this could work out. They went to get the horses, the new ones' eyes wide on the new building, looking for their place. The two other horses were an old grey and a dark ginger coloured mare, still young and fresh.

James looked at Darren after he had given Dandy his ration. "We should clean that room, Sir... 'tis night time soon..."

Darren knew, his heart tight, so they walked upstairs with some garbage bins, and Travis had joined, throwing all the bottles and cigarette butts out, scrubbing the floor and the walls, the windows and door wide open on that chill night. They finished late, the night dark, only the soft snorts of the horses seeping up from the stables, their hooves trampling the hay and straw bedding. Darren sighed, the place cleaner, at last, that smell almost gone.

He patted the boys on the back. "Good job. Thank you." They waited, and he sighed. "Listen, work hard, that's all I ask, and we'll be just grand, alright? But don't abuse my kindness. It can go as swiftly as a flame is fanned out."

They nodded, watching his unsettling blue eyes, and left for the night to their room, which was on top of the hayloft, a tiny room under the roof.

Darren plopped down on the bed, breathing hard, letting his tears flow as his shoulders rocked silently. Clinging to that single hope he had, that maybe Lord Shackleton had not given him away to a hopeless place. He steeled himself though, and unpacked, made the bed, and prepared his clothes for the next day. He undressed and blew the candle out, waiting in the dark in that foreign space, listening to the soft sounds of the horses drifting up. Wondering what this new life would bring.

Early dawn, the sun barely licking the sky, but Darren was up, feeding the horses with the boys, the stables loud with their munching, their curious stares at each other. A tentative sniff through the grates from Dandy earned him some ears pinned back on the mare's head, her teeth snapping at him.

Darren smiled. "Doesn't like you, does she?"

James walked to him with some eggs in his shirt. "Found a couple this morning."

"Great. Let me cook them."

"I'll get some bread."

Darren fried the eggs on the stove; the flames chasing away that night chill. They ate huddled around that single table and went downstairs then to wash the dishes up at the well, a small washroom allowing a quick dip into ice cold water, but there was not time to heat it as a maid hurried up to Darren.

"His Lordship will arrive today. Have the carriage ready when I tell you. I'm Stacy." She smiled at him and hurried away, so he gestured the boys over.

"Scrub and clean that carriage as if your life depended on it. I'll deal with the horses."

They left quickly, and he went to prepare Dandy and Tulip, making sure that their coats shone like diamonds, an extra layer of dark fat spread on their hooves.

Tulip nibbled his neck softly, and he had to laugh, push that soft nuzzle away, the sun warming that chill morning air.

Lord Hampton watched his son's pale face, leaning against the coach's window, his light-brown hair ruffled by that slight wind. He was holding a white handkerchief against his lips, tainted with blood, his brown eyes on the rushing landscape.

Jolting at his sister's hand on his arm, her voice filled with excitement. "At last! I can hardly wait to be there! And that ball on Friday, what a treat!"

He pulled a face. "Sure, sister."

"Don't be such a spoilsport! You should be exhilaratingly happy, brother, to be here, in the countryside. You will get better soon, you will see, isn't that so, papa?"

Lord Hampton smiled. "Of course. This is the whole point."

"Too bad that Lord and Lady Shackleton had to move abroad. I was looking forward to meeting Juliet."

"There was no other choice. Fortunately, I have secured his horses and his stable master. That man is worth his weight in gold."

"New horses? How exciting!"

"We shall see."

Lady Hampton turned to him. "I do hope we are not going to be disappointed. That last stable master was a scandal."

"Do not worry, my dear. The man has an impeccable record. Harry would not sell me short."

"I do hope so. Poor Harriet. I do hope that the gentle climate will be to her benefit. Maybe we should also bring our young Lord to milder climates." Her worried eyes were on her son, who had coughed up another sliver of bloodied saliva.

Lord Hampton's face darkened. "Hopefully, there will be no need. Some fresh countryside air can work wonders."

His son just shot him a tired look, his frail form wedged into the seat, a thick blanket on his knees. *I'm going to die... soon...* a mild smile on his face at the thought, weary of the struggles, the strenuous breaths, his weak body which would not carry him. Trying hard to swallow his despair, being a disappointment to his family, his parents, his friends who could not do anything with him. *Countryside air...* the rushing trees, that mild sparkle on a stream's surface, that lush greenery around with the sun pouring through the playing leaves. *Soon...*

Darren had set up his mirror, dressing, making sure that his clothes were impeccable, a mild stress invading his insides. He went down to check on the horses, the two good friends waiting patiently, their eyes on him when he checked their tack one last time. James gave a last wipe to the carriage gleaming in that afternoon sun, and Darren pulled his gloves on.

He glanced at the boys. "See you later, boys. Make sure the stables are perfectly cleaned."

"Yes, sir."

He mounted on the bench and set off, the horses giddy a bit, but still trotting in unison as the mansion came into sight, a couple standing at the bottom of the stairs, the steward, and a young lady, her eyes smiling as he steered the carriage in front of them. A perfect halt, the horses calm and steady, and he got off and bowed deeply, raising his eyes into the Lord's eyes, to his smile.

"Darren Turner. Your reputation has preceded you."

"Thank you, Milord."

"Welcome to my estate. I do hope you settled in fine."

"The honour is all mine, Milord. All is fine, thank you." Keeping a straight face when his heart was beating against his chest, his tight waistcoat, watching as the Lord's eyes went to the horses behind him with a slight frown.

"Lord Shackleton neglected to tell me that the horses do not match."

Darren swallowed. "They do not match in colour, Milord, but in pace and temper. There is not a pair of such sure-footed and calm horses on this side of the country." He shut up at his boldness, watching as his master circled the carriage, stroked the horses on the neck, watching them stand, staying put, just nibbling on their bits. Lady Hampton had walked closer too, with the young lady clearly enchanted.

"This carriage is beautiful."

Lady Hampton pulled a small face. "It is… but I am not sure about these horses. How will it look when we go to that ball?"

Her husband looked at her. "They were pulling Lord Shackleton to the balls, and I am sure this had not been an issue here in the country." He turned to Darren. "Isn't that so, Darren?"

"Absolutely, Milord." A mild panic in him that the Lord might just sell them, his companions, these horses he had raised and taught himself, watching as they grew with him, from colts to sturdy horses.

The young lady was enchanted, though. "Oh, Mama. It's not such a big deal. Surely it is more important to know that they will not run away, right?" She whirled to Darren, and he had to smile.

"Yes, Milady. They will never do such a thing."

Lord Hampton stood in front of him. "My son is gravely ill, and he will need to be taken out daily on a stroll. I can not afford to have horses which spook or have an uneven gait."

"I vouch for these two, Milord, with my own life."

Lady Hampton's lips pursed up. "Bold statement."

"It is only the truth, Milady." His words drowned, that edge still there of facing the unknown.

Lord Hampton sighed. "Very well. We shall keep them." Almost smiling at the relief flooding Darren's face. "Every morning at ten, report here with the barouche for his Lordship's ride. The top will need to be off as much as possible for him to catch some sun. I trust you know these country roads better than anybody."

"Yes, Milord."

"I am most pleased to have you; it is a rarity to have a man who knows what he does."

"Thank you, Milord."

"The ladies might join you, however, my wife does not like to be jostled around in a carriage, so it might just be my children. The ball on Friday. Make sure that everything is meticulously prepared and cleaned."

"Of course, Milord."

"We shall see how these two horses work out. My son is extremely sensitive, so he will be a good judge. You may withdraw, Darren."

He bowed and watched them leave, exhaling hard. He walked to the horses and stroked their nuzzles. "You better behave tomorrow." Dandy nudged him in the chest, and he had to smile.

Next morning, he got the horses ready, the barouche's top folded down, that crisp autumn air warming with the sun's rays, announcing a glorious day. The horses nibbled their bits softly, waiting for him to get ready and sit. A clack of his tongue and they were gone, trotting swiftly, anticipating that ride, which made their hearts flutter. Pulling up in front of the stairs, checking his watch. Ten o'clock sharp. He got off and watched as two footmen carried a young man down the stairs in a chair, a thick blanket over his knees, his hand pressing a handkerchief to his mouth. His brown eyes were on Darren, though, and he could not help but melt a bit under that soft gaze, even if it had instantly clouded with hostility and veiled boredom. He opened the barouche's door and bowed, waiting until the two men struggled the young Lord on the seat, pulling the blanket tight on his knees.

Darren closed the door and looked up at the young man. "My name is Darren Turner, at your service, Milord."

The young man's hand left his face, just to show a small smile filled with scorn. "I know who you are. Now, drive and let's do this horrid outing." He put his handkerchief on his mouth and averted his eyes.

Darren breathed deep and mounted on the bench, softly taking the reins as the horses perked up, but he just put them in a walk, not wanting to shake the young lord up, dead worried at his frail form and pale skin. A gentle wind perked up as they left the gates of the estate, the road winding down between tall trees, that golden light filtering through leaves which were turning their colour, green into shades of yellow, red, and rust, the road smoother so Darren clacked his tongue and the horses went into a mild trot, pulling evenly, the barouche's gentle sway like a caress. Effortlessly climbing a hill, down that slope, the landscape wide on rolling hills of green.

The young man's eyes went a bit wide, holding that handkerchief tight, his lungs struggling with that harsh air, that mad fright in him that he might cough.

He steadied his voice, snapping. "Slow down a bit."

Immediately, the horses went into a walk, and Darren turned back to the young man. "We will go at your pace, Milord."

He just nodded, vaguely relieved that the man didn't prattle, didn't ask anything, watching his large back, that dark hair gently swaying in the wind, his soft voice as he talked to the horses. Taking another road, this one more in the shades, lining a gentle stream, that soothing rolling of the water smoothing his nerves. He felt vaguely ashamed for snapping at him, but didn't want to apologise either, so he kept quiet, his eyes a bit lost on the birds, that tingling there at the back of his throat. *No... fuck... not this...* He breathed against it and steadied his gaze on the driver's back. What was his name? *Darren...*

A commotion to the left made him turn towards the noise, his eyes a bit wide at that hunting party, horses in full galop, chasing a fox, the dogs howling as they tore towards the road. But Darren just gently reined the horses in, alert, their heads raised as the dogs poured on the roads, the horses, the men shouting, but they stayed put, waiting. They watched them disappear between the trees at the end of that large field lining the road, and the young man turned to Darren's smile.

"Everything alright, Milord?"

"Yes... I am most impressed. Any other horses would have bolted."

"But not these ones, Milord." A bit proud, his love for them warming his voice.

The young man smiled. "I see."

The road home, uneventful, and the young man felt a sudden disappointment that they were already back, but he let those two footmen take him down, sit him in his chair.

He looked at Darren. "This was tolerable. See you tomorrow."

Darren just bowed deeply and drove back to the stables, his mind on those words. *Tolerable...* His heart sank, and he unharnessed the horses, giving them a couple of carrots. James and Travis walked them to the field, and Darren went to change to do the chores around the stables. They had also planned to restore the vegetable garden, even if it was already late in the season, they could maybe grow some corn, potatoes, and pumpkins.

But next morning, Darren was there, ready, his stress eating at him, that entire ride silent, the young Lord's hand on his mouth, pressing that white cloth against his sharp lips.

Another drive next day, in silence, and Darren had given up pleasing him, although he took great care selecting beautiful roads, breath-taking landscapes which even made his heart race after all those years.

Another morning, clouds churning in that lead sky, but the young man just said, a mild irritation in him. "My father insists on this despite the rain lurking. Absurd."

Darren didn't comment, and they set off. Halfway from the estate, the clouds thickened and a few droplets plummeted from the sky. Darren stopped the barouche and jumped down to raise the top, securing it tight as fat droplets fell from the sky. In a matter of minutes, he was soaked, but strapped the top tight, peeking in to make sure the young lord was dry.

His wide brown eyes, on Darren's soaked hair, his smile.

"Are you all sheltered, Milord? We will make haste."

"And you?" Out without thinking, watching the sky pour down on them.

Darren just gave him a wide smile as rivulets of water rushed down his face. "I will be fine, Milord. Thank you for asking."

He sat and urged the horses into a swift trot; the rain lashing down with the wind which had picked up. Darren pulled his jacket tighter, and took a thick blanket out from under the bench, pulling it on his shoulders and back to at least have some warmth, his eyes squinting on the road as they sped towards the mansion.

Once there, they had to wait for that downpour to calm a bit, the horses' coat gently steaming in that air which had become too cold. Darren's teeth chattered softly, but he waited in that icy rain, under that soaked blanket, watching the sun peek out. He got off when the rain stopped and pulled the top down to allow the footmen to take the young Lord out.

His brown eyes were on him. "Thank you."

"It is my pleasure, Milord."

"I'm Archibald. Lord Archibald. Please. Not Milord."

Darren smiled at him. "It is my pleasure, Lord Archibald."

"See you tomorrow, Darren. Warm up."

"I shall, My Lord."

Archibald let it slip, waiting until they put him in his chair, just listening to the horses trotting, carrying the barouche away fast.

His mother rushed to him when they put his chair down in the tearoom. "Archibald! That dreadful weather! I hope you are all dry!"

"Of course, Mama, do not worry. My driver made sure of it, that poor man."

“That is his duty. Nothing to make a fuss about. I do hope you are enjoying those rides, even with those mismatched horses.”

“Those horses are gold, mother. Trust me.”

“Well... if you say so... tomorrow, we shall see, when we go to that ball. Come. Tea has been served, it will do you good.”

Archibald’s eyes drifted towards the stables, barely visible from that large window overlooking the park, a thin stream of smoke rising from the roof. He smiled and sipped his tea, the taste of blood lining his throat.

Chapter 2

The day of the ball had arrived, the large carriage ready in that chill dusk. Darren watched as they settled the young lord and waited until the others got in, then set off to the neighbouring estate. It was still an hour's ride there with a good pace, the dusk lights enough, but the lamps were ready, filled up, and the horses' dinner stashed with his, under the bench.

The carriage swung softly, Archibald's eyes on the setting sun, the colours spreading in the sky. His mind, was on his imminent death, wondering why his mother had insisted on him joining the ball when he could not stand or dance, when every breath was a struggle. Listening to the chattering of his sister and his mother.

He felt his father's hand on his. "How are you doing? You have some colour since your carriage rides."

Archibald pulled a small face. "If you insist, father..."

"It is for your good."

"I know. "*Soon, I will die, father, and that able man can drive me to the cemetery.* His mind on Darren, his smile, listening to his voice as he instructed the horses sometimes. Wondering why it filled him with calm, that he was driving, that he was there, close. He chased his thoughts away, those ridiculous thoughts he had been churning many sleepless nights, burning in his bed, and focused back on the landscape drowning in the setting night.

At last, the mansion, lights on, music seeping out from those large windows. Listening to his father instruct Darren.

"We will possibly finish late."

"It is alright, Milord."

Archibald's heart, tight, watching those coachmen huddled under their large coats, their hats, some walking to Darren to shake hands, to blow into those frozen hands, even if they were bantering, their breaths in the air, mingling with the horses'. Watching as Darren put two large blankets on his horses, stroking them, strapping their grain sacks on their heads when he had removed their bridles and bits.

He had to be carried inside, and he was already fed up, wondering how long they had to stay.

Darren watched him being carried away, his heart tight. Trying to understand what could ravage such a young body, remembering when he had been twenty-five, feeling invincible, riding, and working for twelve hours a day, his body, and mind not tiring.

He got jolted out of his thoughts by George, another coachman working for a neighbouring Earl. "So, how's life treating you? A real shit, that affair with your former master..."

"Yeah..." He clipped his coat tighter, shivering a bit in that deepening night.

"I heard you're driving that weakling of a lordling around every day? I wonder what for... he's as good as dead, that one."

"Watch your mouth. You should not talk with disrespect of my masters."

"Look at you, being all faithful like a good dog... but let me tell you somethin', Darren. They don't give a shit about us, those folks. We freeze here whilst they enjoy the high life in their warm palaces." He spat. "So, respect? Fuck off, will ya..." He barked a nasty laugh and took a small bottle out of his coat pocket. He offered it to Darren just to snatch it back. "Oh, that's right, I remember... you don't drink either... Tsk...tsk... nothin' better than this to warm your blood." He took a large swig.

"You should not drink."

"Fuck off... that's all I have to say. Lick their boots until your tongue rots off... you've been taught well, boy, but lemme tell you the truth. You expect anything from these folks? Gratitude? Respect? They will sooner kick you out at your first mistake. 'Tis ain't Lord Shackleton you working for... How's your new home? I heard it's a right shithole of a place."

He was loud enough for others to hear too, and Darren just swallowed and went to sit on his bench, watching the horses sleep, one leg propped under their blankets. Darren pulled his blanket out too, holding it tight, that icy night air slowly eating through the fabrics, but he was used to it, waiting, so kept his eyes on the stars, counting them, marvelling at their shapes, not to fall asleep. He ate his sandwich too later and took some warm tea out which he'd carefully wrapped in some old rags. Sipping it until it turned to ice too.

Blowing puffs of breath into the air. The sky slowly lighting up, his eyelids heavy, his whole body stiff under that cold blanket and clothes, when finally, the families started leaving, so he lit the lamps on the carriage, stomping the ground a bit to get some blood back into his feet, his hands numb. His eyes were on Lord Hampton and his family walking out, the young Lord's irritation plain on his face when they brought him up to the carriage.

They were trying to lift him inside, but he almost slipped to the ground, and his voice snapped with his fear. "Put me down, stupid idiots!"

The footmen obeyed, and Darren walked close, bowing.

"Allow me, Milord. I'll settle you, if you don't mind."

Archibald looked at him, relieved, but also filled with apprehension. "I am not sure you are strong enough on your own."

Darren just smiled and spread his hands. "May I take you out of this chair and put you in the carriage, Milord?"

"You may. Gladly. Please." He breathed through his fear, but felt his strong arms scoop him up as if nothing, holding him tight.

Darren stepped up inside the carriage, holding that shrivelled body tight in his arms, Archibald's head against his chest. He put him down carefully on the seat, taking that blanket from the young lady and smoothing it on his thighs and legs. Meeting his brown eyes, close. "Are you comfortable, Milord?"

"Lord..."

"I am sorry. Are you comfortable, Lord Archibald?"

"Most comfortable. Thank you." Breathing in relief when a bout of cough raked his body, and he pressed that white cloth against his mouth. Darren was flooded with anguish, but Archibald just smiled feebly. "Do not worry. Just the usual. Drive fast. You need to get home and warm up. Waiting all night... absurd." He gestured feebly and Darren got out, helping the ladies in.

Facing the night roads lighting up with the sun rising, the horses trotting swiftly, that lilting carriage almost putting him to sleep too, so he opened his coat, letting that icy dawn air jolt him awake. Breathing in deep, clacking his tongue softly to urge them forward, the shadows dancing on the road, but he knew it by heart, every line, and curve, the horses too, working with him, their soft mouths connected to his gentle hands.

Home at last, the footmen carrying the young lord out, his eyes half-mast, the ladies almost asleep. Darren drove back in the rising sun, making sure the horses were cared for before he washed quickly with cold water and rushed upstairs to make a fire in that single stove that served as heater. Huddling around it, warming his trembling hands, that icy bed not tempting at all, but he was dead tired, so he drank that scalding tea, almost burning his hands off on the mug, and went to bed, curling up under that thick chilled blanket. A couple of hours of sleep, he knew, before he had to take Archibald for his walk... His eyes closed. Darkness.

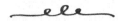

He had to wait a bit the next day, but they eventually carried the young Lord down and seated him. Noticing how pale he was, his eyes sitting in dark circles, but Archibald smiled feebly.

"I could not sleep... that ball was exhausting."

"Should we do a shorter ride, Milord?"

"No..." His breath short, a mild smile at the worry in Darren's voice. "No, for God's sake, this is the only thing keeping my sanity here... in fact, let's make it longer... I need all the air I can get after being stuck for hours in that awful ballroom..."

Darren smiled and drove the barouche over the hills, choosing a longer ride, the weather mild, the sun filtering through grey clouds. He was tired, but also mildly thrilled that the young man found some pleasure in these outings, hoping that they were helping him somewhat, even if he seemed dwindling, that pale shade not leaving his cheeks. They drove near a lake, the scarce sunlight playing on the water's silver surface, and Archibald just wanted to soak it in, this peace, not a soul in sight on that narrow road.

"Stop! Stop here..."

As soon as the words were out, the barouche stopped, a worried Darren turning to him. "You're unwell, Milord?"

He smiled. "No... just wanted to stay awhile here..."

"I can drive down to the shore, if you wish."

"Sure. Great."

Darren drove the horses to a narrow path leading to the shore, lush green grass bordering that crystal lake, and he stopped them, making sure the young lord could see the lake from his side.

Archibald spoke softly after a while, his eyes on the playing waves. "I would like you to drive my hearse, Darren."

Watching as the coachman turned to him, wide eyed. "I beg your pardon, Milord?"

"Drive my hearse. I have my trust in you that you will not let my coffin fall out." He chuckled lightly, but stopped at the look of utter despair in Darren's eyes. He sighed. "Forgive me. Imminent death can make for crude jests."

Darren was too moved to speak, every word he could think of somehow wrong, so his gaze followed the young man's to the lake.

Archibald spoke after a while. "Let us go. But not home. Drive some more."

"As you wish, Milord."

"Leave the title, Darren. Just Archibald."

Darren's face fell. "I cannot possibly..."

"... and I cannot possibly be with you on these rides, if every sentence you utter ends in my stupid title!"

Darren quieted, trying to grasp his request. He blew a small breath. "As you wish, Archibald."

"Much better..." A small smile, which he hid straight away in that cloth. "Just drive."

Darren drove for another hour, making sure they were not too fast, but Archibald didn't speak, his brown eyes on the rushing landscape, trying to force air into his lungs. He was exhausting himself, he knew, but didn't care, a grim determination in him to end it. *Soon... I will be too tired to go out... to get up... to breathe...* Watching Darren's back, his worried face floating in his mind. *This man whom I scarcely know cares. More than anybody. He would bring me to the end of the world if it meant that I healed...* Coughing a bit, watching his blood taint that white cloth. He leant back, exhaling softly, watching their mansion come into sight at the end of that shadowed driveway, the sky laden with low dark grey clouds. *Rain. Soon.* His eyes on his mother rushing down the stairs with their steward. The barouche halted, and she walked up to it, straight to Darren, who had jumped down to greet her.

"Just what were you thinking! You were gone forever! His Lordship is frail, he should not..."

"Mother!" His voice made her turn. "Mother... I asked Darren to have a longer drive. Leave the man alone, please."

"Archibald! Your health! These rides are not good for your body..."

"On the contrary... they are excellent... Now, let these good men help me down. I will retire to my room. Darren..." He turned to those brown eyes, which had softened. "Thank you for this excellent ride. See you tomorrow."

His mother objected. "I am not convinced that you should go out tomorrow."

"But I am, mother. Thank you for your concern."

He let the footmen take him down and sit him in his chair, a feeble wave of his bone hand to Darren, his eyes smiling above that white cloth pressed to his mouth.

Darren just bowed to him, his breath caught with worry. *How long... drive my hearse...* a well-known chill running down his spine, remembering that very same request from his father's dying lips. *Drive my hearse, boy...* he drove the horses back to the stables and let them loose in the field, watching them roll straight away in that dying grass, the others walking to them, nibbles on the neck, soft sounds as they welcomed each other. James and Travis were deep into cleaning the stables, so he changed and joined them, sweat pouring down their backs as a soft breeze chilled their shirts to their soaked skin.

Going to bed very late after having groomed the horses, and he had to help the boys who were not used to his standards.

Their arms were trembling by the end. "Sir... you are going to kill us..."

Darren smiled. "You will need to get used to it if you want to amount to anything."

James washed his face in the bucket near the well. "I want to. Become real good."

"Start by talking properly."

"You speak like the lords, sir."

"I had to learn." Working very hard not to slip back into the language around him, biting his tongue sometimes when a few rogue words slipped out.

He blew the candles out and lay down, dead tired too, his mind on the next day, where he would take the young Lord.

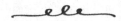

Jolting awake at a loud knock on his door, he sat up straight, eyes wide on that dim room, the harsh moonlight streaming through the windows. He jumped out of bed and opened the door, facing a panting young page, his eyes wide in the candlelight.

"Saddle a horse and ride to town, get the doctor… fast, that's what his Lordship has said… Tell him, boy, he should ride like the wind… 'Tis the young master, Darren… he ain't good…"

But Darren had already turned, dressing quickly, pulling his boots on, his jacket above that flimsy shirt he'd carelessly pulled over his body. Rushing down the stairs to the stables, the horses jolting awake, some neighing. He got a saddle and a bridle, tearing the black horse's door open, Lord Shackleton's hunting horse, his fastest. Raven's eyes went to him, and he saddled him, fast, putting the bridle on.

"Easy… let's go…"

Walking the horse out, who had already perked up. He swung himself up in the saddle, reining the horse in, not letting him bolt straight away. *Calm, calm… warm him up a bit.* A fast trot to the gate in that harsh moonlight, the landscape capped with silver, that mad worry in him. He let the horse fly when he'd reached the road, not needing to spur that fast steed as his hooves ate the road, their breaths in the air. That black shadow among tall trees, only the sound of the horse's ragged breathing, his nostrils wide. Darren's mind bathed in anguish, hoping the doctor would be home, that he would hurry… *drive my hearse…* those drowned brown eyes… *No way…* Spurring the horse, shouting as he galloped faster, a reckless ride, he knew, but he trusted the animal, having trained him and ridden him countless times, he knew every move of that strong body between his thighs, that strong mouth tugging at the reins, and he let go, letting them flow as the horse bolted, even faster, his hooves beating the road. Used to long chases during hunts, Raven didn't tire, even when the foam streaming from his mouth and chest had plastered Darren's thighs, hooves meeting stone, and he slowed, that clattering unnerving in that quiet night.

At last, the doctor's house. He jumped down on trembling legs, holding the panting horse, and hammered at the door.

A couple of minutes when a light glimmered behind that thick yellow glass, the latch, the doctor's puzzled face in his nightgown.

"Darren?" For a fleeting moment, not even understanding as Lady Shackleton had left, but the panting man just pushed the words out.

"It's the young… Lord… Lord Archibald Hampton… You must hurry."

The doctor nodded. "Prepare my horse, will you? I'll get dressed. You can rest yours too, you know the way."

Darren hurried to that back courtyard where the stables were, and tied Raven up, letting the trembling horse rest, his body soaked and fuming in that chill night air. He had found a blanket and put it over him, then got the doctor's horse out of his stall, a sturdy little bay, but he was worried, looking at that horse's stocky legs. Still, he attached it to the cart and led it to the front, waiting for long minutes before the doctor got out, carrying his bag.

"I'll drive there straight away... actually, could you drive me? It will be faster. You can tie your horse to the back if he can manage."

"Without a rider, he will be fine..." He tied Raven to the cart. "Doctor... is it grave?"

They sat on the cart, Darren gathering the reins.

"I need to examine him. The young lord is extremely fragile... but let us hope for the best."

They left, the cart speeding into the night, that sturdy little horse pulling with all his might, and Darren had no trouble guiding him, knowing the roads by heart, even if that silver light made it easy to see. He pushed that sturdy little horse to what he could endure, Raven's panting breath in the back as he followed in a light trot, and the doctor patted Darren's back.

"I couldn't have driven this fast, my good man. You rode like the devil, too."

Darren didn't comment, his blue eyes on the road, on that long alley lined with trees, the mansion's right wing lit up, the frantic butler rushing to meet the doctor.

"At last! You were fast, thank God! This way..."

Darren watched them rush up the stairs, disappear behind those large doors, his breath short, his eyes on the lit up windows. *Please, please...* silent whispers into that empty night, that dark sky void of any gods.

He brought Raven back to the stables, making sure the doctor's horse got a full load of hay and water. He rubbed Raven's dark coat dry, waiting to give him his drink, until he could not feel that mad heat on his skin. Dismissing that his whole body was soaked too, chilled to the bone. Darren then went back to the cart and drove back to the mansion, waiting, holding the horse with ice in his chest.

Hours, the sky dipping into dawn, almost, when at last, the door opened, and the doctor walked out. Darren straightened, trying to read his face, anything, that grim face too familiar when he had come out of his lady's room.

"He lives, but has a fever, and is struggling to breathe. We will see tomorrow. I will come back around lunchtime."

Darren's relief flooded him, even if he knew they were just buying time. He helped the doctor up and gave him the reins. Watching the cart speed away, he then leant on his knees, his lungs burning too with a dull ache. No time to go to bed, the sky's rosy edge too bright, so he walked to the stables and woke the boys up.

They got to work, preparing the horses' meals, their hay, sweeping the yard whilst they ate, the stable corridor spotless. He didn't have time to change, his clothes still damp from his ride, sweeping the yard, when he looked up, straight into Lord Hampton's eyes.

He bowed, holding his broom. "Milord..."

"Up early, I see... Darren, I wanted to thank you... had you not ridden that fast and brought back the doctor with equal speed, my son might not have been of this world anymore this morning."

"It is the least I could do, Milord." He watched the master's drowned eyes roaming that clean yard, the whitewashed walls gleaming in the morning sun.

"You might need to go again... just be ready." Almost as if talking to himself. "My son might not live... despite my hopes of this air invigorating him a bit. He woke this morning, delirious, wanting his ride..." He smiled at Darren feebly. "It's as if those rides were all of a sudden everything he was longing for. I am grateful, truly. There is no need to come to the house today, though. He is too unwell to even get up."

"Of course, Milord..." Swallowing his anguish, that slight pang to his heart, knowing he would not see him, maybe for days... weeks... *maybe ever. Drive my hearse...* His eyes welled up, but he kept his tears in, breathing a bit harder.

"I will be going. You did a good job with this yard. Well done."

Darren watched him leave, and James walked up to him. "Should we take the horses to the field?"

"Yes... there will be no need for them today."

Archibald opened his eyes, the bed unbearably hot, so he threw the covers off, just to have a mild hand put them back again.

He met his sister's eyes, his voice weak but laced with irritation. "I need to breathe..."

"You are also soaked. The servants will come and bathe you soon."

"The doctor..."

"He came during the night. That stable master rode to get him."

"He did... of course..." His eyes on that golden sunshine in the sky. "I want my ride."

"Father forbids it. Do not be unreasonable. You can barely breathe."

"So what.... Rather die in that carriage than in my own sweat in bed!" He coughed, blood spattering on the white sheets, and Francesca wiped his mouth off.

"You need to rest. The rides can wait."

"Call Darren here... I want to thank him."

"Father went already this morning." She frowned a bit, meeting his burning eyes.

"Now. Get him."

"Alright, his Lordship. I am relieved you are indeed alive, brother." She got up and left, slamming the door shut, but he didn't care, his eyes on that golden light.

Darren arrived an hour later, wearing a white shirt and a vest, his black pants, and leather boots, cautiously stepping into that stuffy room with the butler.

Archibald's eyes went to that haughty man. "Leave us." He bowed and left, a swift shadow on his face, and Archibald patted the bed. "Come closer. I am not dead yet."

Darren walked close and stood, his hands laced behind his back. "Milord..."

"What did I tell you? None of this title absurdity. Not when you have possibly saved my wretched life... for which I am truly thankful..." He breathed faster, struggling a bit. "Sit here, please." He patted the bed and Darren sat down, facing him, not daring to object, a mad worry in him seeing his pale face and paper thin skin. Archibald reached out and took his hand. "Much better..." He ran his thumb over that hard skin. "Strong hands..." His eyes met Darren's. "Does this bother you?"

"No..."

"It should, though... you could pull your hand out."

Darren stammered a bit. "If it offers you comfort, I don't mind."

Archibald's brown eyes went to him. "It feels good, it is warm, not like mine, dead cold..." He spread his hand against Darren's, their palms touching, his soft white skin against that large strong palm and fingers, that tanned skin in a harsh contrast with that sickly pallor. He grinned. "What a pair we make..."

Darren's heart raced, a slight fear in him at his words, and Archibald caught that little light of terror in his eyes. He slid his delicate fingers between Darren's and closed them, a feeble touch, not leaving his eyes. "I might die soon, and I might as well tell you... because I trust you more... than any of the people populating my life... but I am not taking this to my grave." Darren almost forgot to breathe, and Archibald smiled. "You understand though... I will not need words."

Not leaving each other's eyes, their fingers intertwined, that golden light filling the room, as Darren struggled with his shame, that slight fright.

Archibald sighed, leaning against his pillows. "I wish we could stay like this forever... in this small moment of understanding... even if you are dead scared..."

"I worry for you..."

His pale lips curled up. "You do. And you care... a rare treat."

Steps on the corridor, so he pulled his hand out, grazing Darren's fingers as they left each other, Darren standing when the door opened, letting his mother in, followed by the butler.

"I do believe you had quite enough, dear. Darren has work to do, do not keep him any longer."

Archibald smiled. "Of course, mother. Darren, I will see you soon. When I am better."

"Milord, Milady..." He bowed and their eyes met, an amused light in Archibald's brown pools.

Darren left, almost rushing outside, raking his hair as his swift strides took him through the park. *What was this? Madness... Sheer madness... but he knows... he knows...* Closing his eyes to his thoughts, to that mild despair, still not fully trusting him when he knew he would never say a word. *Would Archibald?* Instant guilt pouring in, trying to ignore his racing heart. *This is so wrong... so why does it feel so right?*

Chapter 3

"William Willoughby is paying his visit today."

Archibald pulled a face, his bone-white hands on the sheets. "I could not care less, Father."

"Now, now... three days stuck in bed... it will do you good to have company."

"William and I have nothing in common. He is a boisterous, arrogant twat."

"Archibald! Please. Language."

"Apologies... he is only visiting to meet Fran... no doubt looking at courting her."

"It would not be a failed attempt. Should he propose, I am giving her hand without a second thought."

Archibald's lips curled up, bitter. "Sell her on the meat market, like cattle."

"Archibald! Truly!"

"It is only the truth." Mildly fed up, he looked at his father. "I want to be dressed and go on my ride."

"It is highly unreasonable."

"It does not matter, does it? I will die anyway..."

His father kept quiet, but his eyes shone with tears and Archibald sighed.

"Please, Father. I do not want to meet William and listen to him boasting about activities I will never be able to do, nor I have a care for. I need my ride... and I might just live..."

"Your mother will be most displeased."

"She can entertain William then, and dream of marriage and grandchildren... I can not provide any of those, so make sure this works out..."

"Archibald..."

He averted his eyes, his throat tight. *Fran...* thinking of her, how she would end up inevitably married to one of the lords, *maybe that ass twat William... how long since I've seen him? Years... he must be grown, handsome and brash... twat...*

He let the servants dress him, sit that lame body into his chair, holding his handkerchief against his mouth, a mounting nausea, but he held tight, his eyes on the door, that flooding light, those blue eyes which haunted his dreams.

Darren watched them carry him down, his heart beating hard at the look in those brown eyes. Waiting until they settled him and left, he climbed on his seat and turned around, for a while both of them silent, then Archibald pulled the cloth away from his lips.

"Did you miss me?"

Darren swallowed but could not hide the truth. "I did."

"And I missed you. Now, drive fast. I do not want to meet William Willoughby..."

"His Lordship is visiting?"

"You know him?"

"I've met him maybe once, years ago, when he was still a young boy."

"And?"

"He was pretentious... pardon my words... and harsh with his horse."

"That would be him... perfect twat." He laughed lightly, and Darren risked a smile. "Alright... we will have time to chatter. Just drive. To that lake. You know which one I am talking about."

"Yes. I know."

They left swiftly, the horses giddy a bit with that warm autumn air, somehow the summer last breath in that golden sunshine, and Archibald held tight, trying to ignore his nausea, his tight lungs, just trying to live the moment, being free, his eyes roaming the landscape, the colours, to soak them in maybe one last time.

The barouche stopped on the lake shore, the horses waiting, and Darren turned back to him. "You would like to stay a bit?"

"Yes... take me out... Let's sit on the grass..."

Darren frowned lightly. "It might be cold... wait, I'll put a blanket down."

He loosened the horses' reins, letting them graze, and put one of the thick horse blankets down on the grass near a willow. He climbed up and scooped Archibald up in his arms, walking with him to that blanket.

Darren put him down carefully, a mild worry in him. "I am not sure where you could lean your back... that tree bark is hard as stone."

Archibald raised his warm eyes at him. "I could lean against you."

Darren's stomach clenched. "If you wish..."

"I wish it very much. Please."

Darren sat down behind him, against the tree, trying to ignore his galloping heart, and pulled Archibald close between his legs. He held him as he had started to slip aside, mortified a bit, but Archibald just leant his head against his chest, his eyes on the dancing waves.

Feeling that heart beat in that broad warm chest. He smiled, his voice weak. "I could fall asleep on your chest..." Darren didn't know what to say, trying to ignore his own feelings, and Archibald turned his head back a bit to look at him. "I am embarrassing you... and taking advantage of your obedience, for which I am sorry... but I am not sure... how much I have to live... and taking my time with this is not going to happen." He searched Darren's eyes. "I do think we need to be brutally honest with each other, and not hold grudges, if one is terribly wrong..." He lost his breath, that slight nausea sweeping through him, feeling Darren's arms tighten a bit. He smiled. "Nothing... too bad... so... am I terribly wrong? Being in your arms?"

Watching Darren's parted lips, feeling his breathing become shallow, those soft words almost pushed out. "No... no, you are not wrong..."

Archibald smiled, and his hands went to those broad arms. "Would I be terribly wrong... if I asked you to kiss me?"

His eyes, a bit wide. "It is wrong... on so many levels... you know this..."

"Is it wrong... for us, though?" A pained shadow crossed Darren's face, and Archibald ran his hand on his arm. "If... we were just two... beings... just here... forget all else... everything... just us, now... Would you kiss me?"

He sighed. "I probably would..."

"So... it's just us..." Smiling, his head a bit light. "My dying wish... if you want..."

"Don't talk like this... please..."

Their eyes met, Archibald barely breathing, his heart rushing that scarce blood around, warming his chest. Feeling Darren's warm hand on his cheek, tilting his head up gently, so he parted his lips, and closed his eyes, just bathing in that touch, flutters in his stomach when he felt those soft lips press gently against his, so he opened them wider, trembling, clinging to that warm arm. More. Opening wider. Not leaving Darren any choice but to yield to that impatient mouth, kissing him wider, meeting his tongue, letting his teeth graze his lips, that slight metallic taste of blood in that burning mouth, his barely existing breath, so Darren broke the kiss, letting Archibald draw a deep breath, his eyes still closed, his body melted in his arms.

For a fleeting moment, Darren thought he'd died, that pale face bathing in the afternoon sun, but then Archibald opened his eyes, a slight smile on his lips. "Not a dream then?"

"No..." A deep sigh, filled with his remorse, his dread, his feelings, which should not even have been there. He looked down at Archibald when he felt his hand on his cheek.

"No regrets. Thank you." Stroking his face, not leaving those blue eyes. "We do not need to put words on this for now. Let us just enjoy these moments... whilst we can..." His eyes roamed around. "Our little haven..."

Sitting, holding each other, watching the sun play on the waves, drowning them in orange.

Darren spoke after a while, feeling that chill in the afternoon air. "We should go. Your parents must worry."

"Yes... you are right... we can come back tomorrow."

Darren's heart, tight. "Yes..."

"Let us go then."

He closed his eyes, letting Darren carry him to the barouche, settle him in his seat, but his touch was different, Archibald could feel it, so he grabbed Darren's hand, as much as he could, before Darren could straighten, meeting his eyes. "You might just give me a reason to live... one day at a time..."

Darren's eyes welled up. "I do hope so..."

"Do not worry... every moment we have, and will have, is ours forever... no matter what happens... let us go... I am tired."

Darren drove home, and by the time they stopped in front of the stairs, Archibald could barely stay awake. He waved at him from his chair with his small smile.

"I will see you tomorrow, Darren, at the usual time."

"Of course, Milord."

A tiny spark in Archibald's eyes, and Darren had to tame a smile, watching him being carried away into that huge house.

Next day, they drove to the lake again, sitting together under that large tree which provided a shelter from prying eyes. The horses grazing, that gentle wind ruffling the lake's green surface, and Archibald felt for the first time that maybe he would live a bit longer than he'd anticipated. *Maybe a few days... weeks...* lying on Darren's chest, inhaling his scent laced with fresh hay and horsehair, soothing, like a balm to his feeble heart.

That deep voice he so loved. "Are you hungry?"

"No..."

"Sure?"

Archibald looked at him. "This sounded like 'I heard you, but I don't believe you.'"

"Maybe..."

"You brought food?"

"I figured we could eat something. We never make it back for lunch."

"Tempt me."

"Alright..." Darren smiled and got up, holding him, then settled Archibald against the tree, leaving his jacket to dim that hard surface.

Archibald watched him take a basket out from under the bench and bring it back, a swift, loving gaze to the grazing horses before he walked to him and put the basket down, sitting cross-legged on the blanket. He opened it and took two sandwiches out, handing one to Archibald.

"What is it?"

"Just bread, butter, and ham. And some tea. You will have to drink it from the flask."

Archibald's lips curled up. "Nothing stronger?"

"I don't drink."

"Oh... what a relief, truly..." He tentatively bit into that sandwich, so different from the ones he was used to. The bread's hard crust, that strong taste of peasant ham, and the rich butter. He smiled and ate more, a bit surprised that he had an appetite, albeit a mild one, it was there. He could not finish it though, and handed the rest to Darren, who just swallowed it, washing it down with tea.

"Feeling better?"

"Yes... it was excellent, thank you..." He held his hand out. "Come back... please?"

"Of course." He settled behind Archibald, and held him, feeling how his body had relaxed in his arms, his soft breathing. *Asleep...* he had to smile, but didn't need to look down, holding him, his arms aching.

Hours, the sun dipping into dusk.

Darren stroked gently that peaceful face, watching his eyes open. "We need to go..."

"I slept..."

"For hours..." He smiled, meeting his eyes, that slight smile.

"Princes are woken with kisses in tales."

"You mean princesses."

He nodded, waiting, and Darren leant down and planted a soft kiss on his mouth.

"Mhm... I am still asleep..."

Another one, but this time, he'd lingered, and Archibald parted his lips, letting him invade his mouth, pull him closer. "Better..." Kissing him back hard, scorching his lips on his stubble, wanting more of that roughness, wanting his teeth...

Losing his breath a bit when Darren withdrew. "Woah... awake, my Prince?"

Archibald laughed. "Yes... awake..."

"Come on..." Darren shut up, scooping him up not to let his thoughts spill, to tame that insane hunger for his lips. He settled him, his thumb lightly grazing his swollen lips. "Fresh countryside air does wonders..."

"It does, indeed."

Darren drove home, their hearts light, watching the mansion come into sight. A clattering of hooves behind them, the horses' ears smoothed back at the sound of the intruder, a dark bay horse in full gallop, reined in as they stopped, prancing and foaming. A tall figure jumped down, pushing the horse's reins into Darren's hands, who had gotten off the barouche. A young man, with dark hair and blue eyes, his smile wide, and for a fleeting moment, Archibald thought he was seeing a younger version of Darren, his eyes wide on that stranger who just jumped up next to him and slammed his hand on his shoulder.

"At last! I caught you! Phew... I thought I would miss you again, but not a chance! Right on time! Back from your daily outing? I heard from Francesca you do your little health promenade every day?" He laughed, slamming Archibald on the shoulder again, and turned to Darren, who just stood there, holding that panting horse, the foam streaming down his legs and body. "Be a good man and bring my horse to the stables. I am dining here tonight. Have it groomed, fed, and ready to leave for later." His eyes narrowed. "My... my..." He jumped in front of Darren, facing him off, then turned to Archibald. "Who is this man?"

"He's our stable master and coachman. Darren Turner. He worked for Lord Shackleton before."

"Ah! That's right. Peculiar... we have an uncanny resemblance, don't you think, Archibald?"

"Maybe..." Vaguely irritated, quickly meeting Darren's puzzled eyes.

"Ah, well... might be one of my father's bastards. Who knows, right?" He barked a laugh, watching Darren pale. "Shocking? Not so much, knowing my father's ravenous appetite for cunt."

"Excuse me!"

He turned to Archibald, grinning. "I do not like softening words." He turned back to Darren. "Who was your mother?"

Darren breathed harder, watching that young lord, briefly meeting Archibald's eyes. "Lady Shackleton's handmaid, Milord."

"Ah... you might want to ask her if she had a little encounter with Lord Willoughby."

"She died, Milord. A while ago."

"Ah... tragic, I suppose. Never mind." He smiled. "Who cares anyway? I might ask Father... could be fun."

Darren just stood, holding the horse, those words ringing in his head, but it could not be possible, any of those absurd words, thoughts, even if there was something akin to the young lord in his physical features, he was sure of his lineage, his parents... an icy dread in him, watching that young man turn to Archibald.

"These men need to carry you? You are in a worse health than I thought."

Archibald looked at him, grim. "I am dying."

"Don't be daft! Now, to dinner. I can hardly wait to meet your lovely sister."

"You inherited your father's ravenous appetite for cunt?"

William burst out laughing. "Oh, I knew we would be great friends! Let us go."

Darren watched them go, stroking that exhausted horse, his flanks bleeding where the spurs had broken skin, his romp, and flanks streaked with crop marks.

He tied him to the back of the barouche and drove back to the stables, his mind on that young man's words, knowing how they liked playing sometimes, hurt those below them. He focused on the horse whilst James and Travis took care of the other two, and washed his wounds down, putting some healing balm on them. He groomed that strong animal thoroughly and brought him to a stall filled with straw and hay. He ate heartily, and Darren went to help the boys clean the barouche.

Archibald could barely contain himself during dinner, listening to William's stories about his hunts, his travels, and his social life in London, all the while openly courting his sister, and downing glasses of wine. Francesca was enthralled though, he could see, that handsome young man enchanting her senses, and he felt sick a bit, thinking back at the words he'd so carelessly thrown at Darren. *I need to talk to him tomorrow... tell him it was a jest... nothing more...*

He jolted when William's loud voice reached him. "Archibald! We should hunt together."

A mocking smile. "I can barely sit, let alone ride. Besides, I despise hunting with all that it entails."

William roared with laughter, echoed by Francesca and their mother. "Come on! You cannot be serious! Hunting is the pride of this country."

"I am serious."

William just shot him a grin. "When you feel better, we will go. Proper riding, not being carried around in that lame carriage."

"That is perfectly fine."

"They must be awfully boring, those rides, but I have a great idea! Let us ride with you. Tomorrow, Francesca, I would like to invite you to ride with your brother. We ride and entertain him."

"I do not need...."

"But you do. So? What do you say, lovely Francesca?"

She smiled at him. "Gladly. I would like that very much."

"You have a good horse?"

"Darren will prepare mine for me."

Her father objected a bit. "Your new mare is not ready, and Darren will not have time until tomorrow to properly train her."

"I do not fear her, Father."

"I still think you should ride another horse."

William watched her carefully, and she straightened. "I am perfectly capable of riding that horse. Besides, William will take good care of me."

"That is absolutely true. Settled then." He rose, kissing her hand. "I shall see you tomorrow. Archibald?"

"At ten. Sharp. Do not be late." Inwardly fuming, his mind on that ride rotten.

"Perfect. Hey, boy! Tell that stable master to bring my horse. Run!" He laughed when the page took off.

His mother's voice. "Be a dear, Francesca, and escort our guest out."

"Of course, Mother." She rose, and they walked out, lightly laughing.

"Ah... a perfect match."

"That man is a drunkard and a brute."

His mother, prim. "I will not have you destroy this budding relationship. Lord Willoughby is highly estimated and has a solid fortune. The young lord will grow..."

Archibald pursed his lips and coughed into his cloth. "For sure, Mother..."

"You need to retire, Archibald. I am delighted that you have a new friend who might show you some manly ways of living your life." She rose and left, almost storming out.

Archibald's tired eyes went to his father. "I am a tremendous disappointment, Father."

"No, Archibald. You are anything but. Your mother will calm down. As soon as William has proposed."

"You approve of this match?"

"It is as good as any."

Archibald quieted, his mind on his little sister, on that impending doom called marriage.

Francesca walked outside with William, her heart flying in her chest, walking all the way up to Darren, holding that gleaming horse.

"Darren, tomorrow we ride with you, to escort my brother. Lord William will come with his horse, so have my mare ready for me."

Darren's face fell. "Your mare, Milady?"

"You are deaf?"

"No, of course not. If I may be bold enough, Milady, Linda is not ready to be ridden outside..."

"I am perfectly capable of riding my horse. You will be there, and I have nothing to fear with his Lordship by my side."

William kissed her hand. "That is true, my dear." He looked at Darren. "You would do well to just obey her Ladyship, and not run your mouth."

"I am sorry, Milord."

"Give me my horse." He smiled at Francesca. "I will see you tomorrow." He mounted the horse and took his crop out from under the saddle's lapel, beating it down the horse's flank as he spurred him.

Darren and Francesca watched him race away, Darren, sick to his stomach at how he treated that horse, but he turned to Francesca's voice.

"Lord William can be harsh, Darren. I value your advice, but you have nothing to fear. I am an excellent rider."

"Yes, Milady. Your horse will be ready tomorrow, as requested."

"Very well. Goodnight."

Darren watched her walk up the stairs, his eyes drifting to the windows on the right wing, to that single glowing square of light.

Chapter 4

Next day, they were waiting for William in front of the mansion, Darren holding Francesca's horse after he'd helped her up in the saddle, the mare restless, even if he had taken care of lunging her early in the morning. She was chewing at the bit, prancing, despite his best efforts to calm her, but Francesca seemed unphased, her eyes on the road.

Archibald watched that prancing horse. "You could have chosen a calmer horse."

"She needs to learn. I intend to make sure she gets broken in properly."

Darren tried to reason with her a bit. "If I may, Milady... maybe stay behind the barouche, she will not have enough room to bolt..."

"Thank you, but you have nothing to worry about."

Archibald smiled. "You would do better to listen to Darren, he knows a great deal more about horses than you, or that twat. Here he comes..."

Francesca frowned at him, but then her eyes were straight on William, reigning that foaming horse in, that white fluff tainted with blood on his sides. "Ready?"

Archibald arched his eyebrows. "Are you sure you will manage the ride with this horse? He looks proper exhausted."

"Do not worry, my good friend. He can go many more miles." He turned to Francesca. "Marvellous horse... just like her rider."

She blushed, and he winked, making Archibald almost laugh, but he hid his smile in his handkerchief, gesturing to Darren. "Let us go then. I trust our riders will be able to keep up."

William mocked. "With these two mismatched horrid horses? Not an issue."

Darren's and Archibald's eyes met, but they didn't comment, and set off, the two riders riding in the back, chatting. Darren glanced back at the mare when they reached the road, watching her tug endlessly at the reins, the struggle plain on Francesca's face, but she pinched her lips, and tore at the horse's mouth, moving the reins left and right, sawing the bit in the animal's mouth who had smoothed back her ears.

William's voice reached them. "We should let them stretch their legs, your horse needs to fly, that is why she is restless."

"Maybe you are right."

Darren almost turned back to object, but then remembered last night, and preferred to keep quiet, watching as the riders went to the front, the two horses visibly agitated, even if William's seemed tired. The mare swung her head down, and Francesca almost fell forward, but she pulled at the reins hard, her voice sharp.

"Stop this!"

William pointed at the field lining the road. "Here. Ideal. They can just stretch their legs and tire. You will not have a problem with her. Just whip her until she drops." She laughed, and he put his horse into a light canter, down to the field, and Francesca's mare followed.

At first, it seemed she had her under control, galloping behind William, but the mare swung her head down again, and bit down, taking off with a kick of her strong legs. A mad scream escaping Francesca's lips with her fear as she felt the horse almost disappear from under her, but it was an illusion, the trees a blur as the fast mount sped forward, her head tucked into the reins. William took off after her, but his horse couldn't keep up, too tired, even if he was beating his skin off.

Darren stopped the carriage and secured Tulip's reins. He jumped off, quickly unharnessing Dandy, leaving only his bridle on. He swung himself up on his bare back and took off, letting the sturdy bay gallop at full speed. Cursing softly under his breath when he'd caught up with William, who was beating his horse to no avail. Francesca's screams echoing in that large field, a forest close, at the end of it, and he tried to shout to her, to make her understand she had to pull the horse in a circle, but she was panicked, and losing her strength, that mad gallop putting her off balance. The mare bucked once, almost sending her flying, and she'd lost her stirrup, holding on tight to the animal's mane, howling. Darren spurred Dandy faster, watching those fast approaching trees, Francesca's body almost collapsed on the mare's neck. His stomach in a knot seeing that the horse would not slow, rushing straight for those trees.

"Faster, Dandy..." A gentle request, but the horse had heard it, giddy a bit to be out of the carriage, he ran faster, next to the mare's left side. Darren reached out his hand, almost slipping off that smooth back, and yanked at the rein when he felt it between his palms. It slipped a bit, and the leather burnt his skin off, but he held tight, even if the pain was maddening. He slowed Dandy, holding that single rein as the mare slowed, listening to his voice. Both horses stopping just in front of the trees, panting.

Darren jumped off and held the mare tight, stepping to Francesca, her tears streaming with her sobs. "Are you unharmed, Milady?"

"Yes... yes... I think so..."

"Let me take you back." He helped her leg back into the stirrup, and took the reins, vaulting back on Dandy, holding the mare close as Francesca wiped her tears.

William caught up with them halfway, his horse barely walking. "Francesca! Are you alright?"

"Yes... I'm fine... just shaken a bit."

"This horse needs a good lesson. She could have killed you."

They rode back in silence, and Darren helped Francesca down on her trembling legs, opening the door for her.

"Please sit and rest, Milady. I would advise that Linda comes home tied to the back..."

The words were barely out, and William jumped down and yanked the reins out of his hand, lashing his whip across the mare's head, neck, and shoulders, over and over again, Archibald's eyes wide at the scene as Darren stepped close to stop him. A wicked light in William's eyes, and he lashed the whip across Darren's face, hitting hard.

A split second of disbelief in Darren as the pain registered, that mad sting rushing down the right side of his face. His hand flew to it, and his eyes welled up, but he didn't yelp, didn't cry, that soft shock rendering him mute.

Archibald was beyond himself. "Just... just what were you thinking?! William!"

"The man needs to learn some respect, just like the horses under his care."

"You... you have no right..." A bout of cough cut his words, and Darren's concerned eyes went to him.

Francesca leant over, holding his shoulder. "Calm down..."

Archibald breathed in as much as he could, that mad anger clutching his ribcage. "I... I do not have to calm down..." He looked at William, trying to pull on whatever dignity he had. "You... you do not touch my men... ever... especially not Darren..."

William's lips curled up as he pushed the panicky mare's reins into Darren's hand. "You are too soft, Archibald. A servant does not interfere with a lord's actions."

"You were... beating that horse up..."

"As I said, she needed to be disciplined. Nothing unusual." He looked at Darren with a small mocking smile. "Just like you. Your insolence will not be tolerated. Apologise."

Archibald seethed. "He does not have to apologise to you."

"Truly? I am amazed, Archibald, that you are taking his side."

Darren breathed against the injustice of it all, and faced William, his voice calm. "Please accept my apologies, Milord."

"There is a man with some sense, at least." He put the whip under Darren's chin and tipped it up, meeting his puzzled eyes. "Next time, I will not be this lenient. If anything, your negligence almost caused her ladyship's fall today, so consider yourself lucky that you only got one blow, and not more."

Francesca objected softly. "There is no need for this, please, William. Darren warned me about the mare."

"He just neglected to tell you she was this dangerous." Holding the whip under Darren's chin, he raised his eyes to Francesca and Archibald. "Your father had high praises for this man, but I cannot see why. Shame." Darren's face flamed up, despite himself, but he kept quiet, not wanting to make the moment worse. William turned back to him with a smile. "Good thing you are keeping your mouth shut, and not trying to embarrass yourself even further."

"William..." Archibald breathed against that tightness in his lungs.

"Do not exhaust yourself, Archibald. Let us go home. I believe her ladyship had enough for the day."

She nodded and stayed in the barouche, waiting until Darren tied Linda up to the back and secured Dandy to the front. He got in his seat, clenching a handkerchief on his bleeding palm, his heart in his heels. The words hurt more than that blow, even if he could feel it all the way down his face, burning with a dull ache. That trip done in silence, Archibald's eyes not leaving that broad back, a mad anger in him, but he could not speak, his scarce breath stealing his words. Blood, again. Lining his mouth. He sighed, dreading to be home, his thoughts on how he would talk Francesca out of this madness.

They stopped in front of the stairs and William jumped down and tied his horse next to the mare, as Francesca's mother hurried to them from the garden.

"Wonderful! You are back for lunch! Please, stay William..." Her words died seeing Francesca's ashen face, her dishevelled hair. "What happened?"

"Nothing serious, Mama... my horse bolted, and Darren had to catch her..."

"You are being too kind, Francesca." William's eyes went to Lady Hampton. "That horse is dangerous. Something that your man here neglected to tell us."

Archibald breathed, his anger plain. "He tried, but you would not listen."

Lady Hampton looked Francesca over. "Are you hurt?"

"No... I am fine, Mama..."

William took her hand and kissed it. "Thank God and your guardian angel."

Lady Hampton was clearly upset. "I cannot believe this! Darren! Come here at once!"

Darren got off, standing in front of her.

She gestured at his face, puzzled. "What is this?"

William smiled. "Oh... just a bit of discipline, if you do not mind."

"Not at all! I am without words! This can never happen again. I will make sure his lordship is informed. Do not forget that we took you in because we are good friends with Lord and Lady Shackleton. Another mistake will not be tolerated."

"I understand, Milady."

Archibald spoke, his voice weak. "Leave him alone... all of you..."

"Archibald!"

"Leave...him... alone!" That last word stole whatever breath he had left, and he leant back, heaving.

The footmen grabbed him and put him in his chair whilst William stepped to him.

"Must be truly horrific not to be able to draw breath... save it for more worthy words. Now, to lunch. I had enough."

He took Fran's hand and walked her up the stairs, Lady Hampton following, delighted, and Archibald glanced quickly at Darren, his heart tearing at the look in those blue eyes. *It's not your fault...*, but he could not speak.

Archibald whispered to the footmen. "To my room..."

"You do not wish to dine, Milord?"

"No... to my room. Now."

Darren drove to the stables and left the barouche and the horses to the lads' care, washing his face in that cold water of the barrel, his hand. The cut had started healing, but he smeared some cream on it, the one he used for horses' wounds, and bandaged it tighter.

James walked up to him. "You are hurt, sir?"

"Nothing too bad... her ladyship's horse misbehaved a bit today."

"That mare... she bites too..." His eyes grew wide at the red welt on Darren's face. "Sir! What happened?"

"Nothing... leave it."

James shrugged, but left, knowing better than to probe, grateful that he didn't get his mouth whacked in, even if Darren had never even raised his hand once, just his voice, if it had been needed at all.

They worked all afternoon, and settled the horses for the night, a vague anxiety in Darren above that fatigue, that Lord Willoughby had not asked for his horse, the evening dipping into night, that dead tired horse sleeping on his feet.

He went up to his room to eat, and then waited, reading a book, almost falling asleep on his chair, when there was a knock on the door.

Darren opened it, facing that young page. "Milord wanted me to tell you that Lord Willoughby will sleep at the mansion tonight. No need to prepare his horse."

"Thank you."

He walked down to the stables and checked on that horse, fed him, and gave him water, as he was not going anywhere. *All the better...* watching those tired eyes, his flanks drawing in air. *Soon, he will have trouble breathing... and will be sent to the slaughterhouse... worked to the bone...* He stroked that beautiful animal's slender neck, and went upstairs, drowned in his thoughts, that mild anguish not going anywhere in that quiet night. Something he hadn't known until now, living a life of mutual respect on Lord Shackleton's domain, every day filled with the certainty of what he had to do, knowing that all would be fine if he did it right. But there was a mild fear in him to face the next day, not knowing what it would bring, knowing he hadn't done anything wrong, and it still felt like he had, somehow, that nagging guilt pushing at his chest. His thoughts on Archibald, how he was the only reason he hadn't walked away this day, wondering where this was all going, whatever they had, that mad danger tainting those small perfect moments when they thought nothing else existed but them. No disease, no lurking death, no danger, just their lips, their hands, and skin, their eyes... He turned on his side, sighing into the night, forcing his eyes closed. *I need to sleep...*

Archibald averted his eyes from the window, a small lamp glowing in the night near his bed, so he watched the flames, trying to breathe. He knew that William had stayed, having overheard the conversations of their maids, his bitter thoughts on how he had acted, what kind of man he was under that charming smile. His blood cold when he thought of Darren. *I wish I could just get up and walk there... walk into his arms.* He hugged himself, trying to picture how it would be, if he could just do whatever he wanted. *Get up. Walk out. Walk somewhere.* The memory distant, almost like it had never existed, that his legs would carry him.

A bitter smile, his eyes going to the door, his father's cautious form. "Come in, Father..."

He gently closed the door and pulled a chair close, sitting. "I was hoping you would be asleep."

"Sleep doesn't come easily when your head is full."

"I heard what happened today."

"It was not Darren's fault." Clipped, he almost lost it right there.

His father raised his hand, mild. "I know."

Archibald breathed. "Father... this man... William... he is a disaster..."

"It might be too late for Francesca. She is in love. And quite frankly, I have very few reasons to object if he proposes. His family is wealthy, more so than us, and he will inherit everything, being their only son."

"I figured... sad story..."

Archibald breathed harder, his despair clutching his throat, and his father poured him a glass of water, making sure he drank at least a few sips.

Lord Hampton put his hand on that damp forehead. "A slight fever again... you got upset today."

"Like it mattered... my words are stolen by my non-existing breath... and I hate it. Had I been able to walk, or do anything, I would have whacked that twat's mouth in!"

Lord Hampton smiled. "I see your spirit has never left you."

"I cannot remember, Father... how it was when I could still do things properly."

Lord Hampton watched his only son, a shadow of the young boy who had liked to run, ride, and climb trees, who had always had his knees scratched to the blood. "You might still be able to do those things."

"Highly unlikely… I should have ridden after my sister today, not sit there, useless."

"Had you been able to interfere, she would not have ridden that horse."

"Darren had told her."

"I know. But his word does not weigh against Francesca's or her beau's."

Archibald's lips pursed, gutted. "He hit him… that brute…"

"So he said, and he was quite proud of it too."

"If Darren leaves, I will not go on any more rides. It might just end my life."

Their eyes met, silent, and his father patted his hand. "He will not leave. I will talk to him. You should rest and get some sleep."

"Alright, Father."

He left, taking that small lamp, and Archibald's eyes went back to the window, to that cold silver night, hoping that he would wake in the morning.

Chapter 5

Lord Hampton walked towards the stables in that early morning light when the sky was still rosy, just enjoying that morning silence, wishing he didn't have to think about his invalid son. That mad hope in him though, that Archibald would somehow heal, and walk with him. His eyes on the yard, listening to voices drifting from the stables, oats, and grains being poured in mangers, the horses' soft neighs.

He watched Darren walk out with a pitchfork on his shoulder, lost in his thoughts a bit, when he raised his eyes. Darren stopped, that slight puzzled look quickly melting into a mask. Lord Hampton walked up to him, his eyes a bit wide at that angry welt running down his face. Keeping his hands behind his back not to run it his fingers along it.

"Good morning, Milord."

"Good morning... I came to discuss Wednesday's hunt. Lord Willoughby, the elder, has invited me to join him and his son, and others. I trust Lord Harry's horse will do? The black one."

"Yes, Milord. He is fast and reliable, you will not have an issue with him."

"Thank you... Darren, my daughter's mare..." Watching as a slight despair rippled through that mask.

"I would like to apologise for what happened yesterday, Milord."

"It is not your fault. My daughter learnt her lesson."

"You are most gracious, Milord."

Lord Hampton smiled thinly, but his heart raced a bit at that hard look in Darren's eyes. *He's hurt. And rightly so...* "I would like to assure you that what my wife said yesterday is not to be taken by the letter. I have the last say about who goes from this place, and it is certainly not going to be you."

"Thank you, Milord."

"In fact, you have done a lot of good to Archibald, I mean, the rides, so they need to continue. He will not have another coachman, so if you were thinking of leaving after what happened yesterday, I would like you to reconsider it."

Darren sighed softly. "There is no need, Milord. I will not let Lord Archibald down."

Lord Hampton noted his words, but he was relieved, noticing that drowned light in those striking blue eyes. "My son means the world to me... you might as well know... and he keeps talking about his death... Losing a child... I am not sure you can survive that pain..." He closed his eyes a split second, apologetic. "I am truly sorry... I did not want to rip wounds open."

Darren swallowed. "It is alright, Milord."

"You lost your child. It is most inconsiderate of me to talk about my son's possible death when you know the pain I fear."

"He died before he was born, Milord... I did not have time to get to know him."

"A most unfortunate event... losing your wife too..."

Darren kept quiet because he had no words, really. That day, gone in the past, something he had tried hard to forget. He put some strength into his voice. "I have made my peace, Milord."

"Good on you... Anyway, as I said, just continue these daily outings until the weather permits. They do him good. This evening, we are invited to Lord Willoughby's for dinner, so have the carriage ready, we leave at six."

"Yes, Milord."

"Just bring his horse up to the house when you pick up my son. I trust he will have a late breakfast with us."

"Of course, Milord."

Lord Hampton turned and left, a vague relief in him, hurrying back in that morning light to speak to Archibald before breakfast.

Darren went to get some hay, stashing a huge pile on his fork, swinging it on his shoulder, back to the stables. The boys were busy cleaning the mangers and grabbed their forks to get more hay, all silent. They groomed the horses then, Lord William's, Dandy and Tulip, and Travis made sure that the barouche gleamed from top to bottom, sweating with the brush and then the polish.

Darren brought the carriage up to the stairs, waiting, watching William walk down the stairs with Francesca, their wide smiles, but Darren's eyes were on Archibald, carried behind them, his face pale, that handkerchief pressed to his mouth.

He handed Lord William his horse, facing that curved smile, that mocking voice.

"Right on time." He turned to Francesca. "I will see you tonight, My Lady."

"I can hardly wait..."

He mounted the horse and left in full gallop, her loving eyes following his form until he'd disappeared.

Archibald pursed his lips. "Touching... now, let me leave. This is just about the amount of sugar sweet love I can handle today."

"Oh, Archie! You are such a cynic."

Archibald smiled at her from his seat. "That is what you become when you are courting death."

"Archie!"

"Go and make yourself beautiful for that wretched twat. I shall enjoy my ride."

She left, and he looked at Darren, that face he loved pulled into a mask. A sullen anger in him at that red welt running down his right cheek.

Their eyes met when Darren closed the door, and Archibald leant towards him. "You are sulking?"

"No, Milord..."

"Tsk..."

His blue eyes glanced around, a soft despair in them. "Not here..."

"Alright. Let us go."

They drove to the lake, and sat at the foot of their tree, silent for a while.

Archibald spoke first. "Father told me you would not leave. Let me down."

"It is true."

"He also told me you lost your wife and your child. I had no idea you were married."

Darren looked down at him. "It does not matter anymore. They are gone." He sighed, watching that jealous light in those brown pools. "Nobody knows this, so please keep it to yourself… she was my wife, but it wasn't my child…"

"She cheated on you?"

"No… we were married because she had become pregnant… Lord Shackleton wanted to avoid scandal."

"His child…"

"Yes… it would have been his child… she was just a maid, and I was single… understandably… with no intention of getting married… but it was convenient, and my parents were faithful to our master… and who was I to disagree or object? I owed them everything… so we got married and pretended that the child was mine… and then she died giving birth to that dead child…" He shrugged lightly, the emotions still raw, despite that loveless union. "So… now you know… might ease your jealousy." A slight smile at Archibald's face, shifting from a mild sadness to disbelief.

"Jealousy? I am not jealous." But it was a lie, and he had to laugh, as much as his lungs allowed it. "Alright… yes, I am jealous… Yesterday, I wanted to get up and walk to you. I pictured it, rushing through that dark park, to the stables, into your arms… kiss your pain away…" He lifted his eyes to Darren's puzzled eyes. "That is right. Kiss you, maybe more…" His eyes shone. "I have no idea what I am talking about, you know? Just fantasies of how it could be… with a man… but I've known quite early that women were not for me… my body gave up before I could do anything…" He smiled, out of breath, and felt Darren hold him tighter.

"I figured… this is not without its dangers, you know…"

"Yes… but what does it matter? Live today… die tomorrow… I do not want to die not having known how it is to love another man…"

A slight pang to Darren's heart at his words, but he understood, scolding himself a bit for seeing something else there, maybe…

Archibald grabbed his hand and met his eyes. "Let me rectify this… I do not want to die not having known how it is to love you."

Darren parted his lips, moved a bit, but his caution was in flames. "This… this could be our death sentence…"

"Mine is already looming above my head. And would you live without me?"

He breathed. "No…"

Archibald smiled. "All is well then. All in good time… when I am better… Just… maybe show me now how it could be… just a glimpse…"

Darren leant down and kissed him deep, sealing his mouth, then slipped his hand on Archibald's chest, and undid his top buttons, sliding his hand on that feeble chest, all the while kissing him whilst he pushed the shirt apart and down, letting his lips stray on that slender neck, his tongue, his teeth. Listening to his quickening breaths, holding that featherlight body, tracing his ribs with his fingers, his thumb, whilst he ate his neck, gently nibbling that pale skin with his teeth, and Archibald grabbed his arm with his nothing force, a soft moan escaping his mouth. A faint whizz in his breath, so Darren stopped gently, cupping his face, a soft kiss.

"Liked it?"

"I want more..."

Darren stroked his cheek. "When you are stronger... there is no rush."

"I might die... before we..."

Darren's fingers slid on his lips. "No... you will not... and if you become that unwell, we will find a way... to make it happen. Alright?"

I love you... those words, almost out, when he was not even sure if it was love, that mad, warm rush warming his chest, those lips which had set fire to his veins, scorching his skin, that gentle pain caused by his teeth.

"You are unwell?"

"No... just dazed a bit..." He smiled, his eyes straying to the water's rippling surface. "We should go. I need to get ready to go to twat-face tonight..."

"Will you be well enough?" That concern plain in his voice, so Archibald looked up at him.

"I have something to look forward to now."

"Oh..." A slight tint to his cheek, and Archibald stroke that angry welt.

"I wish I could beat the shit out of him."

"Noble young lords don't swear."

"Fuck that."

They laughed, and Darren got up and took him in his strong arms, walking with him to the barouche.

Archibald took his hand and kissed it when he had settled him, a new light in his brown eyes. "Drive me home, Darren."

"As you wish, Milord."

Their eyes sparkling, almost puffing with laughter. That ride home like flying, Archibald's eyes closed as the wind snaked between his brown strands, caressing his burning skin.

William strode into his father's office, sitting in a chair, propping his feet on another one. Grinning at his father's slight frown. "Am I disturbing, Father?"

"You are..." But he could not be mad, that pride swelling his chest, seeing his son. "But never mind. What is the news? Dinner tonight with the Hamptons?" His lips had curled into that dark smile William so loved.

"Oh yes. I intend to propose to lovely Francesca and ask for her hand in marriage... soon. This is a first step."

"A delightful young lady. I do hope she will agree to marrying you."

"I have already charmed her, Father. The rest is mere formality. Ask the old man for her hand, marry her. We will move into the West wing, if you do not mind."

"I would be delighted. The Hamptons are well-off and I would expect her dowry to be substantial... and with Edward's son on the brink of death, there is a high chance you will also inherit the estate after the old guy's death. A winning situation, on all accounts."

They laughed, their mirror smiles and eyes, even if his father's dark hair had greyed over during the years.

William smirked. "Yes... Archibald is extremely sick and weak... I would not be surprised if he died this winter... shame, but what can you do? Blood is not always strong..." He eyed his father, amused. "You know their stable master, Darren Turner?"

His father nodded. "Of course. I met him several times when he was still at the Shackleton estate. In fact, he grew up there, so yes, I remember him well. An able man."

William put his fingers together, musing. "You ever noticed we had a resemblance?"

His father pursed his lips. "Just spit it out, William. You know I like to be straight to the point."

"Is that man your bastard?"

There was a silence there in that quiet room, but his father smiled lightly. "Could very well be... I had... a brief affair with his mother back in the days... we were young... and as such, fooling around... as you do now, with the maids."

"Father...," said with a smile though.

"So... it could be. I had thought about it, seeing him sometimes on that estate, but never asked. She got married to their stable master a while after our encounter, if I may call it that at all."

"Ah, I see... so, not a love story, then?"

His father laughed. "No. I would not call that a love story. It was a one-off, and I never spoke to her after."

"So that man could be... my half-brother?"

"Mhm... I would not call him anything, even if he is mine... and how to prove that? It matches time-wise, though."

William squinted his eyes in amusement. "Fun..."

His father shrugged. "If you think so... I mean, I could have more... considering the number of encounters I had with various maids and peasant girls."

William grinned. "You were not too cautious, then?"

"No... what for? It is not like I would bear the consequences."

They laughed lightly, and William rose. "Time to get ready for my lovely fiancée to be. You will see, father. She is a true beauty."

"I know. I could not be happier for you, William."

"Thank you." He bowed mockingly and left, his father's eyes following his form.

Darren stopped the carriage in front of the Willoughby mansion, that huge house looming in the setting sun. William was already there to greet them and help Francesca down.

"Stunning, as ever, dear Francesca."

She blushed but hooked her hand on his arm to walk inside, followed by her mother, who had started chatting to William. Lord Hampton waited for the footmen to put his son in his chair, Archibald's eyes on Darren standing near the carriage, his breath in the air as that autumn chill settled with the night. His heart tight in his chest, but he could not speak to him, and was carried inside fast, that mild warmth even stronger in the dining room. Lord and Lady Willoughby greeted them, all smiles, that mild pity in their eyes, so Archibald swallowed his anger, sitting thankfully next to his father, facing William and Francesca, with Lord Willoughby taking the head of the table.

He felt a hand on his arm. "Are you feeling well enough?"

"Yes, Father."

"Just let me know if you don't. If this drags on, I might have you brought home."

"We shall see. It is alright for now."

But the prospect of leaving early had made his heart race, so he blew a small breath, and focused on the conversations around him, mainly about the upcoming hunt. His eyes drifted to the window, to that darkening sky, thinking of Darren waiting in that cold, that mild anger at the injustice of it all, seeing the servants and maids around them, the butler, scurrying and making sure everything was spotless and flawless. *Unreal... what makes us better than them? Why are we sitting here, and not the other way around? Why...* He got jolted out of his thoughts by William's brash voice.

"Archibald! We should meet up to play some chess or cards. I gather the weather will be soon too foul to go on your outings."

His eyes went to that arrogant, bold smile, his voice tainted with a mild scorn. "I do not plan on stopping my outings. They do a lot of good."

"Oh... but surely you will have time for us to play a bit. After all, we are almost family." Toasting him with his glass of dark red wine, those feral, mocking blue eyes watching him.

Twat... but he raised his glass of water. "Surely. We shall see."

A mild chill in him, watching Francesca turn to William, laughing when he'd said something funny, surely, but he could not hear it, so he just watched his sister. How her eyes gleamed, her lips slightly parted when she listened to William, and he could hardly understand it, that strong girl, almost melted at his feet, her reason gone somewhere in that burning heart, swallowed by those raging flames. *Is this love?* His heart beating harder. *Surely not... this insane madness... not seeing this man for whom he really is...* His eyes drifting to the maids serving them, how they averted their eyes when they got close to him, or blushed. Something invisible to the people around him, blissfully unaware, chatting, eating. He toyed with his food, sick a bit at his thoughts, at what he suspected, but ate a few bites, no to faint. More food brought out, but he waved it away.

His father turned to him. "Do you wish to go home? I am worried that this might be too much... and where is the end?"

"Would that not be terribly impolite?"

"You are sick, Archibald. They will understand." Not even leaving him any options, he turned to Lord Willoughby. "Excuse Archibald. I will send him home with our carriage, if you do not mind. He needs to rest."

"Not at all." Silence all of a sudden, all eyes on him, so Archibald pinched his lips, hiding them behind his handkerchief, but his grateful eyes went to his father's smile when the footmen picked him up.

William's small smile. "I do hope you feel better. We will have your parents and sister brought home, do not worry."

He just nodded, unable to talk, clinging to that lilting chair until they got outside, breathing in that icy air. Darren jumped from his seat, walking to them, that concern plain on his face, so Archibald gently grabbed a footman's hand, and they put him down.

"I am going home early. The rest of the family will follow on Lord Willoughby's carriage."

"As you wish, Milord."

Archibald's eyes smiled at him, and he got put inside, and covered up. The horses pulling, that mild swing soon put him into a state of mild daze, watching the silver landscape speed by, his eyes heavy. Darren's voice drifting to him, talking to the horses, soft words, soothing, and he imagined that they could just fly somewhere, like in tales on a magic carriage, far somewhere to a place where nothing mattered, but them... a gentle nudge to his shoulder, but he was too weak to wake fully. He still felt those strong arms scoop him up, that broad chest he knew so well, so he curled up in his arms, pretending to sleep, his face wedged against his coat, inhaling his scent, trying to keep it inside of him. Walking up the stairs, down the corridors, turning, somebody opening his room's door, that warm candle light sifting through his eyelids. He felt the bed under him and opened his eyes, looking straight into Darren's, a mild surprise in those blue eyes.

The steward's prim face was behind him. "Thank you, Darren. His Lordship needs to be put to bed, so you may withdraw."

Archibald smiled, wishing he could just reach his hand out and hold him back from leaving, but only their eyes spoke, briefly, watching him turn and leave, his gaze following his broad back in that black coat. *Come back... stay...* but it was impossible, so he let his servants undress him, tuck him in bed, leaving a candle by his bedside. Bitter, feeling for the very first time so lonely, it pushed at his chest with a vague ache. *I just want to sleep next to you... how is it to sleep next to another human?* His memories vague of his childhood, those rare times when his mother had allowed him to cuddle up, but he had inevitably woken alone in bed next morning. *Is this what we are all looking for? That warmth, that other breathing body filled with a soul matching ours? In the best of cases...* A vague chill in him in that quiet room, that he would stay and die alone, even if that mad yearning was there for Darren, the odds of them being anything but those stolen moments seemed out of reach. *A sinful crime which could cost our lives... my family's reputation...* but even as those thoughts drifted like shadows, he knew he could not walk back, stop whatever they were having. *My selfish dying self is going to go all the way with this, because I have nothing to lose. Forgive me...*

Darren went to bed late, that room chilled so he had to stoke the embers up, putting some thick logs on them. Hoping that it would be warmer soon. He was chilled to the bone, but undressed and quickly went under that thick blanket, shivering until his body obliged and heated that space up. That mad rush of fright hitting him in the dark when his thoughts drifted to Archibald. *Because it is wrong, so wrong...* that mild despair floating above his birthing feelings for him, that this was not going anywhere... *how to live like this? Stolen moments... illusions, really... dangerous...* He tried to distract himself, thinking of Wednesday's hunt, but those brown eyes kept interrupting, his gorgeous lips, that soft glass-like skin. He sighed, turning on his side, closing his eyes. *Sleep, sleep... do not think...*

Chapter 6

Lord Edward cautiously peeked into his son's room, meeting his eyes. "Awake?"

"Yes, Father." That voice tainted with disappointment, the rain pouring outside.

"Well... this is not a weather for your ride, but I have a surprise for you." He pushed something in from the corridor, and Archibald's eyes went wide.

"What is this?"

"A wheelchair. Custom made. I had it delivered from London." Archibald could not speak, watching that chair on wheels, a mild panic invading him as his father pushed it closer. "Look. Comfortable, easy to push, you will be a bit more independent with this, not relying on the footmen carrying you."

Archibald pushed that wave of raw anger down, trying to soften it with that light pouring from his father's eyes. Pride, even some joy at his purchase. But he only found an abysmal despair. *This is how they see me... as an invalid... maybe for good... I will never walk...* catching that light drowning in those fatherly eyes, so he forced a smile.

"Thank you, Father. This is most thoughtful of you."

"Oh... I am relieved. To tell you the truth, for a fleeting moment, I thought..."

"No. It is perfect. I shall try it out straight away. Allow me to dress and you can push me to breakfast." He smiled, watching him step outside, eyeing that dark green velvet chair studded with brass buttons, gleaming dark brown wood as the structure and the wheels.

He let his servant dress him, and the footmen put him in the chair. A vague relief on their faces that they didn't need to carry him anymore. His father stepped in and pushed him down those corridors, a strange feeling in Archibald, feeling that chair glide effortlessly, that this would be his new life. *Until it lasts, this wretched thing...*

Meeting his mother's and sister's eyes, dumbstruck, hearing his father's proud voice. "Feast your eyes on this. I had it delivered from London."

His mother got up to have a better look. "Oh, my... how beautiful. You are going to be so comfortable in this, Archibald. And look more human too, not carried around like an infant."

"Thank you, Mother." Inwardly fuming, but he knew her inside out, and looked at his sister, who had walked close.

"May I?" She took it over from her father and rolled him around the room, then spun him around, crouching down to him, laughing. "This is fun!"

"Just don't spin it... I need to get used to it."

"Think of all the possibilities! You can go on a promenade now, even maybe dance at a ball!"

"For sure, sister. I will be the most eligible bachelor in the county." He coughed and quickly pressed the handkerchief against his lips.

"Of course! Why not? You will feel better. And when you do, the ladies will come to you."

His mother sat, sipping at her tea. "They might just take an interest in you with that chair. It is peculiar to have an invalid husband."

Lord Edward blanched a bit. "Archibald is not invalid... this chair is merely here to help him regain his strength."

"We all know that this is a dream, Edward. It would be better if you accepted it and stopped filling Archibald's head with your fantasies."

Francesca pushed Archibald to the table, but he had lost whatever weak appetite he had had and looked at his father.

"Take me back to my room."

"Are you positive? You have not eaten."

"Please, Father." His eyes begged too, and Lord Edward pushed him back, leaving him near the window.

"Anything else you would wish for?"

"No... I would have wished for my ride, but it is not an option."

"Darren could take you in the carriage."

"No. He would be soaking in this rain, without any shelter. I do not want that."

"He is a coachman. This is nothing out of the extraordinary."

Archibald's eyes went to him, veiled with anger. "It may be so, but it is not tolerable for me. Please give me my book. I shall read and try to avoid utter boredom."

"William will come later."

Archibald sighed. "Tell him I am having a nap. A long one..."

"I suppose he will propose. It is almost a formality now."

"Wonderful..."

"I will leave you. See you at lunch."

"Yes."

He closed his book on his knees and looked towards the stables, that roof barely visible behind those tall trees. His mind on his mother's words. *Soon, you will have a son-in-law worthy of your dreams, Mother... patience...* wondering if she was right, his gaze drifting to his legs under that blanket. *I could just get up...* the thought there, but he was too scared. *They will not carry me after all these years... they are probably dead...*

He opened his book and sighed, at peace though, listening to the rain hammering at the windows. Missing Darren like crazy, but there was no way he would ask him to drive in such a weather.

Darren and the boys were cleaning the stalls, the horses tied up, that pouring rain lashing inside through the wide-open door when a soaked footman ran inside, followed by a trotting horse.

The man wiped his eyes. "His Lordship's horse... Lord Willoughby's..."

Darren took the reins. "When does he need it back?"

"You know him... I have not a clue. We will send a page to you. Damned rain! He had to ride here too, could not have taken a carriage or something." He left, fuming, running under that deluge, and Darren led the horse to a stall.

He gestured Travis over. "You know what you have to do."

"Yes, sir."

They worked whilst Travis groomed the panting horse, covering it then with a blanket, as he was steaming.

The day dipping into a darkening afternoon when a page appeared, rushing inside the stables, almost into the grains cart.

"Sir Darren... Lord William wants his horse."

"James..."

"No, sir... he said he wanted you to bring it."

James shot a puzzled look at him, but Darren just forced a smile.

"Of course... feed the horses, boys. I'll be back."

He quickly saddled the horse, helped by James, and put his coat and hat on, walking to the mansion under those harsh fat droplets plummeting from the sky. By the time he got there, he could feel the rain seeping through, despite that thick coat.

Standing, waiting, for what seemed an hour, his eyes on that stubbornly closed door. *Fuck, fuck...* silent words, but his anger was boiling, when finally, the doors opened and William rushed out, laughing, waving at Francesca's form in the doorway.

He stepped to Darren and took the reins out if his hand. "I made you wait? Well, what can you do? My fiancée would not let me leave. That is right, I shall marry your young mistress very soon, and we will see more of each other." He smiled wide, pulling his gloves on, unfazed by the rain streaming down his face.

"Congratulations, Milord."

"Thank you." He stepped closer and ran his hand down the welt on Darren's face. "Barely there. I was most gracious."

"Yes, Milord."

"Wonderful! You will be pleased to hear that your invalid of a master got a nice rolling chair from his papa today. A true beauty." He laughed, and Darren had to compose his face to hide his rushing heart. "Yes, a real treat. He was delighted, of course, you should have seen him. Well, better this than sitting all day in one place, useless. Maybe death would be better. Merciful, don't you think?"

Darren swallowed. "It is not my place to have an opinion on this, Milord."

"Truly well taught. Nice. Your parents must have been proud of you."

He had that wicked glint in his eyes, and Darren chose not to reply, bowing when he mounted his horse. His coat had soaked through, and he could hardly wait to leave, watching as the young lord spurred his horse straight into a full gallop.

He walked back to the stables, to his room, shedding his wet clothes, hanging them on a string strung between the roof beams. Stoking the fire up before he changed and started cooking something to eat. His heart clenching for her, but there was no surprise there, that engagement so predictable. *She was lost the first time she saw him... aren't we all... lost at first sight...* He sighed and sat down to eat that quick omelette, the rain hammering at the roof.

It had stopped by the morning, a glorious sunshine pouring down, and Darren's heart beat a bit harder, because they could go on that ride. He prepared Raven and waited for Lord Hampton to walk to the stables in his hunting gear. James was ready to escort him on the roan, the boy a bit awed that he got chosen, but Darren had briefed him thoroughly, so he was confident he could do this right.

Lord Hampton smiled at the gleaming horse. "A true beauty."

"And fast too, Milord."

"I know... Archibald is very impatient, so please make sure you are there maybe earlier. He can hardly wait to leave."

"Of course, Milord."

Lord Hampton mounted and stroked the animal's neck. "Let's hunt, Raven, and come back in glory." He spurred the horse into a gentle trot, James following, and Darren exhaled in relief, quickly preparing the barouche.

He pulled up to the mansion and within a couple of minutes, Archibald was pushed out, the footmen carrying him down the stairs. They settled him, and Darren took off, not needing words, as he took the roads to their lake. A swift ride in that late autumn sunshine, warming them a bit despite that lingering chill.

He turned to Archibald when they'd reached the lake shore, worry rippling through him at that dull light in his brown eyes. "You are unwell?"

"I missed you. That is all. Take me out."

Archibald was already clinging to him when he took that light body in his arms, settling under their tree on the blanket he'd put there. Just holding him, but Archibald pushed at his arms to turn to him.

"I am not sure I can survive... a day... without you... and the weather is not going to give us any respite."

"Yes, it is true."

That mad little despair in his eyes. "Why does the world have to be like this? I want to just sleep in your arms... I would just like to do that. And it is impossible." Watching the same despair invade Darren's blue eyes, so he reached up to his face. "Sometimes, I am dead scared."

"Me too."

"But... it is not enough for me to step away from you..." He smiled wryly. "That twat is marrying my sister."

"I know. He told me." Almost smiling at how Archibald had evaded those dangerous waters of their fears.

"Idiot. We will have to suffer his company, as he will be part of the family. I do not trust him."

"He can certainly be a bit bold... and tactless."

"That is mildly put... Father gifted me a sublime rolling chair. Isn't this great? I almost blew up.. right there... but it is Father... I cannot be mad at him, he just wants the best for me."

"It might help you move around better."

"My legs... do you think they are dead?"

Darren frowned. "Dead? You had an accident?"

"No... I just haven't used them in a while... spent my years in bed, or sitting, mostly."

Darren pushed him out of his arms and settled him against the tree, taking his blanket off. His hands went to his calves. "May I?"

Archibald smiled lightly. "Touch me? By all means, do."

Darren slid his hands on his right calf, gently probing, squeezing that meagre flesh, and Archibald hissed.

"Ouch..."

"Painful?"

"Yes... a bit..."

He did the same with the other one, a gush of warmth flooding Archibald when he felt those hands on him.

Darren looked up. "I need to inspect your thighs."

"Please..."

He massaged the right thigh, stroking, then the left, and Archibald almost closed his eyes. "You're hurting?"

"No... I mean, a bit, but nothing too strong."

"It looks to me that they are not dead. You feel pain, and you can feel my hands on your skin?"

"Yes..." *and how... you have no idea...*

Darren smiled. "They need to work again."

"Impossible..."

"Not if you set your mind to it." He put the blanket back on Archibald's legs and took him in his arms, looking down at him. "How is your breath?"

"Better... maybe... I am not sure."

"Gain it back. Then you can learn to walk."

"How?"

"I can help you. Lame horses need time too, and rehabilitation."

Archibald's smile was tainted with disbelief. "You are pulling my leg."

"Hardly."

They laughed, and Archibald turned his lips towards him. "Giving me some hope merits a kiss."

"One?"

"Maybe more..."

Their lips met, and Archibald opened up wide for him, wanting to feel all of him, his taste, his breath, his teeth. Moaning a bit when Darren bit his lower lip gently, pushing his lips against those teeth, wanting more.

Darren broke the kiss. "Hey... I cannot leave a mark."

"Sure... sorry..."

"Don't be..." Kissing him again, pinching a bit harder, but careful, just making sure those pale lips pulsed with blood again. Letting him breathe.

"I could get used to this."

Darren just smiled, stroking his face, watching his eyelids flutter, but he didn't fall asleep, just stayed in his arms, watching the light play on those gentle waves. A golden light, maybe the last one.

"We need to leave..."

Reluctant, but they had no choice, Archibald knew. Listening to the horses' hooves cluttering on the road, soaking in those last dying rays. *I might live...* his mind on walking again... *maybe... if I can manage to get rid of that fear.* Realising with a mild ripple of anguish that he hadn't coughed, really, just a bit. He clenched that handkerchief in his palm though, holding on to it, his eyes hard as the mansion came into sight.

His footmen rushing down with his chair, ready.

Darren turned to him, and Archibald had to smile. "This was excellent. Thank you."

"My pleasure, Milord."

Archibald just lightly grazed his lips, blowing him a soft kiss, that movement invisible to the footmen, almost as if he wanted to just wipe them off, but Darren had caught it, squinting his eyes at him with a small smile. Watching them take him away, his heart a bit lighter, that thrill in him of maybe Archibald healing, that mad dream of making him walk again.

Chapter 7

The weather turned colder, rain drizzling into the scarce sunshine, so their outings became less frequent, and Archibald brew his frustration, his eyes on that cloudy sky in his windows. *Yet again a rotten day...* His eyes went to the door, watching his father enter.

"Care for a walk?"

Archibald pursed his lips, sitting in his chair. "I cannot walk, Father."

"I could push you in the park. It would do you good. The sky is clearing a bit, and we might be just lucky between two showers."

"I am not sure..."

"I thought we could walk to the stables? You have not been yet." A small smile seeing Archibald's face light up.

"Sure. Why not."

"Splendid. Allow me." He pushed him to the stairs, where the footmen carried him down.

Coats on, and they were gone, early, that crisp morning air filled with bird songs. Wild geese flying in that graphite sky.

Archibald breathed in deep, holding his handkerchief close to his lips, his eyes on the park, the gravelled road, hearing his father's steps. The stables... his heart racing, knowing that the buildings were there at the end of the road cutting through that immaculate lawn. He hadn't seen Darren for days, and he had to tame his enthusiasm with his father behind him, close. The buildings approaching, that archway leading to the stable yard, voices drifting to them, horses neighing, the sound of hooves on the gravel.

Lord Edward pushed him into the yard, slowing a bit, Archibald's eyes roaming around, James leading Dandy and Tulip to the fields, followed by Travis leading the mare, the old horse, and the pony trotting behind them, free. A slosh of water, and his eyes went to the barouche, water dripping down the side, the sound of a brush on wood. Lord Edward pushed him closer, and Darren stepped out from behind the barouche, holding a large brush, his shirt half-open at the front, soaked, his chest heaving, that slight puzzled look replaced by his smile, just a glint of surprise in his eyes seeing Archibald.

He wiped his hands on his trousers, embarrassed a bit. "Good morning, My Lord... Lord Archibald... I apologise, I am not in the best of states..."

Lord Edward smiled. "No need. We are the intruders here. I wanted to show Archibald the stables."

"Of course, Milord. This way." Darren put the brush down, and quickly wiped his hands, leading the way inside, the stall doors wide open. A bit apologetic. "We are starting cleaning when the boys are back from the field."

"That is fine. I trust the hay is of good quality this year?"

"Yes, Milord. It is excellent..." Archibald caught his eyes, hiding his smile behind his handkerchief, watching as he forgot his words a bit. Breathing in deep. "Uh... we changed the farmer supplying us, so it is much better."

"I am delighted to hear it. Let us step outside. I have matters to discuss." They went to the yard and Lord Edward faced him. "Francesca is getting married, as you know, and my wife refuses to have those two horses pull the carriage..." He raised his hand at the alarm in Darren's eyes. "No need to fret, they will not be sold, of course, but Francesca will need a carriage worthy of her status, especially marrying the young lord."

Archibald pulled a face, mocking. "Unbelievable. There is nothing wrong with some modesty."

"This is not our choice to make, Archibald." He turned back to Darren. "So, please go and find a carriage and a team of four horses. Matching in every aspect, impeccable. Lady Francesca would like them bay in colour."

"Understood, Milord. How fast does her ladyship need the carriage?"

"As fast as you can manage to buy them and make sure they work properly."

Darren nodded, his mind on this huge task. A matching team with winter approaching, secure, well-trained horses... He sighed softly. "I will do my best, Milord."

"Very well. Now, to the other matter at hand. You might not be able to do your outings with the weather being so fickle, but you could walk Archibald in his chair. I did it this morning but will not be able to commit to this regularly. Besides, your strength is greater than mine. Maybe you could come to the mansion in the mornings and push him here. That walnut tree there would be a perfect place for him to read and soak in some fresh air. That is, if this would be to your liking, Archibald."

Archibald blinked at his father. "Of course... I mean, I would like it, father, sure..." His heart in his throat.

"Would that be an issue, Darren?"

"Not at all, Milord."

"It is settled, then. Please come tomorrow, early."

"As you wish, Milord."

"Very well. We shall be going."

Darren bowed and watched them leave, his heart racing.

Next morning, Archibald had been brought down to the bottom of the stairs, and he watched Darren walk to him, that loose shirt under his vest, the wind ruffling his dark hair. He took his chair without a word, and pushed him down that gravelled path, and Archibald reached up to his warm hand, covering it with his ice-cold palm, as if that warmth could seep into his body and make his flesh live again. Feeling how effortlessly he was pushing that chair, his strong strides beating the gravel.

Archibald smiled, and looked up at him. "Isn't this glorious? Sometimes, Father has the most unexpected ideas."

"I can see."

His smile almost melted Archibald's heart right there, that gush of warmth flooding his chest, making it hard to breathe. He closed his eyes for a split second and Darren stopped walking, his broad hand going to Archibald's shoulder.

"You are unwell?"

"Yes..." He smiled up at him. "But not because of my illness... I have another one, it seems... makes the heart do funny things..."

"Oh... I see." Darren pushed him, their hearts flying a bit, and Archibald's hand slipped from his when they neared the courtyard.

The boys were in full work, and Darren pushed him under that tree. "I need to work a bit, but will keep an eye on you, alright?"

"Yes... I have my book..." Only their eyes spoke then in that brief glance before Darren turned and walked to the stables.

Archibald opened his book, but his eyes darted to him, each time he pushed the wheelbarrow out of the stables to the dung pile, each time Darren walked to the hay barn, that heavy load on his pitchfork just casually thrown on his shoulder. He had rolled back his sleeves, those strong arms working effortlessly, his deep voice scolding the boys sometimes. Archibald smiled, and read a bit, his mind at peace.

Later, Darren brought him a glass of water. "I should push you back, you need to have breakfast."

Archibald pursed his lips. "Do I?"

Darren's eyes smiled. "You do..."

Archibald gestured him closer, and he leant down a bit. "Is there any way we could stay alone one of these mornings?"

Darren looked at him. "Maybe..."

"Splendid... I am counting on you."

That slight touch of their fingers as he took the glass away raced down Archibald's spine, and he had to sit back, a bit faint. Choking on his own thoughts which seemed to flame up, burn his mouth, his lips.

A few days later, Darren came to get him early, the sky's edge still pale, and he pushed him back to the stables, the yard empty.

Archibald looked up at him as he stopped the chair near some stairs. "The boys are away?"

"Yes. I sent them to town to the blacksmith. The horses needed new shoes. They will be back much later..."

"We are alone?" His stomach clenched around the flutters in it, all of a sudden unsure, watching his blue eyes fill with an amused, warm light.

"Yes, we are. But you can read near your tree..."

"Or..."

"Or, we could have tea in my humble lodging."

"I think tea would be good now..."

"Tea it is then..."

Archibald held onto his neck when Darren took him in his arms and walked up the stairs leading to a door under the roof. He pushed it open and put Archibald down on a chair near a table.

Archibald looked around that single room, wide-eyed, his heart hammering. From fear. Wrath. "This... this is where you live?"

Darren turned to him from the stove. "Yes, it is."

"This... this is a disgrace!"

He smiled wryly. "Well... it is not too big, but it does the job." Watching Archibald in his neat, elegant clothes, and for a fleeting moment, he thought this was sheer madness, him sitting in this shabby room under the roof. *Us. Having this whatever...*

Archibald caught that light in his eyes. "Come here." He took his hands when he'd ambled close, looking up at him. "Let us not waste time which is precious."

A small sad smile. "You don't belong here..."

"I belong with you. The rest is insignificant." Archibald squeezed his hands feebly. "I wanted us to be alone... but I have no idea what I should be doing... I was hoping you would..."

Those warm brown eyes made Darren's legs weak, so he took the kettle off the stove and stepped back to Archibald. He scooped him up and brought him to the bed, sitting him on it, not letting Archibald think, or talk, sealing his mouth with a kiss, letting those feeble hands go around his neck as his hands roamed his back, the skin taut on those bird bones poking through his flesh. Peeling his jacket off, his cravat, he pulled his shirt over his head, standing between his legs, holding him closer as he ate him up, those burning, trembling lips. Archibald tugged at his shirt's neck, so Darren pulled it off, panting, their eyes meeting, close, as Archibald's hands went to his broad chest, tracing his muscles, around his back, pulling him close, closing his fists on that rippling flesh, moaning into the kiss, that sound, almost out without thinking as he let Darren push him back on the bed, pull his boots off as he took his own ones off too, push him up on the bed with his thigh when he'd claimed his mouth again. Kissing, their hands roaming each other's skin.

Darren broke the kiss, letting Archibald breathe, stroking his face, bathing in his eyes, his voice. "I want more..."

"There is no rush..."

"But there is... for me..." He parted his lips, feeling Darren's mouth, his tongue, just clinging to him, to his shoulders, unsure.

Darren slid his hands on that smooth skin, holding Archibald closer, goose bumps rising under his touch, that soft tremor under his palms. His mouth wandered down to Archibald's neck, soft bites, that feeble chest rising faster, pressed against him, skin to skin, as his hand slid down between his legs, just brushing over that birthing bulge. Archibald laboured breath in his neck, so he stopped and gently cupped his face.

"You will strain yourself..."

Archibald inhaled, deep, and smiled. "Yes... you are right..."

Tears welled up in his eyes, and Darren just kissed him softly. "We will find more time... do not worry..." Feeling Archibald's chest rise, his heart beating against those feeble ribs, a slight worry in him.

Archibald smiled, panting a bit. "Alright... let us stay like this though... I want to stay in your arms..." Darren lay down on his back and pulled him in his shoulder, tight, just holding him close, that nothing breath on his chest, his skin. "I dreamt of this... just being with you... close... wondering how it would be..."

That voice, so filled with sleep, it made Darren smile, so he stroked his bone thin shoulder. "I hope it's as you dreamt it..."

"Better... much better..."

He'd fallen asleep minutes later, Darren knew, that soft breath on his skin, but he held him, watching that ashen face and that dark shadow around his eyes. *So weak...* his heart clenched, that mad feeling in him that Archibald might not live, the thought spiralling him into a panic because he knew he was lost... *in love...* Sighing against that painful glow in his chest, his heart throbbing.

Archibald didn't wake when Darren got up after a while, gently covering him, and went down to do the stables.

Archibald was still asleep when Darren walked back up, half-naked as he'd washed at the well, and he put the kettle on, and made two mugs of strong tea with milk. He planted a soft kiss on Archibald's lips, waiting until he woke, his brown eyes still a bit hazy as he looked around.

"I slept?"

"Yes... for hours..."

He sat up, dizzy, a bit bitter. "Truly glorious..."

Darren put his palm on his cheek. "It did you some good, do not regret it."

"Your hair is wet..." Running his fingers into that mass of dark hair, watching his smile.

"I had to wash. My work is not the cleanest."

"But you love it."

"Yes, I do. I made tea."

"Heaven."

He brought him a mug, and they sat on the bed, sipping that warm, sweet liquid.

Archibald turned to him. "I wish this could be our life... Too soon? But I would like to wake next to you and go to sleep on your shoulder."

Darren's lips curled up. "Yeah... It would be nice."

Just watching each other, sipping their tea.

Archibald spoke after a while. "I feel much better... I never slept this well." He sighed. "What now?"

Darren took his mug. "Now, you will dress, and I will push you back. It's late. Better not have somebody find you here..."

"You are right, of course..." He dressed, and Darren readjusted his cravat, his jacket. Archibald caught his hands, meeting his eyes. "This whole thing is impossible."

"Yes..." Pained, he straightened and took him in his arms. "But this is what we have."

"If you would be a maid, this would not be an issue. Stupid, and unfair." He looked into his eyes, apologetic. "Not that what we have could be compared to that, do not get me wrong..."

"I know..."

Their throats locked, and Darren brought him back to his chair. Hooves beating the ground, close.

"The boys are coming back... let's go."

"Alright..."

He pushed him back to the mansion, the footmen hurrying down to take him up the stairs.

Archibald whispered. "Tomorrow..."

"Yes... see you then."

A quick meet of their eyes, brief, filled with despair and longing, and he was carried away. Darren closed his eyes, exhaling hard, and walked back to the stables, his heart heavy.

Chapter 8

"Ah... your attention drifted away, dear Archibald!"

He met those arrogant eyes, that slight smile, as William snatched his pawn off the chessboard. He couldn't care less, but focused back on the game, his mother and Francesca sitting on the couches, reading their books, and he wished he could disappear with a book, and not play with that twat, but it had been impossible. He pushed his bishop further.

"Nice move... you astonish me, Archibald, considering how you have no time to play. You were modest about your skills." He moved his rook, leaning back.

"I used to play a lot... when my health allowed it and I had more patience."

"Indeed... ah...ah... You missed spotting my knight. Tsk-tsk..." He took Archibald's bishop off and smiled at him over the board, his eyes unreadable. "Horses can be unpredictable creatures, n'est-ce pas?"

Archibald frowned. "I guess. It has been a long time since I haven't ridden."

"But as I have heard, you still spend your mornings at the stables?"

Archibald froze a bit, but held his gaze. "Yes, I do." *So, what's that to you, you insufferable twat. Shut your fucking mouth...*

"Must be refreshing... and you do not need to neglect the company of your favourite coachman either."

"He does not have time to chat."

"Who said anything about chatting?"

Archibald raised his eyes to William's mocking eyes, unsure. Masking his rushing heart. *I'm being stupid... he is just teasing, like the idiot he is.*

His mother's voice made him turn towards her. "Why, I never understood why your father had this idea. It must be awfully dull to sit there and be in the company of the stable staff, truly."

"I read, mostly."

"Still... ah, never mind, I suppose, if it does you good? Next Friday, we have a ball, the last of the season. I can hardly wait to introduce you to some young ladies. Your chair will make an impression, I am sure."

"Mother... Truly, I would like to stay home, please."

She looked at him, hard. "No, Archibald. It is time you did something with yourself. After all, you are our only son and the heir of the estate and the family's fortune. You need to start courting some young ladies, fund a family, have children..."

"If I can have children, at all." Clipped, he could barely contain himself when he felt William's hand on his arm. He looked at him, at his smile.

"Come, come. Surely, this should not be on the table, yet. I will make sure to chaperon you during that ball. We will have a great time." He winked and moved his rook again, wiggling his eyebrows at Archibald. "I might just win."

"You might..." Bitter, he swallowed and pressed his handkerchief against his mouth. More for comfort, as he had scarcely coughed.

His father entered then. "How is everything? Francesca, I brought news. Darren might have found your carriage and your team. I need to go and inspect it tomorrow with him, but as I trust the man, this is mere formality."

Archibald's face flushed at his name, but he feigned disinterest, watching the chessboard.

William's mocking voice. "I sure hope he made a decent choice. My dear fiancée only deserves the very best."

"His knowledge of horses is not to be disputed."

William shrugged, his eyes on Archibald. "We shall see. I am most curious to find out."

Lady Hampton rang for tea. "Me too. You would do well to sell those awful, mismatched horses, dear Mister Hampton."

Archibald raised his head, but his father replied before he could. "No, my dear. Archibald can have them... I mean, it just makes sense. What do you say, son?"

Archibald's eyes went a bit wide. "Have them?"

"Yes. It is high time you had your own horses. That is, if they suit you."

"Of course, Father. They do. Thank you." He couldn't hide his joy, that burst of warmth in his chest, thinking of how Darren would react when he would tell him.

William smiled. "Why… this is a splendid gift, Archibald. Suits you."

Archibald just smiled back, unaware of that dark light in those blue eyes. "Thank you. I am most pleased."

William turned to Lord Hampton. "Does the coachman come with the package?" Lord Edward frowned a bit, seeing the colour drain from Archibald's face. Anger. Maybe something else… William spread his palms. "Forgive me. A bad jest."

"Indeed… Darren is not an animal. I could hardly gift him away."

"Indeed." But his mocking eyes were on Archibald's blanched face, watching him carefully.

Tea was brought in then, and they gathered around the table, conversations drifting to the wedding, the ball. Archibald only nibbled on his biscuits, that warm tea bringing him back to that small room under the roof, the cup burning his lips. His eyes drifted to the window, that iron sky, and lead rain pouring from ashen clouds. He felt his father's hand, so his eyes went to him, to his smile.

"You look better."

"I dare not believe I feel better too, Father. It might be an illusion. A temporary relief." A mad fright in him at the prospect of living because he had buried himself, and the possibility of having a life terrified him. *What kind of life?* The only one he wanted seemed a death sentence too…

"Do not be so hard on yourself."

"I am grateful, father, for your gift. Truly."

"Those are just horses. Nothing of significance. I wish I could give you more."

Archibald's eyes almost welled up. "You are already outdoing yourself."

Lord Hampton just patted his hand, and sipped his tea, a small light of hope in him, that Archibald might live, that he might just live another year, maybe.

Next day, Lord Hampton went down the stairs to meet Darren. He was holding Dandy and Raven, the two horses saddled as Lord Hampton had wanted to ride to check the carriage and the team out. They had an hour of trail ride, and Darren led the way, the sky laden with clouds. Trotting then, side by side.

"Riding is best. I hate to be carried around like an old invalid."

"You ride exceptionally well, Milord. I have heard of that hunt."

"Ah… my famous jump…" He patted Raven's slender neck. "But it is all thanks to this excellent horse. You trained him well."

"He was easy to train. An excellent temper. My father chose him, I remember the day he was brought to us, as a young colt of three."

"How many years ago?"

"Ten, Milord."

"That is a long time to have known him. And the others."

Darren shrugged, moved a bit. "They become like children, pardon the analogy, Milord."

"I am grateful for what you do for my son, Darren. He might just live a bit more."

That kick to his heart, but Darren kept a straight face. "I am glad that the young lord benefits from his time outside."

"He does. Too bad the weather has been foul. We had Lord William over to entertain him, but I had the impression he only got on Archibald's nerves." He smiled lightly, watching that small curve at the edge of Darren's lips, quickly smoothed into a mask.

"Lord William has a forceful personality, pardon my words, Milord."

"Please. You may speak freely, for I do think we share the same opinion. Ah... but what can you do? My daughter fell in love... Love is a tricky beast..."

"Indeed, Milord..." He was hoping Lord Hampton would stop talking, evoke love, or anything related to it, because his heart was in flames, and he feared the words would just tumble out of his mouth, like clumsy little flaming pellets.

"Yes, a fickle beast... unexpectedly attacking when we let our guards down... ah... yes. Nothing can be done when it strikes." He glanced at Darren, but he kept quiet, keeping his horse in a light trot. "Shall we canter a bit? That field looks ideal."

"As you wish, Milord."

They set off, the horses giddy with their freedom, rushing when they let the reins loose.

Next day, the sun was up, and Archibald made sure he got ready early, eager to leave the house and meet Darren. *At last...* several days had flown by without just as much as seeing him, just listening to his father recount their ride, that successful visit to the seller. The horses and carriage had been bought, they just needed to go there and bring the horses over as soon as the stalls were ready. He waited at the bottom of the stairs, turning his face to the sun, that meagre, cold sun, but it was there. Listening to his steps on the gravel, but Archibald didn't open his eyes, waiting until he got close.

Looking at him, breathless a bit. "At last..."

"I am sorry. I could not leave straight away."

"It does not matter... bring me away from this horrid house, and far from William, whom, I gather, will be here soon..."

Darren smiled and pushed him to the stables, under the walnut tree. He smoothed the blanket on Archibald's legs, tucked it in, and Archibald breathed harder a bit, feeling those strong hands on his legs.

Their eyes met. "I missed you..." His voice, so low, but Darren had heard it.

He brushed his hand down his hand. "Me too..."

Archibald looked up at him. "I have news for you... Father... now that Francesca will have her fancy carriage and horses... gifted me the other two horses."

Darren's face fell. "Which ones?"

"What do you think? Dandy and Tulip, of course." A rush of relief rippled down his face, and Archibald smiled. "This is great news, right? For I will never sell them as long as I live, and if I die, I will leave them to you..."

Darren wiped at a rogue tear, clearing his throat. "I could not be happier..." He leant closer, meeting his eyes. "Please do not talk about death. It might be casual for you, but you are ripping my heart open each time..."

"Alright... I am sorry."

"How is your breath?"

"Better..."

"Then we can soon work on your legs... make you walk."

"I have a hard time believing this."

Darren smiled. "Try to believe first. There is nothing without that."

"I wish I had your confidence."

"You cannot have mine, but you can dig out yours. It is there, otherwise you would not be so feisty."

Archibald pursed his lips. "Feisty? Maybe..."

"Time to heal... and forget death."

"It was a comforting thought."

Darren blew a small breath. "I cannot imagine how... but maybe it was for you..."

"And what now?"

"Just live. Now, read your book. I have work to do."

"So simple..."

Darren smiled wryly. "It is. You think too much. That is the main problem."

Archibald smiled wide. "Truly? This is new. Nobody has ever told me this before."

"Well, I'm telling you now..." His eyes softened. "I have to go."

Archibald's eyes followed his broad back until he'd disappeared behind the stable doors, and he opened his book, trying to keep his mind on it, but the lines seemed to blur, his fickle imagination leaping to other thoughts. Of getting up and walking with him. Riding together. Just standing and melting in his arms. His skin burning where his fingers had lingered. He rubbed it lightly with his thumb, his eyes in the golden leaves, that light pouring down from the sky, playing.

A week had passed like this, with some mornings better than others, but the weather kept cooling, and he could pass less and less time under that tree. A mild despair in him, despite his breath coming back, those slight bouts of cough void of blood.

Waiting for the carriage in the dusk lights, listening to his mother's huffing voice.

"I sure hope we will make an impression with your new carriage, my dear."

Lord Hampton pulled his gloves on. "I still do think this is rushed. Those horses have barely been here for a week."

William grinned at him. "Why... your more than able stable master had then ample time to train them, I am sure."

Lord Hampton didn't comment, his hand on Archibald's shoulder, watching as the carriage emerged from the park, huge, the four matching bay horses identical to anybody who didn't know much about horses. James was riding the front left lead horse, the animals a bit nervous, tugging at the reins. A mild stress on the boy's face, but he jumped down, and went to hold the rear horse tight. Darren got off whilst the footmen opened the door for the family.

Lord Hampton stepped to Darren. "How are they?"

"They are in a new place and I am new to them too. They were led with firm bits and their heads tied up high..."

Lady Hampton looked at him. "Well, you better keep those heads tied up. I am sick of our horses dangling their heads."

"Yes, Milady." His eyes went back to Lord Hampton, catching him rolling them.

They waited until she boarded the carriage, and Lord Hampton lowered his voice. "Just do what you think is best. My wife will not notice if you loosen the straps."

"I have loosened them, Milord... but it needs to be done gradually. For now, we will work with what we have. I had to take James to manage the lead horse, until they learn and get used to me."

The rear horse tugged at the boy's hands, hard, and a mild stress rippled through Darren, but he kept quiet and waited until they were all settled.

He stepped to James then. "Do not let them get the upper hand. When we will be back, we will retrain them, but there is no time now."

"Alright, sir." He waited until Darren sat, and went back on the lead horse's back, thankful that he didn't try to throw him off.

They set off; the horses trotting vigorously, alert, and Darren cursed under his breath, holding the reins tight. He had left those harsh bits, as the horses' mouths were used to it. *Too much too...* Holding them with an iron grip, those stone mouths, his arms cramping after a while. *What a drive...* Voices drifting to him from the carriage, Lady Hampton's shrill with excitement, William's smooth laughter mingling with Francesca's, Lord Hampton's measured words, Archibald's slight exasperation. The icy air flowing around him, his eyes on the horses, their ears, every tiny movement, on James' back, the boy doing his best to keep up with the horse's swift strides.

Fortunately, the journey wasn't too long, and he halted the carriage in front of that huge mansion, music drifting from behind those illuminated windows. James had jumped down on trembling legs, holding the horses tight, whilst Darren opened the door.

William jumped out, almost bumping into him. His broad smile. "Nice driving. I bet those horses are a welcome change from those two slowpokes. My dear... allow me." He helped Francesca down, then Lady Hampton.

Lord Hampton followed and waited until the footmen took Archibald out and sat him in his chair. He took the blanket to cover his legs, but his wife tore it out of his hands.

"Leave this horrid blanket! Archibald has legs and should at least look like a decent man, even if he is invalid and has to sit in this chair!"

"Mother..."

"Do not even object, Archibald. I had it with you hiding behind your blanket and your cloth here." She reached for the handkerchief, but Archibald snatched it away, his eyes like murder.

"Leave me alone."

He was shivering, that warmth missing from his legs, and Darren's heart clenched, but he had to stay put, and wait, when William stepped over and took hold of the wheeled chair.

"Now, now... allow me to push you in, it's cold here. You do not need that blanket inside; your mother is right."

"Do not patronise me, William."

"I would not dare."

He laughed and pushed him in, whilst Lady Hampton shoved the blanket into Darren's hands.

Darren watched them leave, that blanket still warm from his skin, and he sighed deep and put it in the carriage, walking to James then. "Are you alright? Not too tired?"

The boy was trembling, so Darren pulled a blanket from under the bench and smoothed it around his shoulders. "Thank you.... sir." His teeth chattering, holding that horse tight.

"Here... relax your hand a bit. They are tired, they won't want to run away... or let's hope so... but we will have to watch them. These are not Dandy and Tulip who would just stand here all night... Better not take the bridles off either, they can eat like this..."

Some other coachmen had drifted close, eyeing the horses, and that arrogant George sneered. "Nice team... at last you get to drive some quality horses... must be a real change after those two you have usually..."

Darren just shot him a look, loosening the straps to let the horses' heads down, those powerful necks stretching with grateful sighs.

One of the men shook his head. "Ain't good to loosen those... you will spoil them, and won't be able to tighten 'em up again..."

Darren just continued as if he hadn't heard it, then strapped the grain sacks on the horses' heads.

George grinned. "He's a stubborn mule, our Darren here. Won't listen to good common sense. Or advice. Who's this boy here? Scrawny thing." He ruffled James' hair who shot an alarmed look at Darren.

"This is James. Leave him alone."

"Hey... no harm done, aye, boy?"

Darren had finished and faced him. "Are you done? Find somebody else to pester."

"Sure thing... always a pleasure talking to you..." George left, ambling to some others, and Darren sighed, and turned to James.

"Hungry?"

"Yes..."

He got their sandwiches out and they munched close to the horses, the reins on their arms, but the horses seemed content, their heads lowered, scrunching their oats. Other men drifted to them to talk whilst the music spilled outside. Their breaths in the air in that chill night.

Archibald's mother had ushered a flock of young women and their mothers around him, and he could barely breathe, listening to them, each time they got introduced. Vaguely overhearing his mother complimenting his chair, how it allowed him to live a normal life. Some shot dubious looks at him, but she assured them that apart from his legs, all else was working fine, eliciting shrill laughter from the mothers, and some embarrassed smiles from the girls around him. He swallowed that deep shame, almost closing his eyes when some mothers inquired about their fortune, what he would inherit, how they had heard he would not live long. His desperate eyes went to his father, approaching with a glass of lemonade. He handed it to Archibald, greeting the women, then turned back to him.

"Enjoying yourself? You are mighty popular."

"Just take me out of here, father, I beg you. I need some air..." He was trying to breathe, that stuffy air all of a sudden unbearable, heavy with perfume and human heat.

"Of course." Edward took his glass away, and excused him, pushing the chair, greeting people as he made his way further from the main room, the dancing couples, William, and Francesca, not leaving each other's eyes. They stuck out of the crowd, that dashing, handsome man and his bride, and some shot her envious looks whilst trying to catch his eyes.

Archibald averted his eyes, drained, a gush of gratitude in him when his father pushed him out onto a large terrace overlooking the driveway. He pushed him all the way to the railing, the carriages visible from that first floor, close, men bantering and talking in that deep night, their hands wedged under their armpits, the horses asleep, breaths puffing in the air, the faint clicks of bits in soft mouths.

"He is a handsome man."

Archibald looked up at him. "Who?" Thinking of William when his father gestured below.

"Darren."

Archibald snapped his gaze to Darren, standing near the horses, his wide smile and then rich laughter, talking to an older coachman. He reached back to stroke a horse's nose when he'd pushed him on the shoulder, talking all the while, and Archibald had to swallow, his heart racing at his father's words.

"I suppose... it is hard to judge... as he is a man."

"So? One can see that, regardless of gender."

"If you say so, Father..."

He shut up, mildly panicked. *Why did Father push me here? Then, maybe this is the only terrace.* His teeth started chattering softly, that bitter cold biting into his skin, wondering how Darren and the others could stand for hours in that cold. Even with that thick coat, he could see he was cold, his shoulders hunched, blowing into his hands. James was half-asleep on a horse's back under a blanket, clutching the harness not to slip to the ground. That old coachman checked his watch, shaking his head.

"What is the time?"

His father took his pocket watch out. "Almost two in the morning."

"We should be heading home."

"I am afraid this is not an option. William and Francesca are having a mighty fine time, and so is your mother. I promised her a dance."

Archibald pinched his lips. "I do not want to come next time. No more balls, please."

"Archibald... I wish I could grant you this request, but it is not possible."

"Unless I feel sick, and I just might." He looked up at him, his eyes glinting, and Lord Edward squeezed his shoulder lightly.

"Alright. We shall see. Let us go inside. You might catch a cold here."

Archibald cast one last glance at Darren, wishing he would raise his eyes, but he didn't look up, holding the rear horse, stroking his neck.

They left much later; the ball dwindling to an end, Francesca flushed, flying on William's arm down the stairs to the carriage.

Darren hastily removed the blankets and woke James up, waiting until they got on board, Lady Hampton just glancing at the horses lowered neck, but she was a bit tipsy and didn't comment. A quick glance at Archibald, their eyes meeting briefly before he was pulled into the carriage, his face chalk-white, that dull fatigue in his eyes. Darren had to breathe against that soft despair invading him, that urge to just step there and take him in his arms, kiss that pale mouth. He sighed and mounted on the bench, starting the horses, some shaking their heads at the sudden freedom, but there was less resistance with their heads free, and he smiled in that icy night, those four horses pulling fast, their hooves beating the gravel of the road. James was riding deftly the front horse, even if he was exhausted, Darren knew, he was not used to waiting for hours in the cold, or riding in the front of a team, but he was managing well.

Still, Darren had to shout at the horses to turn faster when the road wound too sharp, wishing for more light, but the sky stayed stubbornly dark. The horses alert, their ears pricked towards the dark trees, sensing night animals in the dark. They bolted a couple of times, and he had to hold them tight, soothing with his voice, cursing in his head.

Despite the cold, by the time they got back, Darren was drenched, panting, reining the horses in in front of the mansion. Gathering his breath, but he jumped down, holding the rear right horse tight, that steaming horse tugging at his hands.

William got out and turned to him whilst he helped Francesca down. "My, my... what a ride..."

Lady Hampton was beyond herself. "What took you? We almost died in that carriage! This is insufferable!"

There were many things which Darren could have said, but he caught Lord Hampton's eyes, that small shake of his head, so Darren just sighed. "Apologies, Milady."

"I am just about done with your apologies. These horses better work properly next time we take the carriage."

"Yes, Milady..." The rear horse tore at his hand and the harness' buckle caught in his arm, tearing the skin up. He hissed, and pinched his lips at the pain, trying to calm the horse before it would start rearing.

Lord Hampton waited until Archibald got taken out and turned to Darren. "I am thankful, truly, that you managed with these new horses... You are hurt?" Alarmed a bit at the dark blood dripping to the ground.

"It is nothing, Milord... a scratch..."

Archibald's eyes were wide at that trickling blood running down his arm. "This is not a scratch!"

Darren almost smiled at the alarm in his voice. "It is fine, Lord Archibald. Truly. I will take care of it."

Lord Hampton took Archibald's chair. "Well, then. Tomorrow."

"Tomorrow?" Archibald was seething. "It is already today, Father." His eyes went to Darren. "Can you get some sleep?"

Darren glanced at the sky's edge, lighting up. "No, Milord. But it will be fine. Thank you for your concern."

Their eyes met, silent. Archibald's soft despair, his warm calm, even if he felt like crumbling, his arm aching every time the horse tugged on it.

Lord Hampton smiled thinly. "Well, we shall retire. See you later. Good night."

"Good night, Milord."

Archibald watched him climb up, gather the reins as the horses wanted to bolt straight away, holding them until they stilled, but his arms were trembling, his lips, he could see it in that dim light of the torches. *Fuck. Fuck. Fuck.* Just wanting to lie next to him, soak him in, caress that tired face. The horses moved then, that carriage carried away in the dark night, his voice drifting to them as he was talking to them.

His father's hand on his shoulder. "I will have you taken to your room. Get a good rest."

"It is easy for us... we can rest... sleep this out..."

"That is our privilege, yes."

"Splendid..."

Chapter 9

Next day, the sky stayed stubborn grey, early afternoon, when Archibald woke, and let his valet dress him and help him in his chair. He pushed him straight to the library for tea, but he couldn't care less, his mind on Darren, swallowing that lump in his throat. A dull burn on his forehead with a vague ache... *fever, maybe soon... maybe I will die no matter what...*

His eyes went to his father's smile as he handed him a cup. "Had a good rest?"

"Yes..."

"We could go to the stables, have your stroll."

"Sure."

His mother sipped her tea. "What for? It is rather chilly outside. I would not want you to feel worse."

"It is fine, Mother. Truly." Taming the irritation in his voice, surprised at how drained he felt, his emotions choking him.

"Well, if you say so. Do not complain if you get a fever again. The ladies were impressed with you yesterday at the ball. There are a couple of them I could well imagine being your wife. I will invite them over for tea in the coming weeks leading up to Francesca's marriage."

His heart raced a bit with panic. "Mother... it is too early to talk about marriage? I..."

"Nonsense! You are the heir of this estate and of your father's fortune, and you ought to have married first... but who could have known? If you live, you can get married. And sooner rather than later."

Archibald's eyes went to his father, but he was just smiling, hiding behind his cup. *Fuck...* "Father, let us go before it gets too late. I need air."

Lord Edward pushed him to the stables, that crisp air around them and a melancholic sky, some wild birds flying towards silver waters and marshes, maybe... Archibald was close to tears, not even knowing why, that insane longing tearing at his chest, making it hard to breathe. Wondering how long he could live like this, this torture even worse than his illness, clawing at him. Darren's voice made him breathe harder, wishing he could just get up and rush to him as he walked out of the stables, straight to them.

"Milord... what a surprise..."

"Yes... I gathered it would do us both good after the ball."

"Of course, Milord."

"But do not let this hold you up. We will stroll a bit and then walk back."

"Actually, Milord... we were going to pause for tea. So you are not holding us up." He glanced at Archibald, but had to snap his eyes away, that warm brown gaze ramming him in the chest.

"Why, this is splendid." Archibald's gaze went to the bandage on Darren's left forearm. "How is your wound?"

"Oh... it's nothing, Milord. I dealt with it."

"How? You should have had a doctor over." Archibald could barely contain that mild despair tainted with anger.

Darren looked at him, trying not to give away his feelings. "It is alright, Milord, truly. I just burnt it on the stove..."

Archibald blanched. "You did what?"

He smiled at him. "This is common, Milord. It stops the bleeding."

"But... it must have hurt... this is insane!" Just wanting to hug him, kiss his pain away.

Darren shot a quick glance at Lord Edward, a warning light in his eyes when he looked back at Archibald. "Thank you for your concern, but it is fine. It doesn't even hurt anymore, Milord."

Archibald almost spoke, but he had caught that light, so he shut up, just exhaling softly. "Fine then."

Lord Edward smiled. "Well, we will leave you to your tea. Maybe you could go out tomorrow with the barouche if the weather is fine?"

"Of course, Milord."

"Ah... I almost forgot... Monday, you need to go to the train station at eleven and pick up my mother, the Dowager Countess. She will stay with us until New Year's. Take the carriage and your two good horses, no need for Francesca's, it would only cause you more work."

Darren smiled. "As you wish, Milord."

"Granny is coming? Why didn't you say a word?"

"It was meant to be a surprise, but ah... I guess it is out now."

"I will go too. Somebody needs to greet her."

"Splendid idea... I did not dare to ask, with your health..."

"It will be fine." His heart warm at the thought because of all the people in his family, he loved his grandmother best. Smiling at the thoughts of his mother finding out. *Oh, Mother... you are in for a treat...*

"Well, then... we shall be leaving. See you soon, Darren."

"Milord..." He saluted briefly, his smiling eyes on Archibald, those soft brown eyes above that white handkerchief pressed to his pale mouth.

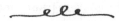

But it was pouring the next day, and Archibald just sat near the window, trying to shut out his mother's incessant complaining about his grandmother visiting, holding on to the thought that at least he would see Darren the next day.

They set off in the morning, the sky clear, almost letting some blue through those milky clouds. Archibald just sat in the carriage, his eyes on the landscape, the cloth pressed to his mouth. He lowered it though, a bit puzzled, watching that white fabric void of blood. That rush of fright racing through him, so he rapped on the carriage's side, as hard as he could. Feeling it slow and stop. His steps.

Darren opened the door. "You are unwell?"

"Just ... can we stop?"

"Here? I need to pull over to the side, but yes, we could..."

"Stop. Just stop for a minute and climb in."

Darren shot him a puzzled look, but then climbed back up and steered the carriage to the side of the road. He let the horses graze and climbed into the carriage, but as soon as he'd stepped in, Archibald grabbed his jacket and pulled him down on his knees.

His eyes burning. "If you don't kiss me now, I might just die..." He pushed himself off the bench and Darren had to catch him as his arms wrapped around his neck, and his mouth found his mouth. Opening wide, pressing his lips against his, hard. Soft moans and breaths as they tore at each other, holding tight, until

Darren had to break it, that painful kiss, before Archibald would lose his breath. He held him tight on his heaving chest, hearing Archibald's tears spill into his voice.

"I missed you... so much... so much..." Silent sobs, and Darren just rocked him gently.

His lips on his ear. "I missed you too..." They looked at each other and Darren stroked his hand down his face. "We need to go, or else we'll be late."

"I know..." But he leant in for a soft kiss, taming his mouth, a bit slack in his arms. Letting Darren sit him back, smooth his blanket on his legs.

"Comfortable?"

"Yes... Just drive. We would not want to face Granny's wrath." He watched him get out, felt the carriage tilt as he climbed up, his voice, the horses pulling, fast.

They arrived just in time, and Darren left the carriage in the cares of a young boy, even if he knew the horses would not move. He had to leave Archibald behind, but he had given a good description of the countess, so he waited on the platform until the train pulled in. Watching the passengers get off in that billowing steam, greet others. Finally, an old lady was helped down from a first class carriage by a servant, maybe her butler, her grey hair streaked with white, neat in a bun, wearing a large lavender dress and a matching hat. Her eyes darted around and caught on him as he was walking close.

Grey eyes, alert, her voice prim. "Are you my son's driver, Mister Turner?"

"Yes, your Ladyship."

"Very well. Help my good servant with the luggage. I only brought him and my maid. Now, let us go. Is my grandson with you?"

"Yes, your Ladyship. He is waiting in the carriage."

She led the way, and they followed, carrying the suitcases, and the butler pushing a heavy cart loaded with trunks.

She turned to Darren. "I do hope all this will fit."

"It will, your Ladyship."

She looked him up and down. "You seem well built... what a great luck... Which one is the carriage?"

"This one, Milady."

She stopped, rooted to the ground. "This? The horses… they don't match. Ah… not that it matters. Where is my grandson? Archie!" She walked swiftly to the carriage when he had peeked outside, and Darren rushed to open the door for her, helping her up. "My boy! Look at you! You look much better since I've last seen you, I must say! This countryside air must do some good."

He hugged her, then faced her as she settled. "Granny… good to see you. Yes, this air did some wonders. I might just live."

"Ah! Of course you will live. Now, I can hardly wait to see everybody and especially Francesca's fiancé."

Archibald's mouth pulled up. "Ah… I am afraid you might be disappointed…"

"I have heard of the young man… and well… let's just say that I am not thrilled… but we shall see… sometimes, marriage does wonders."

"If you say so…"

Darren looked in. "We are ready, Milord… My Lady."

"Splendid! Let us go then."

They set off, and she turned to Archibald. "Very handsome man, I must say, your coachman."

Archibald's face flamed up, so he pressed the handkerchief to his mouth lightly. "Granny…"

"Even an old woman can see that and appreciate it." Her amused eyes were on him. "No need to hide behind that towel, dear."

"I'm not hiding… but I might cough…"

"Oh, well… what a sight! Even in this bleak weather, these landscapes are unmistakable. We had many rides with your grandfather here… lovely times…"

"I went out daily… when the weather allowed it. In the barouche."

"And you did well! I gather your handsome coachman must have been a lovely company."

He averted his eyes, mildly panicked that some warmth was creeping up his cheeks. "Uh… we don't talk that much… usually…"

"Well… you may not talk, but I was thinking of his sight… Ah, never mind. I guess this is not something a young man would notice."

"Maybe…" He focused on the landscape rushing by, listening to Darren's voice drifting in.

The rest of the ride spent in silence, just a couple of comments from his grandmother, when a turn of the road, or a forest and field, brought up some memories. Their mansion coming into sight in that filtered light and her eyes lit up.

"Home, at last! I gather your mother must be thrilled to have me. But never mind, I shall enjoy every moment with you, Franny and Edward."

The carriage stopped and she let a footman help her out, Lord and Lady Hampton hurrying to her, but Francesca got there first, rushing to hug her.

"Granny! At last!"

"Oh treasure... my sweet little girl... married soon? I can hardly believe it."

Lady Hampton hugged her lightly. "Welcome, Mary. It must have been quite a journey."

"Oh... not at all. Your coachman made it very smooth."

"Indeed? I am relieved to hear he has not messed up this time."

Lady Mary just shot her a glance and went to hug her son. "Edward. So good to see you!"

"Mother... it is an honour to have you, and a delight."

"My dear... I brought some gifts... you can have them at tea time. Now..."

She turned and watched Darren help the footmen take Archibald out and settle him in his chair. A slight movement of Archibald's hand, a brief touch on that strong hand which had just left his arm.

She walked closer. "Are you settled well, my dear?"

"Yes, Granny."

"What a chair... truly magnificent.

"If you say so..."

"Let us go to lunch. I am starving."

Lady Hampton smiled thinly. "We had your favourite prepared."

"How thoughtful of you."

They sat later together for tea, a soft rain swishing against the bushes and trees outside. Archibald's eyes drifted to his grandmother from that light grey light pouring through the windows.

She took a sip from that flowery cup and put it on its saucer. "So, all is well, and Franny's marriage soon. What a delight!"

Lady Hampton pursed her lips. "Maybe it would be high time to stop calling her Franny. She will be Lady Willoughby soon."

"Ah... that is right, my dear. A noble title."

Lady Hampton chuckled, picking a light cake up dusted with sugar. "Oh, yes! And what a fortune! And what a man! Young Willoughby is a delight. Exquisite to look at. A true gentleman."

Archibald swallowed the word which had vaulted into his mouth, sipping his tea instead. His amused eyes on his grandmother.

"Oh, my... if he took after his father, he must have a slight dose of mischief in him, too."

Lady Hampton frowned. "Not an ounce."

The countess smiled. "I seem to remember his father as a young man, coursing all the maids and peasant girls he could find." She laughed lightly.

"Well, William is anything but."

Fran forced a smile. "He is a true gentleman, Granny, you'll see. He's due soon."

Archibald put his cup down. "I think it's time for my nap."

Lady Hampton turned to him. "Do not dare disappear. William is counting on your company."

Archibald sighed. "I do not wish to meet him, Mother..." But his words died when the door burst open, William walking in, taking his gloves off.

He stepped straight to the countess and took her hand, planting a kiss on it. That brash smile. "The Dowager Countess. I am deeply honoured to make your acquaintance. Fran was full of praises about you."

The countess checked him out swiftly. "My dear, good to see you again. I seem to remember you as a small child."

William straightened, laughing. "Sure. I do not have your memory, but I am delighted to become part of your family."

"Indeed."

He turned to Archibald. "Good to see that you have not retired to your room."

Archibald pressed his handkerchief to his lips. "I just might, unfortunately. I am extremely tired."

"Ah... Must have been straining to ride to the train station to pick up her Ladyship. I gather the company of your good coachman must have sweetened it a bit."

Archibald let it slip, despite his heart lurching in his chest. "Care for a game of chess?"

"Why not? You might win this time." He pulled a table close, and got the chess board, whilst the countess, turned to Fran.

"Handsome, truly. He is the spitting image of his father. Uncanny."

Fran's face flamed up. "Oh Granny... I shall be exceedingly happy."

She huffed, her eyes drifting back to William who had sat to face Archibald, his legs sprawled as he leant back in his chair, that dark smile at the edge of his lips. "Let us hope so, my dear. Let us hope."

Chapter 10

But next day, the weather had become unusually mild; the sun fighting the impending doom with its last warm rays. Archibald's heart raced, and he could hardly wait for breakfast to be over and asked to be brought down to the front fast, pushed out into that sun as the barouche made a turn and stopped near the stairs. Their eyes locked, Darren only dressed in a shirt and a vest on top, his black pants, and boots. He jumped down and helped the footmen settle Archibald, trying not to touch him, avoiding his eyes. Back on the bench, driving away fast, until they were far, out of sight. He turned back then, meeting his smile, his dreamy brown eyes.

Archibald clutched his handkerchief. "To the lake?"

"If you wish?"

"Yes. Drive fast."

Darren obeyed, putting the horses in a swift trot, letting that warm air caress them, glide on their skins. Straight to the lake where that golden sunshine played on the waves, but the trees were losing their leaves, the shore all too visible. Still, the road was the empty, most families having moved back to town, so he steered the barouche down, letting the horses graze.

He stepped to Archibald when he'd put a blanket down, and took him in his arms, feeling that maybe there was a bit more strength in those feeble arms clinging to his neck. He wanted to put him down to sit, but Archibald just lay down, pulling him next to him, not leaving his eyes.

"We might not have another day like this... this warm..."

Darren glanced towards the road, but they were still sheltered by the hedges and the barouche. He looked down at Archibald. "You may be right..."

Just watching each other, holding hands on Archibald's chest, his ribs rising softly.

That voice, barely there. "Kiss me. Just kiss me, don't stop. Don't stop whilst I have breath left."

Darren leant down to him, feeling his hand tighten on his hand, feeling his soft lips part, letting him invade that mouth void of blood, of the taste of death. Their tongues gliding softly as their breaths mingled, breathing each other in deep. Kissing deeper, bolder when they felt that Archibald could still breathe. Darren hand slid behind his back to hold him closer to his chest and Archibald's hand went to his back, holding him as tight as he could.

Letting his weight crush him a bit, feeling his warmth through his shirt. *Is this making love? Is this how you make love?*

He opened his eyes, breaking the kiss, his palm on Darren's cheek. "Are we making love?"

A glint of surprise in Darren's eyes over that ocean of fear. "You could say that, yes... I mean, we could do more..."

"Like what?"

He blushed a bit. "You don't know?"

"Not really. Father tried to teach me things... and I read some scenes in books... mainly between a man and a woman."

"It would be similar between us too..."

"Ah... some readings on ancient times come back to me now... such as in Ancient Rome and Greece..."

Darren smiled. "Such as."

"You read those books?"

"I read some books. As many as I could when my work was done. I didn't have much time, as you would imagine..."

"You made love before? With another man..." His heart raced, his eyes asking.

"Yes... I did." Darren smoothed his palm on his cold cheek. "I would not call that love making. We were curious and reckless, young. Later, we had needs."

"I understand." His hand went to Darren's chest, pushing under his shirt where it was open at the front. "This is not us, though."

"No."

None of them put that word on it, even if they felt their hearts racing, that hard light invading Archibald's velvet eyes. "I want to make love to you properly."

Darren sighed. "That will be difficult to manage. Nigh impossible."

"Nothing's impossible."

Darren just watched him, silent. Willing himself to believe his words, which seemed mere fantasy, that stubborn light in his brown eyes. He just smiled at him lightly. "We shall see." A sudden idea in him, so he laced his arms around Archibald, rolling with him until Archibald was lying on top of him, meeting his puzzled eyes.

"What...?"

"Just wait and see." He gently grabbed Archibald's knees and pulled his legs apart, then pulled his knees forward. Slowly, until he was straddling him. "No pain?"

Archibald panted, but he managed to push himself on his elbows, looking with slight wonder at his legs around Darren's waist. A rush of blood racing straight down to his groin where their cocks met through their pants, hardening.

He looked into Darren's eyes. "Is this a trick to exercise my legs?"

"Call it what you want." He ran his palms down those thin thighs, kneading those meagre muscles lightly. "Tell me if it hurts." Feeling Archibald arch against him. Meeting his eyes.

"You know full well it doesn't hurt..."

His lips curled up. "Is that so?"

"Yes." Closing his eyes to his touch, that raging fire which had started burning in his chest, racing down his body to where their bodies met. He leant on Darren's chest; his lips close to his lips. "Is this how it's going to be?"

"It could be like this."

"Without clothes on..."

Darren smiled, caressing his thighs. "Ideally, yes."

Archibald closed his eyes and kissed him, not wanting to hear more, because it was not possible to go all the way, and he was desperate, but still grateful for this moment, even if their clothes were in the way, he could feel him, hard, pressing against his own hardness. His touch, those warm palms gliding on his stiff flesh, his muscles clenching softly under his strong fingers. He trembled, and Darren just held him tight on his chest, letting him catch his breath with his quivering lips on his neck.

Long moments in that lush sunshine, the horses' soft snorts close, their bits clicking as they munched that late grass. The swish of a slight wind ruffling the waves and leaves, gliding them to the ground. Archibald almost fell asleep in that warmth, but he pushed himself up, smiling down at Darren.

"Thank you for this moment."

"My pleasure."

"I am fully aware this is probably not going to be a regular feature of our meetings... but you could still help me with my legs."

"As I promised."

"I felt every touch of your hands."

"Glad to hear."

Archibald stroked his cheek, tracing his lips. "I will keep the memory in my flesh. Think of you at night when I lie in bed, alone."

"I will think of you too."

"A comforting thought. I will remember this and cherish this shared moment. Even if we are apart, I know where your thoughts are."

"As do I." Kissing him, pulling his head down gently, letting their tongues roam each other, their teeth. He bit down on Archibald's lower lip, softly, caching that small moan with his breath. "We have to go..."

"I know." His eyes drowned, but they had a new light, a glimmer of hope and warmth.

He let Darren roll him off and pull him up to sit. Taking him in his arms, but Archibald helped a bit, trying to hold his body better, holding Darren'ssmell, neck tight until he put him in the barouche. A last soft kiss, and Darren sat on the bench, picking the reins up.

The horses perked up and pulled, Archibald casting a last loving glance at the lake. *I know, somehow, that I won't be seeing you for a long time...* Saying his goodbyes to that landscape which had become haven, his eyes drifting back to Darren's back, that back he had started knowing, those bumps and ridges under his shirt. His soft black hair ruffled by the wind. They were wedged into Archibald's palms, his fingers. He knew them by heart now, closing his eyes. *Even if we have to be apart, you live under my skin, in me... I can conjure how you feel, smell and taste. I can taste your breath, feel your teeth, your lips...* Smiling at his thoughts, letting the sun colour his cheeks, warm his lips. As the road ran, the landscape rolling in shades of orange, red and brown, he watched the mansion loom into sight; the gravel messed up by a horse's hooves which had been stopped too harsh. *William*. But he could not care less, his skin and flesh still pulsing with his lover's touch and teeth.

Meeting his eyes when he'd stopped the barouche and jumped down to help him into his chair which the footmen had carried down. A swift glance when they seated him.

His warm brown eyes going to him. "I have enjoyed this ride. Thank you, Darren."

"My pleasure, Milord." Bowing, that amused light in his eyes, which he pushed above his despair of leaving him again. Watching him being carried inside until he was out of sight. Closing his eyes to that pain tearing at his chest.

Archibald asked to be brought straight to his room, to the window, fed up, not even wanting to meet William and make any of those fake conversations. He reached for his book and put it in his lap, his eyes grazing that beautiful sight from those high windows. *No way to escape lunch...* a bitter taste in his throat and he was hoping it was not some stale blood lingering, although he hadn't coughed at all.

He jolted a bit at the knock on his door, just turning slightly. "Come in." A relieved sigh when he saw his granny peeking in.

"Am I terribly disturbing your daydreaming?"

He smiled. "No, Granny."

She put a stash of books she was holding on the small table near the window and sat to face him. "I went through the library and brought you some books. May I?" She reached for his book and he gave it to her. "Ah... Botany handbook? Maybe you are ready for some more exciting things."

Archibald frowned. "Like what?"

"Oh... I just picked random books... you know... a few that would interest a young man like you... in his prime." Her eyes smiled, and he just sighed.

"In my prime... you cannot be serious, Granny."

"You will get better and start courting young ladies, and as such, you should know what you are facing. You also did not have time to fool around with anybody... khm... so might as well learn it from books before you get to practise it."

Archibald's cheeks flamed up, but he didn't bring the handkerchief to his face, knowing she had already noticed. "Uh... alright. As you wish." A bit mortified, so his eyes went to the park outside. Those distant stable roofs, somewhere there, barely visible. His voice, soft. "I am not sure I will be able to practise anything."

"As young men do..."

He turned to her small smile. "Like William?"

"Oh! Of course. Franny is blind to it, but they have all been there. Him, his father..."

Archibald's heart raced. "You know about those... what his father did?"

Lady Mary arched her eyebrows. "I just might, dear. Why is this of interest?"

Archibald was not even sure he wanted to know. "William said something to... Darren..." Gathering his breath because it got knocked out by his name. "That he might be his father's bastard..."

"Your coachman? Oh, well... there may be many of them. Willoughby the elder was certainly known for coursing young maids and peasant girls." Her eyes softened. "This is not a story you wish to know, dear."

"I just might want to know after all."

She watched him a bit, then sighed. "His encounter with Lady Shackleton's handmaid cannot be described as anything pleasant, as I recall it. The young lady was most distressed, freshly married, and all, that her maid got treated this way, so it made a bit of a noise. Fortunately, they were already sort of engaged with their stable master, and he turned a blind eye, he loved her so much. Shortly after their marriage, she announced she was with child. Nobody ever questioned that child's father."

She quieted, and he looked at her, his heart in flames. "He forced her?"

"I suppose it was called 'heavily insisted' at the time. After all, he was a lord, and she was a mere handmaid. Young too. It got solved, as I told you."

"But Darren could be..."

She smiled. "You have seen him."

There were no words needed, and Archibald leant back, more bitter than ever, his words barely there. "He doesn't know."

"He probably knows. Ignoring it is perhaps the least painful way to deal with this."

"I will tell him. He deserves to know."

"That is opening a whole new can of worms, dear. Perhaps some things are better kept in the dark."

"Not this. Not how you came to be and of this world."

She reached for his hand. "I will leave this with you."

"Why do men have to be like this?" Bitter, he wrung the handkerchief in his hand.

"Not all men, dear. You are not one of them."

He smiled, bitter. "I am barely one at all."

"Now, now... Read the books I brought you. They might teach you a thing or two." She rose. "It is almost lunchtime."

"I'm not hungry... and I don't want to meet William."

"I see. In that case, I shall tell the folks downstairs you feel ill."

He looked up at her, his heart flying. "You would do this, Granny? I'd be most grateful."

She stroked his hair. "I would do more. A noble lie to buy you some peace. I will see you later, dear. Just rest."

He watched her leave and picked one of the books up. 'Love in Ancient Greece.' Almost dropping it right there, as if that heavy leather cover could burn his fingers off. *What...* His eyes darted to the door, but nobody came, so he flicked it open, lost after the first lines, drawn into a world he had only glimpsed through vague sentences in history books. His cheeks, in flames at some of the illustrations. He got lost in it, his skin burning, but his eyes ate the words, a sullen rage birthing in that weak chest, that this was all normal back in those times, and it was an abomination and a sin now, something so beautiful warped into becoming a sin, something vile which could get you to the gallows. His heart icing over, because he knew his privilege, his father's connections possibly saving him from that fate when Darren would be killed straight away, probably. *My Erastes...* Grazing that soft leather, his eyes drifting to the stables' roof. A vague comfort there though, that this was alright in some distant times, cherished even, this liaison which made him shiver with fear. He pinched his lips, those brown eyes darkening with determination as he rang the bell. *We will not amount to anything if I stay this weak...*

His eyes darting to his servant. "Bring up something to eat."

"As you wish, Milord."

"And I am going to tea later."

He bowed and left, then came back a while later with a full platter of food. Archibald ate, forcing the food down when his stomach signalled that it was full after a few bites. Washing each bite down with a sip of water, that will there to live for whatever lay ahead. A certainty there as his body filled with that warm blood clutching at the food. A long-forgotten warmth as he leant back, exhausted, but his eyes danced at the sight of those almost empty plates. His chest filling with warmth too, close to bursting as he mouthed those silent words flying towards that roof. *I love you. I love you. I love you.*

Chapter 11

Next morning, the air had cooled but that grey light was there behind those clouds covering the sky. Archibald waited for Darren after breakfast, his heart racing, because he was unsure if they could talk, a ride impossible with that looming rain and the cold, but he insisted on going to the stable yard to read, have that small walk, still. Watching him approach with his long strides, meeting his eyes, letting him grab the chair and push him through the park.

Archibald's voice, soft. "I missed you..."

"I missed you too..." His deep voice, so pained, that Archibald had to look up at him.

"I have something to tell you."

"Oh..."

Archibald smiled and dared to touch his hand briefly before they reached the yard. "I'd need you a bit alone? Maybe you could push me to the lake at the end of the park?"

"I might be able to free myself a bit."

"Just tell the boys I'm being the difficult, spoiled lordling whining for a walk near the lake."

Darren laughed softly as he settled him under the tree. "As you wish, Milord."

Archibald whispered. "I wish it very much."

Darren smiled wryly and went to work, that touch burning his skin, that nothing graze of that feeble hand. Relieved that Archibald looked maybe better, even pale, his cheeks a bit more filled up. Even if he had noticed how gaunt his own face had become in the mirror, his blue eyes drowned in that burning love, his appetite almost gone in the burning pit of his stomach.

He walked to James and Travis. "His Lordship is insisting on a walk near the lake, so I might be gone a bit when we are done with the stables."

The boys exchanged a look but refrained from commenting, knowing better. "Sure, sir... I mean, we can manage, you know..."

"I know." He smiled, and they worked for a couple of hours.

Darren went to get Archibald when he was done, after a quick wash at the well during which Archibald's eyes ate every inch of his naked torso, imagining running his tongue over those muscles, tasting his skin. Watching him pull a clean shirt on and his jacket, walk to him.

"I am ready to take you to the lake, Milord."

Archibald made sure to raise his voice. "About time to."

"Apologies..."

"Never mind. Let us just go."

Biting his lips not to burst out laughing, holding it until they were out of sight where he smiled up at Darren.

"I hope I did not hurt you playing the young master."

Darren smiled at him. "But you are my young master."

Archibald's smiled died. "Certainly not. Not me. Hold on, stop here." The lake quiet, not a soul in sight. He reached for Darren's hand and pulled him to the front, looking up at him. "Don't crouch down... I'm not a child." Darren stopped, letting him hold his hand, reach for the other one too. Archibald breathed in deep. "I have to tell you something. And it is not easy." Watching Darren's eyebrows arch a bit. "You remember what William told you? About his father?"

Darren paled a bit. "Yes..."

"It is true." He held Darren's hands stronger, even if he had no strength left, seeing those wide, blue eyes fill with tears. "You know, right? You knew the moment he'd said it."

Darren pulled his hands out and turned away, his eyes on the lake, his hands going to his hair, through it. Blowing a heavy sigh. "I kept thinking about it... Not that it matters now..." His voice drowned in pain, and Archibald's heart raced.

"Forgive me... it might not have been my place to tell..."

Darren turned to him. "No... it is fine..."

"I also know how..."

Darren raised his hand, bitter. "I do not want to know. I sort of guessed... some things come back to me now... which were insignificant then, or I did not understand." He smiled, his eyes drifting back to that vast expanse of cool, grey water. "They loved each other, my parents. They loved me. That is all that matters. Blood is one thing. Heart is another."

"On that note, just come here, please?"

Darren looked at him and stepped close, letting Archibald take his hands again, but he'd glanced around once, nervous. Back at him to that weak tug. Meeting his burning brown eyes.

"I also wanted to tell you something else. And it concerns us..."

Darren's breath caught, because in that moment of despair, he thought Archibald wanted to put an end to whatever they were having, maybe saving them too, and damning them at the same time. His eyes going wide at those soft words.

"I love you."

Darren blinked, his lips parting, thinking he had heard it wrong, but Archibald just repeated it, not leaving those puzzled eyes. "I love you. I know it. And I am sorry."

Darren went to his knees in front of him, his legs not carrying him in that insane moment when his world got knocked over. Clinging to those cold hands which got warmed by his skin. Trying to breathe when his breath had been knocked out, and Archibald's had flown away with his words. Waiting. Hoping. Dreading.

Watching Darren's lips tremble, feeling his iron grip. "I love you too."

Tears rushed out of their eyes, sliding down their cheeks, silent in that crisp, cold breeze ruffling the lake's surface. That confession like a death sentence, flying into the sky with wild geese leaving for warmer climates. Archibald didn't care, in that small mad moment, he pulled him close, lacing his arms around Darren as he knelt between his knees. Feeling his strong arms go around his back, hug him tight. Breathing hard against their sobs wanting to burst up like a stream long held under ground.

Archibald whispered into his neck. "Nothing in this world will change how I feel for you. Nothing."

They looked at each other, letting go of that hug, Darren's eyes filled with despair above his relief. "This is madness."

"Our madness..." Just wanting to kiss him, but he held back, knowing how dangerous it was, even this small moment, even if from afar, him kneeling could have been mistaken for fixing his wheelchair. A kiss would not be mistaken. Not forgiven either, but Archibald's heart was light, bathing in the light of those few words. "Somehow, we will make this work... I don't know how... but I want to live. For you. For us." Trying to push him into some kind of hope when Darren was seeing this from below, from his world which was void of the ease and privilege of Archibald's.

Clinging to those words. "I am glad you wish to live."

"Make me get my legs back and we could run." Knowing there was no other option, utterly clueless how he would even have the courage to leave everything behind.

"Gain your legs back and we shall see."

"You would take me far?"

"Wherever you would wish to go."

"I knew it the first time you took me out... that you would take me to the ends of the world."

"Hold on to that thought."

That madness they had conjured tainting every word, words which they could not even believe themselves, but it felt good, to voice some dreams above that despair, coat that hopelessness with a tale.

Darren rose, knowing that time was rushing, and working against them. "I have to bring you back to the house."

"I know..."

Archibald leant back, his strength gone, letting him roll him back to the house, watching his mother come back from a walk with Francesca on William's arm. Her frown, his mocking smile.

"At last! We were looking for you everywhere!"

"I was at the stables, as usual, Mother."

"Well, never mind that. You could have walked with us. It is anyway too cold to sit in the stable yard. You will be sick."

"Allow me to judge what is best for me."

William stepped closer, looking down at him. "We could play chess after lunch. Like a small family tradition we are building?"

Archibald swallowed his wrath. "Absolutely. I would be delighted."

His mother huffed. "At last, you have some sense in you." She looked behind Archibald. "You may withdraw, Darren. The footmen will take care of his Lordship."

Archibald spoke to him when he felt his hands leave the chair, but he could not see him at all. "Tomorrow morning, usual time."

"Yes, Milord."

Listening to him turn, his steps on the gravel, fading. Archibald closed his eyes briefly, trying to keep his voice for a few fleeting moments.

Meeting William's mocking eyes. "Parting is such sweet sorrow."

"I do not know what you mean."

"Oh... you know... just quoting the great one." He winked and pulled Francesca towards the stairs.

Archibald's heart sank, but he let the footmen carry him upstairs, push him to the salon.

His grandmother turned to him. "Had a nice walk?"

"As usual, Granny."

She poured him a glass of water. "I am delighted to hear. Are you staying for lunch?"

"Yes. I am done wasting away in my room."

"Such a delightful surprise, dear!" She gave him her small, mischievous smile. "Have you been reading my books?"

"Yes, Granny." Trying to tame that flame on his cheeks.

"Good. Highly instructive."

His father stepped in at that sentence. "What is?"

"Oh... just some old books I found for Archibald..."

"Indeed?"

"Yes. He needs to learn; some things have been missing from his education." She toasted him with raised eyebrows and he blushed slightly.

Watching his son's dreamy eyes on the park. "You look better."

"I went to get some fresh air."

"So I have heard. I was looking for you at the stables, but the boys told me you ordered Darren around to take you to the lake."

He pinched his lips, dead scared. "That is his duty. To obey."

Lord Hampton and his mother exchanged a quick look.

He put his hand on Archibald's shoulder, mild. "There is nothing wrong with going to the lake. You could go every day. And no need to order him around, either. Just tell him I am fine with it. A dutiful man should not be jostled around, even if he is a servant. You know this."

He sighed. "I know. I am sorry."

"Nothing to fuss about." He patted his shoulder and left to pour another drink, waiting for his wife, Francesca, and William to arrive before going for lunch. His eyes on Archibald, though, his chest tight.

Conversations after lunch drifted to the upcoming horse race in a few days, the last of the season on hills and fields.

William raised his glass at Lord Hampton. "A grand occasion to win this race this year. Father bought a beautiful ginger gelding, stunning, truly. And fast. Our stable master will have a breeze this year."

Lord Hampton smiled. "Well, this year, we have also entered for the first time. Now that I have Lord Shackleton's hunting horse."

Archibald raised his head. "And who is going to ride that horse?"

"Why... Darren, of course. This is the tradition. The stable masters' race."

William's eyes gleamed at Archibald blanching. "You should not fret about this; it is all too common. Of course, you have never raced, you don't know that for an experienced horseman it is nothing. A mere fun time." He whirled his glass. "Obviously, if all goes well. Shame Lord Burton's stable master fell last year and broke his neck. Shame." He pursed his lips, drinking deep, gesturing to the butler to fill his glass again.

Archibald turned to his father. "Why do this folly? Risk the life of a good horse... and a good man..." He could barely breathe, that mad worry draining his blood away, so he pressed his handkerchief to his lips, out of habit.

"Darren is more than able to ride that horse. I have high hopes he will even win. There will be substantial money to gain."

"More... money? What for?" He was dizzy, so shut up, mad desperate.

William laughed. "What for, indeed? It is always good to have more. To spend it." He toasted Francesca, sitting a bit further away with the women. "To spend it on your love."

Archibald closed his eyes, biting on that soft fabric to keep his words in. *Madness.* Fearing for his life as if it were his own. Even if he knew he rode well, it was everything he could think of.

Those couple of days, flying by under a heavy, icy rain. Impossible to go on a walk, on a ride, watching those churning clouds and that pouring rain. Hoping it would last, that they would cancel the race.

Those hopes killed by a lush sunshine the day of the race, as if that sun was mocking him, drying the grass, pouring that generous light laced with warmth. *Fuck*. Archibald let his father push him to the carriage, Raven tied to the back. Their eyes met with Darren's for the briefest moment before he was lifted in. Too short, not enough time to read those blue eyes. He leant back, that mad worry in him, trying to breathe through his handkerchief.

They settled on a hill overlooking the arriving line, that final line, a mad descent on a field from a hill, then a curve before the last finish line. They could see that arrival from near the gate, the crowd a bit below, or along that long race track cordoned off in the countryside. The start was there too, close. Flags waving in the wind. His father pushed him close to where the riders were getting ready, maybe to exchange a few words with Darren before the race.

Darren had checked Raven's tack, and taken his coat off, only a white, loose shirt on his broad shoulders, his black riding pants, and boots, standing, the horse's head resting on his shoulder, Raven's eyes half-mast, his lips loose. A couple of lords had walked there to check him out, and Lord Hampton stopped in front of Darren, his hand on Archibald's shoulder.

"All fine, Darren?"

"Yes, Milord."

William walked to them then. "This horse is asleep. Are you sure he will run?" He laughed, and Darren just stroked those loose lips softly with his fingers, keeping that small smile on.

Lord Hampton puffed. "Oh, he will! You will see."

Archibald's clipped voice. "This is madness."

William grinned. "Just because you are afraid, you should not spoil the fun."

"I am not afraid."

"What then? Your able coachman can ride like the devil, or so I have heard. Nothing to worry about then, isn't that so, Darren?"

"You honour me, Milord."

William laughed. "You will lose today though. I have a perfect horse and a rider to match your talents."

Lord Hampton laughed lightly. "I highly doubt that. Darren could win with his eyes closed."

William's lips curled up, watching the other lords who had gathered around them. He raised his voice. "I will double my bet against him if he races without the bit."

There was a stunned silence at his words, some murmurs starting. Lord Hampton's eyes flew to Darren, the man unfazed, stroking that sleeping horse.

Darren's blue eyes went to him. "This is your decision, Milord."

"Racing without a bit?"

Darren shrugged. "It is not the bit that steers the horse. Or stops it."

Laughter followed his words, but people were watching Lord Hampton.

Archibald reached up to his father's arm, chalk-white. "Father... please..."

"Alright. I will take your challenge."

William grinned. "Anybody else?"

Some joined in when another lord stepped close. "Let's triple it, and he takes the saddle off, too."

Lord Hampton hesitated, feeling Archibald tug at his arm, meeting his desperate eyes. "No... Father..."

William slammed him on the shoulder. "Leave your father alone. He can decide for himself. It is a fun challenge. And a substantial amount of money. For all of us! There is no way he can win without a bit and a saddle."

Lord Hampton shrugged. "Oh, well... let us have some fun."

Archibald's eyes went wide, watching the bets being placed.

William stepped in front of Darren. "Strip your horse. We shall see what you can do without any riding gear. I would suspect not much."

Laughter followed, but Darren just unbuckled the girth, taking the saddle off. Stroking the horse's nose softly when he had arched his neck back, puzzled a bit. The bridle followed, and he put a halter on, securing the reins to the side buckles. He stood then, waiting, the horse pushing his tongue out, searching for the bit. A bit more alert, but he nibbled Darren's neck, his hair, licks to his neck until he got a caress. Going back to that semi state of sleep, his coat shining under that pouring sun, mirroring Darren's dark hair.

Archibald looked up at Darren when William and his father had stepped away a bit. "This is folly..."

He smiled at him; his eyes warm. "Trust me."

"Nobody can ride a horse without tack."

"That may be right. But I am not nobody."

Archibald shut up when his father stepped to him, taking his chair.

"Good luck, Darren. I gather you know what is at stake."

"Your money, Milord. And my reputation."

"Do your best." His voice had softened, that mild worry in him that he was putting that man at risk, but Darren just smiled.

"I shall, Milord."

Watching them leave, go to their places, hearing the first bell to get ready. He grabbed Raven's thick mane and swung himself on that smooth back, blending with the animal as the other puzzled riders watched him ride to the starting line with only that halter on that powerful horse. Shaking their heads.

One of them rode next to him. "You're gonna break your neck, Darren. Ain't nobody gonna hold that horse back when it bolts."

Darren just smiled at him, at ease, feeling the animal's every move between his thighs, Raven responding to a touch of his finger on the reins. "Sure thing."

A second bell and they lined up, some horses already so nervous, they kept tugging at their riders' hands, foam plastering their chests. Raven just pranced lightly, his neck arched, waiting.

Another rider leaned to him. "Where's your whip?"

Darren shrugged. "There is no need for one."

Some laughed, and William's stable master pursed his lips. "Arrogant twat. I will wipe that smile off your face." He had a strong whip in his hand, holding that golden gelding's mouth tight, the horse nervous, shying at every move of the flags. "This one here is eager to fly. You will only see our backsides, Turner, mark my words." He laughed and tried lining the horse up, the starters taking ages to let them go, winding animals and men up alike.

Archibald's eyes wide on that mass of horses, Darren barely visible towards the middle when William's golden horse had pushed to the front, wondering why he'd stayed back, all the other riders fully equipped, and his heart raced with that mad worry. That he might fall. Die. He startled at that loud bang, the ribbon falling as the horses bolted; the crowd shouting at the top of their lungs, the riders, a mad rush in the trampling of hooves, the soil flying around them as they tore in that soft grass. A dark flash, and Darren was gone, the hooves beating the ground until it faded.

Lord Hampton sighed. "Now to wait until they appear up there..."

Lady Hampton squealed. "Oh... so exciting! I do hope he will not disappoint us! That is mad money you bet on that horse, my dear."

Archibald could barely contain his anger. "There is a man involved. A man's life at risk. It is reckless."

"Have some respect for your father, young man." She almost stepped to him. "He knows best. It is that man's duty to represent his lord best and ride for him. And if needed, give his life too."

Lord Hampton soothed her. "Now, now... maybe not give his life..."

"Whatever it takes!" She had turned, her eyes on the hill, straining her neck as the crowd held their breath, waiting, listening to distant cheers whenever the riders passed some spectators in the distant hills and woods.

Lord Hampton breathed. "Soon..."

William shot him a look; his lips curled up. "I seem to spot my golden horse..."

It had appeared on top of the hill, that golden horse, in full galop, his rider hitting him hard amongst the mad shouting. Breaths held as he was alone, that strong animal and his rider. Archibald almost died right then. Trembling. Choking back a sob when a black horse appeared on the top of the hill, chasing that golden one. Raven. The horse stretching his powerful legs, the rider blended to the animal's back, his black hair, and that black mane flying with that mad speed as he leant on the animal's powerful neck. *Jesus...* Archibald almost forgot to breathe. *Please... please...* The crowd howling as the black horse got closer, at break-neck speed, racing down that hill. The hooves beating the ground, the swish of the whip. Racing towards that large curve where Raven had almost caught up, time slowing as they took the bend, the front rider looking back, swishing the whip harder. Lord Hampton and William cheering in unison for their respective riders, the crowd delighted at that tight finish, almost already thinking that victory was a done deal for the golden horse. William's smug smile as he looked at Archibald. His wink.

Darren watched the last straight line come into sight, his pants soaked with the horse's sweat, his shirt tugging at his body, but he held on tight on that slick back, feeling Raven tug lightly against the noseband. *Soon... not yet...* Coming out of the bend, his knee almost grazing the ground as the horse took the curve, sharp, working as one, man and animal, in that mute understanding they had crafted during long years, when Darren had been the first one on his back, riding him only in a halter before he had put anything in his mouth. Many riders then, lords who had tugged at that soft mouth, but Raven had known, he would be home after exhausting hunts, with his human. Breathing him in, getting some healing balm on his bleeding lips, a soft mash. Not allowing any bit into his mouth until he had been fully healed. Their small secret, that he would do anything for him too. Waiting for a sign, rushing towards that golden horse, adjusting his body under Darren's when he felt him lose his balance, catching that fragile human with a move of his shoulder, his back. Ignoring the cheers, just their breathing in his ears, waiting for that soft voice, one ear pricked back to catch his voice. That last stretch. Waiting.

Darren spread his hand on his soaked neck, letting the reins go. His voice, soft. "Go..."

Raven bolted, that freedom he'd been waiting for there, that mad rush in his large heart to please the man on his back. That being who had meant everything in his life, who was everything, still. Even if he was not a colt anymore, even if many hunts with various masters and strangers had tired his lungs and legs, he gave it all, feeling him clutch his mane tight, squeeze his thighs around his ribs. He ran faster, as fast as his legs could carry him, knowing he had been held back, even when he'd wanted to fly faster. Some strength left in his body, breathing harder as his hooves ate the field.

Darren just leant on his neck, his mane in his face as the horse ran faster, making his eyes water. Not just because of the speed, but because he knew. In that insane moment, Raven had understood and was giving him all he could. Exhausted, he clung to the horse, drawing on his last reserves to stay on that powerful back. Watching in a blur that golden horse get next to them, hearing the swish of the whip. To no avail. He knew. Risking a small smile as he leant closer to Raven's neck. A small clack of his tongue and the horse flew faster even, leaving the golden horse behind, his laboured breathing. Blurring Darren's vision, his breath short. A glimpse of a waving flag in the corner of his vision, the cheer of the crowd blurred as he was panting, trying to breathe, his tears streaming. Stroking the horse's neck, sobbing, but he gathered the reins, wiping at his tears as the horse slowed to a canter, to a trot. Letting him trot, closing his eyes, letting that trot relax his body too, those aching muscles, turning back to a raving crowd, catching Lord Hampton clasping hands with some of his friends who had also bet on him. Putting the horse into a walk, letting that powerful neck stretch, feeling his laboured breathing, the foam sliding down his legs, his own blood still rushing in his veins, but he walked close.

Lord Hampton had pushed under the rope, catching the horse's rein, smiling up at him.

"My good man... I have no words..."

Darren panted, smiling wide. "It was an honour, Milord."

His gaze drifted to Archibald, to his pale face, his handkerchief pressed against his lips, and a ripple of worry rushed through him, but Archibald took it away and made a small wave with his hand, barely visible, but his soft brown eyes shone with a relieved light. Love. That loving gaze warming Darren's racing heart.

Darren looked down at Lord Hampton. "Allow me, Milord."

He jumped down and held the horse whilst a race official put the laurel wreath on the horse's neck, and the other one on Lord Hampton. Handshakes, congratulations on that fast animal, a couple of people trying to buy him, but Lord Hampton refused, knowing what he had in his hands.

Raven pushed his nuzzle against Darren's soaked back, licking his neck to get a taste of his smell, and he got a swift stroke to his nuzzle, that small stroke of his fingers he knew by heart. Content, nibbling on his shirt, he waited, basking in that victory's glory.

Chapter 12

Next morning, Darren pushed Archibald to the stables, the sun still up, and Archibald watched him work, knowing he must have been dead tired after the race, the drive home, and taking care of his chores all afternoon.

He washed that drawn face later in the well, and walked to Archibald. "I'll push you to the lake."

Archibald just nodded and closed his eyes, letting that slight breeze caress his skin. Opening them only when he smelled the lake's sweet, watery scent. Darren stopped the chair and sat next to him, so from afar, it would seem they were watching the lake. He was toying with blades of yellow grass, long stems which had dried up , and crumbled under his strong fingers.

Archibald spoke after a while, willing his hands to stay put, even if Darren was so close, he could feel his heat, his scent. That black hair in the corner of his vision, ruffled by that breeze. "That was some impressive racing you did yesterday."

A small smile, tossing the blade of grass away, plucking another one. "Yeah... I mean, Raven and I, we go back a long way. He is exceptional. Just as all the others, each with their own little personality."

"I never thought of horses as such. Just thinking they were dumb animals you rode. I had to learn the colours though, and some breeds."

Darren grinned. "They are anything but dumb."

"I could see it." Looking at him and Darren met his gaze. "Have you had your own? Horse, I mean."

"No."

"What? During all these years...?"

Darren shrugged, tossing the blade of grass away, picking another one. "Horses are expensive. You never keep that kind of money. Besides, there were plenty to ride and teach..."

"But... they got sold? Surely..." Watching that slight pull of his mouth, that painful smirk.

"Yes... that is inevitable sometimes..."

"But... this is unfair! What if Father decided to sell Raven?"

Darren blew a breath, forcing a smile. "Then I would say my farewells... and hope that his Lordship had sold him to a good place." He tossed the blade of grass away, lacing his fingers together on his knees. "That is all we can hope for. To end up in a good place." A slight pang to his heart, because he was home, but was missing the place where he had grown up, that security.

He turned to Archibald's hand on his shoulder, his outraged voice, and wide eyes. "You are not cattle!"

Darren dared to plant a soft kiss on that feeble hand, squeezing his flesh. "No. But I go where I am needed. Or where I am sent. It is not much different from being sold."

Glancing around so Archibald withdrew his hand, curling it into a fist. "Fucked up. This is fucked up beyond belief..." Tears mounted in his eyes. "Us... being served by you... we are all the same... we should be..."

"I am not sure what I would do with your life... sorry for being so blunt. It seems utterly boring."

Archibald had to laugh softly, not entirely sure Darren had not made the comment on purpose to take that bitter nail out of his chest. "That it is. For sure."

They looked at each other, that silent yearning burning in their eyes, so Darren moved and knelt in front of Archibald, pushing the blanket off his legs, taking his right calf in his strong hand, massaging that meagre flesh. Not leaving his eyes as Archibald breathed harder, letting him knead his flesh on both legs. Darren grabbed his ankles then and straightened his legs, moving them up and down, slowly.

Archibald pulled a face. "Ouch... this hurts... a bit..."

"But tolerable?"

He nodded, leaning back, a bit wide-eyed at his legs moving, even if it was only Darren's hands. He felt the blood course those long-neglected muscles with a dull ache. But he endured it, silent, trusting him.

Darren covered him up after a while. "You should try to move them, even if they don't obey first. A small movement is better than being idle."

Archibald looked at the blanket on his legs. "You believe in this..."

"You feel pain? Warmth? Then they are not lost. They might not be perfect, but you will be able to do something." A sudden idea in him. "How about riding a bit?"

Archibald met his smile. "Are you serious? I cannot even walk..."

"You don't need to walk. The horse will carry you. Just some walking in the pen, nothing too strenuous. But it would do good to your legs."

Archibald sighed. "I am not sure... I don't want to fall."

"I would be close. And Dandy will not throw you off."

Archibald smiled. "I bet he won't... alright. I need to sell the idea to Father... and you need to squeeze it in your day."

"You could ride instead of coming here."

Archibald's heart sank. "This is the only time we can be alone."

"Not for long."

"My mother... I know... she was talking about some ladies coming to visit tomorrow for tea... I could not care less..." He pinched his lips, bitter. The neighbouring wife and the daughter of a lord, somebody he had supposedly met at that ball where he was taken there with his wheeled chair. *Who?* He could not remember, their faces blending, their smiles and eyes above him. Their shrill laughter. He shuddered. "I wish we could just disappear somewhere. Far from here. Just us."

Darren gave him a sad smile and rose. "That would be nice, yes. Let me push you back. It is getting late." He grabbed the chair and pushed.

Archibald sighed. "I will talk to father about the riding. He will be thrilled. I... I can't ride well. I got sick after a few lessons..."

"It doesn't matter. I'll teach you."

"It's winter soon..." Bitter, he let himself sink into that chair, wishing for the road to stretch into infinity so he would never stop pushing.

"You can ride all dressed up too. Winter is ideal."

"Is that so? You are giving me hope."

Darren stopped the chair in front of the stairs and faced him. "Hope is all we have."

Shutting up as the footmen appeared to carry him away. Archibald just waved, pressing that white cloth against his lips.

Next day, they were waiting for their guests when Archibald casually addressed his father. "I would like to pick up riding again. Darren said he could help if that is alright with you."

William shot him a mocking look. "What a splendid idea. I bet he could." Grinning at Archibald's small scowl.

His father smiled. "If you feel strong enough... this is delightful news."

His mother looked up from her embroidery. "Indeed it is. If you can ride, you will seem less of an invalid, and you might even be of interest to the ladies. Now, do not mess up this afternoon. Lady Pembleton is coming over with her delightful daughter, Charlotte. She is a noble lady, young, and awaiting a suitor. They have not been intimidated by your health or physical state, so it is great luck. If all goes well during this afternoon's promenade, you can start courting her and marry her in spring."

Stunned silence followed her words, Lord Hampton just coughing slightly, his worried eyes on Archibald's bleached face.

towardHis weak voice. "Mother? Marry...? I do not intend to marry..."

"Tut-tut! I will not have this. Not from you, heir to this estate. You are gaining back some health? It is time to marry and worry about the rest later. Charlotte is ideal. She has taken a liking to you at the ball and wants to get to know you better, even in your sorry state, so..."

Archibald snapped. "This is not your decision! Not anybody else's either! It is my life..." A bout of cough cut his words, surprising him too, so he pressed the handkerchief against his lips, not even daring to take it away. But he knew, the taste of blood flooding his mouth, a small desperate whine escaping his trembling lips.

His granny stepped to him. "You are unwell?"

Archibald looked at that cloth tainted with ruby red. "Yes... so it seems."

"Nothing unusual. Wipe it off and forget your nonsense behaviour." His mother stepped to him and wiped his mouth crudely with a wet cloth. "There. All proper. Now, I seem to hear them, so behave."

Archibald's desperate eyes flew to his father, but the door opened then, and the guests got announced, Lady Pembleton going straight to Lady Hampton, hugging, her daughter trailing her. William had risen to greet that young girl, her pale brown hair in locks, tumbling to her shoulders. She was wearing a lavender dress with white gloves.

William steered her to Archibald. "My soon to be brother-in-law, Lord Archibald Hampton."

She curtsied lightly, her voice soft. "Lady Charlotte Pembleton. It is nice to meet again."

Archibald gathered his breath. "My pleasure."

Lady Hampton's shrill voice filled the space. "Let us enjoy a splendid walk before we sit for tea. It will do us good and allow our youngsters to get to know each other better."

Archibald looked at her, his voice barely concealed, filled with anger. "And how do you envision this, Mother? I can't..."

"Oh! I summoned your good coachman to push you. After all, he is more than capable of doing that."

Archibald's eyes went wide, and he blanched, despite himself, almost feeling like his heart would give up at that very moment. "You did what?"

"You heard me. He's waiting downstairs, I gather. Let us hurry. Charlotte, dear, just walk next to Archibald. I am sure you have a lot to talk about. Do not mind that man pushing him, he's our stable master, and as such, is as good as furniture." They laughed lightly with Lady Pembleton and William, and Archibald had to dig deep not to blow up, that abysmal despair filling his lungs, his chest.

He got carried down to the bottom of the stairs, facing Darren, who was waiting with his hands behind his back.

Her mother stepped to him. "Just push my son, as you usually do. We are going for a stroll in the park. Lady Pembleton will walk with you and we'll be in the back, to give the young ones some privacy." She smiled, and Darren just bowed lightly.

"As you wish, Milady." His heart racing, watching that young lady put her hand on Archibald's chair, lean to him lightly.

"I am delighted to walk with you."

Archibald just nodded, but his eyes never left Darren, even if he knew that it was madness, trying to wordlessly tell him that this was a trap, that he didn't know. Feeling him step behind, take his chair and push, slower, to allow the young lady to match his strides.

She chatted, delighted, her small fur mantel on her shoulders, her eyes roaming the tall trees lining the path. "How beautiful... mother said you had a nice mansion, but she sold it short, I am afraid."

Archibald was trying to find some words for that idle small talk. "Indeed... it is quite big." Darren's hands, so close, he could feel them, so he had to close his eyes for a fleeting moment, dizzy.

"I would truly like to get to know you better... mother said you might walk again one day?"

"I have no idea..." A mad fright there, all of a sudden, the idea of walking not even tempting him anymore. "I might not. At all."

"Oh, well... I do not care." She smiled down at him, her legs swishing her skirt. "A man has other qualities when it comes to marriage than his validity."

Archibald cleared his throat lightly, all too conscious of Darren walking behind him, silent. "I do think it is hasty to mention marriage."

"Why? Isn't it what we are all longing for? A good husband, a secure future. You may be invalid, but you seem kind-hearted, at least, that is what your mother has said. That you could not do any harm. Well... I mean you could not... in this chair..." She quieted, a bit embarrassed, and he glanced up at her, wondering if she had lost her words out of decency, or she was just plain simple. She caught his eyes. "I would be happy for us to marry. I would take you as you are. In this chair, even."

Archibald was at a loss for words, trying to claw himself out of that despair. "I do believe it is too early... we don't know each other."

She smiled, skipping lightly. "Plenty of time when we got married. Or engaged. We should get engaged first. That is the proper way."

Archibald held his handkerchief against his lips to keep himself from howling. Almost reaching up to clutch Darren's hand when he caught himself. Trying to breathe when he had nothing left in that tight chest. "I... I need to go back... the air... is too harsh... cold..." He felt the chair slow, stop, heard his concerned voice.

"You are unwell, Milord?"

"Yes... yes, just push me back..."

His mother and the others had caught up when Darren turned the chair.

Her puzzled voice. "Just where do you think you are going? Archibald!"

"I... I don't feel well..." And he didn't, a cold sweat breaking out on his back, his eyes wide as he was trying to draw that icy air into his lungs. A mad fright. *What... what...* His vision blurred and he could only feel his strong hands catching him as he fell to the side. *What... Breathe... Breathe...* Darkness. Like a shroud.

His eyelids fluttered open in that semi-dark, that feeble candlelight. *Barely dressed, in bed...* His mouth parched, so he pushed his tongue out to lick his lips. Soft whispers, so he turned his head to the voices drifting to him. Murmurs, *maybe... Father...* he tried to speak, that raspy voice barely making it.

"Father..."

A mere breath, but Lord Hampton had heard it, stepping close. "Archibald! You're awake? At last..." Watching his eyelids open, his brown eyes glazed over, searching his face.

"Where... what...?"

"The doctor is here... Your nerves... it seems your nerves could not handle it... maybe your lungs too..." That despair in his eyes when he had dared to believe that he was better.

Archibald closed his eyes not to see that abyss of fatherly sorrow. "I see... How...?"

"Darren carried you back in his arms. Thank God he was there, that strong man. You would not stay in that chair, limp... William rode to get the doctor..."

The doctor's voice. "Bed rest for a few days, and if possible, avoid distressing company. I would suggest a few days near the sea... but I am not sure it is an option."

Lord Hampton turned to him. "My mother has a cottage near the sea. It is a two-days carriage ride... but it could be done."

"I would say, if possible, with only one accompanying person. Lord Archibald needs some quiet time, alone."

"I see... let me talk to her." He took Archibald's hand. "Would you like that? The sea? Granny's cottage for a couple of days would do you good."

Archibald pried his eyes open, barely conscious. "As you wish, Father..."

Edward patted that feeble hand. "I'll talk to her. Just rest." But Archibald had already slumbered, that laboured breathing filling the shadows of the room.

Darren's eyes drifted towards the mansion, hoping, that Archibald was safe, maybe over the worse. His arms still trembling from carrying him, that limp body, hurrying with that delirious fright that he might be dying, despite everything.

Trying to get him out of that mad shouting around him, his heart in pieces, that heart barely carrying him anymore, bruised and battered. So, he had tightened his arms around that man he so loved, and walked faster, even if every step had seemed the last.

He turned from the window, his body's memory etched in his flesh, listening to the rain hammer on the roof, his eyes lost in the flames of the stove, licking the metal, dancing on the logs as the kettle started boiling. Pouring that scalding water on the tea leaves, the aroma filling that barely warm room, the wind finding places amidst the roof tiles, the beams, that attic room filled with small drafts licking the skin, like tiny, icy beasts. He huddled around his mug, blowing on that scorching liquid filled with milk. That rich taste sliding down his throat. His eyes lost a bit, burning with tears dancing at the edge of his eyelids. He jolted at that hard knock on his door and rose to open, puzzled, the evening bending into night.

Facing his lord, he almost dropped his mug. "Milord...?"

"May I come in?"

Darren almost lost it with worry, seeing his drowned eyes. "Of course, Milord..." He stepped back, letting him walk in, look around as he closed the door.

He turned to Darren then, keeping a small silence, looking for his words. "I will not even mention how grateful I am for today. That you could carry Archibald back fast to the house." A small sigh. "He is awake... but the doctor said he needs rest. A few days by the sea... alone... as much as possible... and I want to ask you to drive him there, to the countess' cottage. She has a maid there; she wrote to her to set it all up for Archibald. It would mean you would need to neglect your duties here for a couple of days... as long as it is needed for Archibald to feel better. Lord Willoughby volunteered to send somebody from his staff to step in, but I was wondering if James could be trusted. I know he is a mere stable boy, but I would not want them jostled around by a stranger. After all, we are not going anywhere... and I could ask Lord Willoughby to lend us a coachman if..." He quieted, waiting, watching that man's drawn face, his wide eyes drowned in tears.

Darren gathered his voice, hoping nothing showed through. "James can be trusted, Milord. I will brief him. When should we be leaving?"

"Tomorrow. As soon as Archibald can be readied. Take the smaller carriage and your good horses." He smiled mildly. "It will do you good too, to be a bit away, take a small break, even if I know you will be at my son's whims."

"I shall take great care of his Lordship, Milord."

"I know. I trust you fully, that is why you are going with him. So, pack, and brief the boys. I will send a page to you when you can come and pick Archibald up." He moved to the door, turning with a small smile. "Thank you again, my good man."

"My pleasure, Milord." He opened the door for him, dazed, closing it then, leaning against it as his silent sobs took over his body, sliding it to the floor.

Chapter 13

Next morning, he was waiting in front of the mansion, the horses munching their bits. Watching the footmen carry Archibald down, but his eyes were closed, even when they lifted him in. Darren helped to secure that wheeled chair and the luggage to the back, turning to his lord, and Lady Mary then.

"My son is not feeling well, but he is determined to go..."

"Very well, Milord."

He turned to the countess, who had gently put her hand on his broad arm. "Drive safely, Mister Turner. Here is the map and the address. I have written to the maid living in the neighbouring village there, and here is a letter for you when you arrive with a list of where to find everything. It is a small cottage, but probably a palace for you." She chuckled lightly. "I haven't been in a long time, but the sea is close, a mere walk from that cliff area where the house stands."

"Very well, Milady." He pocketed the letters and maps in his coat.

"I trust you will sleep at an inn on the way. Make sure Archibald has a large room."

"Yes, Milord."

"Farewell, Darren. Have a safe trip."

He bowed and mounted on the bench, his heart almost leaping out of his chest at the prospect of driving there, just the two of them. Even if they would be not alone, it felt so unexpected, he almost choked on his own feelings. Driving away carefully, the horses only in a light trot.

Lady Mary turned to her son. "That is one good deed done."

He frowned. "I cannot possibly fathom what you are thinking about, mother."

She patted his arm, meeting his smile.

Darren waited until they were far to stop the carriage and open the door. Archibald had been laid down on the bench, but their eyes met, so Darren stepped in, taking his hands which he had reached to him. Silent, his eyes so deep in those dark sockets, Darren's heart lurched.

That voice, barely there. "We... are on our way?"

"Yes... don't strain yourself..." Mad worried, he had gone to his knees next to him, and brought his hands to his lips. Those burning hands, limp.

Archibald wanted to stroke his face, but his hands wouldn't obey. "Just drive... I will be fine. I am with you..." He closed his eyes, feeling his hands put back on his chest, the carriage lilting as Darren stepped outside, then back on the bench. That light swing as they set off. His voice... He drifted away on it, in a dream, of rolling hills, rushing towards freedom... a place where nothing mattered...

Jolting at his warm hand on his shoulder. "We are at the inn..."

Archibald blinked, so weak, he could not even lift his head. "You will have to take me out... I cannot even sit..."

Darren scooped him out, holding him tight until he could put him in his chair. Pushing him into that stuffy common room.

Archibald' stomach vaulted at the smells. "Just... let's just hurry to my room..."

Darren had to carry him up the stairs, following a servant who opened the door for them. He lay Archibald on the bed. "I need to get the luggage."

He smiled feebly. "Hurry..."

Opening his eyes to his smile. "I'm back."

"I have no servants here..."

"May I..."

Archibald's lips curled up. "Of course... you may... I wish it would be more romantic... than just undressing me as the invalid I am..." His words died with those warm fingers lightly dancing on his lips. Their eyes meeting in that dim candle light.

"I'll undress you and tuck you in, but I cannot stay. Servants don't sleep with their masters. Especially not the coachman."

"Shame..." But his eyes played as Darren stripped his clothes off, leaving on his breeches. "You could take those off too..."

"It would not be fair... as you cannot see me naked." His eyes glinted.

Archibald leant back, letting him cover him, tip a glass to his burning lips. "I crave no food..."

"No wonder. Just rest. I will be here to dress you in the morning."

"You may not sleep with me... but you could give me a goodnight kiss..." Parting those burning lips, slipping that nothing breath into Darren's mouth. Panting after a few strokes of their tongues, out of breath.

Darren smoothed his blanket down. "Sleep. Please."

"Alright." His brown eyes burned softly in that warm light. "I love you..."

Darren pressed his palm against that pale, scalding cheek. "And I love you." He left then, softly closing the door.

Next morning, they set off, a small rain showering the landscape, different clouds churning in the sky as they got closer to the country's edge where the land meets that frothing sea.

They stopped for lunch, eating in the carriage, but Archibald could only force a few grapes down, and a small swig of water. Nothing seemed to want to stay down, his head light, almost as if he was buying time. *Maybe I am...* He looked up at Darren's voice.

"When we arrive, the maid will be there, allegedly, and she will be the only one serving you. That is what the countess said."

"Splendid..." He pursed his lips.

Darren patted his arm lightly. "Hey... you need that maid."

"Surely..." His eyes drifted to the trees. "I can hardly believe we are alone... let us not go there. Just drive. Let's leave. Never go back." His heart raced at his own words, and his head felt light, again, that rush of mad emotions sucking his strength away. He leant back, weak. Feeling Darren's hand on his arm. Warm, strong. Meeting his eyes.

"No. It is folly, and you know it. Let us just cherish these few days."

"I am not marrying that stupid girl." His eyes took that hard light Darren knew well.

"I suspected so."

"I am not getting married. Even if I cannot be with you... as partners... I will not betray what we have by bedding a woman..."

Darren's eyes widened a bit. "Alright..." Moved, he couldn't speak, knowing that every single one of Archibald's words were madness.

"Let us go. We should arrive tonight."

"Do you feel better?"

"I would not dare say that, but I can sit. It is progress, right?"

Darren smiled, packing their lunch away. "It is."

"Kiss me. I am not sure when we can kiss again. How wretched!"

Darren just took him in his arms softly, pulling him off that bench, sealing that bitter mouth, which had gone slack under his touch, his lips, and arms. Listening to his breath, but Archibald felt like floating, breathing Darren's breath, bathing in his taste, floating on the caresses of his tongue, that scorching pain of his stubble ripping his soft skin raw. Moaning softly, because it felt just right, because he wanted it never to stop, but Darren broke that lush kiss, gently holding his face until his eyes opened into his eyes.

"We need to go."

"I know..." Letting Darren sit him back, smooth the blanket on his legs. Archibald forced some air into his tight lungs. Nerves. He knew. That mad love eating them alive. Watching him climb out, start the carriage. He leant back and drifted off to that lilting gait.

Night falling when he got shaken awake gently. "We've arrived."

Archibald peeked outside, that small cottage of grey stone wedged on the cliff in a small, lush unkept garden filled with autumn flowers. A rotten blue wooden fence. The horses were waiting patiently. The house, dark.

He frowned. "Where's the maid?"

Darren shrugged and handed him an envelope from his coat pocket. "Her Ladyship, the countess left you this. She said it has the list of where we can find things. The maid might be late."

Archibald opened the letter, barely having enough force to tear the envelope up. His eyes eating the lines in that setting dusk light.

My dear Archie,

I trust you have arrived well at my little seaside haven. That trusted coachman of yours has surely made sure you got to your destination unharmed and in fresher spirits. I am afraid the house has been neglected, but he is an able man, he can clean it and stock the kitchen up. Ah, I forgot. The maid is not available, I am afraid.

I have neglected informing you that she has moved years ago, but understandably, did not want to worry your father, nor wanted him to send one of your mother's spies. I am sure your handsome coachman can take those duties over, possibly far better than my maid ever could have. Enjoy your stay, my darling. I am looking forward to seeing what that fresh sea air has done to you and your health.

Yours ever,

Granny

Archibald had to read it twice, his hands trembling as he handed the letter to Darren, meeting his concerned eyes.

"What is it?"

"Read it for yourself." His heart racing, his eyes on the setting sun tainting the sky blood orange. Seeing Darren's eyes widen, meet his eyes. Archibald smiled. "So, does my handsome coachman think he can take over a maid's duties? Maybe better than the maid herself..."

Darren didn't know what to say, floating a bit, in disbelief. Looking up at Archibald's voice.

"Just settle me, then the horses... we only need one room... because you are sure as hell not sleeping anywhere else but in my bed."

Darren rushed to open the house, his hands trembling, then scooped Archibald up and brought him upstairs to the master room, those large windows overlooking the grey sea, further, foaming at the bottom of that bay's cliffs. That lush sunset tainting the light in violet and red shadows.

Archibald blew him a kiss. "Hurry..."

It was almost an hour to settle everything, let the horses loose in a small field behind that cottage, lock that door, bring some firewood up and start it, bring some food up, their trunks. Archibald's eyes following his every move with a loving gaze. Letting Darren step to him and pull his shirt off, bring a basin close with a sponge, wash his torso and arms off, his face, careful, taming the strength of his hands, his touch.

Archibald caught his wrist when he wanted to rise. "Wash me down. Please."

Darren swallowed. "Everywhere?"

"Yes."

He leant back and let Darren strip him, almost too shy to even look, but it was Archibald who was burning with a different fire, pulling his hand close with that sponge, gliding it on his hips. Meeting his eyes, and Darren boldened up and washed him down, gliding the sponge down his cock, his legs, his feet.

Archibald's eyes danced. "Your turn..."

He just smiled, stripping, standing in a larger basin which he'd filled with water. He took a small pitcher and scooped some water up, letting it glide down his body, those rippling muscles glistening in the fire's dancing flames, in that flaming setting sun, and Archibald had to swallow, his eyes caressing every inch of that strong body lightly covered with dark hair, that firm ass, his strong thighs.

An unknown surge there to have that body close, under his hands, so he whispered. "Come here..."

Darren stepped out, drying himself before he walked close, still a bit in awe, a bit shy, even if he was burning for him, he couldn't know what Archibald wanted, how he had envisioned this moment which seemed impossible and all of a sudden was there. At arm's reach. Yielding to Archibald's hand pulling him on the bed, opening his mouth to a kiss as his feeble hands groped that firm flesh of his arms and shoulders.

Darren boldened up and lay next to him, taking him in those broad arms, that thin body with its nothing force. That way with which Archibald just let himself go in his arms driving him crazy. Because it was new, even to him, that lush abandon, those yearning sighs, his hands gently roaming his back.

He broke the kiss, worried. "Are you sure...? You have enough force? Breath?"

"I don't care... I need you... I dreamt of this... so many times... and I don't know what I'm doing... but I trust you." His brown eyes shone with that warm light which made Darren's heart race.

"Alright... We could maybe just do something lighter... nothing too straining... and then, in a couple of days, when you feel better..."

Archibald put his fingers on his lips, looking up into his eyes. "I want to be yours, then... We are not leaving until you made me yours."

"Oh..." It was so soft, but Archibald just parted his lips for a kiss, pulling him down gently on his mouth.

Letting Darren hold him closer, tighter with his left arm, his right hand straying to where their cocks met, hard, arching against each other. He took them in his broad hand, locking them together in that firm grip, sliding his fist up and down as he kept kissing him, drinking his soft moans, panting in his mouth too. Letting his mouth stray to Archibald's neck, biting that soft pulse, nibbling his way down to his collarbones, stroking them all the while, slow licks to his chest, his neck arched on his arm, his head tossing on the pillow when Darren closed his lips on his nipple, sucking hard then, grazing it with his teeth as his tongue played with it. Feeling him harden, his moans filling the room dancing with fire shadows. Feeling how close he was too, knowing, biting down on his chest softly when he felt him arch against him, flood his hand. Stroking them more, letting go too, moaning against his skin, letting their juices mingle, glide down his fist, slick their skins. Soft, lush caresses. He brought his hand up to Archibald's face, cupping his jaw, wondering if it would be too much, his eyes asking when those burning brown eyes went to him at his touch. His thumb brushing Archibald's lips, leaving a wet trail, watching as his tongue licked that trail away. Kissing him then, their tastes there, just barely as their breaths mingled.

Looking at each other, not needing words. Darren held him tight in his shoulder, stroking his hair as they lay there, the fire dancing on their naked skin, that window filled with stars studding that dark sky. Falling asleep with tears in their eyes, floating on each other's warmth.

That warmth which never left Archibald during the night, even when he woke a bit, just to pull closer to him, when it was not even possible to be closer, feeling his arms tighten around him in his sleep. His breathing which was like a lullaby to his lonely heart. Closing his eyes, trying to soak it in, that feeling of having his skin on his skin, his lips on his hair.

Something like a dream when the sun tore it apart, and Archibald sat up, alert, his hand grazing that empty sheet.

His eyes darted to the door when it opened, relief flooding him, seeing his smile. "Awake?"

"Where were you?" He leant back on the pillows, weak, that lush late autumn sunshine pouring in the window.

Darren put a tray on the bed. "I gave breakfast to the horses and made you breakfast."

"I may not be hungry."

Darren just pushed the tray in his lap and pulled that metallic cover off. "A nice fresh omelette for you and some tea and toast. You can surely eat one bite of each and drink a sip of tea." He sat on the bed, the mattress bending under his weight, and Archibald reached for his hand.

"Don't just go like this. Wake me up before you leave." A mild panic there, above that joy. That fear of not having enough moments filled with him.

Darren sighed, running his thumb over his hand. "You need to rest. I would not wish to wake you. I'm never far..."

"This is all new to me... being with somebody... sleeping together..." He blushed slightly. "I could not miss what I never had... and now, I am not sure how I will live without it."

Watching Darren's face fall. He swallowed, pained. "You will manage... we all do..."

"Your wife..."

Darren smiled, that bitter curve at the edge of his lips. "Ah... maybe. I mean, she didn't love me and resented every moment of our union... even if it had been brief... as you know."

"You had to bed her..."

Darren nodded, his blue eyes going to the sky. "Yes. She... even if she was in love with our lord, she wanted a true married life... even if we had discussed of just sleeping together... she wanted to warm to me... or something..." He pulled a face, but left his hand in Archibald's. "It didn't work too well, but we did what we had to do. And she did all that a good wife would do. Took care of the house, washed, cooked... prepared my tea... I was young and busy, I did not have time nor energy to think about it." His eyes went to Archibald. "It is not the same as what we have here... even if only for these brief moments. She never loved me." Answering his unuttered question. "And no men had ever loved me either." A rogue tear slid down Archibald's cheek and Darren wiped it off with a smile. "You should eat. Not cry and distress yourself."

"I don't think I can..."

Darren picked up a piece of toast and put a piece of golden omelette on it. A small piece which he lifted to Archibald's lips, meeting his eyes. Pushing that bite between his parted lips. Leaving the tip of his finger just enough for Archibald to get a taste, colour his cheeks as he chewed. Another small bite. His finger lingering a bit.

Archibald leant back at the third bite. "Enough."

His eyes danced. "Sure?"

"Enough of eating."

"Drink then."

Archibald shook his head, so Darren took a good swig of that lukewarm tea, and leant to him, close. Archibald parted his lips, letting him seal his mouth, push that warm tea into it with a lash of his tongue, and he had no other choice but to swallow. He had laced his arms around his neck and pulled him close, feeling Darren move the platter to the side, off the bed to the table. All the while kissing him, letting Archibald pull him on the bed, fist his shirt as Darren kicked his boots off. Looking down at Archibald when he'd pulled him down on top of him, but Darren held his weight up on his elbows not to crush him.

Stroking his hair out of his forehead. "What now?"

"I don't know... I just want you..."

"You're not strong enough..."

"I know..." Bitter a bit, lost, his eyes begging, not even knowing for what.

Darren pulled his shirt off and pulled the covers off Archibald, leaning on him just enough that he would feel a bit of that weight, kissing him softly. His mouth wandered down his neck, that heaving chest, nibbling his ribs as his hands glided down his arms, closing on his wrists. Licking a trail down from his sternum to his belly button, his blue eyes burning in his brown eyes, as Archibald watched him, wide-eyed, an unknown feeling above his fear.

Darren stopped and smiled at him, catching that light of fear in his brown pools. "I might just take you in my mouth, if that is fine with you, because it is nothing exhausting for you, but you will still probably see the stars... or so I hope." Amused, he was waiting, holding Archibald's wrists gently.

Archibald's mind raced, battling with his heart. He sort of knew... having read some of those books, but he was mortified a bit, that embarrassment colouring his cheeks. "Only if you want to..."

"I would not be between your legs if I did not want it. But you are in charge. I will not do anything that you deem unpleasant."

"I do not even know what you are talking about..."

"Care to find out?"

"I guess..." Giving in to those playing blue eyes, to that trust he had decided to give him fully.

"You can stop anytime. Just ask me."

"Alright..." His breath caught when Darren planted a large kiss on his hipbone, nipped it with his teeth, that small pain, and his warm tongue sending a wave up Archibald's body, pushing a small moan out. "Ah..."

Darren smiled, kissing his way down the top of his thigh, leaving a trail of fire, and Archibald's back arched when he felt his mouth around his cock, hot, warm, tight... A soft mewl escaping his lips, pulling at that gentle grip on his wrists, but Darren just held him, letting him thrash mildly on the bed as he sucked him, hard. Watching his face, his rising ribcage, listening to his breathing, his head tossing on the pillows. Knowing he could not hold it for long, that body just learning that birthing pleasure. A few harder licks and sucks, and Archibald came with a small moan, heaving a bit, his eyes in tears at that insane pleasure, the waves still lingering, lapping at his spine from the base. His eyes closed, feeling Darren sidle up to him, tilt his head to the side.

Archibald opened his eyes to his smile.

"Sleepy?"

"I don't want to sleep..." Wanting to ask what had happened with his seed, too ashamed to ask, somehow knowing, and it filled him with an unknown thrill.

Darren stroked his hair back. "You should."

"Stay then..."

Darren obliged, pulling him on his chest, covering that frail body to his shoulders. Smiling at Archibald's breathing. He had already fallen asleep, and Darren just watched the clouds chase the sky, not even remembering when he'd stayed in bed last. Not ever with somebody he loved in his arms. Somebody who loved him back. In that mad little moment of perfection, there was nothing else but him and Archibald. At the edge of the world, nothing else existed. No rules, no laws, no families... nothing. Just them. A fleeting dream, he knew, but he pushed those thoughts out, just letting that golden moment etch itself in his mind, his flesh. His taste still lining his mouth.

Chapter 14

Archibald woke to the smell of food, his hand searching blindly when he met that broad warm arm. Opening his eyes, watching Darren turn to him, laying on the bed, but he had his shirt on.

Archibald's heart sank. "You got up?"

Darren put his palm on his cheek. "I cannot stay idle in bed. I had to cook lunch. Take care of the house a bit. When you're done eating, I'll push you down to the beach. If you feel well enough."

Archibald pushed himself up as best as he could. "I have to be... better..."

Darren got up and put a tray in his lap. "This starts with eating." He lifted the lid and gave him an apologetic smile. "I cannot cook any of the fancy dishes you are used to... but I still hope a humble vegetable stew will do."

Archibald caught his hand. "I do not need any fancy dishes... I am not even sure I can eat." But it smelled good, that creamy broth, some pieces of carrots and potatoes floating on that pale yellow cream. He picked up the spoon and gingerly scooped some out, tasting it. "Mhm..." Eating another spoonful.

Darren gave him a piece of bread. "Have a small bite of this with it."

"You have eaten already?"

"Yes. It is a bit late, and I need my food..."

Archibald smiled. "Must be a real treat, having a body that doesn't tire."

"You tell me. You are younger."

Their eyes met, their smiles.

Archibald laughed lightly. "That may be so... but I barely function." He ate a few more spoonfuls, bit another small piece of bread off. Leaning back with a sigh. "Enough... and I know it is not, but this is what you will get from me."

Darren took the platter away. "There is still tea time, and dinner."

Archibald shook his head. "No. Impossible."

Darren took his hands, pushing a smile above his worry. "I will not force you. But you will not get better if you refuse to feed."

Archibald's eyes flamed up. "Get better? What for? If I get better, if I manage to stand, even walk, I will need to get married... I have thought in that mad moment yesterday that I could evade it... but I cannot see how... It is a trap... Because I do want to get better, but every step towards validity and health is a step to my grave." He squeezed Darren's hands as much as he could, watching his eyes drowning with each word. "Life is death without you. No matter what I do, I am walking towards death."

Darren watched him, searching for his words. "You... you will still have me."

"Not the way I would want it. Not as my lover. You would not be there in the morning to wake with me, and at night to hold me. I would see you every day, and talk to you as my inferior, and I am not sure I can bear it." He leant to him, holding his hands tight, his eyes burning. "Would you bear it? Seeing me on the arm of a woman? Knowing I share her bed sometimes? That she could bear my children?"

Darren's eyes widened, shimmering with tears. He looked away; his voice pained. "Why talk about this now?"

Archibald tugged at his hands so he looked back at him. "Because it is truth. It will be truth. You know it."

His despair mirrored in Darren's blue eyes who just ran his thumbs on Archibald's hands. Forcing a smile. "But it is not truth yet. Not now. Just enjoy this gift we got. These few days. Right now, we could just love this despair away... this hopelessness... but I am not going to make love to you out of despair... so let us get dressed and walk down to that sea. So that you get better... even if you do not want it... I would rather have you alive than driving your hearse to the cemetery..."

He almost choked on his last words and Archibald reached for him and pulled his head in his lap. Thrilled, that that strong man just let him, melted into his touch, let him run his fingers through that soft, dark hair. Just staying like this, Archibald's eyes on that light grey sky.

His voice, soft. "Alright. Take me to the beach."

Darren pushed himself up, his blue eyes drowned in tears. "Sure?"

Archibald wiped at a rogue tear which had escaped his right eye. "Yes. You are right. I need to live. Because I want to live... and find a way to live my life with you."

"It is folly."

Archibald smiled. "That is my expression. But you may be right. Even then, folly is all we have already."

Darren took his hand and kissed it. "If you say so..." He got up and took some clothes out for Archibald, who just waved a hand at some of them.

"Dress me simple. I cannot care less about fashion. No cravat, or any of those suffocating clothes."

Darren just put some pants on him and a shirt, a vest, and a thick coat. Boots then which he pulled on his feet and legs, kneeling in front of him as he sat on the bed. Meeting his eyes filled with lust.

Archibald cupped his face and pulled him into a kiss. "I need that walk?"

"You do. I will deal with you later."

"Tonight...?"

"You are not strong enough. Eat, get some sleep, breathe some sea in. Maybe tomorrow, or the day after."

"We are not going home until you make me yours."

"So you said."

Archibald held his face. "You will? Promise me."

"I promise."

Rising, he pulled him up, an illusion there that he was standing when it was only his strong arms holding him tight.

His eyes in those blue seas. "I love you..." Clinging to his shoulders, feeling his warmth, his body under his clothes.

Darren scooped him up in his arms, looking into his eyes. "And I love you."

"Don't drop me..." Smiling, almost limp in those strong arms.

"Would I ever?"

He carried him downstairs to his chair, sat him in it, and pushed it outside. Despite the rough path, it was not too difficult to push that chair towards a path leading down the slope to the beach. A winding path carved in that hill sloping further away from the cliff, a gentle breeze carrying that thick smell of iodine and salt. Archibald closed his eyes, tasting that salt in the air as it found his lips, invading his nostrils, finding his lungs. He breathed in deeper, wanting it inside, that frothing sea, the waves crashing on the shores and against hard rocks, black as tar. That grey sand lapped by that grey sea. Gulls screeching high above. The soft scrunch of wheels on sand. Feeling his arms around him. The sand under him. He opened his eyes, facing the sea in that sheltered bay, the cliffs hugging it, the cottage somewhere up there. He leant back against Darren, who had sat behind him, the waves close, sloshing on that damp sand.

"Heaven..."

"It is nice, isn't it?" Hearing his smile, his deep voice resonating in Archibald's feeble chest.

"You have been before? To the sea?"

"A couple of times. With Lord Shackleton and his family. Training horses for the hunts. They loved running on those beaches."

"No time to rest then..."

Darren smiled. "No."

"Do you even get days off?"

"Sometimes. When I ask for them. It is rare. I do not like to hand over my duties. Or idle around."

"And I am struggling to fill my days..."

Feeling Darren shrug. "I have a hard time imagining what you do with your days, even if I know full well what you are doing."

"Or what I am not doing." Archibald smiled, bitter, but his hands had gone to those broad forearms around his chest, holding them gently.

His grin in his voice. "You could say that."

"When did you start it? Working?"

"Mhm... I am not sure I remember. I had always helped, even little... working properly? Maybe at eleven... I had to do some school before, my father had insisted."

"Eleven... I was still throwing tantrums."

"When you are tired, you do not have the force to throw tantrums."

"I can imagine... only imagine... I have no notion of what you are talking about... My health went soon around thirteen... a slow decent into being what I am now..." He breathed in deep, that sea air like a balm to his tired lungs.

"You will get better."

"If you say so..."

"I have selfish reasons to wish it."

Archibald leant his head back on his shoulder, meeting his smiling eyes. "Is that so?"

"Uhum..." Leaning on those parted lips, pushing his tongue in as his hand went to hold his jaw gently. A swift lick to those lips filled with salt.

"I could kiss you forever..."

"A nice thought..." Darren held him tighter, their eyes on the sea, the playing waves, that gentle breeze ruffling their hair. Black and brown, dancing like flames.

Archibald had almost fallen asleep when he carried him back up to that warm room. He laid him on the bed, pulling his boots off, and most of his clothes. Tucking him in when Archibald caught his hand with his nothing grip.

"I don't want to sleep... those are hours without you."

Darren smiled. "I'm not far. And you need that sleep."

"Nonsense..." But he had closed his eyes, that feeble chest rising softly, a bitter edge on his mouth.

Darren kissed those bitter lips gently. "I'll wake you later..."

"Fine..." He didn't open his eyes, that afternoon glow in the sky highlighting that pale skin, dancing in his hair.

Darren sighed, but left, closing the door gently. He went straight to the garden in the back, the horses neighing and hurrying to him in that small field lined with apple trees. They had gorged themselves, their sticky lips searching his hands, his pockets.

"Nothing for you. You are already full." Stroking those strong necks under that soft hair, running his fingers through their manes, that deep love glowing in his heart each time he was with them.

He walked then to the trees and picket a couple of apples, putting them in his shirt which he had bundled in his hand. The horses following, grazing that meagre grass, their eyes darting to him. A rare peace, a futile illusion, that this was their home, and they would never have to leave. A bright little moment in that late afternoon sun peeking through those ash grey clouds.

He walked back to the kitchen, peeling the apples, cutting them crudely into an iron pan which he had lined with butter and sprinkled with sugar. Flour and butter then, crumbling them together with his strong hands, a hint of sugar, some cinnamon, and he stashed it on the apples. Lighting the oven, he waited until it warmed, just sitting, watching the flames, then pushed the pan in. Glancing at an old clock ticking on the wall. He also put a kettle on, rummaging through all the tea leaves the cook had packed for Archibald... *so many... what for...* unsure, he chose the one he'd used in the morning. Brewing a whole kettle, dousing it with milk and sugar. *So much sugar... unreal...* something he was not used to, having just a small quantity for his whole year, but the cook seemed to think Archibald would bathe in it.

He pulled the crumble out after a good half hour, cutting it up in slices which fell apart, serving two portions. Two mugs, then, and the tea. He picked that huge platter up effortlessly, walking upstairs, the sun dipping down to sleep, that orange and purple painting the sky. Opening the door, watching Archibald stir to his steps, turn to him, his brown eyes silent.

"Had a good sleep?"

"Yes... you brought food? I have no appetite..."

Darren smiled, putting the platter on the bed. "Not even for cake?"

"Cake?" He shuddered at the thought of those powdery sweet cakes that his mother loved for tea. "Ugh... I especially hate cake..." Watching Darren's face fall a bit, so he pushed himself to sit. "But... I will maybe still taste yours..."

"Oh... alright..." He uncovered it and put a plate in Archibald's lap. "It's just apple crumble. There are many down in the garden and around the field. Made some pretty happy horses." Darren smiled, pouring two mugs of tea too.

"Apple crumble..." His eyes on that mass of golden apples layered with what looked like crumbs, thick, that sweet cinnamon smell invading his senses. "You made this?" Looking up into his eyes, in disbelief.

Darren shrugged; a bit embarrassed. "Yes... an old family recipe. My mother's."

"I am honoured."

"Please." He smiled, picking his spoon up. "Taste it first. You said you didn't like cake..." His eyes glinting.

Archibald smiled and scooped a piece up, putting it in his mouth. That sweet and sour taste instantly made his mouth water, the dough just melting together with the apples, that sticky sugar and butter-like cream. A small, surprised moan escaped his mouth, and he scooped another portion up, licking it off the spoon. Meeting Darren's eyes, who was just watching him, mesmerised.

"It is... surprisingly delicious."

Eating more, almost a new light in those dull, brown eyes.

Darren handed him his mug. "Drink too. It will wash it down."

"I want to bask in the taste first. Mhm..."

Eating with a focus Darren had never seen, that plate cleared, that hungry blood rushing to his cheeks as it raced his body with jubilation. Food. Sugar.

Archibald licked his lips. "Might I be bold enough to ask you to bake this every day?"

"Not at all! I would be delighted if it meant you ate with this ravenous appetite."

Archibald met his eyes. "I have selfish reasons to eat more."

"Is that so?"

"Yes..."

Their eyes met, and Darren had barely any time to put the platter on the table, Archibald had reached for him, grabbing his shirt, pulling him close, pulling him into a wide kiss. Wanting that mouth filled with cinnamon, apples, and sugar, that taste he loved, something he wanted more of, mingling their breaths, their tastes. Bolder, he moaned into Darren's mouth, feeling his hands peel his shirt off, pull his pants down. He stripped too, only leaving Archibald's mouth when it got in the way, laying on him gently, holding his weight up not to crush him. Searching his eyes to draw breath, to ask, and Archibald just panted softly, holding his gaze, not even breaking that eye contact when Darren reached down and spread his legs, one after the other, lying back on him, gently, kissing that mouth which wanted him so much, feeling his feeble hands glide to his back, trace his muscles. Pushing his weight on him just enough to trap them together, rocking his hips to make their hard cocks push against each other, glide on each other. His hands in Archibald's hair, stroking softly with each thrust, kissing him deep and slow, those trembling lips, drinking his moans, his breath words. "Oh God... Oh God..." Not letting him squirm away when that crushing pleasure was near, rocking him until he arched against his body, his hips, eyes shut tight, mewling softly, small sobs as he lost it, coating them, that warm slickness just enough to push Darren over the edge too. Rolling off him, but his arms had pulled Archibald with him, cradling him, pulling his limp leg on his thigh, holding it as his other hand held his slim shoulders, grazing his skin, planting soft kisses on his eyelids filled with tears.

Looking into those brown eyes shining with a new glow. Leaning into his touch when his weak hand went to his cheek, his jaw.

"I never want to leave this bed..."

"A nice thought..." Smiling, he ran his hand up Archibald's thigh, from his knee to his hip, turning his palm gently on that sharp bone, gliding his hand to his ass which he gripped. Firm enough to watch his lips part. Massaging that slight pain away straight away, lush caresses to that meagre flesh.

Archibald blushed. "I am not sure what you find in this wretched body of mine..." A bit desperate, his eyes asking too.

Darren cupped his ass gently, leaving that warm palm on that shivering skin. "I know what I have under my hands. Not a body. You."

Archibald's eyes welled up. "That is awfully kind of you."

Darren cupped his chin, holding it with enough force to get his full attention, his blue eyes, dark. "It is not kind. It is the truth. I love every single portion of this body you abhor. This body which still manages to shelter your bitter little soul.

This body I am looking forward to making better… even if it is just enough to make you see yourself in another light."

A rogue tear slid down Archibald's cheek. Love. Shame. "I do not deserve you."

"You seem to think you do not deserve many things. Start by hating yourself less."

He laced his arms around Archibald when he broke down crying. Pulling him close to let him sob into his neck. Rocking him with that pain in his chest.

Chapter 15

They had slept locked together, Archibald in Darren's arms, his head on his chest, breathing his skin in, his warmth melting his stress, soothing his tired nerves. He had never cried so much, and never slept so well, as if his body had been waiting for his body, his soul for his soul, that exhausting search finally over. Stirring when he felt him move, so he opened his eyes, meeting those blue eyes in that dawn glow.

His soft voice. "I'm going to feed the horses and make breakfast. Just sleep. It's early."

"Don't go..." That bed, already empty when he had only moved a bit, leaning on his elbow.

Darren stroked his hair back. "It is necessary. I will come back with food." Smiling, hoping he would calm and go back to sleep. Kissing that pouting mouth deep, pushing him back into the pillows.

Archibald sighed, meeting his eyes. "Alright... as you wish." His eyes, already half-mast.

Darren pulled the covers on him, still warm from his body when he slid out into that cool room, but he was used to it, waking in a much colder room, so he just dressed, and stoked the fire up before skipping downstairs, out the back.

The horses neighed when they saw him, and he stashed a good pile of hay into their pen, and brought their oats in two buckets, waiting until they ate it all, his eyes on that glowing pink sky lighting up with that cold sun. He went inside and fired the stove up, put the kettle on, waiting for it to boil whilst he prepared the tea leaves, and took a couple of eggs. Toasting the bread in a pan with some butter, he also took some jam he found on a shelf, even if the cook had packed some sort of fancier looking one. He couldn't care less, his eyes lighting up at that thick, hardened honey sitting in a closed jar. He scooped some out too, and made the scrambled eggs when the sky had lit up.

Bringing everything up, peeking in, but Archibald was awake, sitting in bed, his eyes on the windows. They went to him, though. "Breakfast?"

"Yes. I do hope you have some hunger in you."

"Maybe..." His lips played, but he waited until Darren put all that food in his lap. "Oh... all this?"

"You don't have to eat it all. I can help." He served him his tea and sat next to the bed on a chair. Spreading some butter and honey on a toast, he offered it to Archibald. "This will do you good. Honey does wonders."

Archibald pulled a small face. "Ugh... I am not sure. It looks thick and hard?"

"That's the best." He swallowed half a toast whole and pushed the scrambled eggs in front of Archibald. "Eat. Please."

The way he chewed, his mouth and jaw moved stirred something in Archibald, kindling a long dead desire for food, so he ate, slowly, but it felt good, somehow, that anticipation there for those simple tastes which had been crafted with love. Even if crude, it tasted of him, of his hands, his whole being, those bites like pieces of his flesh, like an unholy communion he could not get enough of.

Raising his head at Darren's voice. "Oh, my... you ate a fair bit." Smiling, his face glowing with joy.

"I guess I did..." Feeling a bit dizzy, he just leant back, trying to breathe with that full stomach.

Darren took the tray away. "A walk this morning will get you ready for lunch. If you eat like this, I have hopes that your health will improve fast." He ran his thumb over Archibald's cheek. "You have some colour, at last..."

Archibald grabbed his hand, holding it against his lips. A soft kiss. "Thank you."

Darren smiled. "Thank yourself. Now, let me dress you up and we are off."

"Must we?"

He looked down into those disappointed brown eyes. "Yes. Because you need it, then you need a good lunch, then a nap, and after that, we might indulge a bit."

His eyes smiled. "Alright.

He helped Darren dress him, taking care of his shirt, his jacket, helping as best as he could with pulling his pants up. Already exhausted, but he clung to him when Darren scooped him up.

"Oh... much heavier." Grinning.

Archibald laughed softly. "Do not lie."

"I wouldn't dare."

Their eyes meeting, so Darren kissed him gently before he brought him down to the chair.

He pushed him down on the shore; the weather chilled but a glorious sun out, the wind blowing, chasing some clouds. That grey water, dark blue and green, the waves playing on it. Archibald just sat, soaking it in, breathing that salty air in.

He turned to Darren. "Bring me some sea water in your hands. I want to taste it."

His eyebrows shot up, but he obliged, walking there swiftly, and letting the waves lap at his boots. He leant down, and the water leapt into his broad hands, ice cold, the froth tickling his skin. He smiled and held his palms tight, hurrying back to Archibald. He showed him that tiny bit of water and Archibald dipped his fingers in, licking the sea off them, closing his eyes as that sharp taste invaded his mouth.

"Mhm... I almost forgot the taste... it has been a long time, bathing in the sea."

"You could come back in the summer."

His lips curled up, bitter. "I do not wish to be here without you."

Darren let the water slip from his palms and knelt in front of him, taking his hands. "You should come back and walk down to the water. And bathe."

Archibald looked at the sea, avoiding those eyes he so loved, avoiding seeing in them that truth he knew. That these fleeting moments might be the only ones they would ever have. Flying away like wisps of smoke, time running like a wild horse let loose. In that mad moment, he pictured Darren walk with him into those icy waters, letting them be taken by those waves. Far below. Where nothing mattered anymore. Where they would be together... He looked down at him at that gentle tug of his hands.

That concerned voice. "In what place are you?"

"Not a good one, I am afraid..."

"Perhaps we should go back. The sea is tricky, it can mess with your wits."

Maybe guessing those dark thoughts which seemed so hopeful to Archibald. What was there when they went back? Nothing but despair. Darren steeled himself though, because that was all he had ever known, biting down on his own tongue, clenching his jaw, when all was too much, but there was no other choice but to carry on. He pushed him back, turning his back to the waves singing their songs. Tantalising. Wanting them. He pushed harder, up the path, back to the house where he held Archibald tight, bringing him up the stairs to his room. Undressing him, smoothing the covers on that silent man who had turned his mournful eyes to the windows.

Darren hesitated to say something, but then just turned, stopping short at that soft voice.

"Don't go..."

He turned back, meeting his eyes filled with tears, and he was too weak to resist to that plea, so he stripped and slid next to him, letting him snuggle up.

Archibald breathed him in deep, his scent laced with horsehair, sand, and sea, that salt on his skin which he licked away with a flick of his tongue, feeling his chest rise, so he kept at it, playing on his chest with his tongue, gliding up to his neck where he dared to scrape it with his teeth. Gliding his palm up to his jaw to tilt his head to him, to claim his mouth into a lush kiss.

He looked up at Darren. "Let's have that nap together. We might not have many more, and you might not have one ever again..."

Darren smiled. "As you wish."

Archibald pressed his chest against his chest. "I love you... this will never change, no matter what the future holds." Feeling Darren's arms go around his back, hold him close in that tamed embrace laced with his strength.

"And I love you. Just remember this truth. No matter what happens and what you are going to be told."

Archibald closed his eyes not to cry, wedged against him, letting his breathing and his warmth lull him to sleep.

He had brought Archibald down to the garden after their nap, in front of the house, whilst he trimmed some bushes and tried to clear that overgrown small patch. That afternoon sun, glorious, even if a small chill pervaded the air. Archibald's eyes went to the road, to the sound of cluttering hooves, watching as Darren straightened too, watching that small buggy pull up to their gate, stop on the road. An older man with a wide smile.

"Good afternoon!" He jumped from the buggy and walked up to the gate, his eyes scanning them, settling on Archibald. "Pardon the intrusion, I just saw the chimney blowing smoke from afar and wondered who might be here. You are related to the countess?"

Archibald answered, that sullen anger growing in his chest at the intrusion. "I am her grandson, Lord Archibald Hampton."

"Oh! I remember you… from when you were a small child, yes! Long-time no see… How is the countess?" His eyes darted to Darren, so Archibald turned to him.

"Be kind enough to check on the dinner, Darren. Thank you."

He got it and bowed, leaving.

Archibald turned back to the man. "My butler and cook…"

"Ah… good to have a man who can do all these."

"I was sent here to heal, I am ill of health, and as such, should not have company." He smiled thinly, that veiled message there for the man to leave.

He smiled back. "Well, then… I am reassured that you are not intruders. One can never be prudent enough these days. Enjoy your stay. Please tell the countess Lord Branson sends his regards. She will know." He chuckled. "We go back a long way… ah… happy days when she was still passing her summers here with her husband…"

"I will make sure to pass it on. Farewell."

"Farewell, farewell." He left, waving, and turned the buggy around, driving away.

Darren came out when he had been out of sight, meeting Archibald's desperate eyes.

"You know what this means, don't you?"

"We have to leave."

"Soon… not yet, though. One more day. Then we are off. Damn it!" Archibald slammed his palm on his thigh, wincing at that sharp pain, a bit puzzled that his leg had jerked back. His wide eyes going to Darren. "Did you see this?"

He smiled, his arms crossed. "Yes. Not a surprise though, I would hope. We made sure to train them every day."

"But… this was just me." He tried to move his leg, and it stirred, muscles and tendons pulling at that limp leg. "Jesus…" That joy coated with dread. The dread of maybe walking again. "His eyes went back to Darren. "Tonight, we consummate properly our liaison because we only have one more day here. I am going back home as a man."

"You are already a man."

"Your man." He smiled, giddy a bit. "A proper dinner to gain some force?"

"It's almost done." Smiling, his eyes eating him up, and Archibald reached his hand out, so he walked close, taking that bone thin hand.

A soft kiss on that strong tanned hand. "Take me inside."

After dinner, much later when the sun had dipped behind the horizon, and the sky got covered by that dark velvet studded with diamond stars, they went to bed, amongst candles lit on the bedside tables, the fire burning softly, casting dancing shadows on the walls, in their eyes as they lay, facing each other, Darren's strong fingers tracing Archibald's side, from his shoulders to his hipbone, sending shivers down that pale skin. Not needing words as he pulled him close, into a deep kiss as their bodies melted together, that touch familiar, warm, Darren's hand gliding down to Archibald's ass, so he breathed a bit harder, unsure of what he was going to do, but he just stroked him softly, wandering into his cleft, pushing that flesh around a bit, and Archibald stiffened, that slight fear intruding into a moment when he wanted to give him all.

Darren broke the kiss, looking at him. "We do not have to do anything that you might regret later on."

Archibald reached up to his face. "No. I will not regret anything."

"Sure? This is... If we do this... we could die..."

"I will die if we don't do it..."

He licked his lips, trying not to cry. "Alright..."

Darren kissed him softly, and moved behind him, pushing his arm under Archibald's shoulders to pull him towards him, meeting his slightly puzzled eyes which quickly warmed with a new light. Kissing softly, until he felt him relax, melt on his arm, so he reached behind him to dip his fingers in a glass of oil he'd put on the bedside table. Not leaving those brown eyes when he pressed his finger against him, drawing lazy circles on that firm flesh, kissing him all the while, listening to his breathing, his soft moans. Long minutes, reaching back to coat him some more, drench him, until Darren felt him relax, so he pushed his finger in, slightly, just the tip. Stopping, meeting his eyes, but Archibald didn't flinch, those warm brown eyes glowing in the candlelight. He was so beautiful in that small moment, waiting, limp in his arms, that Darren almost forgot his breath, awed a bit.

Archibald just reached up to pull him down into a kiss, to give him that small encouragement to push further into that slick warmth. Trembling at the feeling when he felt him move his finger, in and out. Gasping when he twisted it, reaching a spot Archibald didn't even know existed, and his eyes went wide. He grabbed Darren's shoulder, feeling him stop.

"No... Don't stop."

"Oh… all fine?"

"Yes…" Panting when Darren resumed, floating on something out of this world, that birthing pleasure rolling like tide. He whined softly, almost losing it right there when he felt another finger pushing in, that stretch almost too much, a dull ache which got instantly swallowed by that insane pleasure. "Ah…"

"Still fine?"

"Yes…" Soft kisses. Archibald got lost in that languid rhythm, knowing that he wanted him, all of him. Not just those teasing fingers. He met his eyes, asking, his words gone.

Darren pulled his fingers out gently, and reached down, pushing his hard cock against that slick entrance, holding Archibald's shoulders all the while not to lose his eyes. Watching as those eyes grew wide when he pushed in, his lips parting. He put his hand on his hip softly, pulling him close, pushing in ever so slowly, watching his face, but Archibald just clung to him, to his neck, panting softly. A shuddering breath when he felt him in, all the way, or so he thought, and Darren didn't move, waiting for him to adjust, to give him a sign, that small moment of wonder almost too much for both of them, breathing hard, fighting their tears. Archibald went slack on his broad arm, leaning his head back, parting his lips, so Darren leant down to kiss him, roll his tongue on his tongue as he started rocking him slowly. Just moving his hips, holding that sharp hipbone softly, that slight movement enough to make Archibald moan, mewl in his mouth. Gasping when those slight moves of his hips sent shock waves up his spine, that now familiar feeling at the base building.

He opened his eyes, a bit desperate, but Darren just held him tight, his voice soft. "It's fine… let go…" Reaching down to hold his cock in his hand, and Archibald lost it then, arching against him as he came with a moan.

Darren just kissed him, staying in until Archibald had stopped shivering and clenching around him. He reached down then to pull out but held him at the same time not to hurt him. Meeting his eyes.

"And you?"

Darren smiled, holding him, massaging his ass with his strong hands to kill the last remnants of that slight, dull pain. "Do not worry…"

Rogue tears pearled out of those brown pools filled with a new light. "I love you…"

"And I love you."

"I'm yours now."

Darren smiled. "If you insist."

"I do… I want to belong to you. Body and soul."

Darren just pulled the covers on them in that overwhelming moment, holding him tight against his warm body. Archibald's eyes half-mast in that warmth he so loved, his body blended against Darren's muscles, a dull fatigue there in that quiet room filled only with the logs burning, and their soft breathing. A grim determination birthing in Archibald, that he would not let him go, not let anybody stand between them, because this was where he belonged, in these strong arms, under his mouth and hands.

He turned his head back to him. "If I told you I will find a way for us to be together, could you hold on to that thought? In case something hopeless happens... even in the deepest of despairs?"

Darren's eyes widened a bit. "I would think so..." Not even believing that any of his words could be truth, but he was willing to give Archibald that hope. A bit thrown by that stern light in those brown eyes.

"I mean it. I belong with you. Not anybody else. I am sure of it."

Darren's eyes softened. "If you say so."

"And you?" Searching his blue eyes, hoping.

Darren just smoothed his palm on his cheek. "I was lost the moment I saw you."

"Truly?"

"Truly."

"You trust me then? To carry it through."

"I trust you blind."

They kissed and Archibald turned on his back, wanting him closer, wanting more. His eyes playing. "Sleep seems to evade me..."

"Is that so?"

"Yes... I wonder what we could do to pass the time..."

"What indeed..."

"I was hoping you would have some ideas..."

"I might just have some..."

Pulling him close as he sealed his mouth with a wide kiss, the flames' shadows dancing on their skin.

Chapter 16

They woke lost into each other's arms in the morning, a new light in their eyes, a new curb at the edge of their smiles, everything else erased in that small perfect moment with that golden sun pouring into the room. Waking with soft kisses, their hands finding those familiar places on their bodies which they had discovered the night before. A new strength in Archibald, his blood coursing his veins as his senses awakened under Darren's touch, his lips. Wanting more of him, of that new love which had burst his dwindling life apart and given him a new one. Pulling Darren on top of him, wanting his eyes, his mouth, his whole being. Letting him push his arm under that limp leg, lie on him between his legs which he had spread, arching his neck back when he pushed in, still careful but bolder, rocking him with more force as Archibald clung to his broad back, chest to chest, his breath in his neck, his tongue on his skin, lavish kisses, teeth, nips, making him float, breathe harder, his breath picking up the same rhythm as his hips, his eyes in his eyes then, his fingers digging in his flesh when he lost it, closing his eyes, his trembling lips meeting his lips, that deep kiss stealing his voice, his breath.

Opening his eyes to his touch, his fingers grazing his brows, his forehead. "Breakfast?"

Archibald smiled. "Alright…" Shutting up at his thoughts. That it was the one before their final one the next day. That next morning, they would leave, because it was not possible to stay, not with people driving in front of the house since that man's visit.

Archibald watched him get dressed, already missing his skin, his weight. "When we are back, we can start the riding lessons."

Darren smiled at him, pulling that loose shirt on. "I am looking forward to it."

"I am not sure... not sure how to bear my days without you loving me..."

Darren walked close and took his hand, guiding it to Archibald's cock. Watching him blush. "You know now how to pleasure yourself..."

"Oh... but... it is not the same."

He straightened. "True. But better than you burning from yearning."

Archibald smiled, pulling the covers on himself. "Alright. Absurd, but I might just give in to temptation."

"You will. Trust me." Watching how Archibald's face had changed, a new glow there, that pinched, frustrated dark look gone from his eyes. Those dark circles still there around his eyes, but they were not due to his ill health, but that newly found exhaustion coursing through his body, making his blood rush to those pale cheeks.

"What is it?"

"Nothing. I'll bring your breakfast."

"Our breakfast. We eat in bed."

"Oh..."

"And then... I'd like us to stay here until lunch."

"I see..." Meeting his small smile, a wave of that feeble hand.

They had not even left that bed, just for a quick stroll to the beach where they watched the raging waves, that icy wind not letting them stay too long. Winter on their necks, they knew, soon, that golden light dull, swallowed by that grey sky spewing a slight drizzle. Back to the house, they dried in front of the flames, sipping some tea, then went to bed after Darren had packed their clothes and prepared the carriage for the next morning.

Holding tight, just watching the flames in the fireplace, too tired and overwhelmed, even if they knew it was their last night, none of them moved, in that moment of dread when making love maybe for the last time was almost the only possibility left.

Archibald looked up at Darren as he was lying against his shoulder. "I should be loving you... and I am unable to..."

His heart tight, but he squeezed his shoulder softly. "It does not matter... what we had here cannot be taken away. We need to sleep because tomorrow will be a long day. You feel better, but you are far from fully healing, still."

"Sleeping is a waste of time..."

"Not in each other's arms."

They looked at each other, silent, soaking that moment in, and Archibald slid down into the pillows, lacing his arms around Darren, who had followed. Watching his face in the candlelight to remember every line in that soft glow, every curve of his lips.

Archibald breathed against his lips. "I love you."

"And I love you."

Kissing, still, wide. Because it felt right to fall asleep breathing each other in.

In the early dawn light, Archibald woke to his kisses, as if the night had not even existed in that haze. Thrilled, because he knew his touch now, knew what he wanted, rolling him on his belly, covering his back with his body as his arm went around his chest. Sliding inside of him as Archibald arched his back as much as he could, feeling how careful he was, holding his weight, that body which could just crush him, squeeze his breath out. Soft moans in that dawn light as their pleasure built, lost in each other's bodies, holding tight as they lost it, squeezing their eyes shut to keep their tears in.

Archibald watched later Darren pull the carriage to the front, the trusty horses stopping short as he jumped down to scoop him out of his chair. He sat Archibald on the bench, and smoothed his blanket over his legs, but Archibald could feel it, they felt different, warmer, stronger somehow. His flesh still pulsing with every touch of his hands, teeth, and lips. Their eyes met, a soft kiss before Darren stepped out, securing the wheeled chair to the back, then stepping on the bench, clacking his tongue. The carriage jolted and Archibald cast one last loving glance at that small house wedged atop the cliff, that haven of love. His eyes on the rushing landscape then, a bit bitter that Darren was sitting in the cold, but there was nothing to be done about it, so he relaxed, his thoughts a mess, his old self gone somewhere, pulverised by that raging love they had found. Another young man's reflection in the window's glass, his brown eyes hard, a sharper edge to his jaw, a more determined light in those brown pools.

The mansion came into sight the next day, under a pouring rain. Footmen rushing outside with umbrellas to help Darren take the chair down and the luggage. Wanting to take Archibald out but he waved them away.

"Let my coachman do it. He is much stronger than all of you."

Darren stepped in and took him in his arms, even if he was soaked, Archibald blended against him. Sheltered by the carriage, they stayed in that strong embrace for a few fleeting moments as Darren planted an icy kiss on his warm neck. Not needing words as he took him out and put him in his chair. Their eyes meeting, rivulets rushing down Darren's face. Tears, maybe. Archibald could not tell, holding his tears in, but keeping it together, for him. Steadying his voice not to give his feelings away in front of the waiting footmen.

"This was a most pleasant trip, Darren. Thank you."

"My pleasure, Milord." His voice, heavy with tears, but he was standing under that pouring rain, so they could not see anything.

The footmen took Archibald swiftly away then, and Darren just stood a bit, unable to move, his chest aching so hard he had no breath. Dandy pushed him softly in the back, so he turned with a smile to stroke his nose. That small push jolting him out of that pain, so he steeled himself and climbed up, the horses pulling fast straight away, home to their stables.

"Archibald! Thank God! At last! It must have been straining, the trip under this icy rain. Warm up! Quick!"

He didn't react to his mother's shrill voice, his eyes lost a bit in his thoughts as he got pushed inside their tea room. William and Francesca were sitting near the window, and William shot to his feet when he saw him, hurrying there.

"Archibald! How good you look! I am amazed!" Grinning, he slammed his hand on Archibald's shoulder.

"Thank you." Puzzled, that his flaming rage was somehow gone, or at least William couldn't kindle it anymore. His eyes went to his father, who had walked close with a smile.

"You do look better. It is a delight to see. Welcome home!"

"Thank you, Father. It was an excellent idea. Push me to Granny, will you?"

He obliged, and Archibald let his grandmother take his hands, meeting her eyes.

"Now... I am thrilled that you have gained some health back in my small haven. I hope all went well with the maid?"

Archibald smiled. "She fulfilled her duties to perfection, Granny."

His mother interjected from her seat. "Good to hear! I hope that the coachman did not try to play games with her. We all know how men can be."

Archibald sighed. "Mother... please..."

"Nothing shocking. Just the truth about servants and low-class people. Jumping on whatever moves."

Archibald felt that familiar anger rise up, sizzling his nerves. "He has not done anything... the maid is older, anyway..."

"Good to hear."

He turned back to his grandmother, catching her small smile.

She patted his hand. "Good to hear. You can go back there any time, you know, dear. If it did you this good, it would be a waste to have that house sit there, unused."

"Thank you, Granny." His heart flying a bit, but it had also iced over with dread, realising that they were accomplices of the same lie. *What if she knows?* The thought filling him with dread. He clenched his fists, realising that his handkerchief was missing. *I haven't even used it, at all...* He looked up at his father's voice.

"An excellent idea. I would take advantage of it if I were you." That same smile on his lips.

Archibald blinked. "Of course, Father..."

His mother's voice. "But not anytime soon! We are going back to London after Christmas for the ball season, or at least not to miss the whole event. I am delighted you feel better. It is high-time you..."

"No, Mother." It had been said softly, but with that new voice he now had. That edge in it which had not been there before, determined and calm.

She looked at him, stunned. "What did you say?"

Archibald turned to her, using his hands on the wheels, the way he had practised. "I am not going to court any young girls and getting married in the spring."

"Archibald... Edward! Say something!"

Lord Edward just buried himself in his cup to hide his smile.

She turned back to her son. "What took you? Of course, you are going to choose a bride by the end of the season!"

"No, I am not. And do not even insist, Mother. I am a grown man and can make my own decisions. I am not ready for marriage, and this is my final say on the matter."

She could not speak, searching for her words when William rose with his glass to tower over him with his smile.

"My, my... that sea air sure did you some good... you are almost a changed man..." Watching him carefully, and Archibald had to avert his eyes from those blue eyes, too familiar, but filled with a wicked light that was missing from Darren's.

His blood ran cold. "It did some good, yes... now if you will excuse me, I had a long trip, and need to rest. I shall retire to my room." Casting a glance at his father but he was already taking the chair.

"I shall take you." Pushing him out of the room fast, he only spoke when they were out of hearing range. "I am most proud of you."

"I do apologise, but I am not going with Mother's plans."

"You did not upset me. I am proud of you and that you are so firm in your decisions." He pushed him into his room and faced him. "I shall call your valet."

"Wait, Father... before you go. I wanted to thank you... for letting me go there..."

"I was right. You look much better. I have some hopes."

"I'm starting my riding lessons tomorrow."

"Hopefully, the weather will be better too."

"Let us hope so."

His father squeezed his hand. "I am glad to have you back."

"And I am glad to be back with you."

He watched him leave, waiting until his servants filled his bath, and his valet arrived to help him bathe. Watching that steaming water, wondering what Darren was doing.

Darren had brought the carriage back to the stables, James and Travis rushing outside to help him take the horses to their stalls, that rain falling incessantly, but the stables were dry, the stalls done, fresh hay and oats waiting for those tired horses.

James beamed at Darren. "We have fired up your stove, sir, hope you don't mind. Figured you'd be cold and all..."

"Thank you, boys. All went well?"

"Aye... I mean, yes... we cleaned proper too, like you taught us and all..."

Darren ruffled his hair. "Leave the 'and all'..."

"Alright." Smiling, his eyes shining.

Darren hurried then up to his room, which felt so much warmer than the outside, despite it being still just barely warm. He put a kettle on with trembling hands, shedding those soaked clothes dripping water, shivering then, but he rushed down to wash at the well, half-naked, even if the rain bit into his skin. Rushing back up then, drying with chattering teeth. He collapsed finally on his chair, holding his palms to the raging flames, trying to soak in some warmth. Even in dry clothes, he was cold, trembling, and he buried his face in his hands, rubbing his tears away before they could spill out. Drawing a deep breath to unclench that painful throat. He poured that boiling water on the tea leaves, waiting a bit before he poured a large mug. Sipping it to warm up, calm his nerves. Casting a glance at that empty cold bed, that whole trip, like a dream, as if it had just entered their life to leave it even emptier. *I can't let myself sink into despair...* He stood then, downing the mug, and walked to the bed, stripping his pants but leaving his shirt on, sliding into those ice cold sheets. He hugged himself tight, closing his eyes, his exhaustion pulling him into sleep.

There was not time though to sleep late next day when Darren was up with the first lights of dawn, the room so cold he could see his breath, so he dressed hastily and stoked the fire up, that dull fatigue sitting on every limb, that miserable night still lingering, when he had missed him so much. Waking, his hands searching the cold sheets, just to curl up again, knocked out. He fried a couple of eggs and washed it down with tea, then skipped down to the stables, the boys hurrying too, the horses' heads up, their soft neighs as they heard their steps. This was comfort, the only one he could find solace in, stroking their heads poking above the stall doors, lingering a bit with Raven, letting him nibble his neck, chase that sadness away which seemed to sit on his chest and on his throat.

They fed them, and Darren went to work on a saddle he wanted to adapt to suit Archibald, the rain pouring outside, those sharp drops like razor blades falling from the sky.

Archibald just watched the rain fall, incessant, drenching everything, rushing down those long windows. Feeling his father's hand on his shoulder.

"I guess you will ride tomorrow. Let us hope it will pour down today."

"Yes. I hope so."

Choking on his words after that agonizing night when he could barely find sleep, clutching the covers to his chest to have something against his body, that bed without him empty as a tomb. His eyes on that dark night behind the windows, the shush of the rain, his own heart hammering in the dark as he swallowed his tears. Near unbearable, his absence. Even more so with this hopeless rain, the weather wedging another chasm between them. Hearing his mother and Fran enter, in big discussions of the wedding plans. Fran and William were insisting on tying the knot fast, not wanting to wait for spring, so it had been agreed to have that grand wedding before Christmas, so they could then leave on honeymoon. Archibald couldn't care less, a hollow ache in his chest, his hand on a book, but he couldn't even pick it up again, the words not making any sense. Feeling Fran's hand on his shoulder.

"William will be here soon and you will not have time to get bored."

"I am not entirely sure I will find him entertaining." Keeping his voice in check, polite, because he loved her, and didn't want to upset her.

She laughed, spinning him around, meeting his eyes. "Oh... not in a good mood today?"

"Not exactly..."

His mother sat down, gesturing for tea. "You are always so sour, Archibald. You should be rejoicing in your improving health and enjoying another young man's company, more so that soon you will be related. You could not dream of a better brother-in-law..."

Her words got cut by William walking in, his hair wet, his wide smile. He took his gloves off, flinging it to the footman rushing behind him.

"I apologise. I rode here, and I am soaked." He kissed Fran's hand, winking at Archibald, then sat down, a cup of tea served straight away.

Fran had sat close, her eyes eating him up.

Lord Hampton smiled at him. "Riding in this weather is no small accomplishment."

"Ah... nothing to worry about. My sturdy horse took me here, as ever. It is just a bit colder and wetter. I left him in the good cares of your staff, he must be at the stables by now." His eyes went to Archibald with that arrogant smile he knew so well. "Your excellent stable master will bring him back in due time."

Lord Hampton raised his hand. "Oh... well... a stable boy can do that."

William just smiled at him. "Oh no. I insist. I would not trust my horse to a mere stable boy."

"As you wish, of course."

Archibald swallowed and looked away, but there was no escape, he knew, watching William chat with Fran and his mother, wishing for time to fly faster and bring that night, the next day, so he could see him, hear his voice. Just be close. He clenched his fists, resting them on those legs which were aching dully.

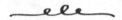

Late into the night, William rose when the butler walked to him. "Your horse is waiting for you, Milord."

He pulled his gloves on. "Fantastic!" Turning to Fran to kiss her hand. "My dear... a couple of weeks and we shall be married. I can hardly wait."

"Yes... what a delight."

She was burning for him, Archibald could see, and a bitter envy invaded him, because he knew that love, but it was impossible for him, for them, so he just looked up at William when he'd stepped close.

"Archibald? I am delighted you feel better. Much stronger at chess too? I will see you soon."

"Yes, thank you. We had a great time." A straight lie, said with that ease he had now, that secret locked in his heart, covered with lies too.

"Indeed." His lips curled up, that wicked light in his eyes, but he left, hurrying outside.

Darren watched him walk out into that pouring rain, holding that exhausted horse. Facing him when William had stepped close with that curb of his mouth.

"Darren... so good of you to bring my horse."

"You asked for me, Milord." Throwing this in, because he was boiling at the state of that poor horse, almost asleep in his hands, his flanks rising as he was trying to draw in breath.

"Indeed I did." Those mocking eyes went to him, facing each other in that mute knowledge. William stepped closer, his voice soft, meeting his eyes. "Do not forget your place though..."

"Yes, Milord."

"Ever the obedient... so help me up. I pulled a muscle during my last hunt."

Darren just laced his fingers together, holding his palms to him, letting him step into his hands with his boot dripping mud. William put his whole weight into them, and Darren almost collapsed right there, but held tight, clenching his jaw as William settled in the saddle.

Looking down at him as he gathered the reins, spurring that horse awake. "Next time you talk back to me, I will whack your mouth in. My father's blood coursing through your veins does not give you the privilege to address me like one of your equals."

Darren blanched. "I did not..." He shut up when William wedged his whip under his chin.

"What did I tell you? Good to see you are learning. You've been spoiled, but I can assure you that once I have married Lady Francesca, I will endeavour teaching you some manners." He flashed a smile and turned the horse, whipping him into a full gallop.

Darren watched him leave, his heart hammering in his chest. Those words tearing up memories he didn't want, unearthing a truth he didn't acknowledge, even if it was plain now, looking into the mirror every morning. Liches clawing to the light, warping what he knew into something else...

He was sitting in front of their house in that small garden, on a bench, holding an apple which Mama had put into his hands whilst she washed the rest in a big basin, that late autumn sun glorious, playing on butterfly wings. He raised his head at the cluttering of hooves, as he loved horses, even at barely five, he would rush to them when his father drove by and stopped sometimes for his lunch, a quick kiss. He rose and hurried to his mother, her hands over her eyes, squinting to see that lonely rider. He watched him too, that dark horse, one hand in her skirt as a man stopped short in front of them, jumping from the horse. He felt her back a step, reach down to him, and his child mind somehow sensed it, that dread, so he hid behind her, clutching that apple tight, his eyes on that dark-haired man with his blue eyes, his smi le.

"My, my... long time no see..."

"Milord... It is an honour..."

"No such formal talk between us, Evie..." He had stepped close, and his eyes went from her soft brown hair to him. A glint in those blue eyes, his lips curled up. "And who do we have here?"

"My son, Milord..." That dread in her voice, but it had taken an edge, her fingers digging into his shoulders.

"Show me."

She had to obey and grabbed his hand, pushing him to the front where he wedged himself against her, looking up at him as he looked down at him. Silent, that small smile on when he looked at her, a mocking curve of his mouth.

"Pretty little boy. His father's spitting image." He laughed softly, and she held him tighter, her breathing shallow. "You like apples, little one?"

He nodded, not having words for this fancy man and his beautiful horse, and his eyes darted to his mother, scared a bit seeing her so pale, her lips pinched.

"I will not hold you back any longer. It was nice seeing you again."

"Likewise, Milord."

He seemed to hesitate, but then looked at him again, and turned to mount his horse. Leaving fast, in full gallop. She sighed, deep, and let him go.

He looked up at her. "Who was this, Mama?"

"Nobody. A lord. Go and eat your apple."

He had sat again and bit into that sweet apple, his eyes lighting up at the familiar sound of the carriage. He rushed to his father who had jumped down from the bench, scooping him up in his strong arms.

"Oy! My boy!" Hugging him tight, biting into the apple he had pushed against his mouth. Unaware of the adults' eyes meeting, hers in tears, his warm smile to her, extending his hand which she took, trembling, letting him pull her into a hug. Breathing in his neck as he hugged them tight. "My boy..."

Chapter 17

Next day, the rain had stopped, and even with that chill in the air, Archibald was waiting in front of the mansion, his heart drumming in his chest when he saw that familiar form approaching, that gait he knew so well. Grabbing the armrests to tame his hands which only wanted to fly to him, meeting his eyes.

"Good morning, Milord."

"Good morning." Closing his eyes at that fake formality when he knew it was the only sane thing to do with his footmen standing behind him. Feeling the chair roll away, so he risked tilting his head back, silent, just their eyes speaking for a while.

It was Darren who broke it with his smile. "Ready for your ride?"

"More than ready."

Chuckling at the words, their hearts in flames.

Darren stopped the chair near Dandy who had been prepared already, his curious nose going straight to that human in the chair, sniffing, giving a quick lick to his hands.

Archibald patted that nose clumsily. "I do hope he does not bite."

"Do you think I would give you a horse that would?"

"No, of course not... apologies."

Darren smiled at him, flipping a strap on the saddle's side. "So, I fixed these straps for you on the saddle. Once I hauled you up, I'll strap your legs in, and you won't fall."

"And if the horse falls?"

"You will only walk around today and find your balance, no need to rush anything." He patted the horse's neck, looking down at him. "So, still up for it?"

"Yes..." Unconvinced, but he wanted Darren's hands on him so badly, that he was willing to take the risk.

Darren stepped to him and pulled him up, holding him tight until he was facing the saddle. Holding him close as he spoke, not leaving his eyes, their bodies melting. "Alright... I will turn you around and you will grab the top of the saddle, then pull, and I'll push your legs until you hang there like a sack, and then I'll arrange your legs. Just don't move."

"I'm not sure you are strong enough..." Teasing a bit, watching his eyes light up.

"Just wait and see... Ready?" Archibald nodded, and Darren turned him around in his arms, his hands on his hips as he lifted him up a bit. "Grab the saddle. Good. Hop!" He pushed him up, fast, strong, and slid his hand down his leg, walking to the other side to pull his thigh over the saddle. He kept his hand on Archibald's thigh, squeezing a bit, meeting his eyes. "Sit up..." Another caress when he buckled the strap, sliding his hand down his calf to put his foot in the stirrup, and Archibald could hardly sit, closing his eyes to his touch, wanting more. He watched Darren circle to the other side, buckle his leg, his hand wandering on it to make sure he was secure. He handed him the reins, grazing his hands through his gloves, closing them in his fist. "Hold these... you learnt how, right?"

"Yes..." He managed to remember, already dizzy a bit, even if Dandy was not too tall, the world seemed to unfurl from his back, his eyes roaming the yard. Looking back at Darren when he patted his thigh.

"Ready? We'll walk to the exercise pen."

"Alright." Jolting a bit when Darren moved and the horse followed, but he also felt somehow safe, those limp legs strapped tight to the saddle, the fresh air pouring into his lungs, watching Darren's dark hair dance in that slight wind as he swayed in the saddle.

Darren opened the gate and let Dandy in, closing the gate behind them as the horse stood patiently. He took the bridle then and pulled the horse near the fence.

He looked up at Archibald. "I'll stand in the middle and you just walk around. Feel the horse, just let him do his thing, and focus on your body, your hands."

"Hold the reins?"

"Yes, but loose. No need to spoil his mouth. Just a gentle contact, like you are holding a ribbon which could break any time."

"Alright." Breathing in deep, that mild stress invading him, something he had always felt on horseback. *This huge animal... he could kill me...* Memories of

Fran's mad gallop made him weak when he felt his warm hand on his thigh, so he looked down into his eyes.

"You are stressed? The horse will feel it. Dandy won't do anything bad, but you better put that under control if you want to ride other horses."

"I am not sure... he's my horse now, right?"

Darren smiled. "Yes, he is." Stroking the horse's neck.

Archibald's heart lurched. "I am sorry... I know what he means to you..."

"Why apologise? He means a lot, but you mean more... and I am thrilled he is yours."

Their eyes met, that longing there in Archibald to just lean out of the saddle and seal his mouth. *So close...* But he just sat, pouring all the yearning in his eyes.

Darren licked his lips and stepped back, backing to the centre, a soft clack of his tongue. "Go, Dandy."

The horse started walking, following the fence, one ear pricked towards him, one towards Archibald. Slowing a bit when he felt him lose his balance, his hands going to his mane, which he clutched tight.

Darren smiled. "Relax. You can't fall. In fact, let the reins go."

"What?"

"Let them go, spread your arms."

Archibald was trembling when he let the reins go, but he spread his arms, fighting his panic. His legs twitching when his hands could not help anymore.

"All good?"

"Yes... no... I am scared a bit..."

"That's just fine on horseback. Feel the horse, your balance, soften your hips, just follow his back, his steps."

Archibald did, his arms trembling, but after a few laps, he felt more confident, even if he had to drop his arms out of exhaustion, he felt better, his hands just loosely touching the reins. Darren made Dandy change directions, checking his watch so they didn't overdo it and exhaust Archibald, but he seemed fine, a small smile on his lips. Archibald leant forward and dared to stroke Dandy's neck, and Darren just watched them, his heart burning quietly, that horse he loved carrying the man who had his heart. A deep wish there to make them a pair because he knew Dandy was safe with Archibald, that he would never sell the horse if he touched his heart. *Soon... sooner than he thinks...*

"I think we can stop for today."

"So soon?"

Darren walked close, taking the reins. “Your enthusiasm is exemplary, but believe me, you don’t feel it yet, but your ass will be sore in a few hours.” He grinned, trying not to laugh.

Archibald smiled at him. “Is that so?” He leant down, whispering. “I wish you would make my ass sore.” Watching Darren’s face flame up, their eyes meeting as he was trying to find his words. “Speechless, my good stable master? Too bad.” He straightened, grinning, and Darren wished he could just pull him out of the saddle and wrestle him down on the ground, kill that smug mouth with a kiss.

But it was not an option, so he just shot him a look. “Bold words, Milord. I shall remember them.”

“I hope you will.”

They puffed a bit and Darren led the horse back to the stables, James already there to hold Dandy whilst Darren undid the straps. His fingers lingering, still, because it was innocent and invisible, but that feeble touch rippled up Archibald’s skin.

Darren held his arms up. “Just let yourself slide towards me, Milord, and I’ll catch you.”

He did, that mild fright there as he slid from the saddle, but his strong hands were already under his armpits, his arms around him, holding him tight as Travis pushed the chair close. Darren lowered him in it, smoothing the blanket on his legs.

“I hope your lesson was satisfactory, Milord.”

“It was most pleasing.”

Travis gave Archibald a few carrots, and he fed them to the horse, laughing when his lips tickled his palm. Stroking that head poking for more. “This is a great horse.”

“Indeed, Milord.”

“Push me back. I need to have my lunch.”

”As you wish, Milord.” He grabbed the chair and his long strides took them back to the mansion.

Archibald looked up at him. “I hate this game of pretending...”

“It is not fully pretending.”

“You know what I mean...”

“There is nothing to be done about it when others are around.”

“You are so right. I should not even brew on this, right? It cannot be changed. Wretched!” Pondering a bit before he snapped. “Stop!”

Darren stopped pushing and stepped in front of him, glancing around, meeting those eyes dark with anger. “What is it?”

"I... I fucking love you... I miss you... it is unbearable... my nights... are so empty. I want to be with you."

Darren sighed, looking around again. "We can't talk this through now." He lowered his voice. "You are not supposed to exchange so many words with me... and you are not supposed to care... I miss you too... but there is nothing we can do about it... Not now." A mild despair in those blue eyes, so Archibald sighed, bitter.

"You are right, again. Forgive me."

Darren went back to push him, his voice soft. "I love you... you know this. Hold on to it."

"I shall try."

"Eat and rest, drink plenty. You will be sore tomorrow, but your next ride will make it better."

"I am determined to learn and get better."

He looked at Darren when he'd stopped the chair in front of the stairs, the footmen rushing down. "This was a most excellent lesson, Darren, and I am looking forward to the next one."

He bowed slightly. "You honour me, Milord."

"I will see you tomorrow."

"As you wish, Milord."

Only their eyes speaking above that formal, cold exchange, but Archibald masked his despair, as did he, still casting a warm look when the footmen were not watching, a small wave of Archibald's hand, barely lifted off his blanket, enough for Darren, filling that hollow heart with warmth.

Weeks passing with the weather getting colder, but Archibald did his lessons, bolder, going into a trot after a few lessons, trying a mild canter, that relationship with Dandy growing when the horse had realised that he would be regularly riding him. Waiting for him to bring him apples and carrots until one day when he had made Archibald's heart burst when he had neighed at him. Archibald could feel it, his legs getting stronger, the straps looser, even if he had protested at the beginning, Darren had smiled it off, waving his concerns away. Both of them trying to settle into those stolen touches, those stolen moments when their words could be free.

Until a few days before Francesca's wedding when they were practising in the pen, and, after a fabulous canter, Archibald had stopped Dandy, smiling wide, and Darren had stepped to him, sliding his hand under his thigh, smiling up at him. A gentle squeeze, soaking in his smile, his joy, and Archibald almost leant down to him when Dandy raised his head, and they turned at the same time towards a rider cluttering in front of the pen, reining his horse in. *William.* Archibald's face fell, feeling Darren pull his hand out, fast, but his heart was racing, hoping William hadn't seen anything, that familiar mocking smile unreadable as he spun his horse around, grinning at them.

"So... how are your lessons going, Archibald? I came to check quickly before lunch."

"They are going fine." Composing his face when he felt like melting under those wicked eyes.

"Ah, all the better. Soon, we can ride outside together, I would hope?"

Archibald smiled, patting Dandy's neck. "I doubt I could keep up with your speed. I am not that skilled yet."

"Ah, I see... I gather that is why Darren had to readjust your leg?"

Smiling, his eyes unreadable, and Archibald licked his lips, determined not to give in.

"Yes, precisely... they are misplaced sometimes. I am not that strong yet."

William looked at Darren. "You are driving my beloved's carriage for the wedding in a few days. I trust the horses are ready?"

"Yes, Milord."

"Do not mess it up." He winked and spurred his horse into a gallop.

Archibald breathed out. "Twat... I do hope he has not seen anything."

Darren followed his gaze. "I doubt it. And even if... I am not sure he would know..."

Archibald scoffed. "He might be a twat, but those are the most dangerous. Fortunately, he will be busy with Fran soon..." His words died, thinking of her becoming a woman under that man. He shuddered, too tired. "Let's just walk back, and take me down. I am tired beyond belief."

Darren grazed his thigh, meeting his eyes. "But stronger, and you have not coughed in a while."

"Yes, you are right. Something to cherish, however long it lasts." His lips parting, but nothing came out, because all those words he wanted to say were knives, all those tender words flying into the wind to no avail because he could not even hold him, his lips missing his kisses, his mouth his taste, his skin his touch, those rough, warm palms which he loved to feel on his body. "Let's go back. Please."

"Alright..." He didn't talk either, weary of being apart, of those lonely nights when he could not see what was ahead, when he thought that this was all they would have. Stolen moments, light hidden touches, soft words. Anything else impossible, dwindling into an existence which was both torture and the only existence they could imagine having.

The day of the wedding had arrived, and Darren dressed in that new livery that Lord Hampton had bought for the occasion, that piece of clothing so expensive, it made his back drip with sweat. Still, he dressed, and walked down to the carriage, the horses ready, that bay team which now knew him, his steps, his hands gliding on them before he pulled his white gloves on. Their heads tied high but they were used to it, weeks and weeks of practise, their bits lighter, with less pain, knowing that their necks would be released as soon as they were back from work. The carriage had been polished to excess, decorated with flowers and ribbons, even if winter was breathing down their necks. He sat on the bench, and James let the front horse go, watching as that huge carriage floated out of the yard, making its way to the mansion.

A perfect stop, the horses calm and ready. Francesca was breath-taking in her wedding dress, her fur mantel on her shoulders, but even in the cold, she was flushed, barely being able to breathe. That dreamt day, finally at her feet. Lord Hampton helped her in the carriage, then his wife followed, and finally, Archibald and his grandmother. A quick meet of their eyes, a soft look, and he was sat inside.

Lady Mary stepped to Darren then, putting her hand on his arm. "What a magnificent team and carriage. I must say you look dapper, Mister Turner."

He blushed a bit. "Thank you, Her Ladyship."

"Dapper, indeed." She looked him up and down with her small smile. "Well, let us go. The Willoughbys must be impatient."

He helped her up, and they set off, the horses pulling evenly with their elegant gait, that short ride to the village church almost just a breath, the streets decorated, the folks standing on the side, cheering as the carriage stopped in front of the church. Francesca was the last one out, waiting on Lord Hampton's arm.

He turned back to Darren. “This might last awhile. Just wait for us here. Francesca will leave with William, but we will need a ride to the Willoughby mansion.”

“Of course, Milord.” He watched them walk in when somebody came outside to signal that they were ready for the bride, his heart clenching, because he knew that man better than her, that slight hope in him that maybe William had some love for her in that selfish heart.

Archibald watched his sister walk in, her veil in place, her head a bit bowed as people gasped at that stunning white dress flowing around her, that huge veil trailing behind her. Their father’s pride shining in his warm, brown eyes, their mother quietly crying next to him, and Archibald’s heart sank, because he knew all this would be impossible for him. Marrying a woman. Marrying him. Something out of this world, the thought so sinful, he thought the church roof would collapse. Watching William, his dashing smile tamed as he lifted her veil, and for a fleeting moment, Archibald almost believed his words, that he loved her, but his eyes were cold, and he knew the light of love, had seen it in those candlelights in his arms. *You don’t love her, lying piece of shit... my little sister...* Watching, powerless, as she took her vows, to love him until death, his smile, that kiss still chaste, but Archibald knew what was coming, or at least knew that much from books and his own nights, and his blood ran cold at her innocence. Knowing Granny had talked to her, but Fran had been too embarrassed to listen all the way, trusting William blindly. Walking out on his arm, waving amongst the cheers.

His father pushed Archibald outside, watching Fran and William mount into that open barouche pulled by four white horses. They waited until the family got into the carriage too, and Archibald’s eyes closed to Darren’s voice, that deep voice urging the horses forward, calling the lead horse’s name sometimes.

Lady Hampton was still wiping her tears. “What a day! What a day! A mother’s dream.” She glanced at Archibald, but his eyes were on the landscape.

Lady Mary laughed a bit. “Why, soon, you will be a grandmother, dear.”

The air froze as Lady Hampton realised the meaning of her words. “Oh... well, maybe not soon though... they are young.”

Lady Mary laughed, leaning on her stick. “He will make her a baby so fast you will not even be able to draw breath. The Willoughby men are prolific, as we all know.”

“Well, I would hope not to become a grandmother too soon. Not that this danger would lurk from Archibald...”

Their eyes met, but Archibald just turned away, unable to argue. Feeling the carriage speed up as they had left the village, but the horses were pulling evenly.

Lady Hampton huffed. "Some progress, at least, from this coachman. The carriage is smooth, at last."

Lord Hampton soothed her. "He needed time with the horses. As I told you."

"Do not lecture me. I know about horses too. We should keep them."

"There is no way I can afford them any longer. Lord Willoughby has graciously agreed to take them, as they are Francesca's."

"He could take the coachman too."

Archibald's eyes went to her, but his father just smiled. "No way, dear. He is much too valuable."

"I cannot see how."

"Archibald rides again."

"I suppose I can give him that credit. As for the rest..." She huffed, but kept quiet when the mansion came into sight, the family waiting on the stairs for the young couple, as the parent's carriage had been first.

They halted, Francesca and William already in Lord and Lady Willoughby's arms whilst the Hampton's got down to greet them. As Archibald watched, powerless, that Lord Willoughby stepped to the carriage, looking it over, the horses, and stopped in front of Darren who was holding the rear horse. Facing him, silent, their eyes meeting. Same height, those blue eyes like mirrors, Darren's straight face, even if all colour had left it.

Lord Willoughby smiled. "A most pleasant team and carriage. I gather Lord Hampton told you that they are moving to our stables."

"Yes, Milord."

"Bring them tomorrow morning. You can hand them over to my stable master and explain to him what there is to know."

"Yes, Milord."

He just gave him a small, amused smile, and turned to leave. Darren watched Archibald being pushed inside, holding the horse tight not to collapse on the ground.

Waiting for hours, late into the night. Darren had let the horses' head down, watching them sleep as he sat on the bench, watching those cold stars clouded by his breath, hugging himself tight as the noises and music of the wedding drifted into the night. Other carriages waiting, the horses asleep under their blankets.

Deep into the night, the guests finally started leaving, and Darren helped the family in, that slight touch of Archibald's hand on his arm as he helped to take his chair away burning him even through his clothes, sending a shock to his heart.

He drove back, careful not to jostle them around, the horses alert but responding to his voice, his hands. Archibald just sat quietly, dead tired, but his feverish mind was on his sister, on her first night. Hoping, that William would have the decency to love her properly, even if she had no idea what that meant. Hoping it would not be horrible, that he would feel something, know what he had under his hands. Listening to Darren's voice with that ache in his chest, that mad urge there to be in his arms, not even to be loved. He would have been content with a strong hug, his lips on his neck. Fuming at the unfairness of it all. That this was denied to them just because they were men. *I love him, so why? Why this injustice? I only want his arms, his embrace, how is this wrong? How can it be wrong? And why? And who had decided of this?*

He looked at his grandmother when she put her hand on his arm, his parents asleep on the bench facing them. "Lost in your thoughts, dear? Missing Franny already?"

"Yes, Granny..."

"Do not worry. That William might be a strong lad, but our Franny will soon show him her teeth."

He laughed softly. "If you say so..." His smile dying when he realised that they were sort of alone, his parents fast asleep, almost snoring. Knowing that she had lied about that maid. "Granny..."

"Darling..." He met her eyes in that dim coach. Feeling her hand on his hand. "I love you so dearly... and I only wish for your happiness. But it comes at a terrible price for you, Archibald."

His eyes widened, but he left his hand, unable to speak.

She squeezed it. "A dangerous game, dear... one that is far from finished. You know this."

"You know..."

"I am not blind, dear." Her small smile. "But nor are others who would wish you harm. Be careful."

"We already are... it is... torture..." Pinching his lips because this was as close as he got to a confession, his own reality terrifying him when he was letting it to the light to the being who counted the most in his life after his father.

"I am just saying that you need to keep it together if anything happens that may risk exposing you... You need to stay strong for both of you... because you have the power to have an influence on events. He has not."

He sighed, squeezing her hand. "Alright. Let us hope nothing will happen..."

"A hope we can only cling to."

Holding hands whilst the carriage sped into that cold night, that dread in Archibald's heart icing his thoughts over.

Chapter 18

It happened weeks after Francesca's wedding, shortly before Christmas, a cold morning like any other, cleaning the stables, only wearing their shirts and pants as the work was strenuous, when a carriage rolled inside, fast, into the yard. They raised their heads, and Darren walked outside to check, the boys behind him, thinking it was maybe William, even if he usually just left the carriage in front of the mansion to be taken away.

Darren's eyes went wide at the sight of that dark police wagon, his eyes darting to the stunned boys.

Two policemen walked to him. "Darren Turner?"

"Yes?"

He didn't even have time to react; they jumped him, twisting his hands behind his back, snapping the handcuffs on, tight. One of them talked to him then as he was struggling to maintain his balance, his heart racing.

"Darren Turner, you are under arrest and will be brought in for questioning. Your name came up after we have arrested a couple of men accused of buggery and gross indecency, and we need to investigate further."

Darren blinked, trying to understand his words, but he kept quiet, his mind racing. *Who?* Trying to remember when he had had a quick encounter last... *maybe years ago...* Breathing against the pain invading his shoulder blades, so he squirmed a bit, just to have the man holding his cuffs pull them up. He moaned, the pain like lightning.

"Stop fighting or I'll break your arms."

He got shoved forward then, the boys at an utter loss... watching that wagon speed out when they'd pushed him inside.

At the mansion, a detective was waiting for Lord Hampton to walk downstairs to his office. He watched him appear with his smile, gesture him in.

"I apologise, detective. I was having breakfast."

"I am sorry to interrupt, Milord, but you must know that we have arrested your stable master this morning."

Lord Hampton turned to him, wide-eyed. "What? Darren? The man is beyond reproach!"

"Well... this is mighty embarrassing, Milord, but his name came up after we have arrested a couple of men... doing what they should not have been doing... if you know what I mean... and he might be one of them too... We will question him, and let him go if he can prove himself."

"This... I have a hard time believing this... that man is a widower, he had a wife..."

"Many of those men have a wife, families even, Milord... that does not absolve of crime."

"What crime?!" He had to calm down, seeing that man's prying eyes. "Alright... Apologies... this is just unexpected and most upsetting."

"I understand, Milord."

"I will send you my lawyer."

"I do not deem it necessary, but you are free to do as you wish."

"How long will you hold him?"

"As long as it is needed." He turned his hat in his hands. "This is not a stain you wish to have on your household, Milord, pardon me for being so bold."

"You just said you have no proof yet..."

"This is the countryside, Milord, and words fly fast. I am just saying you should consider the impact on your family. True or not, it is a stain. I shall see myself out. Thank you for your time."

He left and Lord Hampton had to sit, out of breath, trying to compose his thoughts before he rang for his butler. "I need to have a telegram sent. Hurry to the post office once I have written down my words."

"Yes, Milord."

He had to go to see Archibald then, walking to his room where he was getting ready for his riding lesson. He knocked and stepped in, gesturing at the valet. "Leave us alone."

Archibald looked up, puzzled. “I need to get dressed, Father. I am late as it is already…”

Lord Hampton waited until the valet had left. “I am terribly sorry, but I am the bearer of bad news, Archibald. You will not need to dress for riding this morning.” He took a deep breath, watching his son lose his smile. “Darren has been arrested this morning and taken to the police station.”

“What?!” That distress plain, something he could not hide in front of his father. “Arrested? Father!”

“Yes… the detective came this morning. Allegedly, his name came up when some men got arrested for… how to say this… you know what the crime of buggery is? Gross indecency? You know when two men…”

Archibald blanched. “I know…”

“So… it seems he has been named, but this does not prove anything, he needs to answer a few questions and will be sent back.”

Archibald was trying to breathe as his vision blurred, that panic rushing down his spine, heaving when he remembered his grandmother’s words, so he steadied his breathing, clutching his chair’s armrests. “What now?”

“I sent a telegram to my lawyer, but he might only be here tomorrow… Darren might be out by then. I am adamant this is a mistake.”

Archibald didn’t comment, his eyes drifting to the landscape, his chest so tight he thought he would throw up. Utterly at a loss at where this would lead.

They had sat him in an almost bare room, his hands cuffed to the back of the chair, so tight, he thought he’d pass out just because of that shooting pain in his shoulders. Breathing hard to try and stay focused when the door opened and two men walked in, their shirt sleeves rolled back. They stood in front of him, their arms crossed.

The burly, dark-haired one spoke first. “I’m detective Polland, and this is my partner, Ryan.” Gesturing at a smaller man with sandy brown hair. “Suppose you’ve been told why you’re here?”

Darren nodded, but didn’t talk, determined not to give them anything, not even knowing why they had him tied up.

Ryan spoke then with a nasty smirk. “Won’t talk, will ya? I bet you’ll change your mind soon…”

Without any warning, the pain burst behind Darren's eyes as his head snapped to the right. A hard slap, probably with the back of a hand. Blood flooded his mouth, when he got another blow, this one snapping his head to the left. He tried to blink through the tears, swallow that blood as the pain registered in his cheekbones, his mouth, his lips. Somebody grabbed his hair and tilted his head up. He squinted, trying to make that blurred face out.

Polland's voice. "Ryan's right. 'Tis but a small slap... start talking if you don't want no more..."

Ryan snickered. "Not a tough one, this one. So... your good buddy Frank said you are one of those mollies whom he had affairs with, that's why you're here... is it true?"

Darren's head swam, but he just let his head fall when Polland let his hair go, breathing through those split lips which had started swelling.

"Better for you if you talk. You might just get jail."

Darren kept quiet, even if his fear was eating him, this seemed the better option. *Frank....* The memory distant, the baker of a neighbouring village. One encounter, so quick it seemed to have not even existed. *They beat him up too...* Moaning when he got punched in the stomach. He bent forward out of instinct and cried out at the pain in his shoulders, trying to breathe when his breath had been cut. Almost in a panic when he could only suck in some air, that pain flooding everything. Another punch to his left ribs, hard, another slap on the left, sending his head flying. He rolled it back, almost knocked out, bathing in that pain throbbing everywhere. Jolting at a fist landing next to him, but it had hit flesh. Not his. A fist slammed into a palm. He cried softly, listening to them laugh.

"Pathetic... will you talk or must we continue?"

Darren just breathed, letting his head roll to the front, his eyes shutting at the pain, but he had to lean into the cuffs, too weak to sit. Another hard punch to the stomach made him throw up.

Laughter. "Look at this... we can go on all day..."

"Let's go and have lunch... he might be willing to talk when we come back."

The door opening and closing. He risked a look, but the room was empty. The blood had drained from his head as his vision blurred, knowing he would faint, but he couldn't do anything, tied up, so let that darkness take him.

Waking later, his arms cramped. He straightened painfully, his senses awakening at that agonizing pain coursing through his body. His eyes on the door, panting through that bloodied mouth. It had dripped on his shirt, his pants, the floor, and he dared not even imagine how he looked, licking those split lips oozing blood. Jolting at the door opening with a bang. Meeting their grins.

"Ready for more?" Polland closed the door and slammed his fist into his palm. "I sure am."

Darren almost lost it then, tears blurring his vision, but he steadied his breathing, not wanting to give them the satisfaction of hearing him cry. *Fuck you*. A hard light seeped into his eyes, and they smiled.

"Tough, aren't ya? Well, let's see how tough you are..."

The door opened then, and a detective walked in, his eyes going wide. "What are you doing?!"

"He won't talk..." But Polland had lost his bravado, unsure.

"Are you out of your mind? This is not some random man; he is Lord Hampton's stable master! His Lordship's lawyer is on his way, or so I have heard from the postman, and you better make him presentable by the time he arrives.... Better... Fuck it! Let him go!"

"What? But..."

"Not a word! Untie him and let him go. Better this than facing a lawyer."

Polland huffed, but undid the cuffs. Darren slid to the floor, unable to do anything else, his arms numb. Ryan and Polland pulled him up by his armpits.

The detective faced them. "Let him wash his face and bring him out of the village... he can walk from there."

They nodded and dragged him to a basin.

Polland set him to his feet. "Fucking stand, motherfucker. Wash up."

Darren squinted, trying to focus with his head throbbing, but he brought his trembling hands to the basin and washed his face, his lips, the water tainting red. Watching those dark bruises on his wrists, a bit wide-eyed, dazed, when he got grabbed and dragged to a small cart. Polland sat at the reins and Ryan held him by the arm in the back, dashing outside of the village to the road where they stopped after a while and shoved him down on the gravel, turning then.

Darren sat up, that icy wind tearing into his shirt, his skin, so he pushed himself up not to freeze on that hard ground. Hugging himself tight with those aching arms, he put one foot in front of the other, swaying, trying to keep his eyes on the road. A good hour of walking, at least, he knew. Utterly clueless if he would arrive alive, every breath a stab, that nausea lingering. He let his tears fall, crying softly at the pain and the cold, but he ploughed on, having no other choice. Knowing too, that he had to mourn his job, his home, his father's words swimming into that hazy mind.

"When you do something that brings taint to your lord's family, you need to be gracious enough to avoid them sending you away. You keep your spine straight by resigning on the spot and removing yourself. No matter if you have just been accused wrongly or you have committed a mistake. There is no leniency for our kind, and our loyalty comes first. To the family. To our masters."

He had listened, but at fifteen, his words seemed so distant, as if it could never happen. And yet, it had arrived, that dreaded moment. He knew, though, what he had to do, watching the sun set slowly on that bare landscape he so loved. The mansion's gates, finally in sight when he thought he would collapse, his lips trembling, that abysmal thirst above the pain. He had to steady himself against some trees, but kept going with that sole focus to arrive at the stable yard, somehow. Knowing that he had not spoken a word, that thought bringing some comfort when he could have told them many names, those men getting ready to go to dinner, to bed then. And Archibald. Safe, his reputation sound. A relief there which washed some more tears out as he stumbled in the yard. James caught him, yelling at Travis, the last sound he heard before the world went dark.

"A real shame, this affair with your stable master." William drank from his glass, whirling that dark red wine in it.

Edward turned to him. "I am positive this is a mistake. My lawyer will clear him out of there, and then we will discuss this."

William looked at him. "It is too late to make this right. Word travels fast on this side of the county. Even if he has not done anything." He pursed his lips, as if he would not even believe his words.

Lady Hampton chimed in. "I always knew something was not right with that man... and to think he spent so much time alone with Archibald!" She looked at her son's impassive face. "Has he..."

"No, Mother." It had come out clipped, even if he had wanted it to be calm, he could not hide that wrath from his voice, that despair in him toiling like tide.

William smiled. "Of course not. Your good mother is rightly worried, though... you could hardly defend yourself."

"He has not tried anything... and what is this? Talking about him like he would be one when we do not know..."

William grinned. "Ah, you are right. Apologies... but a man who has been widowed so long... raises questions why he has not married again."

Lady Hampton put her cup down. "True! My dear William, always on the spot!"

Archibald's lips parted, but he felt his grandmother's hand on his, so he stayed put, letting them discuss the possibilities, his heart in pieces.

Darren had woken to James' gentle slaps, and he caught his hand feebly, opening his eyes. The horses watching. The stable corridor...

He looked at James, painfully forming the words. "I got enough slaps, lad..."

He smiled, his eyes filled with worry, Travis' too. "We was worried, Sir..."

"Were... ah, help me up." His throat tight, but he sat, dizzy, his eyes going to those two boys crouched down to his level, holding a bloodied rag which they had used to wipe him off. He had a blanket on too which he clutched not to lose it. "It is farewell, boys... I cannot stay after this..."

They sort of knew, even if Travis frowned a bit, glancing at James, who just patted Darren on the shoulder. "We know, sir... I am sorry. I loved working with you... stay the night though?"

"Yes... I have to talk to his lordship tomorrow morning, and then I'm off..." His eyes went to the horses, and they flooded with tears. "Take good care of them... you know how... let Lord Archibald ride Dandy. You could go with him on Tulip, James. Make him see the countryside from horseback."

"His Lordship is gonna miss you, sir."

"Yeah..." He stood then, painfully. "Thank you.... For sorting me out. Thank you for everything."

They hugged, tight, the boys holding their tears in, watching him walk out, his hand grazing the stall doors not to fall.

Up in his room, he stoked the fire up, put the kettle on and then took his mother's writing kit out of a box, sitting to that single table, searching a bit his words, but then, he just wrote what his father had taught him, making him remember the words. Hesitating to write to Archibald, but it was too dangerous, to have any of those words on paper, so he just sealed the letter, and put it aside. He went to pack whilst the tea was brewing, but he barely had anything to fit into a large backpack, leaving all the uniforms which belonged to Lord Hampton anyway, taking only his pants and shirts, those two sweaters his mother had knitted, his vests and his coat. An idea taking shape, to go to town maybe, first, then see what job he could find there. *Maybe work at another house, if they needed anybody at all...* He was in a shock, he sort of knew, not his usual state of mind as he sipped that scalding tea, hissing when it hit his split lips. *Shit...* He went to bed then, curling around that painful stomach, his throbbing ribs, trying to find sleep with Archibald floating in his mind, so he let his tears stream, not caring anymore if he cried, knowing that a farewell was impossible. Hoping that he would know that he loved him more than his own life.

Next morning, he was up early, and drank his tea, then hauled his bag up, walking down to the stables where the horses neighed at him, the boys already busy. They stopped when they saw him, trying to give him some cheer with their smiles, and James just dragged Travis out, pretending to get some hay. Leaving him some time to say his goodbyes to the horses. This was so painful, Darren thought he would not be able to make it, stroking the pony first, that small pony he had trained as a teenager, age old. That pest of a mare then who still pinned her ears back at him, just to lick his hand. The roan, that trusty, aging horse. Dandy and Tulip then, the two friends living in the same large stall, rubbing their heads, his tears flowing as they nudged him, licking his tears with questions in their large eyes. Trying to make that grieving human smile, nibbling his neck.

He just gave them a large kiss on their soft noses, stroking Dandy one last time, soft whispers. "Be good, boys..."

His eyes going to the last stall then, that black head poked out above the door, waiting, his ears pricked towards him, that mouth almost in a small smile. Darren wiped at his tears, and opened the stall door, pushing that black horse in, melting against him as he lost it, sobbing, hugging his neck, his face in his flowing mane, and Raven just nibbled his back, puzzled, neighing softly. Waiting until that man he loved had stopped, and started stroking him, looking into his large eyes, and Raven couldn't understand, but sensed something, nudging him in the chest, leaving his head to rest on his broad shoulder. Darren could not talk, all the words he had to say to that horse not enough. Leaving him behind, possibly almost as painful as getting beaten up, as his heart ripped in two, closing that door softly, a last caress to that slender neck, getting a last lick to his trembling hand.

He turned then and hauled his backpack up, closing his eyes to Raven's desperate cry as he left the stables. Hurrying not to hear him, to have the will to carry on, walking to the mansion where he asked the butler to talk to Lord Hampton, that haughty man's eyes filled with contempt. Darren was past caring, carrying that shame which he shouldn't have felt, but it was there, sitting on his chest, his heart, waiting until Lord Hampton hurried down the stairs, slowing when he saw him, his eyes flooding with pity.

"My good man... what did they do to you? I am speechless..." His eyes went wide at the backpack at Darren's feet, raising his eyes to his soft voice.

"May I talk to you, Milord?"

"Sure. Come in."

They walked into his office, and Darren pulled an envelope out of his jacket, handing it to him, holding in his tears. "My resignation letter, Milord."

Lord Hampton could not speak, taking that letter, trying to find anything reasonable to say when he just wanted to tear that letter up. "I am deeply sorry, Darren."

"Please, Milord... If anything, it is I... I, who..." He had to shut up, his tears clogging his voice, only his eyes begged in that bruised face.

Lord Hampton opened the letter and read it, his vision blurring. "Alright." He looked at him. "Archibald will be devastated."

Darren had to breathe in deep to mask his emotions. "Please give my regards to his Lordship. He should continue riding... he could ride outside with James... His Lordship is skilled enough."

"Thanks to you, my good man. I want you to know that although I understand why you are leaving, it is deeply upsetting. Where will you go?"

Darren shifted on his feet. "I am not sure, Milord. Maybe to town first... see if anybody needs a man..."

Lord Hampton pulled a small face. "I must tell you that Lord Willoughby has made sure that everybody in this county, or around it, is informed of what happened. He thought it was his duty... so, you will not find a job here... or anywhere near, for that matter."

Darren's face fell. There was then only one option left, the one he dreaded the most. He steadied his voice. "London it is then, Milord."

They looked at each other, both knowing. That it was the ideal place to disappear, nameless, the odds of him ever finding a place with a good family slim to none.

Lord Hampton pulled a drawer and stashed some bills in an envelope, handing it to him. "This is but a small token of my appreciation for all you have done. Please take it."

Darren just took it, moved. "Thank you, Milord."

His drawn face. "I would wish that you write to me, Darren. When you have settled. I would hate to lose you forever. I would think Archibald would want that very much too."

Darren had to hold tight not to break down crying at his name. "Alright, Milord. It will be my honour to write to you." He took his bag, eager to leave, to be allowed to let his tears flow. "Farewell, Milord. It was an honour working for you."

"I could say the same. Please do take care. And we shall take great care of the horses."

Darren just bowed, unable to talk, and swung his backpack up, leaving fast before he would break down crying. Walking away from that mansion where Archibald still slept, unaware, and his heart tore again for him. Letting his tears flow as soon as he had hit the road, walking fast despite that shooting pain in his stomach and ribs, that dull ache in his cheekbones and lips. His eyes on the road, his mind on that long walk until the city where he could catch a train to London.

Archibald just listened to his parents talk, keeping a straight face when all he wanted was to howl. Keeping his tears in, that abysmal despair, that mild anger at Darren, for leaving without saying a word to him, knowing that it would have been impossible anyway, listening to his mother's incessant complaining, how this was a scandal avoided, how him leaving was a confession, even if his father was trying to persuade her otherwise. She had stormed out, and he walked to his son, laying his hand on his shoulder, meeting those mute, brown eyes drowned in sorrow.

"He asked me to give you his regards, and to tell you that you should ride out with James. That you are skilled enough." He sighed, squeezing Archibald's shoulder softly. "I have asked him to write once he's settled. So that we know where he is, that he is fine."

"Thank you, Father."

He averted his eyes to the windows, to that light rain which had started pouring, his thoughts on him, on not seeing him ever again, sending a rush of panic down his spine. Taming that mad thought of getting into the carriage and drive after him, take him back. Because it was impossible, he knew, having heard William tell them that he had made sure that Darren would not get employed anywhere decent. *Such men should not be near others, especially not noble ladies, and gentlemen...* A small determination birthing there, remembering Darren's words. *You would not be so feisty... Indeed... you may be right...* He swallowed his tears, closing his eyes, still, trying to find some strength in that still weak body to carry out his plans. To find him, no matter what.

Chapter 19

He had managed to catch the last train, having walked all day, near exhaustion, a late one which would arrive at night. Huddled against the window, his backpack between his legs, his eyes on the rushing landscape. Holding his tears in, trying to stay awake but it was torture, that lilting wagon almost making it impossible, the human bodies heating that space up. He kept his eyes open though, wanting to soak in one last time those landscapes he loved, the rolling hills, those winding roads, lush fields, and tall trees. Glinting lakes... He had to shut his eyes at the memory, opening them again just to meet stares, so he turned as much as he could towards the window, not to face those stares, those questioning eyes.

He got off, looking around that busy train station, utterly lost, even if he had been to London with Lord Shackleton and his family, even if he sort of knew the city, there was nowhere he could go at that moment, no place he could call home, the hour late, so he started walking, following an old map his father had left him, just to know at least where he was, letting the crowd carry him, but he knew he had to get out of those wealthier places, going towards the edge of the city, wondering if he could sleep on the streets, his legs not carrying him anymore. But he was also scared in that dark night, the people scarcer as he walked towards shabbier houses, smaller ones, the whole place dirty, the streets filled with horse manure and garbage, the smell overpowering. He breathed in deep, against that deep despair, and his eyes wandered to a sign. An inn... maybe better than nothing. He went in, noticing the innkeeper's stare, but he just paid, out of that small amount of money he still had, and went to a small room upstairs. One night. He knew he could not afford more, this already being a folly, but he could not face sleeping outside.

He washed in a small basin near a mirror, looking at his face filled with dark bruises on his cheekbones, his lower lip split on both sides, his top lip too on the right side.bread Washing that dried blood off gingerly, his hands trembling from fatigue. He ate too, whatever was left in his bag, some bread, and apples he had stashed in there whilst still at home. *Home...* He sat on the bed, dazed, letting his tears stream, just to wash out that deep pain. That shame. Thinking of his parents, what his father would think if he still existed at all, even if he knew... he had known, in that mute acknowledgment, that small disappointment there. Mildly relieved when he had gotten married. And he had never said anything, scolded him, or beaten him up. More worried than anything at what would happen to him. *And now... I am sorry, Dad...* Remembering his warm brown eyes. His voice. *Stay true. Do not give up. Ever. Our kind only survives if we work hard. Hold it together.* He steeled himself and went to bed, determined to sleep, to be fresh to face the next day, drifting off on his pain, the one in his heart greater than the one coursing through his bruised body.

Next day, he was up early, and left, walking towards post offices to check the billboards. He bought a paper, reading the job postings, but there was nothing, really. Being a cab driver requiring owning a horse, at least, or money he didn't have to get started or to even rent one. He dismissed it, the postings for a coachman too, as he didn't have a recommendation letter, and word travelled fast anyway among the rich, especially now that they were travelling back from the countryside for Christmas and the ball season... Wandering in the city then, marvelling at that bustling crowd, the noise, those rushing cabs, carts, and horses ploughing on, noticing with a clenching heart how some of them barely walked, how thin they were, worked to the bone.

Late in the afternoon when another homeless night started looming, and he had walked far, not even really knowing where he was on those shabby, narrow streets, his eyes caught on a ragged yellow piece of paper.

Looking for experienced drivers for delivery carts. Decent pay and lodging provided.

The address was under those bold letters. He tore the paper down and looked the address up on his map. A bit farther, but not too far. A slight hope in him.

He walked there, a good hour, the night setting, people hurrying home, or picking up night shifts. Walking into a dark yard, barely lit, the smell of ammonia catching in his throat, making his eyes water. He breathed against it, looking around, the carts parked for the night, that unmistakable smell of horses all around him, their soft snorts. A large man walked out of the shadows, eyeing him, his eyes dark. In his fifties, maybe, it was hard to tell with that greying hair, and Darren felt a bit unsure, almost thinking better of it when he spoke.

"What do you want?" Watching that tall man, his peculiar blue eyes wide a bit in that bruised face. That handsome face and his height made him stand out from the rough folks he was used to, their faces like they had been sculpted with a hatchet. Save for his clothes, he would have mistaken him for a lordling on the run. His lips curled up. "You ain't on the run, ain't you? We get 'em those lordlings fleeing their homes sometimes."

"No... I am not fleeing... but I need a job and saw your advert." He showed that piece of paper, keeping his eyes on him.

He walked close, taking it. "I see. And you can drive?"

"I was a coachman for Lord..."

"Nobody gives a shit about that here. Which lord, or other fancy pants. You can drive then. That is all that matters." Eyeing him, catching that kind light in those blue pools. "This ain't no lord's stables here. I give you a cart and a horse for the day, you do the deliveries, as many as you can, cos you're paid on them numbers, got it? Ain't no pity for that horse, get it? I buy 'em cheap, you work 'em 'til they drop, and get another one. 'Tis how we work here. You get paid after your day and can sleep in the hay attic, or wherever the fuck you want. Some prefer in the straw barn. I don't give a shite." Waiting, a slight impatience in him, even if he needed a driver badly, and he could see how strong he was, even with his sweater and coat on, those large hands holding his bag tight, his eyes darting around.

Darren's heart, tight, but he had no real choice, this being possibly a blessing, finding a job so fast. *I can always move on...* Swallowing his pride. "Alright. I will gladly take it."

The man slammed his large palm on his shoulder. "Alright, fancy talk. Your name?"

"Darren Turner."

"I'm Clayton Snyder, that's Mister Snyder for you. Nickname's the Butcher cos you know, I butcher horses and men alike." He laughed, showing a crooked grin. "Got family, Turner? A wifey? Kids?"

"No..." He swallowed, unsure again, his heart clenching.

"All the better. Ain't nobody gonna miss you when you drop dead from work." He laughed again and gestured towards those dark stables. "Get comfy. You start early tomorrow. Get some sleep in ya... Grab a blanket on your way up, there's a stash there."

He walked back to a small flat then, banging the door shut, and Darren turned towards the stables, clutching his bag, his eyes a bit wide in that dark as he made his way to a ladder he could make out in that dim glow sifting in through grimy windows. Horses asleep, stirring, tied in between wooden beams, barely enough place to stand or lie down, that straw barely there on that damp dirt floor filled with filth. He tried to ignore it, the smells, the shade of bones poking skin on those tired animals, and took a coarse blanket from a pile, filled with holes, climbing up to that loft then, forms sleeping on the hay in that chill night. He found a space, and sat down, closing his eyes to that rush of despair invading him. *Madness... to sink this low...* but nobody had asked about who he was yet, nobody cared, and he had a place to sleep, so he swallowed whatever pride he had left, and lay down on the hay, covering what he could of his body with that coarse blanket, sleep pulling him straight away.

He woke with the sun, as was his custom, others waking around him, a few 'hellos' thrown his way from those crumpled men. Darren was not sure what to do with his bag, but the others just left their stuff, so he left it too, climbing down with them, watching them take a piss near the horses in the straw, warm their hands on a single barrel where a fire was burning, an old metallic stove with a big pot on filled with tea, or so it seemed.

Snyder walked to him and slammed an enamel mug into his hands. "'Tis yours. For tea and cooking whatever the fuck you want in it. Guys, 'tis the new guy Darren Turner."

"Fancy looking." One of them grinned, a thin man with a scar on his face.

Snyder laughed. "Aye. But he ain't gonna be fancy for long." They laughed, and Darren just stood, brewing a small anger above that mild stress. "Alright. Time to work some." He handed pieces of papers out to all of them, and a map to Darren. "Your addresses. Pickup and delivery. A map for fancy boy here. Come."

He gestured to him and Darren followed him to the stables, his eyes going wide in that dawn light at the sight of those animals, starved, their skin taut on their bones. Almost tumbling into Snyder's back when he had stopped behind a ginger horse. White socks on three legs, the neck lowered, maybe still slumbering. The manger empty, not even a lump of hay in front of that animal.

Snyder looked at Darren. "Told ya. No pity. She is yours 'til she drops."

Darren just breathed, taming his voice. "Her name?"

Snyder snickered. "Name? Fuck knows." He howled at that thin man harnessing a grey horse. "Hey! Smith! What the fuck's this one's name?"

"Last time, it was Mandy." He laughed, pulling the straps tight on his bone-thin horse.

"Mandy it is, fancy pants. Her stuff is there, get her ready and start working, you ain't got all day."

He left and Darren squeezed between that beam and the horse, running his palm on her hipbone, her ribs, down her legs then. Swollen a bit, but no pain. He gave her his hand and she sniffed it, but without any curiosity, just out of instinct, maybe, her eyes dull, her lips loose. He checked her teeth gently, his eyes going wide. *Maybe seven to eight years old...* Looking her over, that long strip on her head, that body which had seen better days. *She must have been stunning in her prime...* that blood still there, lingering on that near skeletal body. *Fuck.* He swallowed, jolting at the thin man's voice.

"Get ready, Turner. You're wasting time." Grinning, pulling that grey horse outside who could barely follow.

Darren went to get a bucket of water still, making her drink, her grateful eyes on him when she had drained it all, so he went for another one, and another when she had enough. Patting her, looking for the brushes, but there were none, so he picked up two handfuls of straw, and groomed her, hard, making her groan, and her coat cleaner. Combing that meagre mane with his fingers, his throat tight. *No pity. Fucker.* The carts leaving amongst shouting and whips lashing, until he was alone, putting the tack on that mare, careful to adjust the harness when it was too big. Turning to Snyder's voice.

"What the fuck are you doing? Hurry up!"

"I'm new... sorry if I'm taking my time to find things..."

"Just leave already, asshole. Time's flying." He spat and left him, fuming.

Darren led her outside and tied her to the cart in that bitter cold, that tired animal, and he sat on the bench, his eyes on that large whip planted next to his seat. He just picked up the reins and clacked them on her, but she started in a panic and he had to rein her in, almost falling off as she darted ahead, until she realised that no blows were falling, so she slowed and walked outside, the streets still fairly quiet, other delivery carts hurrying past. He checked the address, the map, and started driving, trying to play with her mouth until she understood that he would not pull on the reins unless she put her head into them, so she stopped, and got rewarded with slack reins in that second. Munching her bit, she walked on her stiff legs, until they arrived in a courtyard to pick up some sacks of wheat. Darren's eyes went wide at the quantity.

He stepped at the man who was in charge of loading his cart. "Is there a mistake? This seems a lot for one horse."

The man laughed at him. "You're new at the Butcher's? You'll learn soon." Laughing, the others joining, the cart groaning under that heavy load.

Darren had to leave, though, his heart in his heels when the mare put all her weight into the harness, jumping to start that heavy cart. She lost her grip more than once on those slippery streets, but pulled hard, foam plastering her chest by the time they got half-way, and his heart broke for her, cursing softly each time she stumbled. Finally, the mill came into sight, where they had to unload.

Somebody stepped to him. "Hurry up, you're late."

Darren just stood, blinking, and the man yelled at him. "Hey! Unload! Now!"

His eyes went wide, but he climbed and started unloading those heavy bags, throwing them to the men below whilst his horse panted, barely standing. *And this is only the first trip...*

The miller came out and gestured at the horse. "I'll give him some hay if you don't mind. Tis a disgrace, to starve a horse like this."

Darren's face flamed up, even if he was not at fault, so he just nodded, panting too. "Many thanks..."

The miller just shook his head and somebody threw a stash of hay in front of that horse who started nibbling it eagerly. Darren waited until she had eaten it all, glancing at his watch, time running like quicksand.

Looking at his addresses, *so many...* He had to start her though, reluctant, and drove to the next address, crates of vegetables to be delivered to a market, the streets busy. Fortunately, she was responding well, even if they had to stop abruptly to let a faster cab speed by, or avoid another cart. Getting some comments on the state of his horse, but Darren chose to ignore them, because there was no time to explain, and he had no excuses for himself either, allowing this to happen, using that poor horse.

By the end of the day though, he had made sure that she had eaten everywhere she could, sometimes just snatching a couple of carrots or apples from a rotting pile.

At their last trip, he was sure he would resign, and leave, but when he stopped the cart in that dirty yard, and met her tired but grateful eyes, he could not leave. Instead, he untied her and walked her inside, tying her up. Rubbing her off with whatever clean straw he could gather from that filthy pile under her.

He went to look for Snyder then and gave him his delivery tickets.

Snyder snickered. "You did the bare minimum, fancy boy. Shame. The others came back for more. Here. Your wage." He counted it into Darren's palm. "Not a lot, right? Work harder."

"That horse is on the verge of dying."

"Yes. So? I told ya. No pity. She drops, you get another one. No biggie. I buy 'em cheap."

"I'd like to give her more hay."

Snyder barked a laugh. "If you buy it?" He held his palm out and Darren opened his hand, letting him take his wage out. "There. She eats. You starve. Fair deal?"

He swallowed, but met his eyes. "Deal."

"Suit yourself."

He laughed, shaking his head as he left, and Darren walked back to the hayloft, scooping a generous amount in front of her, letting the other two next to her nibble a bit too as they were stretching their scrawny neck towards her to snatch a few strands.

Smith walked to him, shaking his head. "You are crazy, Turner."

"This is no way to treat a horse."

"You'll soon change your mind when you'll be hungry."

Darren just crossed his arms on that painful stomach, knowing he had some stale bread left in his bag. He stroked her neck and went to scoop some tea out into his mug, flinching at the taste. Bitter. As if that tea had been reused a thousand times. *Maybe it is so...* He climbed up to the hayloft and took that single piece of bread out of his bag, washing it down with that foul liquid, his muscles aching after that first day of loading and unloading. He collapsed then on the hay, his thoughts drifting to his old home, to the lakeshore where they could hold each other, to their kisses, to that cottage by the sea where they had loved each other. Closing his eyes on the memories, on Archibald's face floating in his mind, his smile, his lips, his taste, those deep kisses when nothing mattered anymore, just them... He curled up under his blanket, trying to find sleep, almost thinking that he was in a dream and he would wake up in his room above the stables, stroke the horses in the morning...

Archibald's eyes went to James when he had ridden up to the mansion on Tulip, leading Dandy.

He jumped down, bowing. "Milord... I am ready to take you out."

Archibald just nodded, his heart racing, but he let his footmen and James help him up in the saddle. James strapped his legs in, but not too tight, and sat on Tulip, waiting for Archibald to settle, look at him.

"We may go, James."

"Very well, Milord."

Stressed out of his mind, his grief of losing Darren still raw, unaware that Archibald's heart was bleeding, sitting on that horse which had meant the world to his lover. *I am riding for you. I am getting stronger. I will stand on my legs and walk that city to find you.*

"James, how is Raven?"

The boy shrugged, but then caught himself. "He is a bit sad, Milord. Has no appetite, really. Keeps looking at the door, waiting for Master Darren..."

"He's missing him..."

"Aren't we all, Milord? I mean, pardon... we are missing him, this is the truth."

I am missing him more... But he kept quiet, enjoying those familiar landscapes, these roads were Darren had driven him many times. "Let us trot a bit."

"As you wish, Milord."

Lord Hampton watched from the windows Archibald ride back, taken down into his chair, but his face was bitten by the cold, red patches on that pale skin, his brown eyes a bit more alight, covering that deep sorrow. He could see it, that grim determination in his eyes, how he was forcing the food down, how he had insisted on his ride, how he wanted to ride every day. Quiet about Darren, not a word, as if his departure had not left a mark, but Edward knew, it was in Archibald's eyes, in his voice, that dull taint to them, that slight pull of his mouth each time his mother still found something to say. Conversations inevitably drifting to Christmas. To that last hunt before they would leave back to London in the spring to start the ball season.

He turned to his son when he got pushed in later, bathed and changed, handing him a cup of warm tea. "I am delighted that you decided to ride outside today."

"It was a delight indeed."

William and Fran had come over for tea, and he turned to him, grinning. "I bet the company was not such a delight since the departure of your trusted coachman."

Archibald looked at him. "James is perfectly capable of leading that ride."

"Oh, I am sure of it. I can only hope your lonely promenades with your coachman left you intact, my dear brother-in-law."

The air froze a bit, but Archibald composed himself fast. "I do not know what you mean."

"You know, with that man being a molly, one would think..."

Archibald flamed up at the word. "There are ladies in the room, so please refrain from using that word!"

"Oh... as you wish..."

"As for your insinuations, he did not try anything!"

"Good to hear."

He toasted him, his eyes gleaming at his rage, so Archibald turned away, gutted, sipping his tea which had turned in his mouth.

His mother spoke then. "Good to hear, dear. One can only wonder what they are capable of. Not that it matters. He went to London and will sink in the slum where he belongs. Let us not even waste one more word on that foul man."

She turned to chat with Fran and William whilst Lord Hampton walked to Archibald.

He met his eyes. "Nothing yet?"

"No... it is too early... let us wait a bit."

"He is not a foul man, father."

"I know, Archibald." He put his hand on his shoulder, watching the falling snow.

Chapter 20

A bitter cold had settled with Christmas fast approaching, a blanket of snow falling delicately over the landscape, over the cities, people busy with the preparations. More deliveries as the festivities approached, and the Butcher's business was busier than usual, despite the sloshed over streets slick with snow, horses and men working hard in that falling snow, squinting in the cold.

Darren had been there for weeks, a grim determination in him to save enough money to leave to some place better, but it seemed that the more he worked, the less money he had, somehow, whatever extra he could gain gone as his kind heart could not bear seeing his horse dwindle, even if he paid for her hay, it was not enough in the cold with that horrid workload. He had to tighten his belt too, sometimes choosing between feeding the horse or feeding himself, a steady diet of bread and potatoes not being enough to keep his body up. His face had healed, only a small scar on his lip as a reminder of the blows, his ribs still aching, but he had no time to rest, barely enough to get some sleep in that attic filled with drafts. Bitter cold nights, shivering under that blanket, breathing in his hands to be somewhat warm. Hazy dreams of Archibald drifting in his exhausted mind.

Archibald's eyes went to the drifting snow, his heart numb at the approaching festivities, the hunt next day where he would not go, refusing to take part in senseless bloodshed, his heart tearing for those innocent animals. William had obviously offered to hunt with Lord Hampton, priding himself in his new horse, as he had worn the other one to the bone, then sold it to slaughter.

Archibald shivered, trying to close his eyes, that soft burning in him at his absence, that painful yearning burning him alive. Knowing he had touched himself many times during those lonely nights, thinking of his lips and hands on his body, his mouth on him, around him, his tongue, closing his eyes as his hand closed on his cock, stroking, meeting his own hand with his feeble hips, biting his lip as he came with a moan, hard, shooting his load all over his stomach. His hand lazily grazing it, that warm semen, bringing his fingers to his lips, letting them wet them, a quick lick, his eyes in tears. His hand wandered down under the sheets, pulling his nightgown up, but he just stroked that semi-hard flesh, not wanting to feel more, to have these lonely, useless pleasures, this emptiness which could not be filled by his own hands, his own mouth, lips, and tongue. Tears pearling out as he closed his eyes, clenching his jaw. He moved his legs, just slightly, as he had told him, and they obeyed. Every day a bit more. Just the thighs moving a bit, his knees better, his calves twitching as the muscles swelled again. *I will walk. Walk out of here to find you...*

Darren had written one day, when he knew that he would stay for a while, winter being a harsh time to find a job, and he posted that letter written in pencil in a rough envelope, not even knowing why. Maybe that slight hope there that Archibald would know that he was doing fine. Laughing at himself, his hands trembling as he put the envelope in the postal box, climbing back on the bench then, starting that poor horse, her breath in the air, steam rising from her body in that cold.

Days later, the day of the hunt, the mansion was busy, when the post got delivered, and Hanson, the butler, was walking towards the tea room to leave the post to Lord Hampton.

William caught him on his way there and snatched the letters off the tray. "Do not bother, Hanson, I shall give the letters to his lordship." Grinning at the butler's slight shock and disapproving look, but Hanson just bowed and left.

William walked to the room, leafing through the letters, when his eyes caught on that crude envelope in coarse paper, stained, those neatly crafted letters in pencil. He raised his eyebrows and put the other letters on the mantelpiece, flicking the envelope around. A nasty little smile, quickly looking around, but he was alone, only a hearty fire burning. He tore the envelope open, reading that single letter.

My Lord,

I am writing as you have requested. I am well settled and working in London. If you ever would like to find me, I am residing at Snyder's Deliveries. Rest assured that all is well. I do hope that all is well with you and your family.

Yours truly,

Darren Turner

William scoffed, but his eyes had taken a hard light. He put the letter back in the envelope, and his eyes went to the flames dancing in the fireplace. His lips curled up as he stepped there. Just a split second of hesitation, but then he tossed the envelope into the flames, watching them catch it eagerly, burn that paper to crisp. Watching it curl around those letters, turn them to soot and ash. His eyes went to the door when Lord Hampton entered.

"Oh, William! Delighted to see you have already arrived."

"Indeed. I wanted to be here early so we can get ready together. Ah! I got the post from Hanson. I hope you don't mind."

"Not at all." Watching Edward flick through the letters, a visible disappointment on that stern face, so he bit back a smile, feigning interest. "You seem most disappointed."

Lord Hampton smiled thinly. "Ah... nothing of interest. I am expecting a relative to write."

"Shame, truly. But I am sure they will. Let us go and hunt some foxes. It will cheer you up." He took his arm and pulled him outside, casting one last look at that letter burnt to ashes, his heart flying.

Archibald watched them leave from the window, the dogs howling as they tore into that fresh snow, the horns blaring. *Stupid shit...* He turned from the window and opened his book, his mother and sister working on their embroideries, whilst his grandmother read sitting close to him. A mild stress in him that Darren had not written, wondering if he would write, ever, but he also knew that he was loyal and would not disobey his father's request. *So what was going on?* Weeks dragging like years, and still nothing. *Maybe he's busy... or jobless... freezing on the streets...* He chased his thoughts away, trying to concentrate on his book, but it hardly made sense, even if it was interesting, the letters blurring with his nerves on edge, so he closed it again and rolled close to the window, just watching that white landscape, the skeleton trees reaching for that milk sky.

Later, when he had gone back to his book to kill that utter boredom, he raised his eyes at the commotion downstairs, hunters coming back in full gallop, jumping from their horses. A cart stopped in front of the house, shouting, William jumping from his horse too. Archibald's eyes wide at his father being helped down from the cart, his face filled with blood.

"Father!"

His mother and Fran had jumped up at his voice, turning to the door when it burst open, William and another hunter carrying Lord Hampton in, his blanched face filled with blood.

Archibald had rolled close, raising his eyes at William as his panic built. His mother had fainted, so the footmen were busy reviving her.

"What... what happened?"

"A bad fall. But he will be fine. It is a cut on the skin, but the bleeding is profuse. The doctor has been fetched, do not worry."

Archibald took his father's hand when his grandmother had pushed him close, that mad worry in him. "Father..."

Lord Hampton opened his eyes, squinting. "Hey... I'm fine..." Pained, he had to close his eyes, looking back at his son. "I am so sorry, Archibald."

He frowned. "It is alright, Father. Do not apologise to me. Accidents happen on these stupid hunts."

"Yes..."

William put his hand on Archibald's shoulder, waiting until he looked up at him. "What your father is trying to say is that his horse is hurt, Archibald. Raven..." Watching him drain of colour, his lips parting. He smiled sadly, squeezing his shoulder. "We will see how serious it is... and decide accordingly."

"What?! Do not dare touch that horse!"

William's eyebrows shot up. "He is hurt, his front legs. The veterinarian is on his way, Travis went to fetch him, but the horse is lame, barely able to walk, so we shall see... Obviously, I am not going to do anything to him. This is your father's decision."

Archibald looked back into his father's glazed over eyes.

He just smiled at his son. "Do not worry. He is a sturdy horse."

Their eyes, in tears, both knowing what that horse had meant to Darren.

The valet made sure he was covered, his wound washed, and by the time the doctor arrived, it was clear that he only needed a couple of stitches and a few days of bedrest.

William smiled. "Great luck! I have seen that fall, it was spectacular."

Edward waved feebly. "I should not have gone for that jump with that devastated horse who had no spirits..."

"Nonsense! Horses do not mourn. This was not your fault. He should have jumped better."

A knock, and the butler stepped in. "The veterinarian is here, Milord."

"Let him in."

He walked in, grim, and stood in front of Lord Hampton. "I do not have good news, I am afraid."

Archibald froze, squeezing his father's hand, William just standing near the fireplace with Fran and the ladies sitting, wide-eyed.

The veterinarian sighed. "He has partially torn his ligaments on his front legs... which means a long rest and a lot of caring, daily ointments and bandaging. I have briefed James and Travis, and given what is necessary. I will check back in a couple of days... but, this means his career as a hunting horse is over... I had to burn both his legs with a strong ointment, no hair will grow on them from his knees down... for now, they are also a bit bent towards the back, we shall see how it looks in a few weeks. In any case, he will not be able to be used as before, maybe only for light rides. He could possibly still pull, as it requires the hind legs more... That is what you are facing."

William pulled a small face. "Useless then. Wonderful..."

Archibald snapped at him. "You've just heard he needs rest and being taken care of. He is not useless! He will heal..."

The veterinarian spread his hands. "It is up to you, Edward. The young lord is right, he will heal, with time... but he will not be of use to you, not with those bent legs void of hair..."

Lord Hampton closed his eyes, pained. "We shall see. Thank you."

Archibald tugged at his hand until his father opened his eyes. "You cannot get rid of him, Father. It's Raven..." Knowing he should not talk like this, not in front of William, who was drinking every word with his small smile.

"I know. We shall see... I need to go and rest too..." He patted Archibald's hand, and the valets helped him up, walking him out.

William sipped his wine. "Shame. A great horse. But this is a horse's fate. Serve until the very end."

Archibald just turned away, gutted, trying to wall his feelings in, remembering Darren's smile, his face alight after that race, or each time he spoke of that horse. *His horse, damnit! No matter what.* He needed a few moments to collect himself, but then rang his valet.

"Bring my coat, and have somebody push me to the stables."

William stepped to him. "I can push you if you wish."

Archibald looked up at him, for a fleeting moment his tired brain tricking him, that dark hair and blue eyes so familiar, he had to blink, that arrogant smirk and his vicious eyes chilling him to the bone, so he just waved him away.

"No need to tire yourself further. I am sure Fran will appreciate your company after that long hunt."

One of their servants, a man he had never seen before, pushed him to the stables, a small struggle on that fresh snow, but Archibald didn't care, his heart in pieces when he saw the stable yard, the stables alight. The man pushed him inside, into that mild warmth, Dandy poking his head out with a soft neigh. Archibald reached to stroke him, but his eyes were on Raven, the horse's head lowered, panting softly through that pain. He was standing, trembling, sweat trickling down those bent legs, soft moans and groans as James rubbed a thick white paste on his bare legs.

He turned to Archibald though and scramble to his feet. "Milord..."

"How is he?" His eyes had welled up, despite himself, watching that suffering horse.

"In pain, Milord..." James was in tears too, that kind boy, trembling for that horse he loved so much. "We will do what the doctor told us..." He shut up, knowing that no matter what he did, the horse would not have his full capacities back, that gracious speed and body, those swift legs.

"Just do your best, James."

"Yes, Milord."

He went back to kneel in front of those trembling legs, rubbing the cream into his skin, those swollen legs curved where the tendons had been injured.

Archibald had to avert his eyes, trying not to lose it, stroking Dandy who had sensed that distress in the air, the smell of human tears.

Darren's eyes went to the stars in that dark yard, only the barrel burning, giving some heat as he was sipping that foul tea, munching a piece of bread. A peculiar feeling in him, as if something would be wrong, somehow. That sadness sitting on his chest a bit deeper, breathing against tears which had flooded his eyes, salting the bread in his mouth. He swallowed, drinking deep, trying to chase that despair away, that dark little moment. *Why?* The stars silent, cold. Listening to the horses' snorts in their sleep, knowing he had to go to sleep, that wretched night lying ahead where he could hardly rest, dreams chasing him like demons in the night. Where he would walk after Archibald but never reach him, despite running, he was faster, never turning around, even when he begged, waking in tears. Shaking his head, he finished eating and rinsed his mug out, hanging it on a rusty nail next to the others. He stroked the mare's hindsight before climbing up to his place, going to sleep fully clothed, as there had not been any other option.

He washed though in the morning, stripping to the waist at the well, that ice cold water burning his skin. The others just laughed at him, warming their hands over the fire.

"You're crazy, Turner. You'll freeze your cock off."

Smith smirked. "You look fine though, man."

"Fancy-pants washes his clothes too."

Snyder joined them. "What's up, fancy guy? You feel dirty?"

They laughed, but Darren had caught that shift in his voice, that glint in his eyes which roamed his body.

He dried himself and dressed quickly, avoiding those eyes which did not flinch away. He got his mug then and scooped some tea out, blowing on that fuming brew. Snyder started handing the assignments out, and he stopped in front of him with his crooked smile.

He pushed the papers in his hand, grazing his palm when Darren pulled his hand away. "Here, fancy guy. Knock yourself out. Hope you are clean enough." He winked at him, and Darren stepped back, maybe out of instinct, that mild worry rippling through him.

Noticing the others' smirks, some averting their eyes, maybe embarrassed a bit, busying themselves with preparing their carts. He hung his mug up and hurried away to the mare, hastily grooming her with a brush he had bought the other day. The harness then, and he tied her to the cart, leaving fast, avoiding looking at Snyder. *Fuck.* That touch, unmistakable, so he rubbed his palm in his pants, just to even kill that feeling on his skin.

His mind was on it though, all day, even if he had worked so hard that his shirt and sweater were soaked in that cold when they made their way back. His chest tight, but he was set not to give in, not to let him get at him in any way.

Lining up for their wage, Darren faced him, looking him square in the eyes, but Snyder just grinned, counting his tickets. "Good day... you could work more. Maybe next time." He counted the money in his palm, stopping when he'd reached half. "You take it all or feed your horse more?" Mocking, waiting. Darren closed his palm. Snyder scoffed. "Stupid idiot."

Darren just left, and fed the mare, even if he knew he was wasting that money to no avail. She wasn't getting stronger, if anything, it was a slow slide to death, something he could not make right, not here, not when it had been too late for her when he'd taken her over. All he could do was slow it down and make her life a bit easier. Hoping she would die fast, not in agony. Not sent for slaughter.

Waiting for a reply to his letter, not even believing that they would write back. *What for?* Lord Hampton had been polite, and he had fulfilled his wish, there was nothing more to expect.

Christmas Eve arrived then, the town snowed in, decorated in fancier streets, people rushing home, carrying baskets and packages under their arms, the kids playing snowball fights on the streets, and it would have been probably magical if they hadn't worked all day, an exhausting day filled with last-minute deliveries and a frantic traffic.

Darren arrived back soaked, the horse too, barely walking, and his legs and arms were trembling too from the effort, but he unharnessed her and rubbed her down whilst his own shirt and sweater froze on him. Walking to Snyder, then, with the others.

He handed their wages out with a small extra. "Merry fucking Christmas. Tomorrow is your only rest day of the year, make the most of it. If you're going home, be here early dawn on the twenty-sixth. If not, you're sacked."

They laughed and most of them packed a bag and left, only Darren and Smith stayed behind, drinking their tea quietly.

Smith counted his money. "Wanna eat somethin' decent? It's Christmas, man, fuckit. Let's go to the tavern. Drink a couple of beers."

"I don't drink."

"Whaaat?" He laughed. "Fancy boy! But you eat, right? C'mon."

He tugged at him, even if they were both dead tired, and Darren followed Smith, not having any better ideas to kill that lonely night. The first one when he didn't have a tree, didn't spend it on a lord's estate, with the others, realising that he had nobody, really. No family. That illusion there with the other servants populating his life that they were somehow family. Following that wiry man into the night, to that crowded tavern where other loners had gathered.

Smith pushed his way to a small table and pushed him down. "There. We eat, and I drink for two. How's that?"

Laughing, and Darren just sat, still cautious because he barely knew him, at all. His eyes going to him when he felt his hand on his arm.

"I ain't going to eat you. We're both alone, right? Might as well be together, ya know. Even if you're weird as fuck!"

Darren had to grin, and they pushed their money together to buy some food, spend that night in that friendship born out of misery and loneliness.

At the Hampton mansion, the festivities were full on with a dinner that could serve an army, even if only the Willoughbys had been invited, and William rose at the end, raising his glass.

"Dear family, we have an announcement to make with Francesca." He looked down at her flushed face, her eyes in tears. His arrogant smile as he addressed the table. "We are expecting a child."

That stunned silence was followed by the adults rising, raising their glasses, and Fran had to rush to her mother, lace her arms around her. Archibald just watched them, his mother in shock, and he exchanged a look with Granny, who just winked at him. Remembering her words, so he had to stifle a smile and raised his glass, like the others, congratulating them.

Lord Willoughby laughed when they had sat down. "Well, no surprise there. I mean, we knew, of course, living together, but it is a delight, nevertheless. Especially when it is your only son giving you an heir."

Archibald looked at him. *You, lying piece of shit.*

William smiled. "I am honoured, Father. We do hope it is a boy."

Fran put her hand on his arm. "We would obviously be delighted with a girl too..." Meeting his eyes, so she quieted.

William patted her hand, but his eyes were cold. "Of course, my dear. I did not mean it any other way."

"I know..." Her voice had wobbled, but she left her hand under his.

Archibald's heart iced over at the look in her eyes, but he could not do anything, conversations drifting to that child, the season starting in London soon, a couple of months, barely, and they would go there. His eyes on the window, but it was dark, he could not see outside. *He has not written... he will not write...* Feeling so bitter for the first time in that festive night, he thought he'd choke. *Maybe he's moved on, found a lover...* His voice drifted though in his mind. *I love you. Just remember this. No matter what happens, what you're told... And I love you. I will find you.*

Chapter 21

Those harsh winter months had flown by, and Lord Hampton walked to the stables to check on the horses. He had hired a new coachman in the winter, and he was doing his work, but did not have Darren's experience, nor skills. *Nor charisma...* He walked into the stable yard and James hurried to him from the hay cart.

"Milord... Good morning."

"I am here to check on Raven."

"Yes, Milord. He is in the small field, getting some fresh air. Spring is almost here, you can feel it..." He shut up, his face flaming up, and led him to the field near the pen.

Raven raised his head at them approaching, smelling Lord Hampton on the wind, so he walked to the gate, waiting. Lord Hampton petted his head, stroking that slender neck, his eyes welling up at the sight of those bent legs.

James spoke softly. "He walks, trots, and even cantered a bit now that he can go out." A small pull of his mouth to quench his mounting tears. "He won't be the same, Milord."

"I know. Deeply unfortunate." He sighed. "I shall decide what we do with him."

James kept quiet, but his heart tore a bit, almost knowing what would happen, unsure if he could survive it at all. Watching him leave when he let his tears fall, stroking that black neck, letting Raventearoom nuzzle his chest.

William turned to Edward in the tea room. "I have a good friend who would take great care of your horse. He would possibly just pull their small carriage, and spend his days in a field. I could ask him to have a look..."

Archibald turned to his father, barely containing himself. "He could be in a field here, too."

"Archibald... we cannot afford a horse who does not work. I am sorry... and if this man would take him... he would be cherished."

"Oh, yes..." William smiled. "He has kids too, they love horses. And you could sleep with your conscience clear."

"We don't know this man."

William turned to Archibald. "It is nice to see how deeply you trust me, brother."

He was visibly disappointed, but Archibald couldn't care less, his heart racing at the thought of letting Raven go.

"Father... please... please think it through."

"I am sorry. I will trust William on this. And we could go and visit him, right?"

William smiled. "Of course... I mean, he lives a bit farther away, but it could be arranged, sure. I would offer taking your horse myself, but I know how Archibald would feel about that."

Archibald had to compose himself not to lose it. "Let us just keep the horse. Father, please..."

"He is so awfully important to you? I wonder why." William waited, his eyes gleaming, and Archibald just swallowed.

"No... but it's a beautiful horse... and he has served well. He deserves to retire here."

"He is still fine to work for more modest people, like my vicar friend."

"Your friend should not sell him..." Archibald's voice died in his throat, and he turned his chair to the window, closing his eyes.

"Of course not, Archibald. What do you think? A golden retirement he shall have."

His father's voice, weak. "Take care of it, please, William?"

"As you wish. I shall have him taken away tomorrow morning, straight to my friend, and bring you the payment. I will negotiate for you, if you allow it."

"It would remove the pain of doing it myself. Thank you."

William left then, hurrying on his new mission, grinning as he skipped down the steps.

Lord Hampton walked to Archibald. "I know you are angry at me."

"Angry is not a strong enough word." His eyes went to his father. "It is Darren's horse..." He raised his hand at Edward's lips parting. "His horse, Father... you know it."

"Darren is gone. I have not received any news." He tried to put some strength in his voice, mildly annoyed, still.

"He may not be able to write."

"I cannot afford to keep that horse. He is going to a great place."

"You don't know that."

"William just told you... I am trying to get a liking to the man because he is my grandchild's father and Fran's husband. And so far, he has not proven himself wrong."

"He is the same arrogant twat he ever has been. A brute."

"Archibald..."

"Just leave me and let me grieve." *That horse, the man I love...* His eyes went to the window, to that clear grey sky showing shades of blue where spring was trying to break through.

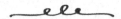

William handed Raven over to the man, who counted the money in his hands. His lips curled up. "Just bring him to a market, and sell him."

"Yes, Milord. I mean... I could get a decent price, still. Thank you for being so generous."

"Your discretion will be appreciated."

"You can count on me, Milord." He tied the alert horse to the cart, and William watched them leave, Raven neighing, tugging at the rope until the cart went into a fast trot, and he had to follow, his head high, his eyes wide.

Bye-bye, Raven. William mounted his horse and galloped back to their mansion, taking more money out of his desk, stashing it in an envelope. Back to his horse, he steered it towards the road, racing towards the Hamptons.

A couple of days later, one of those milder days when you could smell spring in the air, Darren's horse collapsed when they got back, right when he'd stopped the cart. A couple of kicks with her legs, and she was gone, that faithful mare, even if he had torn the buckles open, and taken her harness and bridle off, her eyes were wide on that clear sky. He held her head, stroking her, closing his eyes to his tears, but they rushed out, unable to stop them.

Snyder walked close, and gestured some others over. "Alright. We are feasting today, boys."

Darren looked up at him, the words not making any sense when he saw him walk away, and come back with a hatchet and a knife.

Darren stood, his anger flaring up above that horror birthing in his chest, taking his breath. "What... what are you doing?"

"Cutting her up, fancy boy. She's still fresh, that's good meat. You can eat your fill too." Watching him blanch. He barked a laugh. "Just where do ya think my name comes from?"

Laughter around him, but Darren barely heard it, his head swimming.

Somebody shoved him in the back. "Step to the side. You're in the way."

He stumbled, but caught himself and looked at Snyder, his voice shaking with that wrath. "Don't you dare touch her!"

Snyder snickered. "I ain't got time for your bullshit."

He glanced at some of the men, and they grabbed Darren, dragging him away as Snyder swung the hatchet into her neck. Darren lost it at this moment, throwing up, hard, as they let him collapse to his knees.

"Pussy. Coward." Laughter. The sickening sound of metal meeting flesh.

Darren scrambled to his feet, blind with his panic, his tears, and rushed out of the yard, down the street, his vision blurred, heaving until he had to stop, his legs not carrying him anymore. He slid down a wall, sobbing, that horror opening the floodgates of months of misery and pain.

Unable to gage how long he had stayed there, sitting against that wall in a daze, the thought of going into that yard almost impossible. Archibald's brown eyes floating into his exhausted, grieving mind. *In the deepest moments of despair... hold on to that thought... I will find a way for us to be together... I trust you blind...* His lips trembled, but he breathed in deep, holding on to the thought that Archibald would fulfil that promise. That hard light seeping into his eyes. *Keep going. Do not give up.* He pushed himself up from that frozen ground and walked back, the streets dark, only the fire and some torches burning in their yard. The smell of blood and roasted meat pervading everything. The men silenced when he walked in, not even looking at them, his arms crossed tight on that aching stomach.

Smith caught his arm gently. "Just eat, Turner. She ain't coming back, but you need your strength..."

He wrenched his arm out, looking at him, his eyes like murder. "No. Forget it. Fuck you. And fuck all of you, fucking monsters!" The look in his eyes killing their laughter.

He turned to Snyder's voice. "Ain't no big deal, right? Tomorrow is market day, I'll get ya a new horse. No need to be all upset, fancy boy." He laughed, unafraid, grinning then.

Darren just turned and climbed upstairs, avoiding looking at her empty place. He curled up, shaking, his nerves on edge with that abysmal hunger he had been nursing for days, but there was no way he would eat her flesh, or any horse's flesh. *New horse...* almost crying at the thought.

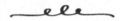

Next day, Darren had stayed behind as he had no horse, and a couple of other men too, as they were new, so he decided to clean the stalls as best as he could with that small quantity of straw. Taking extra care of that place where the new horse would be, near the wall where it was a bit bigger than the others. He had chosen that place and Snyder just barked a laugh at it, letting him do what he wanted.

They walked to the yard when they heard the hooves close, watching those horses being led in, three bays in the front and a black one in the back. The bays looked almost in good shape, but Darren had seen at a glance that one's back was already sinking, one's legs were swollen and the third one was already thin, his ribs showing.

He could not get a proper look at the black one when Snyder gave them a grin. "The three bays go to Karl, Wilson, and Sam." He looked at Darren. "You have a less good one, but hey, you are a wonder boy, you will make it right." Laughing already as he had bought the horse a misery, on purpose, to make Darren's life hell.

The others took the bays away, and the black horse was led forward by a man. His head high, he sniffed the air, and Darren stood, frozen, his blood drumming in his ears. That moment when the animal knew, breathing his scent in on the wind, his eyes going to that man, in shock. Trying to understand what he was seeing because it was impossible. That shock broken by the horse's shrill neigh, that desperate joy, prancing a bit on those bent, stiff legs, his muscles almost melted in that long recovery.

Raven. Raven... Darren walked to him, dazed, reaching his hand out, oblivious to the looks, to Snyder's eyes, reaching to that soft nuzzle, the horse leaning into his touch, pushing his head into his chest as Darren's arms went around it, to his neck. Stroking, his tears blurring his vision, trying to find the horse in that ruined body. *How... How...* He went to hug him then, letting the horse nibble his neck, his back.

Snickers around him. "Love at first sight, Turner."

"Wow... maybe you should try horse cock?" Laughter.

Darren composed himself, knowing how dangerous this was, to give away anything, but he also knew that he did not understand how the horse got here, how he got ruined, wiping at his tears which kept spilling when he saw his injuries, his legs.

Snyder stepped close. "What a crybaby. Now, stop being a woman, or I'll give you another one. Maybe I should if you're this much of a sissy."

Darren looked at him, holding the lead rope. "No."

His lips curled up. "Feisty fuck. I do what I want. Tell me why I should not give this horse straight to another guy? I do what I want here."

"Because I'm buying him from you."

Snyder's breath caught before he burst out laughing. "You... what?" Looking into those hard blue eyes. "Buy? With what?"

Darren almost lost his assurance, but then he just shrugged. "Name your price, and you can deduct it from my wage. Every day."

Snyder scoffed, conscious of the others listening. "You can't afford him."

"You said you buy 'em cheap." Using his words, he was daring him, standing with that horse who had stood behind his back. Darren was ready to fight at this stage, die if he had to.

Snyder gave him his lopsided grin. "You fucker. I buy 'em cheap, but I ain't selling 'em cheap. He's gonna die before you pay him off, but you're a crazy bastard, and it's a deal for me. But we are not sealing it here. Tie him up, and come to my room."

Darren breathed out and led Raven to that place which he had prepared. Still in disbelief, he stroked his neck and hooked the rope to his halter.

Watching his puzzled eyes. "I know... this is not the lord's stables..." Raven just pushed his head into his chest, then waited, but Darren just stroked him. "I will be back, with food..."

Hoping he would manage to agree with Snyder, crossing the yard to his room, knocking.

The door opened and he walked in, a single table there, with a bed in the corner, the fireplace lit. His gaze settled on Snyder who had walked close.

"This is the price..." Smiling at his wide eyes. "Yeah... not cheap... still up for it? Your little madness?"

Darren swallowed, trying to figure out how many months, maybe years, it would mean to work it off. "Yes."

Snyder stepped closer. "'Tis the money only... I need a little extra to seal this deal..."

Darren frowned. "What?"

"See... I just happen to know why you showed up here with your face broken in..."

Darren's eyes went wide, but he didn't say anything, waiting.

"Yes... so I also happen to know what you are into... and let's just say that if you do me a little favour, I may just seal that deal with you, and let you buy that horse with your sweat. Ah, and keep my mouth shut about what you are..."

Darren barely had a voice. "What favour?"

Snyder reached up to his face and placed his palm on his cheek. "Tsk... don't step away..."

Darren froze, his lips parting.

"Good boy... see, I figure, you are anyway into sucking cocks, right? I ain't into fuckin' asses, but I'll take a good blowjob any day of the week... so? How does this sound? Our deal for your little favour."

There were many things Darren wanted to do. Swat his hand away, punch his nose in, and leave. Bang the door shut and leave. Never to look back. None of these being an option with Raven tied in those stables of death. Knowing that the deal was also impossible, if the horse did not die first, he would. *But at least, we die together.* Shutting everything out of his mind because it would have meant madness to think of Archibald, their love, in that deepest moment of despair.

He breathed, steeling his voice. "I need it in writing first. Our little deal. Two papers. One you keep, and one for me."

Snyder scoffed. "That is how much you trust me?"

"I don't trust you at all."

He smiled, taking his hand away. "Fine."

Walking to a small desk, he wrote two small pieces of papers, and they signed. He gave one to Darren, which he put in the pocket of his pants.

Snyder put his hand on his shoulder, pushing a bit. "On your knees."

Darren just obeyed, trying not to think, clinging to that single piece of paper warming his skin. He looked up at Snyder when he felt his fingers clench in his hair, tilting his head back.

"If you bite me, the horse is killed first in front of you, then I'll have the men go through you before we pick you apart."

"We have a deal."

"Good to know." His other hand slid down to Darren's jaw, his thumb pushing into his mouth. "Open wide..."

He did, closing his eyes.

Later, he stumbled outside and shoved his fingers down his throat, throwing up near the well. Washing then, with that hard brush he had, scrubbing his skin, rinsing his mouth. Drinking a full mug of that scalding tea, his hands trembling. Holding back his sobs, steeling his heart, all his being not to lose it. But he took the paper out, reading it in that dim glow of the fire. It was there, and he would make sure that scumbag honoured every letter of it.

He went to the stables and gave a generous lump of hay to Raven, the horse famished, eating with a grateful light in his eyes. He neighed softly when Darren walked towards the ladder, but he climbed, just to have the men sneer at him.

"You should not sleep here with us."

"You think we don't know whatchya did there?"

"Fuck off, molly!"

He froze, meeting their eyes, but Karl just spat at him. "Fuck off, will ya?"

Darren just turned and scooped his bag up, leaving whilst they were throwing whatever they could find at him. He scrambled down, a bit lost at where he could sleep, but then, Raven neighed softly and he hooked his bag up on the wall, lying down at the horse's feet in the straw. It was almost warmer than in that dark attic, and he put his hands behind his head, watching him eat, his head close to his head. Raven nudged him with his nose, his eyes smiling, and Darren's eyes drifted to his legs. He smoothed his hand on the left one, knowing what the horse had, but he was confident he could bandage them so they held better, even if his heart tore at seeing them bent at the knees. Unsure if it would work out, at all, that deal, unsure how long they would live, if Raven could pull at all, even if he had trained him to pull young, Raven had only been ridden for the past nine years. Darren was only sure of one thing. That the price he had paid for that deal was worth it. Even if he wanted to throw up just at the thought of those few minutes, even if he felt ashamed beyond belief, he had his mind set on that single goal. Buy him off. Lead him out of that yard. The two of them, walking towards a better life.

Chapter 22

Archibald sat up in bed, that soft early spring sunshine trying to sift through his curtains. He gingerly pulled his legs up with his hands, turning to let them hang off the bed, touch the floor. Breathing out as his feet hit the carpet. Sitting in that dread. Knowing his strength was there, his muscles, as he could trot, his feet in the stirrups, his legs not tied down anymore. *I could stand... maybe I can stand.* His eyes lost a bit on his thoughts. *What if I fall? So what? Nothing... I'll just say I fell out of bed.* Breathing out, his eyes on the rising sun. That sinking feeling in his chest which raced down to his stomach, kicking it. *I miss you... so much...* Clenching his jaw, that determined light invading his brown eyes. *Fuck. Fuck all this.* Breathing out, he reached for the chair near the bed, and pulled it close. Putting his left hand on it, he pushed off the bed with his right hand, letting his weight go on his legs, his eyes wide when they didn't collapse, but he made sure they were as stiff as possible, holding the chair with his trembling hand as he slid on the ground. Standing. Trembling, still a bit wobbly, but he was standing, his heart almost leaping out at that shock. Crying as his right hand went to his mouth. *I'm standing... oh God... you would be so proud... so fucking proud...* Closing his eyes at how he had wanted to share this moment, stand with his help, stand in his arms, reach up to kiss him. That despair taking his strength, his legs wiped, but he had sat back with a racing heart before they would give. *I'm standing today... tomorrow, one step... and then another... until I can walk out of here.*

He was pushed to breakfast later, and his father smiled at him. "Had a good night?"

"Yes, thank you, Father. I am riding out straight after breakfast."

Edward watched him pile food on his plate, waving the servant away. A small joy in him seeing his son's flesh filling up, his body straighter in his chair, his moves more focused.

Archibald looked at his mother at her voice. "I do miss Fran... she used to brighten up breakfast..." Looking at him pointedly, but he just ate, unfazed. She sighed. "Ah... there is no point... you are always so serious, Archibald. Life is great. Next week, we are moving back to London. About time too! The ball season is starting. We need to get there fast to sort out your wardrobe, even if you are going to be confined to your chair, you should look decent. I am having tickets bought on the train to..."

"Mother, I am taking my carriage, thank you."

"What? Edward!"

Lord Hampton wiped his mouth. "Oh... the horses in London? You are sure?"

"Yes. I am positive."

His mother huffed. "They are mismatched... How will that look in the park? Or in town? We have the bays there..."

Archibald looked at her. "I am taking my carriage and my horses. I intent to ride too there, and Dandy is the only horse I trust. He knows me." A small warmth there, knowing that he loved that horse so much, nothing could stop him from taking him and his friend.

"Well, you are a disappointment, Archibald."

"As usual, mother. Nothing new. Now, if you will excuse me, I shall be getting ready for my ride."

His father smiled. "Enjoy! The weather is glorious today."

"I wish you could come too." Throwing that tiny dart in, watching his face fall.

"Well, now is not the time to buy a horse, we are leaving..."

"I know, Father. Forgive me for tearing old wounds up." He shot him a look and waved his valet over to roll him to his room.

Lady Hampton looked at her husband. "What is taking him? He is insufferable."

"He is alive..."

She threw her napkin on the table. "Sometimes, I wonder if this was the better option."

His eyes went wide, but she had already stood, storming out with her head high.

Darren woke with the sun, Raven lying by his side, their heads close on the straw. He stroked that half-asleep horse, almost like in a dream, when his shivering body and aching throat reminded him that it was indeed reality, the cold, dawn air seeping in through that gaping door.

He sat up, raking his hair, letting the horse slumber, and went to wash before the others woke. He looked around to search for something he could use for bandages, but there was nothing, that yard almost bare, save for the necessities, so he stoked that fire up in the barrel, putting logs on it. Fired up the stove under the tea, not even knowing why, because he shouldn't have cared about them at all, those men. He went to his bag, and fished his old shirt out, almost in tatters. *This will do...* bringing them down to three better shirts... unsure if he could ever buy one, but he sat, and took his knife to cut it up in long stripes.

Raising his eyes when Snyder stepped out of his room, stopping a bit when he saw him, but then he made his way there with his crooked smile. A cool calm in Darren, somehow, and he just went back to cutting up his shirt, sliding the knife all the way from the bottom to the top.

"Whatchya doing, you, crazy bastard?" Laughing as he scooped a mug of tea out.

"Bandages."

"For your head?" He laughed, sipping his tea.

"For the horse's legs. They've been injured."

"Know that. That's why I got 'im cheap... until I sold him to a madman for triple the price." He laughed and stood close, leaning against a pillar holding the roof.

"That's right. How clever of you."

He scoffed. "Right... you better work your ass off today... cos you ain't gonna pay him off if you slack around."

"Of course." Darren had finished, smoothing those pieces of fabric out, a small hope that they would be enough if he washed them every day after work.

Meeting Snyder's eyes when he had grabbed his chin and yanked his head up. "Watch it... Having had my cock in your mouth does not give you privileges." Those dark eyes bore into him, but Darren just held his gaze, cold.

"Indeed?" He stood and tore his chin out of Snyder's hand. "Being my boss doesn't give you the right to touch me." His eyes flashed, that growing anger bringing up old shades of his personality to the light. Long forgotten ones, hiding in the depths of his soul. Clawing to the light.

Snyder scoffed, but he had seen those dark shadows whirl into his blue eyes. "Watch your mouth."

Darren put his knife away, the bandages smoothed on his arm. "I need to work. Don't have time for your bullshit."

He didn't even wait for an answer, walking away, his old obedient self kicking at him. But Snyder was no lord. Still, his heart leaped in his chest, but Snyder didn't follow, didn't grab him by the neck, so he went and crouched down to Raven's front legs, bandaging them with the stripes. Stroking his nose when he sniffed at him, looking for food then, his questioning eyes back at him.

Darren smiled thinly. "No food in the morning, pal... Only after work."

He had finished and went to give him to drink, as much as he could, watching the men amble to their tea, some of them just casting a glance at him, but Darren was in a different world, his eyes dark with that hard light in them. He harnessed Raven, the horse nibbling at the straps, puzzled when the bridle went on him with the blinders.

Darren patted his neck. "Yeah... you know this... we'll see how much you remember..."

Smith walked to him, holding his mug to him. "Here... I figured you could use one before you leave."

Darren took it, but he was cautious, that tiny hate seeping into his eyes.

Smith sipped his tea. "I ain't no enemy, Turner."

Darren shrugged, but at least Smith had kept quiet the night before, didn't pelt him with anything. "Whatever..."

Smith gestured to the horse. "'Tis horse... worth it?"

Darren smiled. "Yes. Worth anything."

Smith patted his back. "Just watch yourself."

Darren sipped his tea, beyond any fear, then went to get his assignments from Snyder.

Reaching his palm out and he put them in it, grinning. "I wonder if you'll manage finishing your day with that new horse. Looks fancy for a cart..."

Darren just took them and left; his heart tight. *So many...* He counted them and there were more than usual, a mild worry in him as he didn't know how Raven would react. Not just to the cart and the pulling, but the city, this gentle colt of the countryside, never torn out of those lush fields, and endless blue sky. That grey sky above them, thick with smoke, dust and fumes. They made the throat dry and seeped into the lungs, that dry cough always there now, even if winter was moving away, Darren could not get rid of it. Wiping his brows when a bout of cough ended, and he spat in the straw, breathing in deep then to draw some air into his lungs, his mind on Archibald, on how he had struggled, that mild worry in him that he might be sick, maybe bedridden too... He had to swallow those mounting tears, try not to think of him when he had to make sure Raven worked, leading that wide-eyed, cautious horse outside, putting him in front of the cart. He tied him in, soothing, but Raven seemed just a bit worried, sniffing the wood of the beams, licking the chains. His eyes on the other horses then, reaching his neck out to get a sniff, soft neighs.

Darren took his bridle tight. "Come, Raven, let's go." Pulling, and the horse moved, the cart jolting, and the rattle made Raven jump forward, surprised at the noise, the pull on his body. Tearing at Darren's hand as he struggled to hold him back, wedging his back against his chest. "Whooaaa! Easy, boy..."

Laughter around him, Snyder's voice. "Great start... You walk all day, Turner? Will be a treat... Finish your missions or I'll skin you and your fancy horse!" Howling after him, but Darren had led Raven out on the street, the cart jolting on those uneven cobblestones, and he had to dig his heels in, hold the horse tight as they struggled.

Raven got it though, his love for his human stronger than his fear, some memories pouring in on those times when he had learnt to pull, so he slowed, pulling as best as he could, his eyes darting to the other carts, cabs, carriages as the traffic got denser. His mind drenched in panic, but he felt Darren's hand, breathed him in as his nose went into his back, his neck, bathing in his voice. *Calm down, easy, easy...* Breathing out, like a dragon, snorting, his head high, tugging on him, still, when they passed a noisier street, people watching that prancing horse and that man latched on his bridle, sweat pouring down his body, drenching his shirt.

Darren stopped him after a while in a quiet street, utterly drained, letting the horse breathe, calm down. He stroked his soaked head. "Uh... I am so sorry... so sorry, boy... but we have no choice, alright?" Panting, his eyes on the sky, time rushing, and they hadn't even gotten to the first address. He breathed out, hard, and tugged the horse forward, all the way to the mill.

The miller was watching the street already, his hands in the air when Darren turned the cart into his yard. "Thank fuck! You're late! What's this horse?"

Darren gathered his breath. "He's new..."

"Fuck this, man! Get packing!"

Darren loaded the cart with the other men, mildly worried again at the load, even if Raven was stronger than that skeletal mare, he had never pulled such a weight. He grabbed his bridle and clacked his tongue, but the cart wouldn't budge, even when the horse pulled, and it confused Raven, so he danced a bit in his harness, panicked a bit, and Darren had to soothe him.

"It's ok, just pull..." Almost begging, but the horse just shook his head, his neck, pacing in one place, unable to figure out what he should be doing.

The miller and his men shook their head and went behind the cart, pushing hard. It went into the horse and Raven kicked at it, panicked, bolting then to free himself, and the cart moved, rolling with such a rattle that it sent Raven into a flight, but he could not run, tied to that heavy cart, so he started thrashing around, mad.

Darren held tight, soothing, in tears. "Easy, easy, Raven, please, please... Easy, boy... Woaaa...woaaaa... "

The gate approaching fast with that busy street behind it, but his voice somehow got through that panicked mind, and Raven calmed, his eyes still wide, snorting, but he was just prancing, pulling too, his ears darting around. Darren just led him until he calmed, chewing on the bit, foam splattering from his mouth, frothing on his body where the harness was rubbing his sweat. That fatigue there too, so he gave up a bit, his wild eyes on his human.

Darren walked with him to the bakery where they had to unload, and Raven calmed a bit, eating a lump of hay, getting some appreciative look from the men there, despite his legs.

Darren took the reins then, smoothing his palm down the horse's body, his ears pricked towards the back when he sat on the bench, holding the reins.

He clacked his tongue, just as he had done when he had trained him, hoping he would remember, somehow. "Go, Raven. Come on." And the horse moved, bolting still, but Darren held him back, gently, soothing, and they set off, the horse still rushing a bit, still tugging at the cart when he got scared, and Darren had to jump down more than once on busy streets to rush and hold him.

No time to stop, a gruelling day when the last address got delivered almost into the night. Raven's eyes wide on the lamps, the scarce light, jolting at rushing cabs into the night, people spilling with roaring laughter from houses, theatres, or pubs, drunk, dragging some music behind them. A foreign world.

They arrived back to the yard way after the others, and Darren jumped down from the bench, his hands on his knees, panting, the night chill sticking his icy shirt to his body. Just trying to catch his breath next to that steaming horse, his flanks rising with his fear, his eyes wide on the dark.

He jolted at a hand landing on his back, straightening. Meeting Snyder's mocking smile in that semi-dark yard. "Back at last? I thought you died."

Darren just breathed out and handed him his papers.

"Nice... all done? I bet it was some day!" He scoffed, but counted some coins into his palm. "First payment taken off, ya know? Better write it down somewhere for yaself, ya know, as ya don't trust me..." He barked a laugh, grinning.

Darren just pinched his lips, pocketing that nothing money. A tiny despair there at where this was all going, watching that exhausted horse, almost asleep.

Snyder slammed his hand on his shoulder. "Second thoughts?"

Darren looked at him. "No."

He laughed and left him, banging his door shut.

Darren almost collapsed right there, but he wobbled to Raven and took him to the stables. He took his harness and bridle off, rubbing him clean and dry, brushing that beautiful coat which had not lost its shine yet. He went for the hay then, knowing that Snyder had also taken off the price of the extra portion. He took the bandages off, probing his legs, a bit relieved that they seemed fine. He stashed a bit more straw in the stall too, and went to the well, stripping that soaked shirt which he washed out, the bandages too, laying them out to dry. His stomach grumbled, revolted that it was so late and it hadn't seen food, so he walked to the teapot and filled his mug. Ambling to his bag where he had his bread, he tore a good piece off and ate it, washing it down with the tea. It swelled in his stomach and gave that false sensation that he had eaten his full, even if at that moment, it seemed to trick him, but he didn't eat more, knowing he only had that bread for the whole week. His muscles trembling, but there was nothing to be done about it, so he drank another mug of tea, and went to Raven's stall, lying down near the horse munching his hay.

His eyes on him, he stroked that soft nose. "At least, you get to eat some..."

Raven nuzzled him, munching, that sweet scent of the hay laced with his breath, and Darren pulled that rag of a blanket on his shoulders, and closed his eyes, letting that deep sleep take him, breathing him in, his heart glowing.

Their luggage ready, Lady Hampton got taken to the train station to join Fran and the Willoughbys on the way back to London.

Archibald was a bit relieved that she was out of the way as he got pushed to his carriage, James waiting too, sitting with the coachman. Archibald didn't care about that older man, averting his eyes not to even see that bench where he only wanted to see Darren, still seeing him somehow, hearing his voice. He breathed against those mounting tears, refusing to give up, even if no news had come, as if Darren had disappeared off the earth. This love found where it wasn't supposed to exist, at all, driving him crazy. Even he had thought of forgetting him, moving on, it was not possible, his absence magnifying his love, that love growing, filling his chest to bursting with the ache of not having him, not seeing him, at all. That soft despair at knowing he existed somewhere in the world, living a life without him. He let them put him inside, feeling James climb too, the carriage jolting, leaving that huge mansion the servants were closing up for the season. *Fucking madness... these huge houses filled with useless furniture...* He had snapped once at dinner, questioning this, and William had laughed at him, and his parents too, save for his father, who had just shot him a desperate look. He leant his head against the window, watching those landscapes he so loved now. Remembering when he had arrived, convinced he would die, and now, he was alive. *For what...* his absence burning him alive.

Archibald arrived much later than the family; the trip taking longer, and let James settle the horses in those city stables, knowing he had taken their freedom for a short while, but hoping that somehow they would help him in his quest. He then asked his valet to push him to his father's office. Knocking.

"Come in."

His valet pushed him in and left him, closing the door. Lord Hampton rose and walked to him with a wide smile. "Archibald! Not too tired, I hope?"

"No, all is fine... We need to talk, Father."

"Oh, alright..." He sat to face him, waiting. Marvelling at that determined light in his eyes, at how his body had filled up.

"I need some money from you to spend as I see fit."

"Of course... I mean, you should have had an allowance, truly. It's just that... you were not too active, so..."

"It's not necessary to explain. I know."

"I will give you an allowance. I am beyond thrilled that you would like to do some things on your own." He rose and walked to his desk, taking the money out, and he put the bills in an envelope, handing it to Archibald then. "A generous amount, so you start doing young man stuff." He winked, but Archibald just took the envelope, unfazed.

"Thank you, Father. I hope you don't mind if I run some errands on my own."

"Not at all."

Archibald's heart softened at that defeated look in his eyes, wondering why he got a bit distant with him, why he could not forgive selling that horse. *This is father... he just wants the best...* He sighed, taming his vengeful heart. "Forgive me if I have been distant lately..."

"A lot happened which justifies it."

I am missing him, father. I love him. I want to find him... "Indeed... I hope we can do some things together." Wondering why his words had frozen in his mouth, that loneliness almost eating him up alive when he wanted to trust him. *Maybe I should... maybe he knows...* But he wasn't sure, so he just smiled at his father's voice filled with joy.

"Of course! I would be delighted."

"Let us talk then tomorrow. I need to go out in the morning, but we could go to the park in the afternoon."

"Wonderful!"

Archibald let him push him out to lunch, his mind on the next day.

Next day, when he asked to be driven to an address further, the horses a bit alert in that thick traffic, missing their driver, the coachman's hands harsher, tugging at their mouths. Archibald had taken his valet, but asked him to step out when he had pushed him into a small office at the bottom of a building. Waiting to be received, he watched that thick wooden door open, a man stepping out, looking at him.

"What can I do for you?"

"I am Lord Archibald Hampton and I would like to hire you."

The man's eyebrows shot up, but he gestured him in and Archibald just waved at him. "Push me in, please."

He did and faced him then, sitting behind a small mahogany desk, the room filled with shelves of dusty books. His small dark eyes under his dark hair, he watched Archibald and took a small notebook out.

Archibald looked at him. "I need you to find a man... my former coachman. He left and is allegedly in London. Or, at least, that is the last information I have."

"Name?"

"Darren Turner."

The man scoffed. "There might be hundreds of Darren Turners in London."

"Tall, blue eyes, black hair." He paused, thinking that he didn't know Darren's age, at all. Swallowing. "Maybe around thirty of age, a bit more... He doesn't have that rough exterior that might come with low-class origins."

The man grinned. "What is that supposed to mean?"

"You know what it means." His eyes hard, that delicate face laced with anger.

"I mean, if you think that will help me... still too vague. A guy with this description and his name, might be still a lot around... any idea what he is doing?"

"He will be around horses..."

The man laughed, hard. "Oh, man... sorry, Milord, but... I mean you have seen London, right?" He laughed, and Archibald's heart sank. Horses were everywhere... crowding the streets.

"Driving, possibly. Maybe in somebody's service... or driving a cab..."

"That is the lowest I should go? Cab driver?"

Archibald's heart sank. "What do you mean?"

"I mean that where should I look? Middle-class families? He had money to buy horses for a cab? One horse? Enough to rent one when he arrived? Or should I look lower? London is big, and there are layers to his profession... how low should I go?"

"He... he was highly ranked with us... stable master, so..."

"Alright. I will look first in richer and middle-class families, ask around. Then I will move to cabbies... that might take some time... then we talk, and I go lower if need be..." He shot him a look. "I assume you have enough money?"

"Yes, enough. And I can always get more."

"He's that important, aye?" He grinned at him.

Archibald composed his face. "We want to hire him back. It was a mistake to let him go."

"That's what they always say..." He had kept his grin, but handed Archibald a paper he had torn out of his notebook. "My rates. Half ahead for my searches, then we talk."

Archibald didn't flinch, even if it was expensive, and paid him out of his envelope.

He pocketed the bills, smiling. "I am not cheap, but I might find your man."

"I appreciate it."

"Talk to you soon, lordling."

"It's Lord Hampton."

"Sure thing, Lord Hampton." He sneered and pushed him out, fetching the valet then.

Archibald watched the streets rush by, his heart beating faster at the thought of having him somewhere, maybe close. His eyes trying to check the cab drivers' faces out in that blur when one of them rushed by, trying to see the other coachmen as they passed them, and it was madness, he knew, but he couldn't help himself. *And if that detective finds him... then what? Do I even want to know? Does he even care about me still?*

Chapter 23

A week had passed since Raven had been led into that dire yard, and every day he got better, pulling those heavy carts with more assurance, his head still high at some of the noises on the city streets, but the heavy work and scarcer food had sapped that fire he had in him, all his energies focused on working. Pulling with a heavy breath, same as his human when he unloaded and loaded those heavy cargos, breathing hard whilst the horse rested a bit between two fares. Darren had sacrificed another one of his shirts to bandage his hind legs too, to protect them somewhat from that gruelling strain, his other two shirts greyed over, but at least he could shed his jacket, the weather warmer, the work not letting his body feel that slight cold still lingering in the air on that gentle spring breeze.

He had stopped to eat though after a delivery to a market, letting the horse rest a bit, just standing next to him, feeding him small pieces of his bread, his heart tight. Turning to a voice behind him.

"Hello... does your horse need a bit of hay? He looks tired a bit." A young man, his gentle eyes on them, on that panting horse.

Darren patted Raven on the neck. "Yeah... he could use some..."

"I have some I could share. Brought it for mine, but they won't eat it all." Gesturing at two solid horses tied to a cart, waiting behind a stall of fruits and vegetables.

"Sure. I would be grateful."

He just smiled and left, coming back with a huge forkful of hay which he lumped in front of Raven, watching the horse dive into it. Darren's eyes welled up, but he just patted Raven's neck, avoiding that man's eyes.

"Not your horse, right?"

He lifted his eyes. "No... not yet..."

"I figured. You don't look the type who would let him starve." Smiling, he raised his hand. "Hold on. I might have something for you too." He walked away and rummaged in a crate, walking back then with a few apples. "You look just as famished as your horse... take these. It's not much but I won't sell these... folks here don't like them damaged... I mean they are not rotten, just got some scratches to the skin." He rolled his eyes and gave four large apples to Darren. "Don't give them to your horse..." Laughing.

Darren took them, moved. "Thank you..."

"It's nothing... you come here often?"

"When I have to deliver... some days... I don't know when though..."

"Doesn't matter. When you see me, just come over. Rest here, I'll have hay for your horse and something decent for you to eat too."

"I am not sure what to say... I am eternally grateful already..."

"Your speech is nicer than what a simple delivery driver's should be. Seen better days?"

Darren looked away, pained. "Yes..."

"So, why stay where you are? Just leave. I could help you find a better place to work at."

Darren stroked Raven's neck. "I can't leave him... I need to pay him off..."

"Oh... well, it's just a horse?"

He smiled. "No... it's not just a horse."

The young man just shook his head. "I mean... you know it better than I do, I guess... but my offer still stands."

"And I'll gladly accept it... but I would like to lend you a hand then. You know... if you need loading or packing."

He extended his hand with a wide smile. "Deal. I'm Jonathan."

"Darren."

"I'll see you around, Darren." He waved and left back to his stall with a smile.

Darren waited until Raven had eaten it all, even if it was making him a bit late for his other deliveries, the horse worked better with the food and he ate one apple, stashing the others away for later, feeling a bit better too. Driving to his next address, the sun warmer, watching all those hurrying carriages and barouches, their tops down, well-off families back to the city populating the streets, and it brought up memories he would have wanted to forget, those brown eyes swimming in his mind, his smile, his hair in the wind when they were racing on those winding roads. Wondering where Archibald could be, what he could be doing, whether he was still thinking of him. Even if he remembered his words, his life of misery had sapped his confidence away, the sight of those well-born youngsters in their barouches making his heart clench, tight. Why would Archibald bother, at all? *Just get on with your life... marry one of these young ladies... forget me... Maybe you have forgotten...* He swallowed, bitter, trying to reason himself that he was wrong, but he could not forget him, those few days spent near the sea when they had loved each other, madly. That hardened heart spitting at his gentle soul. *Forget him. Forget it. I love him. I still love him.*

William and Fran came to visit next day, the shopping for the balls ongoing with her mother, so she spent more time with her than at home, even if home was still just the Willoughby house, William being reluctant to find his own one when his parents' was huge.

Sipping tea, conversations drifted to the next day's picnic in the park, Lady Hampton beyond excited because it also meant Fran could show her growing belly around, strolling on William's arm. Her eyes darting to Archibald sitting near the window, nursing his cold cup of tea, his eyes on the trees growing near the house.

William followed her gaze and smiled. "Ah! A splendid occasion to introduce you to my cousin, dear Archibald."

Archibald looked at him, a barely veiled contempt in his eyes. "I am not going, but thank you for your efforts."

His mother was beyond herself. "Of course you are going! Nonsense! My dear William... please reason with him. I am just about done."

William stepped to Archibald and grabbed his chair. "Let us go somewhere quiet, and talk a bit." He started pushing him out, ignoring Archibald's seething voice.

"Stop pushing me! At once!"

He leant close, pushing him on the landing, swinging the chair to face that huge flight of stairs in that empty staircase. "Stop shouting..."

Archibald's eyes went wide, his feet facing the stairs, feeling William lean down to him, holding the chair, his lips close to his ear. "Have you calmed down? Now... You will come with us tomorrow at that little picnic, and walk a bit with my delightful cousin. Katie is beautiful, smart... a true Willoughby... and much as I hate to picture her in bed with you... I would prefer that than imagining you and my bastard brother frolicking around." Archibald's breath caught, but he didn't turn, hearing his smile in his voice. "Surprised? You should not be, knowing me. Now, I can keep my mouth shut, of course. If you are a bit more agreeable and less of a pest... otherwise I might just let your chair go, and watch you fall down the stairs. An unfortunate accident, n'est-ce-pas? Knowing how you brood all the time, one could even think you wanted to end it..."

Archibald turned his head at his words, breathing hard, watching him straighten with his smile.

"Shall we go back? Tell your good mother how delighted you are to join us and meet Katie."

Archibald gripped the armrests. "You... fucking monster."

William laughed. "You have no idea... I shall take the compliment." He turned the chair and leant on it, tilting it back a bit, his hands curling on the armrests. Leaning close to Archibald to meet his eyes. "I am saving your family's reputation, your father from ruin, and you... You should be grateful..." The chair swung a bit, and Archibald didn't even dare breathe, that void looming behind him. William snapped the chair back, turning it towards the door. "What great luck, right, to have me?"

He chuckled and pushed him back, all smiles. "Archibald changed his mind. I just needed a few private moments to convince him of Katie's charms. Nothing suitable for ladies' ears, I am afraid."

Archibald met his father's puzzled eyes, utterly lost, his heart drumming.

His mother rushed to hug William. "My dear son! I knew he would listen to you!"

"Oh, he does indeed. And he will." Squeezing Archibald's shoulder, that mild warning in his touch, and Archibald just leant back, feeling so defeated he thought he could not breathe.

That picnic under a glorious spring sun when he watched Katie Willoughby walk to them with her parents, her dark hair in a beautiful hairstyle, her lavender dress, and gloves highlighting her light grey eyes. She was pretty, and she knew it, holding her head high, bowing when she had arrived in front of him, that hint of a mocking smile on her lips, almost like William's.

"Nice meeting you, Archibald. William had only praise for you, and I can see why."

"I... likewise. Nice meeting you."

"Just Katie. I do not wish for formalities between us. After all, we are family already." She smiled wide, and looked at a servant. "Be good enough to push Lord Hampton. We shall have a stroll." He bowed, and she walked next to Archibald, her large dress swinging against the chair. "So, I heard from William you are looking at getting married soon?"

Archibald looked at her, his heart dropping in his stomach. "Uh... No, not really..."

"The season is here, and you know it as well as I do that we have been introduced for a reason. I could have my pick of suitors, and frankly do not wish for an invalid husband, but you have enough fortune to be considered, and William is already married to your sister. This makes it easier as we would essentially share the same wealth on both sides. I could do with you being in a chair, if you can fulfil your marital duties and make me children."

Archibald's face flamed up from shame and anger. "It is highly inappropriate to talk about such matters when we barely know each other."

Her lips curled up. "William said you were a bit on the aggressive side. No matter. I will assume you can have children then. Not that it matters. Children can be arranged any other way."

Archibald raised his hand, stopping his valet. "Enough."

She looked at him. "I beg your pardon?"

"Enough. Enough of this talk. I do not intend to marry you, nor court you for that matter. We have met, and it is clear we are not compatible."

"Do not be so hasty. This is hardly our decision anyway." Her gaze drifted back to their parents in a big discussion and Archibald followed her gaze, swallowing his despair, that mad anger which he could not show to her. "So, shall we walk a bit more? I mean, I'll walk."

He just nodded, signalling to the valet to push, drained, his mind racing with his rising panic.

A couple of days later, Snyder walked to Darren after he'd arrived back from work. "I don't give a shit about you..."

Darren grinned, loosening Raven's tack. "Good to know."

"Let me finish, asshole." He grabbed his shoulder and made Darren turn to face him. "Face me when I'm talking to you, dammit."

Darren waited, fighting the urge to swat his hand away, but Snyder just removed it, his voice low. "I don't give a shit about you... but I don't give a shit about lords and fancy folks more..."

Darren crossed his arms, vaguely annoyed. "So? What's that supposed to mean?"

"Means a fancy pants showed up today looking for you."

Darren's face fell, that mad hope flaming up too in his chest. "Who?"

"Fuck knows. Ya think he left a name? On horseback. Your hair and eyes, too, same colour. Young though. I thought I drank too much, still hallucinating."

William... Darren blanched. "What... what did he want?"

"Nothing... asking if you worked here..." His lips curled up. "Thought he could trick old Snyder but I ain't helping any fancy ass rich guy storming into my yard find what they looking for..." He gave Darren his lopsided grin. "Your lover?"

Darren shuddered. "No..."

"But you know him?"

"Yes... from back when..."

"Fuck cares. But old Snyder is like a tomb... until a certain point. So I told him you ain't working here anymore... and he left... but he's looking maybe, so watch out. If he ain't your lover, he ain't no friend either, right?"

"Right..."

Snyder slammed his shoulder with his palm, making him wince. "Knew it! Now, you owe me a mighty one... just thinkin' how I'll cash it." He grinned and left him.

Darren leant against Raven, his legs almost giving at that point, but he just breathed in and out, deep, leading the horse then away from the cart to his place.

Archibald went to see his grandmother, desperate a bit, the talks at home after the picnic being almost only about him and Katie Willoughby, how this was the ideal match, his mother raving about it endlessly. Only his father kept moderately quiet about it, and Archibald had no words, trying to think about how to get himself out of that trap.

He let the countess' butler push him to her tea room, letting her hug him in his chair, sit to face him. They waited until the servants were out of hearing range, their teas gently fuming, a pile of cakes Archibald knew he would not touch. The taste of those apple crumbles still lingering in his mouth somehow, tightening his heart.

He looked at his grandmother, that deep sadness in his brown eyes. "You know why I came."

"Ah... I heard, dear... Katie Willoughby... the young lady is highly praised."

"I will not marry her."

She sipped her tea. "I am not sure how you will carry this through."

"By not proposing in the first place." He sighed, his eyes going to those green leaves playing in the sun. Knowing he would spill everything to her, even if it meant death, or whatever. He could not care less, his heart bleeding dry. "I cannot propose, and I will not marry her, because I love somebody else." His eyes went to her, her silence. "I love him... I don't even know where he is, what he is doing, whether he is still of this world, and yet, I love him... I love him so much, it hurts... It is agony."

She sighed, putting the cup down. She reached for his hands, holding them gently. Watching as his tears pearled down his cheeks, silent, those brown eyes shimmering in tears. "I would like to thank you for this confidence."

"You knew..." Soft, his voice drowned in that ocean of salt.

"I knew, but not how much you loved him." She patted his hand. "I told you. A dangerous game."

"William knows too..."

"Oh... Most unfortunate."

"He threatened me, Granny..." A sudden idea in him. "Does Father know?" His heart racing, watching her straighten, put her hands in her lap.

"Your father... I suspect he does have some ideas..." She pinched her lips. "Threatened? How?"

"He said I could have an accident, if I didn't cooperate..." He closed his eyes. "I need to talk to Father... just in case something happens, so that he knows... that I would never..." He felt her hands again, gripping him with that force she had.

He met her eyes filled with a new fire. "Nothing will happen. Not while you have me."

Archibald almost lost it then, but steeled himself, his voice. "I hired a detective to find Darren..." His name made him weak, and he had to draw breath through those tears threatening to spill.

"Oh... any success?"

"Not yet... He started looking at families like ours... we might need to look lower..."

"I would have known if he had a job at another family."

"How?"

She rolled her eyes. "Darling, I know every gossip in this town... at least the gossip of the rich. He is not working for anybody in our circles."

"And no luck with cab drivers so far, either."

"I doubt he had that kind of money to start even there..."

"Then... where?"

She sighed. "All I can think of is farmers, or delivery drivers... but those are not places where you wish to look... your detective might even refuse. Some of those men are rough and dangerous. I would hope he found a better place."

"I will tell him to look..." His mind almost bathing in a mild shock at her words. *Dangerous...* He pushed the words out. "Do you think... what if he has forgotten me? Found somebody else in his new life?"

She took another sip of her tea, holding his hand still. "Do you honestly think that of him?"

Archibald's face flamed up. "I don't know..."

"You love that man... does he love you?"

"He said so..."

"Now... this is not appropriate in any shape or form, but I must ask, still... Have you loved this man... properly... in my little seaside cottage?"

He averted his eyes, so ashamed he thought he would sink right there. "I... I suppose I did..."

"Now then... what does your heart tell you? He has forgotten you? That man who held you and loved you? Could he have found another man to fill his heart?"

He shook his head, another tear racing down his cheek.

"So, all is hopeful... he is somewhere, and we will find him. Talk to Edward first. He should know... he might as well know..." She sighed. "It is going to be extremely difficult... you have to watch William and your mother. Let them believe you have tamed."

"Alright, Granny..." Trying to believe her words when his hopes were dwindling. But he also remembered his own promise. That he would find a way. "I need a doctor who could look at my legs."

"Oh... most certainly. I might have just the person."

"Please arrange an appointment."

"Those riding lessons did some good?"

"Yes..."

"Splendid! I shall arrange it for you in all discretion."

"Yes... that twat shouldn't know..." He closed his eyes, close to blowing up. "And to think that they are..."

"I know, dear. All the more of a hate to fill William's heart."

Archibald shot her a tired look, but he was determined to talk to his father. Even if it meant he would lose him, knowing that what he had to say would probably break something. *After all, I am his only son... and I am breaking the lineage...* Above his hopes, that abysmal shame, cutting his breath. He looked at his grandmother when he felt her hand.

"Lost a bit in your thoughts again? All will be as it should be."

"I am the ruin of this family."

"All families come to an end at one point... Fran will have a baby, so all is not lost."

"I could marry Katie Willoughby and live another life on the side..." A bit desperate, but he felt lost, facing that abyss of the unknown. A chasm of crime and sin.

"Now, now... Despair should not push you into a life of lies, Archibald. And it would not be fair to Katie either. Besides, William would find a way to get rid of Darren."

"Then... how? How to live? Even if I find him... it is impossible for us to live together without scandal."

"I know... and we will think of something. Talk to your father, watch your back, and find him. That is what you have to focus on."

He sighed, deep. "Alright... Granny, I am most grateful." Kissing her hand, and she rose to hug him, tight.

"Archie... I wish it were easier for you, but these are the times we live in now... Love is not free."

"It is not... and comes with heavy compromises and dangers..."

"This is what you have to face... what some have to face... but we have all been there at one point in our life." She winked.

"Truly? Then..."

"Sometimes, you do not have a choice. You do what you have to do."

"I could do the same."

"You do not even believe your own words, dear." She chuckled, and he had to smile, his dreamy eyes on the playing leaves.

Chapter 24

Archibald waited until his mother went to bed to talk to his father, the night late, but Edward just watched him in that silence, the room barely lit, his dreamy eyes on the outside. Almost rising when Archibald's voice nailed him to his seat.

"Stay, please..." Edward sat back, watching him turn the chair. "We need to talk."

"Alright..." His heart racing a bit at that hard look in his brown eyes.

"I went to Granny, and she said it's best if I tell you everything... even if it means I might lose you, Father..." He swallowed that lump in his throat. Blowing a small breath. Grateful for his silence. "I will not marry Katie Willoughby, despite everybody's wishes."

"Oh... I mean, your mother is most enthusiastic, but I would understand if she would not be to your liking. There will always be other ladies..." He smiled, that smile dying in Archibald's eyes.

"No. That is what I want to tell you. There will be no other ladies, Father." Watching his face fall, a bit confused.

"You do not wish to marry at all?"

"The kind of marriage I would like does not exist..."

Edward blinked. "I am not entirely sure I am following you."

"What I want to say is that I love..." *A man...* But it seemed indecent, somehow, as he was not just any man. His chest on fire as he pushed the words out. "I am in love with Darren... I love him. That is all." Not leaving his father's stunned eyes, even if they had blurred, his tears rushing to his eyes at his own words. Soft, almost barely there. "I would understand if you would send me away, disown me... I cannot be the son you wished for... and I will only bring you shame and disgrace." He quieted, swallowing his tears which had slid to the back of his throat. Waiting.

Edward spoke after a few moments. "I... I mean... I sort of knew... I had guessed, at least..."

"Truly... I thought those were unexpected ideas of yours... for us to be together... in the stable yard..."

Edward smiled mildly. "Not entirely... I knew you took a liking to him... as a friend... maybe more when you were sent to the sea, but I guessed there would be no harm..." He sighed, his eyes a bit wide. "He is gone though, Archibald..."

He shook his head. "I have hired a detective, and he is looking as we speak... I am determined to find him."

"And then?"

Archibald looked at him. "You are not mad? You should be shouting, and throwing furniture around."

"Have you ever seen me do that?"

His face flamed up. "No..."

"So... this is not easy, to say the least... Even if he would be your age and rank, but he is not..."

"Not by status maybe, but by birth..."

Edward raised his hand. "Do not even go there. Willoughby is never going to acknowledge him as anything, especially not his son."

"But he is his son!"

Edward sighed. "By blood, maybe... there is nothing that can be done about this. It cannot be proven, and Willoughby will deny it."

Archibald scoffed. "As if he could!"

"Even if it is plain, it has not been announced in any shape or form, and on paper, he is a Turner, and that stable master's son. Nothing can be done, even if we all know..." He sighed. "I am not going to disown you, what were you thinking? You are my son."

"But useless as it is... I will not marry, nor have children, and if I find Darren, I will be with him. There is no other way around this. I refuse to have him in my service and see him in hiding when we can steal some time from prying eyes."

His voice was flying, his eyes alive, and Edward smiled above his rushing heart. "Let me think, Archibald. I need time to figure out how I could help you best."

"Father... I cannot drag you into this..."

"Well, you already have? Let me think."

"You would do this for me?" Losing his voice, looking up at him when he had risen.

Edward walked to him, and took his hands. "Sometimes, we get a second chance to make things right. You should live a true life." He smiled a sad smile, squeezing his hands gently.

Archibald's eyes went wide. "You..."

Edward just patted his hand and left, giving him a small wave when he closed the door, and Archibald just sat there, his speech gone, drowned in his tears filling his chest to bursting. He pushed his hand on his mouth not to lose it. *Father...* Breathing hard as he let his tears spill.

A lush spring day when Darren started work early, leaving the yard with the sun barely up, the deliveries being more numerous with crops growing, markets more populated as the country was dragged out of winter. More merchandise too, changing hands, fabrics that needed to be delivered, wood and other construction materials, potatoes, flour to bakeries, milk, sugar. Heavy loads which made for gruelling days, trying to keep some strength with that meagre diet of bread and potatoes, mostly. Street kids had taken a habit of climbing on the carts, but they usually got swatted down. Daren didn't mind, the urchins providing a welcome distraction, and they were grateful, those little weasels, rushing to garbage cans when he stopped to unload or load, rummaging through those stinking piles to find some treasures. Mouldy bread, discarded vegetables which were on the verge of rotting, sometimes leftovers of meals, when they were in better neighbourhoods.

One of them who regularly rode with Darren, Tommy, loved going to butchers and scrape the blood off the stone slabs, the wooden blocks, and gather it in a big tin mug. Grinning when he ran back to the cart, climbing on the bench, shouting to Darren who was packing, sweat pouring down his face and body.

"Oy! Got some blood!" Grinning with his teeth shining in his grimy face.

Darren shot him a look. "Great!" He meant it too, that blood a rare treat which they could cook with a bit of salt, eat it with bread. Sometimes, they could fry an onion with it if Tommy was lucky enough to scrape some out of the garbage.

Going back late, he put Raven to his place, carefully grooming him and giving him his hay before he went to make some kind of meal out of all that gathered food. Tommy just waited for him, sitting on the table, dangling his legs. Ignoring the men who just sneered at him sometimes, holding that mug of blood like treasure. Waiting until Darren joined him, taking the mug out of his hands.

Karl snickered. "'Tis your little puppy dog, 'tis mongrel. Guarding that filth like it's gold."

Some laughed. "Eating out of garbage cans now?"

Darren shrugged, putting that blood up with some water. "It is better than nothing."

"You would not starve if your money didn't go to that horse!"

Snyder had walked to them, listening, sipping his beer. He kept quiet though, his dark eyes on Darren and the child.

Sam spat. "Fuck that horse! You think you gonna walk out of here? You outta your mind, Turner. Ain't nobody leaves from here."

Darren smiled, stirring that thickening blood. "You might not be walking out, but I will. Once I paid him off, I'll walk out, and you can watch my back, and that horse's ass."

Smith and some others laughed, and Sam just scoffed. "I believe it when I see it."

Snyder's voice cut the dark. "Pay it off first, fancy boy..."

Darren looked at him but didn't stop stirring. "I seem to think I am doing just that."

Snyder scoffed. "You still have a long way to go... and I didn't seem to remember I allowed this kid to be here."

Darren turned this time, pulling the blood off the fire. "I don't need your permission. Tommy finds the food, he eats too. That is all."

Snyder walked to him, facing him off. "You ain't the boss here. And you could eat... seems to me we ate that horse yesterday..."

"I'll eat you first before I eat horse meat."

"Right!" He stepped closer, giving him that crooked grin. "Tell me what is keeping me from cutting your horse up in front of you and shoving his flesh down your throat."

The men stood, silent, only the fire burning.

Darren stood his ground. "You won't."

"And why is that?"

"We have a deal."

"I shit on it."

That cold light in his blue eyes was mirrored in his voice. "If you kill him, I will kill you next. Gut you and roast your flesh. Then we feast, and do whatever the fuck we want with you gone."

Somebody whined a laugh, and it got picked up by the others, by Snyder who just stood there, shaking.

He grinned at Darren, but that fright had settled in his eyes. "Is that a threat, fancy boy?"

"No. A promise."

He slammed him on the shoulder, trying to ease that moment. "You're great fun, Turner. Would be a shame to lose you."

But even with the laughter, him leaving, something had settled into that dark yard, the men watching Darren sit with that small boy, share that dark blood which had cooked into a thick paste. Eating, a new light in his eyes. That kind light coated by a colder one, hardened by the back-breaking work, and that utter loneliness.

Days passed, and William was waiting for Fran to come out from a doctor's appointment, utterly bored as he sat in the carriage, watching the traffic stroll by, his mind on how he would make sure Archibald married Katie, even if the thought made his skin crawl, he wanted him to be under the family's rule, knowing how Katie was and how she would order that invalid weakling around. Hearing a familiar voice, so he raised his head and looked out the window, a small kick to his chest seeing that man with dark hair stop a cart and jump down, leaving the reins as a small boy darted from the cart in his dirty clothes and dived head-first in a garbage can. William's breathing quickened when that man turned and shot a glance at the boy before he climbed on the cart and grabbed a large sack of flour, swinging it to another man standing on the pavement.

William just watched Darren work, his chest warm, his eyes drinking in his sight, that body with those hard, lean muscles, the skin taut on them, any fat gone, and even if the strength was there on that half-naked torso, the ribs were there too, showing when he moved, gliding against his glistening skin. His collarbones, his hipbones too. Harder lines on his face, that smiling crinkle gone from around his eyes, his hair unkept, jaw clenched as he lifted those heavy loads, sweat dripping down his temples, his back, and chest. He wiped his brows and raked his hair, working hard, and William just smiled, watching him, knowing he could not see him at all. Not recognising that black horse tied in front of the cart, his head lowered, one leg resting as he was catching his breath.

Turning to the door of the carriage opening, to Fran's smile. "All is fine. The baby is moving around and we could hear the heart."

"Splendid, dear. Care for a stop at a cake shop? We could buy some and celebrate." He kissed her hand, and she blushed.

"Oh yes! Thank you. You were not too bored?"

His lips curled up. "No. Street life is fascinating." Closing the curtain, he sat next to her and held her close, his heart flying with his thoughts. The carriage jolting then, leaving fast in that dense traffic.

Afternoon tea was at the Hampton's and William just walked next to Archibald in the garden, giving him a cup. "Excited for the weekend picnic?"

"Excited is probably not the right word, as I hate social gatherings."

"Ah... ever the sour." He laughed, sipping his tea. "Well, maybe it is time to concentrate on my lovely cousin, and forget your heart's longing for my scumbag, bastard brother."

"He might be your brother by blood, but you have nothing in common."

William grinned. "Indeed, we do not. He leads a life of misery, and I don't. I could go on..."

"You know nothing of his life."

William leant close. "Do you think so? I just happen to have seen him this morning." He straightened, holding his cup, watching with his smile Archibald decompose.

"What...?"

"Oh, yes... believe me, better forget him. He looks but a shadow of the man you remember..."

"Where is he?" Archibald had to put his cup down, his hands trembling.

"Wouldn't you like to know? But I don't either. He drives a miserable cart from what I could see. Probably not his either. A fitting place for a man such as him."

"Just... just get away from me." He had to close his eyes not to let his tears stream.

William squeezed his shoulder, waiting until he looked up at him. "You are not giving orders here, brother. I am looking forward to our picnic, and so is dear Katie. See you then."

Archibald watched him leave, but then he waved his valet over. "I need to send a letter."

"Yes, Milord."

He chased his despair away, focused on that single task of finding him, William's words churning in his frayed mind. *A shadow of the man you knew...* But if he said the truth, Darren was alive. That thought only made him shed a warm tear which he wiped swiftly off. *I will find you...*

On Sunday, when they could finish work earlier a bit, the men were sitting in Snyder's yard, drinking tea and munching on whatever food they could get their hands on, bantering, repairing their horse's tack with bits of wire and threads. Smith sat on the table, leafing through a paper he had picked up from a garbage can.

"Listen to this... motherfuckin' fancy folks news... like who cares about them fancy folks and their promenade..." He mispronounced the word, but kept going, mocking. "Who cares, honestly, where they stroll? Strolling, get it? Going nowhere... beats me... Listen, I'll read you..." Chuckling, he took a haughty voice whilst the others snickered. "Lady Francesca Willoughby was seen on the arm of her husband, Lord William Willoughby, and by the looks of it, she is heavy with child, a blessing..." He laughed, hard. "Oh, boy... making the wife pregnant is a feat now?" He shook his head, reading further. "Lord Archibald Hampton was seen strolling with Lady Katherine Willoughby. The young lord cannot walk, but he seemed to enjoy her company in his wheeled chair. By the looks of it, the Hamptons and Willoughbys seem to strengthen their ties, with rumours of the young man soon proposing..." He threw the paper down, laughing. "Fuck, man... them fancy folks... who gives a rat's ass about who I marry or fuck?"

They laughed, but Darren's heart had wrapped in ice, even if it had raced at Archibald's name, a bitter feeling invading him, a mild anger at himself for believing at all that Archibald would care, try to find him... He put the tack down he was working on, lost, his heart torn.

Smith scowled at him. "Somethin' the matter, Turner?"

"No... I don't feel well..."

"Must be all that garbage you're eating." Karl laughed, and shook his head, threading a wire into his horse's bridle to keep the leather strap from tearing any further.

Darren thought of leaving and just going on a walk, but the mere idea was already exhausting, and he could not stay with the men either, their eyes asking, seeing that mild distress on his face, so he walked to the only being who could give him some comfort. He walked to Raven, lacing his arms around the horse's neck, breathing him in whilst his tears pearled in his mane. Raven just pushed his nose in his abs, waiting, breathing against his skin, warming that ice heart in his tight chest. *I have to mourn him... our love... he went on with his life... and he's right...* It still hurt, even if Darren knew Archibald was doing the right thing, his hopes shattered, so he clung to the horse, this horse he was paying off with endless days of hard work, hoping, that they would both make it out of that dark yard alive.

Chapter 25

Archibald went to the doctor his grandmother had recommended, still weary of that picnic where he had to play the perfect gentleman and walk with that awful girl. He shivered at the memory of her talking about their possible life together, where she wanted to live, go to balls, unashamed when she mentioned his condition, how she would not mind not even bedding him. All his hopes in his father and his grandmother, and his detective, who had assured him he would do the utmost to find Darren, now that he sort of knew where to look for him. Still a needle in a haystack, in that buzzing city filled with delivery drivers...

The door opened and an elderly man smiled at him, white moustache and hair, gold-rimmed glasses. "Lord Hampton? Please do come in. I'm doctor Hanson."

Archibald let his valet push him in, and then dismissed him. He looked at the doctor. "Did my grandmother tell you why I'm here?"

"Yes. You want to be examined in all discretion."

"I want to know if I could walk one day."

"Allow me to have a look."

He spent several long minutes examining Archibald's legs, moving them, banging his knees with a small hammer, then straightened.

"There is hope. Can you stand at all?"

Archibald nodded. "I tried. Once. I slipped from the bed, and managed to hold on to a chair."

The doctor nodded. "I would say come here three times a week for special gymnastics. I have an excellent specialist. My hopes are in you walking, maybe, with a cane. Your left leg might not work properly, and your muscles are still weak. This will take time, and a lot of patience."

Archibald sighed, but he was determined to carry it through. "Alright. I'll come."

"Very well. I shall send you a schedule."

"Please send it to my grandmother. My family should not know."

"As you wish."

"Thank you, doctor."

Archibald went home then, his tired eyes on the London traffic, the barouche's top down as the weather was milder, the city alight, and he remembered their rides, wishing that he could just have him sit on the bench, not that old coachman.

Once home, he had to go for tea, and William and Francesca were already there. Archibald set his face into a mask, letting his valet push him near the window, near the sofa where his mother and Fran were sitting.

William was sprawling in an armchair, his blue eyes on Archibald, his small smile. "Had a nice ride?"

"Tolerable. It's becoming quite hot."

"You keep busy..."

"I have to. My health is better. I cannot idle around."

William smiled. "When will you propose?"

The air froze, Archibald's lips parting in fear, when his mother perked up.

"Yes, truly! It would be high time to seal this union!"

"Mother... it is still too early..."

"Hush-hush! Nonsense! Katie is the perfect wife to be, and you should not evade your duties, as ever!"

Fran put her hand on her mother's arm. "It could wait a bit... let them get to know each other better."

William shot her a dark look. "We didn't need that much time. I am afraid Archibald is just delaying the inevitable." He grinned, sipping his tea then.

Archibald held himself back from just yelling his head off, knowing he could not even storm out if he wanted to. "I am not delaying anything... Fran is right. We need a bit more time together."

His mother shrugged. "I cannot understand you. The paper is full of you and your impeding proposal. Might as well do it."

Archibald kept quiet, feeling that trap close on him, but his heart was also burning with that fire he had now. He composed his voice. "I shall think about it."

William smiled. "Do not take forever."

But Archibald took his time, weeks flowing by during which he went for his gymnastics sessions, practicing at home too in his room, away from prying eyes. A grim determination in him, even if the detective was still looking, sending apologetic messages each week. Spring bending into summer, the picnic season full on with the parks filled with folks, so they had to go on weekends for their promenade, but he sat in his chair, not wanting to give anything away, that he could walk a few steps, limping, with his cane. With great pain, but his arm had become stronger, that left arm holding the cane to aid that lame leg. *No matter.* It was steps towards something that could be called walking, the world unfurling at his feet from his height. He couldn't remember being tall, having sat in that chair for so long, and it thrilled him mildly to see the world from a different perspective. Every muscle aching after those gruelling sessions, after having ridden daily in the park, twitching when he lay in bed, burning with desire, that mad lust which he tried to tame to no avail.

Rainy days, when the sky poured down in that beginning of summer warmth. Hard days for man and beast alike, as the deliveries never stopped, even under that pouring rain and the muddied up streets, they had to plough on, soaked to the bone. Darren didn't know anymore where his sweat started and the rain stopped, both flowing down his body, too exhausted to even shelter when he was just sitting for a few minutes, catching his breath. A mild worry in him, running his palm down Raven's body, that his hipbones had started showing, despite him starving himself to get that extra portion of hay to the horse every day. He made sure to bandage his legs though, even if the others had called him crazy, he would not let that horse injure himself. Watching, weary eyed, as Tommy ran to him, clutching something to his chest.

He hoped on the bench, his grimy face somewhat cleaned as the rain poured down on it. "Darren! I found some bread! All good too!" He sat and pushed a big loaf of bread in Darren's hands, his face alight.

Darren's eyes went wide, but he quickly tore the loaf in half, and hid one half under the bench in a small basket. He tore then the remaining piece in half and handed it to the kid. "Let's eat then..." Smiling under that pouring rain which had soaked that loaf in seconds. It still tasted divine, but he held back his tears, those tears which scarcely spilled anymore, his soul buried under that crust of hard work and the shards of his broken heart.

Tommy watched the rain pour into the puddles, creating circles upon circles. He munched his bread. "I might find some more..."

"That would be great."

He gathered the reins, and clacked his tongue, Raven perking up from his slumber, pulling hard in that thickening mud. They set off to the mill, and Tommy just sat, watching the hurrying coaches, the people rushing by.

Tommy left Darren after a couple of hours, jumping down in a run-down neighbourhood, the houses huddled against each other, howling and shouting coming out with that yellow light pouring from the windows.

Darren waved at him and drove home, dead tired, but Raven knew the way and didn't need his hands, eager to be home to eat, at last. That single portion of hay swallowed too fast. Darren halted the cart in the yard, untying the horse. He brought him to his place, rubbing him off, and put his dinner in front of him. He also went and washed in the rain, letting it stream down his upper body, then dried near the fire, sipping that scalding tea. He could not remember anymore how tea tasted, just that foul dark liquid, which had become familiar, almost comforting. Pulling his other shirt on, he lay down near Raven, stroking his legs as he ate, letting him nibble his hair as he pushed the hay around. His mind still inevitably drifting to Archibald, that accursed mind which kept showing him those torturous pictures of his eyes, his smile, his lips... *Forget him... How...*

Snyder caught him in the morning when he was harnessing Raven, the sun glorious, a promise of warmth in the air.

"There was a man here... lookin' for ya... but I ain't no snitch... so said I don't know ya..."

Darren sighed, worried. "Who?"

"Fuck knows. Not a fancy pants, but almost... You hidin' somethin'? Trouble?"

"No."

"Figured. Just watch it... ain't no good, these men lookin'" He barked a laugh. "I need you to live to pay off this wreck!"

Darren almost smiled, but a mild worry had settled in him, thinking of William maybe trying to find him. *So what? I could die... who cares? Who would care?* Clinging to the horse's dark eye, his soft lips nibbling his dark thoughts away. He caressed his head. "I will take you out of here, boy. We'll ride away, far, and live under the stars..." A small smile, imagining that life of roaming, knowing it was a dream, at best, but he sat on the bench, and set off to work, soaking in the sun, letting it run in his dark hair.

Archibald was sitting in his carriage, dead tired after a session at the doctor's, but he held his cane, his eyes on the street as they snaked through that dense traffic. Dinner was set with the Willoughby's, and he knew what Katie would be there, utterly at a loss how he could avoid proposing, he was brewing his stress. Thankfully, his looks, whatever that meant, had been noticed by the ladies during his rides and promenades, and his mother had relaxed a bit, even enjoying that Katie had some opponents. Not something that pleased Archibald, but it allowed him to delay that proposal, which was hanging over his head like a blade. The carriage halted then, and he heard his coachman shout at the horses. *Fuck.*

James was sitting next to the coachman, his eyes on Dandy, tied on the right, who had stopped near a black horse tied to a delivery cart, sniffing that other horse, their noses meeting, neighing softly. The coachman cursed and whacked his whip on Dandy, but the horse didn't move.

He looked at James. "Jump down, will ya, and pull that donkey! We'll be late."

James jumped down, hurrying to the front, when a man walked out of that bakery, wiping his hand on his forehead, his grey shirt stuck to his body. Time slowing as he looked up, stroking his horse, his eyes going wide when Dandy neighed, loud, raising his head, prancing a bit. James rooted to the ground when that man's hand went to the horse's head, his wide blue eyes filled with disbelief. Stroking that frantic horse, Tulip reaching over too to sniff him, neighing softly. The black horse raised his head and arched his neck then, and James almost fainted right there, oblivious to the coachman's shouting. He rushed to that man, straight into his arms, hugging him tight as he almost lost his balance. Thinner, but it was him, James knew.

Any modesty gone in his heart flooded with joy. "Master Darren!"

Darren's legs wobbled, but he just hugged him back, his voice weak. "James?"

The coachman howled. "Oy! Stop this! James!"

Darren pushed the boy away. "Hey... good to see you... But you must go... this is no way to behave..."

James shook with his tears. "But... but you can't leave... the master..." James' eyes went wide when that black horse looked back at them. "Tis Raven? Raven, here?" He looked at Darren, who just shook his shoulders.

"Pull yourself together." He glanced at the coachman's angry face. "James? You must leave." His heart breaking because Dandy was nibbling his shirt, content.

Archibald opened the window and looked up at the coachman, irritated. "Why on earth are we standing?"

"It is that lad's fault... hugging a man right there when I sent him to start the bay..."

"What man?" He looked then, seeing James' shoulders held by a man with black hair, his shirt stuck to his lean body. His heart skipping when that man looked up and their eyes locked. *Jesus... God...* Archibald's eyes went wide whilst those blue eyes veiled with shock.

James had noticed and beamed a smile. "Lord Archibald will be most pleased to see you."

Not understanding why Darren didn't move, as if frozen, the coachman utterly lost when the door opened, so he jumped down to help his master step out. Holding his hand until Archibald stepped down and wedged his cane into the ground. Pale, eyes wide, he wobbled to face them. James had stepped aside with a large smile, watching them, and Darren had to tame the trembling of his hands, his heart almost breaking his chest.

Archibald couldn't speak, his eyes roaming Darren's face, his body, back to his wide eyes which had flooded with tears. He cleared his throat, knowing he could not make a scene, nor hug him, when he was so close.

Composing his voice but pouring all his love into his eyes. "Darren? A most pleasant surprise to find you here... what great luck." He had to shut up, his lips trembling, his tears threatening to spill.

Darren just drank his voice, his words, having seen that light in his eyes, it melted the ache in his chest. That deep shame in him too, knowing how he looked, but he straightened, trying to find his voice. "Milord... it is a surprise indeed... I hope you are well..." His eyes in his eyes, as Archibald was almost as tall as he was, in disbelief that he was standing, walking too. Holding his sobs back, he breathed hard, fighting for air and to stay conscious.

Archibald steadied his voice, knowing they didn't have much time, people already looking, his coachman too. "I was looking for you, to no avail. It would be good if you didn't disappear. Father would be most pleased to meet you."

Darren licked his lips. "As you wish, Milord."

"James, be a dear, and fetch my book and my pencil from the carriage."

He darted off, and brought them back.

Archibald handed it to Darren. "Write down where we can find you. Please."

Darren took it, and opened the first page, jotting down the address, Snyder's name. He handed the book back and Archibald made sure their fingers brushed under it, watching Darren's eyes light up, his lips part.

Archibald smiled at him. "I shall look for you. And find a way for us to be together again."

Those few words lit up Darren's heart, the words barely making it. "No matter what, I will be waiting for you, Milord."

Archibald smiled, his eyes darting to that black horse, his heart burning with rage, but he just waved at Darren. "See you soon, Darren. I shall give the good news to Father."

"It's my honour, Milord."

A last glance, a last goodbye, only their eyes speaking behind their masks, their despair plain in them, their love.

Archibald limped back to the carriage and looked up at the coachman. "To my grandmother's. Hurry!"

The carriage shot off, James jumping up, waving at Darren, who just stood, his shoulders shaking as he could finally give in to his feelings, holding the harness not to slip to the ground, crying against Raven's dark coat.

Archibald was lost in his thoughts during that awful dinner, barely listening to conversations around him, as his heart was racing. He hadn't said anything to his father, but had confided in his grandmother, and there was a plan there which thrilled and equally terrified him.

Jolting at William's voice, his hands on his chair's handles. "Care for a walk?"

"No, thanks..."

But he had already started pushing, and Archibald pinched his lips, letting him push him outside on the landing. He was mildly fed up, when the chair lurched, and tipped down the first step. The staircase swung towards him, but Archibald had clutched the railing, fast, hard, and held on tight as the chair was torn from under him, racing, and then bounding down the stairs. He breathed hard, wide eyed, clinging to the railing when he felt William's hand on his shoulder, that mock fright in his voice.

"Archibald! Are you alright? How clumsy of me... the chair just slipped out of my hands..."

An abysmal rage in Archibald, so he pushed himself on his feet, holding on to the railing as he faced William, his wide eyes. Standing, facing him, eye to eye. "Lying fuck..." Archibald smiled. "Who will believe you, now that I am here to tell them what happened?"

"You... you're standing..." William looked him over, a mild fear above that arrogance.

"Oh... a miracle, surely. Bring up that chair, and let us pretend nothing happened. Push me back, and let's have coffee and a nice talk. As for proposing, that can wait a bit longer... until I forget your clumsiness."

William's eyes had darkened, but he didn't say a word, just went and brought the chair back up. Archibald sat down, letting William push him back, his heart burning with rage.

Chapter 26

The carriage stopped in that shabby street, the sky dark, ambling people already eyeing it, those gleaming horses. Archibald stepped outside, straight into that thick mud.

His coachman's eyes darted around. "This is not safe, Milord. We should leave."

"I have business here."

The coachman sighed, worried. "Please, hurry, Milord."

"Just go. It's not safe, then go."

"I cannot possibly leave you here."

"Then shut up. Let me deal with this."

The coachman stepped aside and bowed. Archibald limped into that dark yard, checking the address one more time, but there was no mistaking it, that faded red painted sign spelling Snyder's, so he walked in, dead scared, but determined. His eyes wide on that dark yard, the burning fire in that barrel. Carts lined on the left and in the back, the soft snort of horses somewhere in those dark stables on the right. He turned at the voice behind him, his heart leaping in his throat.

"What does lord fancypants want here?"

Facing that man with his crooked grin. Archibald steadied his voice. "I have come to meet a man... he said he lives here..."

Snyder arched his eyebrows. "What man?"

"Darren Turner. My former coachman."

Snyder smiled. "There ain't no Darren Turner here."

Archibald didn't flinch, even if that man was oozing danger. "I am positive you are mistaken. He told me himself the other day that he lived here."

"Well, he lied. They all do." His lips curled up. "What's that to ya, a coachman? Leave, and don't come back. We don't like fancypants here... 'Tis a dangerous place..."

"Milord?"

They both turned to the voice, relief flooding Archibald at Darren's sight, even if his face was drawn beyond belief, even if Archibald had to hold back to just hug him tight.

"Darren! I am most relieved to see you."

Snyder snickered. "Told ya to stay put, Turner. Now, talk fast coz you ain't got time for this."

Archibald turned to Snyder. "I haven't come to talk. I have come to take my man away."

There was a small silence at his words, Darren's breath hitching as he was trying to process those words.

Snyder's laughter boomed in that dark yard. "What? A good joke... but he ain't going nowhere..."

Archibald let his anger grow. "He is coming with me. Just release him from his duties, and we are off."

Snyder smiled. "No. He has a debt to pay off first. Then, he may go. Maybe in a few years' time."

Darren's heart raced when Archibald turned to him. "What debt?" Trying to cut that despair out of his voice.

Darren's spoke, weak. "We have a deal. I work to pay off my horse..."

Archibald frowned. "It's just a horse. Leave it." Panicked a bit, as in that small moment, he thought Darren didn't want to leave, maybe not wanting him after all...

Darren sighed. "It's Raven, Milord..."

Archibald's eyes went wide. "What? But... he was not supposed to... how?"

Snyder snorted. "Are you done, fancypants? Get the fuck out of here and don't come back."

Archibald closed his eyes, clutching his cane. He turned to Snyder. "How much?"

"For what?"

"The horse... and the man." He almost sank right there, but held tight, avoiding looking at Darren.

Snyder's lips curled up. "They ain't for sale."

"Even if the price is right? You name it."

"He's that precious, aye?" Eyeing Archibald, then looking at Darren. "He's a good driver... I'll give you that. Those are rare, so it has a price... and the horse too... a good one."

Archibald's eyes flashed. "Just name a price."

Snyder looked at him. "A hundred guineas."

Archibald swallowed, but he had enough money, he knew, so he just reached into his jacket. Taking the money out, counting it in Snyder's palms. "I need it in writing."

Snyder smirked. "Wait here." He looked at Darren. "Get the horse, fancy boy. His lordship bought you, so you can fuck off, and take that lame donkey with you. Must be real good to have worked for nothing." He laughed, hard, and left to his room.

Archibald faced Darren, his heart sinking at the light in his eyes. "I am sorry... I didn't know what to do... that you..."

Darren just gave him a wry smile. "It is fine... I'll go and get Raven."

In disbelief, still, his heart aching, but he walked to the horse and untied him, taking a lead, and swinging his bag on his shoulder. He had nothing else, and the others were asleep, so he pulled the horse out, dazed, looking around in the night, as if in a dream. Meeting Archibald's eyes who had limped close, stroking that lean horse. He looked at Darren, standing close, just lost in his eyes, even if those blue eyes were filled with hurt.

Archibald dared to brush his fingers on Darren's hand, his voice soft. "Forgive me..."

Darren just blew a breath, his tears threatening to spill, and he averted his eyes, just giving a small smile to Archibald.

Snyder walked to them then, handing a paper to Archibald. "Here it is. The price you paid, and that they are sold to you." He took another piece of paper out and tore it up in front of Darren. "Our little deal. Ain't no use for it now that your horse got sold to this lord here..." He laughed, grinning. "Never forget the price you paid for it. I sure won't." Laughing, he left them, and Darren had to close his eyes.

Archibald spoke then. "Let's go... you can tell me later what he was talking about." Waiting until Darren opened his eyes. "He is not my horse, alright? He's yours."

Darren swallowed. His shame. His anger. "I cannot accept it... he will be better off in your stables."

"With you."

Darren sighed, his chest so tight he thought he'd choke. "I cannot work for you, Milord..."

"Not for me. Come. I will take you there. To your new place." Pleading a bit, trying to get him out of that desperate place. "Please. Please come."

Darren sighed, but followed him, tugging the horse. He tied him to the back of the carriage, and Archibald gestured at it. "Please, ride with me."

Darren wasn't sure, dead scared, but he yielded to Archibald's pleading, the whole moment like a dream, climbing after him, sitting to face him, their knees almost touching in that dark carriage. It jolted then; the horses put into a swift trot as the coachman had been eager to leave. Archibald's eyes not leaving Darren's as the carriage swung under them.

Darren broke the silence, unable to shut up any longer. "You walk..." Trying to put a smile in that bitter voice.

"Yes... a bit... I ride too. I did what you told me.... Rode out every day..."

Losing his words at his eyes, losing his breath, unable to talk further about idle topics when he was there. At arm's reach. And Archibald reached out and grabbed Darren's shirt, pulling him close, down on his knees, cupping his face so that he wouldn't flee, pressing his lips on his mouth. Moaning when he felt Darren reach for him, pull him close, opening his mouth, hungry, their tears flowing as they tasted each other, their tongues meeting. Hard kisses, muffling their crying, holding onto each other when they had lost their breath, holding their rocking shoulders tight. Sobbing silently in each other's arms.

Archibald looked at him when they could talk. "I missed you... so much... every single day was torture..."

Darren smiled, that deep sadness settled in his eyes. "I had lost hope..."

Archibald's eyes veiled with a slight reproach. "You said to Father you would write. And you didn't."

Darren frowned. "What? But I did. I did write... maybe it never arrived to you. Happens..."

Archibald seethed. "That scumbag! I knew it!"

"Who?"

"William! I am sure it was him. Who else?"

Darren ran his hand down his cheek. "It doesn't matter anymore. What now?"

"I'm taking you to grandma's. You can hide there, and recover. And we can see each other there, in all discretion."

"How?" Lost, scared.

"Grandma knows. And so does Father."

Darren sat on his heels, in shock. "What?"

"Yes." He gave him a smile, stroking his hair back. "They know and they want to help."

"It is folly."

"Isn't it just?" Archibald's lips curled up, and Darren was lost in his sight, how he had strengthened, his body more filled up, his eyes which had taken a hard light. "I will never let you go. And I will find a way for us to be together. I told you."

"I know..."

A bit mad at himself for having lost hope, just holding his hands, that whole trip like a dream when the carriage stopped and they had to sit and part.

They climbed out and Archibald lead him to the stables, James rushing out to take Raven out of his hands.

"Give him to me, Master Darren. He shall have a large dinner, and all the hay he can eat."

Darren smiled. "Careful with the grains... just a small amount. He hasn't eaten much."

James nodded, and left with the horse, the others neighing, welcoming their friend.

Archibald turned to Darren. "Maybe he hasn't eaten enough, but nor have you." His eyes in tears.

Darren smiled. "I still live..."

"Come. You can pet the horses tomorrow."

He led him to a door near the stables, small rooms giving on a corridor, and he opened one of them. A bed, a bedside table, and a washbasin on a stand, a small cupboard. "Your room for now. There are clothes in that cupboard... might be a bit loose. I knew your old size only."

Darren looked around, his heart tight, not even fully believing that he was there.

Archibald took his hand, making him face him. "I will sleep in the house tonight, and we can talk in the morning. I gather you can use some sleep." He stepped to the table, and gestured at a covered plate. "Your dinner. Please, eat."

Darren smiled, on the brink of losing it. "Those are my words to you."

Archibald smiled. "Not anymore." He hugged him then, feeling how his body had shrunk. "I love you... I still love you..." Kissing his neck, cradling him.

Darren's lips went to his neck, breathing in his scent. "And I love you. I always have."

Letting their tears pearl in that soft night, holding tight.

Archibald had left him then, reluctantly, but knowing he could not stay in the servants' quarters for too long, and Darren turned to the room, almost afraid to move. His eyes roaming the bed, the walls, and the table, as if he had forgotten that such things existed, that deep misery he had lived wiping all normal things out of his existence.

He walked to the table though, and lifted the lid off the plate, almost dropping it at the sight of that simple dish, some mashed potatoes with a piece of meat. He had to cover it back up, whirling away, his hands going into his hair not to lose it. Squeezing tight to let that pain tame his fear. That mad fright of being safe. *Maybe...* Breathing out hard, he steeled himself and walked to the washbasin, the water still lukewarm, so he stripped his shirt off and washed his torso with soap, his hair. Stripping everything, he glided that wet sponge down his body, washing, his movements slow, numb, but then he dried himself and changed, taking some clothes out of the cupboard. They were loose a bit, but it didn't matter, they were clean, so he sat on the bed, utterly drained. Unable to cry, even if the tears were stuck right in his throat, his eyes.

He rubbed his face, sighing, and got up to walk to the table. He sat and took the lid off, trying not to think, taking the fork and knife. Slicing a piece of meat, he chewed it slowly. Scooping some potatoes up then, letting it slide down his throat. A few more bites, but he couldn't eat more, that shrunk stomach assaulted by nerves not taking any more in. *But then it's wasting...* Unsure, a bit ashamed, he still put the lid back on, knowing that if he forced himself, he would be sick. His starved body clutched at the unexpected treat though, and a wave of warmth raced down his body. He made it to the bed, somehow, and collapsed on it face down. Gone. That welcoming darkness like a blanket on his bruised soul.

Archibald undressed, his eyes on the street outside, the rushing cabs, the few people still hurrying somewhere. *He's here... close...* Barely believing it, his hands trembled as he pulled his shirt off, but he avoided the mirror, that body still not a friend, even if it had filled up, some muscles birthing there on his ribs and bones. He pulled his nightgown on, wishing he could just walk to Darren and hold him in his arms. His heart rushing when he thought of the light in Darren's eyes. A foreign light which scared him. *A shadow of the man you knew...* William's mocking smile and voice. *Fuck you!* Archibald was burning with a new fire, something he had never known wallowing in his own misery, and awaiting his death. But he had somebody to protect now, and he knew he would move heaven and earth to make him safe. He turned and went to bed, blowing the candle out, hoping that the next day would bring some light into their life.

Next morning brought sunshine, and Darren woke with a start, almost falling off the bed as he was used to sleeping on the ground. Blinking, he sat up, looking around, his heart racing. *The room... It wasn't a dream...* Blowing a breath, he raked his hair, unsure what to do. He knew where he was though, so pulled his boots on and hurried outside, the light still feeble. *Early*. He walked to the stables, wanting to be close to his only companion. Pushing the door open, he glanced around, the horses perking up, and his eyes welled with tears when Dandy's shrill neigh filled that silence, followed by Tulip and Raven, the horses' heads poking above their stall doors, ears pricked, their nostrils flaring. Darren rushed to Dandy first, hugging the bay's head, letting him nibble his shirt, neigh into his chest. Caressing Tulip too who had pushed close, he let his tears flow. He walked to Raven's stall then, and opened the door, hugging that lean horse, rubbing his head then, meeting the animal's large eyes.

"You're safe now, Raven... nothing's going to happen to you." Losing his voice, that bitter feeling in him that the horse was gone, yet again, from him, but he also knew that Archibald would never sell him. Unsure what he would be doing, at all. He jolted at James' voice.

"Master Darren!" James walked to him, straight into the stall, and hugged him tight. "So good to have you back!"

Darren just patted his back, giving back that hug. He looked into James' eyes when he'd pushed him away. "Back?"

"Yes, back! Her Ladyship said you'd be back to work as her stable master. I'll come when his Lordship will visit... I don't work here..."

Darren swallowed. "You've grown a lot..."

"Yes, a bit..." Embarrassed, he raked his hair, smiling. "Come, let's feed the horses and then eat. The masters will wake soon." He grabbed Darren's hand and pulled him to the hayloft. "I'll climb, and throw it down to you."

Darren waited, in a daze, but the familiar movements of work brought back some comfort, still that mild stress in him that he would soon hear Snyder's voice, leave on the cold dawn streets for another gruelling day. They went to eat then with James, who brought him to the kitchen to grab some bread and jam, and some eggs. This was already too much for Darren, who barely ate not to override his stomach.

A maid hurried to them then. "Darren Turner? Her Ladyship wants to see you."

His stomach clenched, but Darren followed her, up the servants' stairs to the third floor, to a large door which got pushed in.

The maid curtsied as they stepped into that living room flooded with light. "Darren Turner, Milady."

Lady Hampton was sitting, and she gestured Darren to the chair in front of her couch. "Come and do sit down, Mister Turner."

He walked close and hesitated, but she just gestured with her hand, so he sat, putting his palms on his knees. Mad scared, but he managed to push the words out. "Milady, good to see you..."

Her eyes roamed him. "I trust you had a good night."

"Yes, Milady..."

"Archie hasn't told you anything, I gather, too busy to find you again." She smiled at his face flushing. "Mister Turner, we have devised this little scheme with my grandson, so you can rest at ease. You will work for me in my stables. I cannot let you drive my carriages because we both know that your enemies should not know about you working for me. Lord Willoughby is most keen on Archibald marrying his cousin, as you have probably heard from the papers, but we both know where Archibald's heart lives."

Darren stammered. "I don't want to be trouble... I can just leave, and not stand in the way of Arch... his Lordship's happiness..."

She arched her eyebrows, amused. "And his happiness is with Katie Willoughby?"

Darren lowered his eyes. "I don't know..."

"Mister Turner..." She waited until Darren lifted his eyes to her. "Should you walk away now, Archibald would be devastated. I am not saying anything new here, I gather? We both know his happiness is with you, however dangerous and challenging this already is. Should people find out, it would be prison and disgrace for Archibald, and the gallows for you."

Darren swallowed, nodding. "I know..."

"Still, what is life good for if we are not ready to face its dangers? So, I hope my employment offer is to your satisfaction, and you are eager to get started. Archibald will come and visit me, but he will obviously be visiting you. Discretion is highly advised; my staff cannot be trusted. This means that you will need to make sure you do not give away your feelings when others could see you.

I will make sure though to give a room to Archibald where you could meet undisturbed... for a short time. Khm." She smiled. "That is all I can do for my grandson. Lord Hampton and I will see what we could do for future plans... This is not easy, as you may gather."

"I understand, Milady." He sighed, in flames. "And I am not sure how I could thank you... ever..."

"It is I who owe you gratitude, Mister Turner. Archibald lives because of you." She raised her hand when his lips parted in protest. "He lives because he loves you. Unfortunate times for you... but we will see what can be done. In the meantime, just work as thoroughly as you usually do. I have two horses which pull my carriages, and another retired one, my late husband's. Ah, and of course, your Raven."

Darren smiled. "He is not mine, Milady..."

"Curious... Archibald said you had a horse... oh well, here he comes, he can clear this."

Darren turned back to watch Archibald limp in, leaning on his cane. He sat next to his grandmother, but his eyes ate Darren up.

Lady Hampton looked at him. "Now, Mister Turner here seems to think he doesn't have a horse. But you told me he does."

Archibald's amused eyes never left Darren's. "He does."

Darren's heart sank. "I don't... I haven't paid him off... and..."

Archibald smiled. "Yes, you have. Granny will take his price off your first wage. Not the price I paid... but what you owed. Do you know how much?"

Darren nodded, dazed. "I do..."

"So, all is well." His eyes pleading a bit at that hurt light in those blue pools.

Darren's voice wobbled. "I am not sure what to say..."

Lady Hampton smiled. "It is not necessary. That horse is in a piteous state, which is a shame, but he is safe now with you. His price and his food are not going to impact that substantial wage I am going to give you as a valuable stable master, so no need to worry."

Darren had lost his voice at her words, trying not to break down crying, and Archibald watched him, his eyes welled up, knowing he could not hug him.

Lady Hampton rang her bell. "Now, tea, because we all deserve it after all these emotions."

They waited until tea was served, and Lady Hampton dismissed her servant. "So, it is time we plan a bit, as William will no doubt try to figure out what is going on. Archibald, you will need to play the perfect gentleman with him and Katie, not to arise suspicion. How is your French?"

Archibald blinked, swallowing the tea in his mouth. "My French? I have to practise... it has been a while..."

"Well, practise then, it is most important not to neglect a foreign language."

"Granny, I am not sure how this..."

"All in good time. Refresh your French, and your botanical knowledge of lavender, and fruit trees."

Archibald blinked at Darren, but his eyes mirrored his cluelessness. "Alright, as you wish. I trust you know why you are asking me all this?"

"Yes. Now, to the matter at hand. You will come and visit, yes? Then, leave your horse at the stables and come and see me, we will have tea. Then, you can meet in your grandpa's old reading room. I'll give you a key, it opens from the outside, and is a bit hidden from prying eyes. Quiet and discretion is advised." Smiling at that colour creeping up on their cheeks. "All good?"

"Yes, Granny." Archibald sipped his tea to hide his embarrassment, but he was thrilled, his heart racing at the thought of holding him in his arms, soon.

Lady Hampton put her cup down. "All is well then. I am most pleased to have an excellent stable master. Archibald, you have to go home now. Do not come tomorrow, but the day after. And practise your French."

Archibald stood, leaning on his cane. "Yes, Granny. I shall."

Darren stood too, mad worried that Archibald would fall, but he just walked to him.

"Come, escort me to my carriage. See you soon, Granny."

"Yes, dear. Take care."

They left, Archibald pretending to have difficulty walking so he could lean on Darren's arm, let him lace his arm around his waist to help him. Archibald leant against him, cheating a bit, relishing in the heat of his body, feeling his lean, hard muscles press against his flesh, his skin.

His voice, soft. "Thank you for helping..."

Darren smiled, his heart racing. "My pleasure, Milord..."

They walked to the waiting carriage in the yard, Darren's heart tight, seeing Dandy and Tulip led by that old coachman.

Archibald turned to him. "See you soon, Darren."

"See you, Milord."

He helped him up and Archibald slid his hand down his arm when he let his elbow go, squeezing gently when he got to his hand. Mouthing *I love you*.

Darren smiled at him, his skin burning where they had touched briefly, all his thoughts madness in his exhausted mind. Watching the carriage leave. He went to work then, petting the horses, letting them sniff him, lick his palms. Working hard, a slight hope in him that he had arrived home, maybe. That shame there, still, clinging to the edge of his soul.

Chapter 27

Archibald stayed away next day, keeping quiet at home, politely taking part in conversations, even if William was getting on his nerves, as ever. His thoughts on the next day when he could see him again.

He went there early, leaving Dandy at the stables in Darren's hands, just a brief touch of their hands as Darren took the reins, the horse delighted, pushing his head into his chest.

Archibald smiled, whispering. "I'll see you soon..." Leaving, he glanced back at Darren, his drowned eyes, his heart beating a bit faster.

He walked down to the yard later and gestured at Darren, who just followed him to the back of the house, to a door giving on a small garden. Archibald opened it with a key and they walked inside, Darren's eyes roaming the room whilst Archibald closed the door. Darren jolted a bit at Archibald's hand on his arm, but he turned to face him.

"What's wrong?" His heart choking his voice, Archibald had noticed that light in his eyes flooded with anguish.

Darren licked his lips, his voice soft. "I need to tell you something... before we... before we do anything..."

Archibald smiled to ease his dread. "Alright..."

Darren sighed, stepping to the window to avoid looking at him, crossing his arms. "You remember what Snyder told you? About me not forgetting the price I had to pay... for Raven..."

"I know..."

"That deal with him... of me paying off the horse... he would only do it if I did something else..." He sighed, steeling himself, and turned to Archibald's wide eyes. "It is not what you think... maybe? But... he wanted me... to take him in my mouth... and I did..." He clenched his arms tighter around him, his fingers digging into his sides. "I did it because there was nothing else to do in that moment of despair... it was either that or the horse given to somebody else in those stables of death, and I could not... could not let him..." He had lost his words, avoiding those wide eyes which had filled with tears. Feeling Archibald walk close, put his hand on that rock-hard arm.

"I am grateful for your words..." Waiting, so Darren raised his eyes to him with great pain. Archibald smiled. "I don't care. It doesn't matter. It didn't mean anything to you, and you should not be ashamed."

Darren sighed, trying not to cry. "Thank you... even if I am still deeply ashamed..."

Archibald reached up to his face, tentatively, hoping it would not be too much. "We can just sit and talk... I am not going to ask anything of you. Maybe this is just too much... this place, having a proper room and food... maybe you are not ready for us..."

Darren's lips parted, drowned in his brown eyes, his voice, the heat of his palm on his skin, his scent invading his senses. "I will forever be ready for you..."

Unfurling his arms, reaching for him as Archibald stepped into his embrace, melting into his arms which pulled him close, straight into a kiss. A hard, deep kiss, but filled with tenderness, their tongues softly playing, finding their lips and teeth as their hands roamed each other's bodies, and it just felt good and right to Archibald, to be in his arms, as if his heart had found his home, beating against Darren's heart.

They backed to a sofa, and Archibald lay on Darren, eating his mouth as his hands cupped his face, just lost in that moment of peace when they were alone, that danger pushed back with the door closed and the white lace curtains masking the view. A lush sunshine pouring through the windows into that quiet room filled with floor to ceiling bookshelves, that sofa, and an armchair and a large desk. The scent of old books and wood polish.

Archibald looked down at Darren. "I'm crushing you?"

He smiled. "No... but you are heavier..." Caressing his back, letting his hands push Archibald's shirt up to roam his skin.

Archibald breathed faster. "We don't have to do anything if you need time..."

"We don't have time... the only time we have is the present moment... and I love you... I have never stopped loving you..." He kissed Archibald softly. "I'm so proud of you, too."

Archibald's chest flooded with warmth. "Oh... I was hoping you would be... I wish you would have been there when I stood for the first time..."

"I'm here now..."

Archibald leant down to kiss him, wide, impatient. He only sat up to pull Darren's shirt off, letting him pull his shirt off too, laying back on him as their mouth met, their chest, skin to skin. Breathing hard when Darren's hands slid down his back and grabbed his ass.

Archibald's face flushed, his eyes shining. "I see..."

"Too soon?"

"No..." He got up and kicked his boots off, pushing his pants down. He pulled Darren's boots off too, his pants, a bit unsure what to do, but then he straddled him, pushing him back on the sofa.

Just watching each other, how their bodies had changed, Archibald a bit more filled up with those birthing, lean muscles, and Darren's leaner body, his bones poking through those hard muscles, his ribs pushing at his skin. Archibald slid his hand on his chest, leaning down to kiss him, his fingers playing on those ribs, his voice a whisper as he felt Darren's cock arch against his erection.

"Mhm... what to do now?"

Darren breathed hard. "What indeed... I don't want to hurt you..."

Archibald swallowed against his fright. "I know..."

Darren pulled him down into a lush kiss, and reached down between them, taking their cocks in his hand, slowly stroking as he clenched his fist harder on them, locking them together as they grew harder at his touch, his strokes. Feeling Archibald pant in his mouth, his lips quivering against his lips as his pleasure built. He was much stronger, holding himself up, letting Darren play, because it was just enough, his warm palm, his hard fist, their cocks rubbing against each other in that tight warmth, skin on skin, hard flesh against hard flesh. Archibald moaned softly, and Darren felt his slick pre-cum coat his fingers and hand. He smiled into the kiss, and stroked harder, letting that pre-cum wet his skin, their cocks, his other hand holding Archie's back tight so he wouldn't flee, but he was lost, just kissing him, moaning, panting, letting his pleasure build as his skin soaked in his warmth. Trembling. Lips. Body. Arms. Fingers lacing in his dark hair. Moaning into his mouth when Darren cupped his neck, holding him tight, trapping him against his lips, as Archibald came, pulsing in his hand, that wet warmth throwing him off the edged too, their cum mingling, flowing down his fist to his abs and thighs. They parted, their eyes shining, their breaths short, and Archibald reached down to take Darren's hand, not leaving his eyes as he brought it to his mouth, watching his lips part as he sucked his fingers off, licking that thick cream, letting it slide down his throat. Mad scared, dead thrilled, he pushed his fear away to bathe in the light in Darren's eyes, in their tastes invading his mouth. He pushed his fingers between Darren's then and leant down to kiss him, thrilled that he let him, closing his eyes and opening his mouth wide, and Archibald had no shame anymore, madly in love. He kissed him, letting him lash his tongue in his mouth, get a taste too. Darren pulled him then on his chest, cradling him as he kissed his hair, his fingers grazing that shivering skin on his back.

Archibald closed his eyes, breathing him in. Just holding each other in that silent warmth, drunk on love.

They dressed later, Archibald grinning as he readjusted his cravat. "William and Fran are due for dinner. Not that I care. I could sit in a pit of death now, knowing I have found you."

Darren tucked his shirt in. "I am in awe of you... small talk over a never-ending dinner? Must be a treat."

Archibald smiled and stepped to him, cupping his neck to pull him into a kiss. "Mhm... I am missing you already..."

"Me too..."

"I'll be back soon... I have to space these visits out not to arise suspicion. Fucking William is always on the lookout. He might not come here, but if he does, just hide. Let us hope Franny doesn't want to bring him when she visits Granny."

"When is the baby due?"

"Autumn..."

"You'll be an uncle."

Archibald pulled a face. "I won't be anything to that kid, I hope. I don't want to see the massacre that William's parenting is going to be." His face flamed up, that well-known anger flooding his eyes. "He told father and I that he sold Raven to one of his friends... What a liar!"

Darren shrugged. "Unless that friend sold him further... Snyder bought him at a horse market in London." His voice, soft. "What happened?"

Archibald sighed. "I can't believe he somehow found you... There was a hunt before Christmas and Father jumped over something... the horse fell and..."

"I know... I've seen his legs."

"So... that is it. We kept him until spring, and despite me begging, Father managed to let William deal with getting him a good place. Some farce!"

Darren smiled, but his eyes were veiled with that sadness which could not leave them. "It is fine now... he will be fine to do light work."

Archibald grabbed his arm, smiling. "I do hope so. I need a riding partner once we are out of here, somewhere, just the two of us."

Darren's lips parted. "Oh... truly?"

"Truly..." Archibald cupped his face. "I told you... I will find a way... even if right now I have no clue... You are stuck with a limp, lame, sickly aristocrat, Mister Turner..."

Darren smiled. "How about you? Stuck with a coachman..."

"I wouldn't want it any other way..." Archibald kissed him softly, letting him hold him tight as his arms pulled him close. He rested his head on Darren's shoulder, breathing in his neck. "I love you... just having you is close to a miracle..."

Darren's chest flooded with warmth and he held him tighter, cradling him. "I love you too..." Hoping, that they were not chasing a dream, a futile dream which could just be burst apart.

Archibald sat at dinner, his weary eyes on William and his endless boasting about his new horses and hunting dogs, which he was planning to send to their countryside estate for the autumn and winter hunts. Fran was bigger, and she just pushed the food around her plate, her eyes a bit drowned.

William looked at Archibald. "I am impressed at how you are looking better with every passing day... still your usual pale self, but at least you are not in that chair anymore."

Archibald wiped his mouth. "Thank you. Most kind."

"I am hopeful that you will propose to Katie soon. She is head over heels with you, now, that you are not a full invalid anymore, and she has some hopes that you will be able to fulfil your duties as a husband." He drank deep, his shining eyes on Archibald.

Archibald smiled. "I will take my time, as I said. Your cousin deserves my honesty, nothing else."

His mother huffed. "You are insufferable, Archibald."

"As ever, Mother."

His father smiled, trying to ease that sudden tension. "Let us go, and have a drink. The ladies will excuse us, surely."

He stood, and Archibald followed, letting his father help him stand, clutching his cane.

They walked to the salon, and Archibald collapsed on the sofa, drained, but at ease, that unbearable tension gone from him after that afternoon in his grandfather's old reading room. He took a glass of water from his father.

William mocked. "Nothing stronger, Archibald? Wine or brandy would put some colour on your cheeks."

"Nothing stronger, thank you very much. I don't drink."

William sipped his brandy, that dark gold liquid whirling in his glass. "How utterly boring. A man should drink. It fires up the soul, and makes you feistier."

Archibald pursed his lips. "Is that so? Thank you for imparting your bottomless wisdom."

William scoffed, but his blue eyes never left Archibald.

Lord Hampton sat down, and Archibald turned to him. "Have you got any news of Raven?"

His father's eyes went wide, shooting a swift glance at William. "No... I mean, why now, Archibald? I thought you got over that horse."

"No, Father. I am merely curious. Perhaps William could enlighten us?" He smiled at William, who had kept a small smile.

"Sure. I have heard from my friend just recently. He is doing well and is cherished by the whole family. The kids love him especially. Truly spoilt." He smiled, lying with ease.

Archibald smiled back. "How good of you to have some reassuring news."

"You can always count on me, brother."

Toasting, Archibald let him believe he had sucked up his lies, inwardly boiling, but he knew Raven was safe. A dull fatigue in him, and he stood, leaning on his cane. "Excuse me. I am exhausted and shall retire. I may walk, but it is taking all my strength."

William smiled up at him. "I do hope you will be strong enough to hunt with us when we move back to the countryside."

Archibald smiled, dark. "Even if so, I despise hunting. This has not changed. I bid you a good night."

He left then, limping, gritting his teeth at the pain in his legs.

William looked at Lord Hampton. "I would be grateful if you could help me a bit persuading Archibald that he should propose. A wedding then when we are back at the countryside would be grand. I am sure you are eager for him to settle now that he is very much likely to stay alive?" He had forced a smile, but inwardly, he felt like blowing up from that cold rage.

Lord Hampton sipped his brandy. "I have talked to him, but he is just discovering what it feels like to be truly alive... I would not mind leaving him a bit of time."

William huffed. "Katie might not wait. After all, she has many suitors."

"Then let her choose one if she so wishes. I would not wait for Archibald if I were you. Maybe he does not want to marry yet."

"Staying a bachelor is not well-viewed."

"We shall see. Months ago, he was on the brink of death. I am just grateful for every moment."

William rolled his eyes, but stayed quiet, his mind on Archibald's words. *Why ask about that horse now? Unless...* He sipped his brandy, the flames' shadows dancing in his eyes.

Archibald went back two days later, and had tea with his grandmother, just as they had planned, before he went down to the stables, discreetly catching Darren's eyes.

He had to wait a bit in that quiet room when the door opened, soft, and Darren stepped in, carefully closing the door, and turning the key.

Archibald rushed into his arms and Darren just held him, apologetic. "I had to make sure nobody sees me come in here... Not easy, as you may gather..."

"I know... It doesn't matter. Every day apart from you is torture."

Just bathing in those blue eyes, feeling his chest rise against his chest. He parted his lips, and felt Darren lean close, kiss him. Opening wide to him, he let him hold him tight, hold him up as their breaths mingled, their tongues dancing, Darren's stubbles scorching his lips, his skin, and it was not enough, even if Archibald had more strength and was pushing hard against Darren's strong jaw. He wanted his teeth, to feel that warm pain which made his heart race. Backing to the sofa, he let Darren push him down on it, lying back, pulling him close, wanting his weight, everything. Trembling when they parted, breathing hard, their faces flushed, their blood rushing.

Archibald licked his aching lips. "I want you..." Reaching into his pocket, he pulled a small bottle of oil out, his eyes glinting.

Darren smiled down at him. "Came prepared, I see."

"I want you. All of you..." Undressing, frantic, letting their clothes pool on the floor. Archibald pulled Darren on top, spreading his legs. "I could not do anything with you before... really... but I feel better now..."

Darren knelt up a bit, just to coat himself with that slick oil, rub some on Archibald's flesh. He pushed a finger in, gently, watching his eyes go wide. He stopped, waiting, but Archibald just grabbed his wrist.

"It's fine..."

Darren pushed in, to the knuckle, letting him adjust, clench around him as he threw his head back. Soft moans as Darren pushed and pulled his finger out, curbing it up, making Archibald moan harder. Pant, his lips parted.

He looked at Darren. "Just take me... hurt me... I don't care... I have waited an eternity for this."

Darren pulled his finger out and grabbed his cock, leaning over Archibald, pushing it against his slick entrance. Pushing in as their eyes never left each other. Love. Lust. That small dent between Archie's eyebrows at that slight pain, but it was quickly gone, even if he felt stretched, shivering around his hard flesh. Darren waited, just stroking his cheek with his fingers, his hair, until he felt him relax, their lips close when he tentatively rocked his hips. Archie gasped, a moan escaping his mouth which Darren sealed with a kiss.

Rocking him gently, swallowing his moans, breaking that kiss just enough to whisper. "Shhhh... no noise, remember?"

Archie nodded, keeping his voice in somehow magnifying that pleasure which had started building. He rocked his hips back, as much as his strength allowed it, kissing Darren so he wouldn't moan, his rolling hips pushing that pleasure up to his chest, waves and waves of it, down to the base of his spine. His eyes wide when he realised he could not hold back, seeing the same pleasured pain in Darren's eyes. Too much. For both of them. As their eyes met, they came with a trembling moan, barely a breath on those quivering, burning lips. Holding tight, Darren's weight, like a blanket on Archie as his tears pearled. Darren kissed them off, holding him, letting him cry in his neck, letting his tears pearl too, soak his brown hair, his skin. That love there in that golden afternoon light pouring through the curtains. Wordless. Blazing.

Chapter 28

Later, at home, just as they were waiting for dinner, Archibald's mother turned to him from the couch where she was sitting with Fran.

"Archibald, you have waited long enough, it is time you proposed to Katie, she has waited long enough!"

Archibald looked at her, still in that haze clouding his mind a bit, his flesh still pulsing from his lover. Searching for his words when all he wanted in that weary state was to jump up, and shout out the truth. He parted his lips when his father's voice cut those unborn words.

"I do think Archibald should go on his Grand Tour first."

An icy silence followed his words, Lady Hampton's eyes going wide. "Grand Tour? He is too old!"

Edward smiled. "That may be so, but he has had no opportunity so far because of his ill health. It would be a sad affair to deny him this wonderful experience."

"Truly, Edward! A Grand Tour! And with what money?"

Lord Hampton shrugged. "There is enough money for this." He looked at his son's stunned face. "What do you think, Archibald?"

Archibald caught that pleading light in his eyes, trying to form some coherent words when his heart had iced over at the prospect of leaving. "I... I am stunned, Father..."

Lady Hampton huffed. "So am I! truly! A folly!"

Archibald swallowed. "But... if that is your wish, father, I shall go. Gladly." Almost smiling at the light in his father's eyes.

"I am delighted!"

William walked in at that instant, and Lady Hampton turned to him. "My dear son! His Lordship wants Archie to go on his Grand Tour! How absurd?"

William stopped short, his eyes unreadable, but a small smile crept over his lips. "Is that so? Well, young people should travel, right? Shame, that you had to wait so long. What about Katie?"

Archibald tamed his voice. "I do believe your delightful cousin shouldn't wait for me... I might be away years..."

Lady Hampton screeched. "Years? Don't you dare! You need to get married, as the heir of this family!"

Edward put his hand on Archibald's shoulder. "Maybe not years...? You are right, my dear." He squeezed gently.

Archibald smiled. "Of course, Father."

Lady Hampton was still clearly displeased. "What an absurd idea! Absurd! But it seems that you have all made your decision, and I have very little to say in the matter! And when should he leave?"

Lord Edward spoke. "As soon as possible. After all, the nice season is on us soon."

Fran stammered. "But then... he won't be here for the birth of the baby..." Her wide eyes on Archibald, whose heart wrenched.

"I will be back, sis... Don't worry."

William smiled, mocking. "Sure you will be back. You have a duty to this family."

"I know." Archibald's clipped voice died in his father's grip on his shoulder. "I know, do not worry, brother."

They smiled at each other, but William's eyes were dark, brewing that hate Archibald knew so well now.

He looked up at his father. "Shall we go and discuss this in your office, Father?"

"Yes, come. It would be good indeed. Excuse us."

They left, Archibald leaning on his cane, his father's arm under his arm. Walking to the office where Lord Hampton made sure to close the door, check on all the other doors too, that nobody was listening.

He sat Archie down then and pulled a chair to face him, taking his hands. "Archie... I hope this didn't shock you..."

Archibald swallowed, that despair rushing into his voice. "I am not leaving. I cannot leave Darren... not now when..."

"Hear me out." He squeezed his hands, not leaving his eyes, even when his own eyes welled up, those tears tainting his voice which he had lowered. "Archibald, you are not leaving on your own... you are leaving with Darren..."

Archibald's eyes went wide. "What...?"

"Yes... this is the plan we devised with your grandmother... the one which arouses the least suspicions... the Grand Tour... leaving abroad... who would suspect anything? This is what young nobles do..."

"But... take him? How?"

"As your coachman, and travel companion. I have a friend who has a boat. You can take the horses too, yours, and Raven..." He steadied his voice against the tears threatening to spill. "You are going to France, buy a small carriage, and travel to the South... There, you will find a house... with some land... your grandmother has had it as a heritage, and now she is giving it to you. Lavender fields, and fruit trees, mainly..."

Archibald remembered then his granny's words. "Then what? How long do we have to stay? This Grand Tour... you said not years... but then..." His words died when Edward pressed his fingers gently against his lips. Squeezing his hand in an iron grip.

His tears rushed out with his voice. "You are not coming back, Archibald..."

Archibald's lips parted, in shock. "What...? Father..."

"This is not punishment... The French... they are more lenient with your kind... you would not be in danger there, on that remote estate, with those people who don't have our strict laws... You could live there, in peace... with Darren. A recluse aristocrat and his butler, and coachman... and whatever else you wish him to be..." He smiled, letting his tears spill. "And I will remember you, and know that you are living your true life... as it should be... and come to visit sometimes, when I can afford it..."

"Fran..."

"I'm afraid it is goodbye to Fran, Archie... you know full well why... William can't be trusted to the last minute..."

"I know..." His voice drowning in tears.

"You can think about this. Take your time, if needed."

Archibald watched him, trying to etch every line of that loving fatherly face in his memory. "No, Father. I shall accept your gift... and cherish your name until the day I die."

They hugged then, sobbing, pouring all their love into that embrace which was also a farewell. A last hug of love from Edward whose heart broke at that moment, but he held Archie tight, knowing too that he had given him life a second time.

Archibald hurried to his grandmother's the next day, and they talked the plans over, how he would not say a word to William or Fran about when he was leaving, just spend a few days at her place, and then leave with Darren and the horses to take the boat which would bring them to Calais. He rushed then, down to their room, waiting for Darren, meeting his wide blue eyes when he'd closed the door.

Mute, facing each other in that common knowledge, as Darren had been told by the countess, and he could barely believe it, dead scared of leaving, but thrilled at the same time. Their dream, at arm's reach, something even Archibald could not have anticipated, so they just sat on the sofa, holding hands.

Archibald spoke first, dazed. "I am not sure what to say... I just hope you're coming with me..."

"I am. I'll go wherever you want me to go."

"We're going together. I am not your master ordering you around."

"I know..."

Archibald pulled him into a kiss, whispering against his lips. "I love you... and maybe this is our chance... France... where we would not be killed for our love... where we could live in peace... even if far from this country... these landscapes we know... but the sea close, that warm sea I only read about in books..."

"I would follow you to Hell..." Meeting his eyes, their love burning in that quiet room.

"Would you drive me far, Darren?" A small smile, his tears spilling.

"I would drive you to the end of the world, Milord."

Kissing, their tears pearling, flowing in their mouth as their tongues rolled on each other.

The preparations were frantic from then on, packing, and Archibald made sure he didn't have much luggage, knowing they had to travel there too. Knowing that he couldn't care less about those trunks filled with fancy clothes. Hoping, that he could ditch them, and live under the sun in a shirt and pants, letting that sun warm his skin and blood. Hold him under that sun until their skin blended... He jolted from his day dreaming at Fran's hand on his arm. They were alone, the parents still on their stroll, and William away at a horse market.

He looked at her as she sat down. “Hey sis...” Realising how distant they’d become, his heart tight knowing he could not tell her anything.

“Archie... I know we’ve pulled a bit apart... with my marriage and all... and I know you hate William...” He parted his lips, but she raised her hand with a smile. “I understand... but I love him... still... even if I know he is not exactly what you would call a good man...”

“Franny... does he take good care of you? I mean, does he... is he...”

“He is... This is mighty embarrassing... but yes, you do not need to fear... as much as he is a boisterous man, he is also mighty proud of his... skills... so I am a happy woman... alright? We had fights... and you know me...” She smiled. “You don’t need to worry. Mr Willoughby knows my true temper, and can behave when needed...” Her eyes drowned. “You are leaving though, and I am not sure how I’ll bear it.”

Archibald took her hand. “If I told you that nothing makes me happier than this trip, would that make you feel better?”

“Yes, for sure.”

“It is so. Nothing could make me happier. And I will think of you and write to you whenever I can.”

“You seem awfully serious... It’s just a short goodbye.”

“Yes, you are right. Forgive me.” He kissed her hand, smiling. “I do hope your baby and you will be safe. I told Father to write straight away when you give birth.”

“I am sure it will be fine. My husband already made sure the best doctors will be around us.” She laughed lightly, stroking Archibald’s cheek. “You take care, Arch. Please. Be as happy as you can be.”

For a fleeting moment, he thought she knew, but he swallowed that confession teetering on the edge of his lips. “Sure, sis. I shall be.”

Leaving then, the carriage packed to go to his grandmother’s, who lived closer to the harbour.

Archibald hugged his mother, letting her ramble. “Do take care. Make sure you are not cold. And do remember your duties here. No French girls, or anything of the sorts.”

“Yes, Mother.”

Hugging his father then, both of them holding back their tears, whispers as they held each other. “I wish you all the happiness possible, Archibald.”

"Thank you, Father. Thank you." Giving him a swift kiss as they parted, Archibald turned and mounted in the carriage, letting his tears spill as he leant back, knocking the cane against the wall. Crying, unable to look at his father's drawn face, those eyes filled with bottomless sadness.

He had calmed by the time they arrived at his grandmother's, and dismissed the old coachman, knowing that they would ride to the harbour the nextis too day, and his luggage would be driven there by James. Briefly meeting Darren's eyes as he took the horses to the stables.

Archibald sat then with his grandmother after dinner, letting her take his hands. "My dear, this is farewell. I do hope you will write to me, though, and let me know how you make that little estate prosper. It has been neglected for far too long, but it is yours now, make it thrive."

"Come and visit us, Granny."

"No dear. I am too old and the voyage too long. But I shall read your letters with great delight."

"Granny..." Realising he would never see her again, Archibald had a fleeting moment of panic, almost thinking better of it, but she squeezed his hands with a smile.

"Darling... my time is almost up, and do not object, Archibald! But you, your whole life lies ahead... and I hope you will live it in the arms of your lover. That is all you both deserve. To be safe and be loved. I shall think of you both, fondly, and that should be enough for you."

"I am not sure how I can repay you, ever..."

"No need, dear. Just be happy, and live your life to the full. That is all I ask as a payback."

They hugged then, Archibald choking on his tears, even if his heart raced at the thought of leaving.

Next morning, they woke early and Archibald hurried to the stables. The horses were ready, Dandy and Raven saddled, Tulip in a halter, waiting to leave.

Archibald faced Darren. "All ready, Darren?"

"Yes, Milord. James has already left with the luggage."

"Let us go then."

Only his eyes smiling above that official behaviour, but they mounted and left, Darren holding Tulip's lead as they walked on the busy streets. Putting the horses into a light trot when the traffic allowed it. A lush sunshine, their hair in the wind. Archibald smiled, letting the sun caress his face. The harbour. Soon. As if in a dream.

They arrived there despite the heavy traffic and treacherous streets, the sea battering the docks. James waved at them, his smile wide, standing near the countess' small cart.

"Hey! Over here!"

They walked there, and James gestured at a small steamboat. "This is it. The captain is on board, waiting for you."

Darren jumped down, and hugged him tight. "This is goodbye, James. Never forget what I taught you..."

"I will not, Sir..." His eyes in tears, giving a caress to the horses. "His Lordship will buy new horses... but I know a lot now... and I will make you proud, Sir..."

"I have no doubt."

Archibald got off too, and Darren handed him his cane, taking Dandy's reins.

"I'll load the horses... just rest a bit, Milord."

Archibald smiled. "I shall. Thank you."

James mounted then, and saluted with his whip, leaving, his tears streaming, but he smiled wide not to upset them.

Archibald turned to Darren. "Just load the horses, I'll follow."

Darren did so, and when he'd tied them up in the cargo bay, he went down to help Archibald up, so he would not slip on that plank. Taking his arm.

"How sweet..."

They turned to the voice, meeting William's eyes. He was standing next to his horse with his small smile, but his eyes were cold, roaming them.

Archibald's stomach flipped. "William..."

"Rude of you to leave without saying goodbye, brother, don't you think?"

Archibald glanced at Darren, who just stood, frozen.

William pursed his lips. "Oh... my bastard of a brother... you found him? How fortunate..."

Archibald swallowed, letting his wrath invade him. "We're leaving... this has nothing to do with you anymore..."

"Oh, but it does, doesn't it? I can't let this molly go with you, brother. After all, your reputation is at stake."

"Leave us alone..." But his voice had died in that mad worry, feeling Darren let go of his arm. Hearing his soft voice.

"Just go on board."

"No!" Meeting his calm eyes, dead scared.

"Go, Archibald. Please. Tell the captain to be ready to leave."

"No..."

"Please." Darren pushed him gently, his eyes pleading.

Archibald backed away, his heart sinking, but he obeyed, somehow catching a dark light in those loving eyes. He walked up the plank, helped by the sailors, and turned to watch Darren.

Darren, who had walked up to William, facing him off. "So, what do you want? Take me to prison?"

William's lips curled up. "That would be the only reasonable thing to do. Let them hang you and watch you rot."

His eyes went wide when Darren's fist landed in his stomach, but he didn't have time to double over, those strong hands grabbing his shirt. Murmurs around them, but nobody dared interfere.

Darren held him tight, watching him trying to draw breath. His voice, soft. "This is all you will get, scumbag, because you are going to be a father, and I will not carry the burden of widowing Francesca, or making an orphan out of your unborn child. But if you call the police, I will kill you before they have a chance of seizing me... So, fuck off."

He pushed William, hard, watching him land against his horse. His face contorted with wrath and pain, but he could not shout, his words still cut by that blow.

Darren turned, and hurried up the boat as distant whistles could be heard, but the captain raised the plank, and the boat backed off, leaving the harbour to the open sea. Policemen spilling on the dock, crowding around William, who had stood, frantic, shouting. To no avail.

Darren and Archibald watched the shore grow distant, and Archibald breathed, knowing he could not hug him, that mad fright there, almost thinking he would still lose him, even if they were farther now, the waves rocking the boat.

He looked at Darren. "All good, Darren?"

"Yes, Milord. We had a small matter to settle."

Their small smiles, their hands close to each other as they watched the harbour shrunk, the shore blur in that white light.

Chapter 29

France, the arrival frantic on that busy harbour, that foreign language around them, even if Archibald could still grasp some words.

They walked to an inn nearby, and Darren took care of the horses whilst Archibald took a room, his heart tight knowing that Darren would sleep in the stables, but they dined together, still keeping that distance out of security. Darren a bit overwhelmed with that language around him he could not understand, but his love for Archibald overrode everything, not even daring to believe they were alone, at last. Almost.

Archibald had asked the innkeeper about a carriage for sale, and fortunately he had one, left as payment by another English lord who had no money to pay. Darren inspected it and they sealed the deal, buying the harnesses too.

Next day, they were on their way, the luggage in the back, and the map with Darren. Archibald resigned himself to sit in the carriage, but when they had left the city, and roads became less populated, he knocked for Darren to stop. He climbed out, and climbed up on the bench next to him. Sitting so close, their thighs met, warm.

Darren smiled at him. "So close, Milord?"

"Not even close enough."

Driving, the landscape rolling as the horses pulled, giddy, finally having found Darren's hands again, his voice. Raven had been tied in the back, and he followed, neighing sometimes to horses in fields.

A long journey where they had to stop in inns, playing their roles when they were dying to be together, but Archibald bid his time, knowing they would be there soon.

Finally, the house, on a gentle hill, lavenders still green lining the front to the stone wall surrounding it. The sea there, at the edge of the horizon, close. Its scent on the wind. Orchards in the back, fig trees lining the entrance of that single, small stone house, age old olive trees reaching their tortuous limbs to the sky. The stables and fields in the back. Darren stopped the carriage, the horses panting but sniffing the air, alert, as rogue seagulls screeched in that azure sky.

Archibald stepped down, leaning on his cane, exhausted, but his eyes were on that small haven, the key warming his pocket. He looked up at Darren, his blue eyes mirroring the sky, his black hair in the wind, and Archibald could barely breathe as he pushed the words out.

"We're home..."

Darren's eyes welled up and he jumped down, lacing his arms around Archibald. Not a soul in sight, and he couldn't care less, even if they had had a crowd around them, he could not hold back hugging that man he loved. Kissing then, crying softly as they rocked each other.

Archibald opened the house then, letting Darren drive the carriage to the back, deal with the horses. The luggage stayed outside, but Archibald had torn his cravat down, unbuttoning his shirt. The house was chilly, so he opened all the windows, letting that warm air rush in with a sigh, letting that long forgotten house breathe. Walking upstairs on those creaking wooden stairs, he pushed the windows open, that large bedroom giving on a breath-taking view of the sea, the waves glinting in that golden sun. That large bed covered with a sheet, and Archibald pulled it off, letting it pool on the floor. Hearing his steps on the stairs, he turned to him, watching as his eyes roamed around the room to settle on him. Archibald pulled him into a hug, that man warmed by the sun, his scent laced with horsehair and leather, kissing him wide.

"To bed, Mister Turner..."

His eyebrows shot up. "Already, Mister Hampton?"

"I can't wait any longer..."

Kissing him, tugging at his clothes, feeling him melt in his mouth, under his hands. Peeling each other's clothes off as their hands roamed each other. Hard. As if those tamed touches had been released all of a sudden, because nothing mattered anymore, that lurking blade gone, the shadow of that rope hanging above their heads.

Archibald pulled him to the bed. “Mark me… I want you to leave marks… I’ve been dreaming of it… your mouth… your teeth… I want all of you… I’m yours…”

Kissing whatever words of protest Darren might have had, but Darren just pushed him on the bed, covering him, his mouth roaming his neck, sucking, and biting that soft skin and flesh, and Archibald floated on that pleasured pain, trembling, letting Darren roam his body, bite him all over as his tears flowed with his moans. Gasping when Darren took his cock in his mouth, sucking hard, pushing his fingers in him as he teased that sweet spot, licking his hole, hard, and Archibald arched his back, heaving, but Darren didn’t let him come, leaving his cock and ass to seal that panting mouth with a drenched kiss. Pushing inside of Archibald with a moan, rocking his hips, hard, watching Archibald’s face, hoping it was not too much, that loving face bathed in pain and bliss, his tears glinting in that golden light. Not another sound but that gentle breeze, their breathing, the cicada's song in the air.

Darren cupped Archie’s face. “Let your voice out… Nobody can hear us anymore… let me hear your beautiful voice, love…”

Archibald mewled, moaning hard when Darren filled him, his flesh clenching around that rock-hard cock which kept teasing that spot, making him tremble and his body flush.

Gasping, panting, clinging to Darren’s shoulders, his back. “Ah… I love you… my love…”

Kissing, Darren hooked Archibald’s leg on his arm, fucking him harder, panting in his neck as he felt himself close. Moaning at Archibald’s voice laced with pleasure. “Come in me… Come, love…” Darren lost it then, filling him to the brim, his cock pulsing inside of Archibald who let his tears flow, letting go too, waves and waves of cum flooding his abs, coating Darren’s too. That slick juice enough to have Darren rock him even more. Panting, he had collapsed on Archibald, and felt his hands roam his soaked back. His lips kissed his neck as that gentle breeze cooled their burning skin.

Darren pushed himself up, looking down at Archibald who just reached up top stroke his face. “I love you… Love me all day… we have all day… every day…”

“I love you too…” Kissing him, rolling him on top as their bodies blended, drenched. As their hands found skin, hard.

They woke much later, sprawled on the bed, and Darren sat up, still that fright in him that somebody could see them, know... He sighed, glancing at Archibald's silent eyes.

He smiled at him. "Had a good nap?"

"Yes..." Archibald looked at his chest, his arms, his pale skin filled with light purple and red crescents, love bites throbbing with a gentle pain.

Darren grazed them softly. "I would say I am sorry, but they suit you so well..."

"Some colour on my paper skin."

They laughed, and Darren pulled him in his shoulder, their eyes on the setting sun colouring the sky. Shades of blue drowning in violet and gold. Orange flames licking the horizon.

"How beautiful..."

Darren smiled. "A sight to behold..."

"Until our old age..."

They looked at each other, still incredulous, still not fully believing that mad chance they had gotten to live a life filled with their love.

Days to set up the house, weeks to furbish it, to find peasants to work the fields and the orchard, to explain who they were, realising that the next neighbour was an hour's ride away. Making love and cooking their meals, dressed just enough not to melt under that warm sun. Archibald wrote his letters one day, remembering his promise, and a peasant took them to the nearby village to the post.

One morning, Darren asked him to dress for riding, and they went to saddle Raven and Dandy, riding down the road then, winding down to the sea. Their hair in the wind, shirts half open, they faced that long beach stretching into the distance.

Archibald smiled at Darren as the horses danced a bit, sensing the sea, the waves lapping that soft sand. "Ready to race?"

"Sure! Careful though, Raven's legs are not what they used to be."

"Of course."

He spurred Dandy, and the horse took off, but Archibald made sure he held him back a bit, watching Darren catch up, Raven giddy with his freedom, the horse's bones coated with flesh, that dark coat shining in the sun. Drinking in their sight, that loving graze of Darren's hand on that black coat, his smile. He held his hand out and Archibald caught it, laughing, holding hands as the horses galloped head to head. Giddy, that rush making their heart race, their pulse in their palms as they held tight. As they breathed in that sea air, hard, letting it fill them up, their tired lungs, fill up their flesh, make them glow.

Jumping down when they had stopped to hug, tight, kiss, hard. Collapse on the sand, kiss until they had no breath left, nothing. Just their eyes, their chests heaving against each other, their smiles.

It had prospered, that small estate, the summer months ripening the fruits, the fig bushes laden with sweetness, the lavenders pouring their heady scent in that crisp air filled with cicada songs, and nobody seemed to care about the young English lord, and his butler and coachman. Nobody cared that they were living alone, that there was no wife, no children, the people around them smiling when they came to work, bringing them cakes and honey, their children coming to help sometimes, having a great time feeding the horses apples they had picked.

Archibald sat outside one day, reading his letters, letters from his father and his grandmother, his heart tight, but he had a smile on, imagining their voices, their faces as he read those lines, ink letters formed with love flowing on that delicate paper.

He looked up at Darren when he put a platter down on that wrought-iron table, and sat, pouring them some tea.

Archibald sniffed the air. "Apple crumble?" His eyes lighting up.

Darren smiled. "It's the season. Would be a shame to let it go to waste." He took the lid off, and cut a large slice for Archibald, watching him eat, drunk on love.

Archibald looked at him. "Won't you eat?"

"I'm filling up just by looking at you..."

"Flatterer..." But he laughed and pushed a bite into Darren's mouth. "Eat. You'll need your energy soon..."

"You have plans?"

"Afternoon snack, then it's time for our nap, as it's custom here."

"Nap?"

Archibald grinned. "A long nap... in your arms, I hope?"

Darren stood, pulling him up. "I hope you ate enough..."

"I'm still hungry...."

"Is that so? Come."

Smiling, they walked to their room, shedding those scarce clothes, rolling on that huge bed, their limbs intertwining. Skin to skin, their scent drenching everything out as they kissed and their tongues roamed their skin. Tasting, wanting more.

Darren rolled Archie on top, spreading his legs around Archibald's hips. "I think you are strong enough..."

Archibald frowned. "To do what?"

"You know what..." Not leaving his eyes, his thighs framing those delicate hips lightly.

Archibald's eyes went wide. "What...? I am not sure..." But he was hard, arching against Darren. Panting as his stress invaded him, but Darren just held him gently by the waist, those strong, warm hands comforting.

"I would like you to love me... just as I have loved you..."

"I don't know if I can..."

Darren reached for the oil and poured some on his hand. Reaching between them, he oiled up Archie's hard cock, spreading it under his foreskin, rolling his fingers on that slick skin. Archie moaned, hardening in his hand as he stroked him. Coating his hole then, he guided Archie's cock against it. Pushing a bit, waiting until Archie put his weight into it. Feeling him breach, pop in as Archie's eyes went wide. Darren grabbed his hips gently, pulling him inside as he laced his legs above his waist. Waiting, meeting his eyes.

Archibald moved, slowly, feeling a bit clumsy, but it also felt incredible, his cock squeezed in that tight warmth. An insane surge of lust in his chest as he got lost in Darren's eyes, rocking his hips, feeling his hands hold him tight, his legs frame him as he rolled his hips into him. Moaning, eyes wide in his blue eyes as he picked up a stronger rhythm, clinging to Darren, watching his lips part, those soft moans driving him crazy, that power he felt, as he fucked him, gliding on his muscles, kissing his neck as he put his weight on him. *Feel me.* Pushing deep inside, smiling at Darren's deep moan. Rocking him harder, even if he felt tiring, he didn't stop, wanting him to lose it. Their eyes locking, mouth wide, panting as Archie lost it, feeling his hips snap into Darren with a force he could barely control, that insane feeling of filling that clenching flesh almost too much as Darren lost it too, coating them.

Kissing then as he collapsed on his broad chest. Catching his breath in his neck, licking that salty skin laced with his scent. Darren gently moved his hips and let Archie slide out, letting him slide to his side, holding him tight then in his shoulder. Stroking his hair as Archie did the same, running his long fingers in that dark mass. Not leaving each other's eyes, glowing with love.

Darren brushed his hair back. "I love you..."

Archie smiled, clenching his fingers in his soft, black hair. "I love you too..."

Kissing then, drowned in their burning love.

Acknowledgements

My eternal gratitude goes to all my author friends who keep pushing me and cheer me on. Especially to some close author friends on various social media platforms, online communities which have become invaluable friendship groups over the years.

Special thanks, as ever, go to Bjorn who keeps helping me with my covers. To Su, my critique partner and alpha reader, for her relentless support, friendship, mentorship, her precious advice and sharp analysis. To Luana, my trusted friend and beta reader. To all my ARC readers, but especially A.E. Bennett who is always eager to read my books, and is an ardent supporter of my writing.

A massive thank you to all my readers whose constant support and fidelity mean the world to me.

Also By Maxime Jaz

All of Maxime's books are on Kindle Unlimited.
Omnia Vincit Amor trilogy, a dark, queer trilogy set in Ancient Rome
Donum – The Gift Book I of the Omnia Vincit Amor trilogy.
https://getbook.at./Donum

Avis Aurea – The Golden Bird Book II of the Omnia Vincit Amor trilogy.
https://getbook/Avis

Pulsus Cordis Mei – The Pulse of My Heart Book III of the Omnia Vincit Amor Trilogy.
https://getbook.at/Pulsus

Fall - a contemporary MM romance
https://getbook.at/Fall-MaximeJaz

Home - a contemporary MM romance
https://mybook.to/HomeMaxime

Khirion – a dark MMF polyam fantasy romance
https://mybook.to/Khirion

In Aeternum – a dark vampire MM romance
https://mybook.to/inaeternumMax

About the Author

Maxime is a queer author who writes about guys falling in love in various places and times. Although the books could be labelled as queer romance laced with erotica, they do not fit a single genre, and are filled with drama, and sometimes darkness. Maxime likes to explore complex emotions, the journey to self-discovery, and living a life true to oneself, and their characters often struggle before finding happiness.

Maxime has an MA in language and literature, and a long international teaching career as a teacher of English language and literature. Being multilingual, they also love incorporating various languages in their works.

On top of being an avid reader, Maxime loves horse riding, hiking with their dog, and spending time with their family.

All of Maxime's links can be found here.
https://linktr.ee/MaximeJaz